I0747308

HITCHED

A CHAMPION SECURITY NOVEL

LUCY LENNOX
MAY ARCHER

Copyright © 2022 by Lucy Lennox and May Archer
All rights reserved.

No part of this book may be reproduced in any form or by any electronic or mechanical means, including information storage and retrieval systems, without written permission from the author, except for the use of brief quotations in a book review.

This book was not written with AI. This author does not give permission for any portion of this book to be used to train AI.

Cover Photo: Michelle Lancaster @lanefotograf
Editing: One Love Editing
Beta Reading: Leslie Copeland
Proofreading: Victoria Rothenberg and Lori Parks

HITCHED

Former Marine Percy "Champ" Champion has never encountered a problem he can't handle. Flying bullets? Daring rescues? Building Champion Security from the ground up? Making people seriously regret using his hated first name? No problem. He's gotten the job done without a hitch each and every time.

But it turns out there are some situations Champ can't handle alone, like:
• Going undercover as a wedding planner to retrieve some missing cartel data in time to avert an international crisis.
• Keeping his jerk of an ex from threatening his business.
• Preventing Quinn Taffet, Licking Thicket's gorgeous, charming new wedding planner—and Champ's fake fiancé—from getting into danger… or from getting the wrong idea about their relationship.
• Fighting the pull that lands him in Quinn's bed night after night, despite his very best intentions.

• Stopping the pun-happy matchmakers of the Thicket from destroying the sane, well-ordered life he's built for himself.

• And, most troubling of all, protecting his traitorous heart from all the romance in the air.

In short, Champ needs an extraction plan ASAP before he finds himself well and truly… *hitched*.

Note: Although *Hitched* is the second book in the series, it can be enjoyed as a standalone.

1

QUINN

I was *not* a morning person.

I hadn't been one back when I was a kid spending summers in Licking Thicket, even though my Aunt Cherry had bribed me with baked goods, blasted '80s pop songs loud enough to make the windows of her old Victorian rattle, and reminded me crisply that, "Spending your time dreaming is as useless as pining for a man, Quinn. Reality never lives up to expectations."

And at age thirty, despite founding *two* successful event-planning businesses, accumulating a roster of incredibly demanding clients, and having enough failed relationships under my belt to recognize that Cherry had been spot-on when it came to men, I'd accepted that I was never *going* to be a morning person either.

Dreams were just more compelling than reality, period-period.

So when I sensed morning light filtering through my curtains one January morning, was it any surprise that my first impulse was *not* to jump out of bed or even to roll over and check my phone for the onslaught of messages from the half-dozen nervous brides on Taffet Events' current client list?

Heck no.

In fact, I pulled my pillow over my head to block out the light, yanked my quilt up to my chin, and slid right back into a dreamy, sensuous slow dance with the handsomest, most charming man I'd ever met—a man whose tan skin set off his sun-kissed hair and blue eyes, who was witty and intelligent, whose biceps were as big as my thighs, whose lips tasted like amaretto and secrets, and who said my name all hot and slow, like...

"Quinn? Hey, Quinn!"

Um, *no*. My personal Prince Charming wasn't supposed to say my name in that curt, impatient tone. He was supposed to *rumble* my name from the depths of his chest, the way he had the first time he kissed me. Or to *shout* my name, hoarse and helpless, like he did when I made him mindless with wanting. Or even to *whisper* my name sleepily, like he sometimes did when he wrapped his arms around me in the dark of night. He was definitely not supposed to say—

"*Quinn!*" A big, callused hand shook my calf, knocking me out of my dream entirely. "Fuck's sake, man. I've seen dead bodies that were easier to rouse. Did you see where my T-shirt ended up? I have a meeting at work this morning, and I'm running late."

I heaved a sigh, shoved the pillow off my head so hard that it tumbled to the hardwood floor, wiped the drool off my face, and sat up to confront reality—all six feet and several blond-haired, blue-eyed, grouchy-as-fuck inches of him.

Staring directly at the magnificence that was Percy Champion was a little like staring at the sun. He wasn't actually a dream man, I reminded myself. Just a regular old guy.

With a run-of-the-mill gorgeous face and garden-variety broad shoulders, trailing down to a plain-as-dirt narrow waist and dime-a-dozen eight-pack abs that glistened with tiny water droplets from his morning shower like a benevolent god had encrusted them with diamonds.

And while he might bear a slight resemblance to the Prince Charming of my dreams, there were many critical differences. For example, my Prince Charming smiled a lot, and not just when we were drunk on Howling Turtles and flirting at the Thicket Tavern, like the night we met.

Prince Charming wouldn't avoid even the most harmless personal questions as if the answers might incriminate him.

He'd also never say something egotistical (and patently false) the morning after our first night together, like "I can tell you're a relationship kind of guy, Quinn, and I need to tell you, I'm not into relationships," which really should have been my first red flag where Champ was concerned, because if he'd simply *asked*, I'd have told him I was *soooo* not into them either.

Prince Charming would be as sweet and funny when the sun came up as he was when he came by the shop at night to "check on you, because I saw your light was still on."

He would not have a weird split personality that enabled him to talk sweetly to me for hours about everything from our favorite movies, to funny stories about Champ's time in the military, to the ups and downs of owning a business, *then* sex me up until I was cum-drunk, *then* spend the night in my bed...

only to freak the fuck out the next morning like he thought I might tattoo his name on my forehead as a symbol of my undying love if he acted the slightest bit friendly.

And Prince Charming—

The bedroom door opened so fast it hit the wall with a *bang*, and a tiny fluffball predator attacked my discarded pillow with glee.

Oh, yeah. Prince Charming wouldn't be the most irresponsible dog owner in the entire freakin' universe.

It was a good thing Aunt Cherry had decided to spend her retirement traveling around the country with one of her Bunco friends, because she would legit disown me if she knew I'd spent not one, not two, but *twenty-six* nights with someone like Percy Champion. Hell, I was ready to disown myself.

"How the heck should I know where your shirt is?" I demanded. My voice sounded rough and wrecked, which was partly because I was still half-asleep and partly because of, you know… other things.

Things like blowing Percy Champion's monster cock the night before.

Twice.

Despite solemnly vowing on Sunday morning that I would break the cycle of booty calls and morning-after regrets by absolutely, positively never going anywhere near said cock again, and that this time, I meant it.

Damn it. I flopped back onto the mattress and squeezed my eyes shut. For real, Aunt Cherry could never know about this.

"It was my favorite vintage Harley T-shirt," he grumbled.

"Oooh. Bummer."

"It was faded to the perfect softness."

"You should probably have taken better care of it, then, hmm?"

"And this is the third time one of my shirts has gone missing over here," Mr. So-Not-Charming barked, like he was back in the Marines and expected me to give him a jaunty salute. "So could you sit up and help me look?"

Seriously, why did the universe make the hot ones so damn annoying?

"M'kay." I rolled to a sitting position for the second time and gave the man a piece of my mind. "I'm gonna do the world a great service right now and clue you in on a little secret. That deep, commanding voice thing? It only works on me if one of us is about to get our dick sucked. Otherwise, if you want me to do you a favor, there'd better be a bag of fresh, honey-glazed donuts from Annie's in your meaty paw and a big ol' smile on that pretty face, *baby*."

He stared at me for a second, and then his gaze heated. I couldn't tell if he was turned on by my attitude or just imagining getting his dick sucked—again— but my stupid, traitorous body didn't know how to *not* respond to that look. I was *this close* to sliding out of bed and getting rid of his bad mood the old-fashioned way…

And then he went and ruined it.

"Don't call me baby. I hate pet names. And I am not bringing you donuts in bed, Quinn. Ever. That's not… that's not what we *do*. You know that, right?"

Ugh. Seriously? I flopped back down, pulled the blanket over me, and muttered, "I am aware that we are not in a relationship. Just because they're ring-shaped does not make them a symbol of commitment, Champion."

He shook my leg again. "I'm being serious. We need to discuss this—"

"I assure you, we do not." But I was probably running late for work, so I sat up once more—*three sit-ups counted as an ab workout, right?*—and threw off the covers.

Champ made a kind of strangled noise and rubbed a hand over his mouth like he was fighting a smile.

I narrowed my eyes. "What's funny?"

He shook his head. "Nothing? It's just that you're…" His eyes strayed up toward my hair. "Cute."

Cute? Oh. Oh, *fucking fucksticks.* I glanced in the antique oval mirror over the dresser and confirmed my worst nightmare. While Champ looked like a freshly laundered Captain America with his perfectly coiffed blond locks and ogle-worthy pecs, I'd gone to bed with my hair wet and product-free after a postcoital shower, and it was at that moment doing a spectacular impression of a chestnut-colored cotton ball.

The morning got worse and worse.

I slid out of bed in just my boxer briefs, shouldered past him, and padded down the hall to the kitchen, where the coffee was already brewed and waiting, which I guessed was the silver lining of Champ's visits…

Okay, that and the truly phenomenal sex. And the laughter. And the witty conversations.

But these mornings after were killing my mojo.

I poured myself a cup and called over my shoulder, "I don't think we need to discuss anything. We covered all of your concerns during your freak-out on Sunday morning. And Friday. And Thursday. And last Monday. You don't want a relationship. *Terrific.* Neither do I. Don't blame *me* because you find me irresistibly attractive, okay? If you're ready to put an end to this, then stop coming around."

And I would be fine with that, I told myself, despite the pang in my stomach that called me a liar.

A huff of laughter from the doorway was the only thing that alerted me I'd been followed down the hall. The man was too damn sneaky by far.

"Obviously, I find you attractive. Very attractive. Too damn attractive. I'm just concerned you're making this into something it's not, Quinn. I don't want you to get hurt."

Sincerity rang in every syllable he uttered. The man truly, truly believed what he was saying.

It was very sweet.

It was also utterly maddening.

Which was pretty much on-brand for my interactions with Percy Champion.

"Sweet Jesus." I sipped my caffeine juice. "Let me make sure I understand. You're being a jerk to *save* my feelings, you assume I'm a 'relationship guy' even though I've given you no reason to believe this, and you're confident that any man who *did* want a relationship would want one with you. Have I got that right?"

Champ spread his hands. "You're a wedding planner," he said softly, like that explained everything.

"No shit," I shot back, because it kind of did explain everything, just not the way Champ thought.

I loved my job—loved the challenge, and the romance, and the pageantry of it—but there was something about planning a bride's third wedding in eight years that took the bloom off the rose when it came to "forever." Most wedding planners I knew felt the same.

Plus, I'd been partly raised by my Aunt Cherry, who liked to remind me, "Lovers are like baby tigers,

Quinny—adorable at first, but more dangerous the longer you keep 'em around."

And if all that weren't enough, the last time I'd decided to play the odds and risk a commitment, I hadn't just gotten burned, I'd been *charred*, thus proving once again that Cherry was always right.

"I keep telling you, but you keep not hearing me, so this time, please pay attention: I do not want a relationship. Not ever again," I said bluntly. I set my empty cup in the sink and dusted my hands. "And I'm tired of waking up to your assumptions and regrets and… and… weird, totally unfounded accusations of clothing theft."

"They're not unfounded. Shirts don't just disappear—"

"When you're ready to apologize," I interrupted, "I *might* consider listening. But until then, maybe spend your evenings at your own house—the house you *claim* to have, despite never inviting me over—"

"I told you, it's under renovation. And you're missing the point—"

I lifted my chin. "Are you going to apologize for yanking me out of my dream and killing my morning vibe?"

Champ set his jaw.

"Just as I thought. Then this discussion is over. See yourself out." I strolled down the hall toward the bathroom, stripping my boxers into the hall hamper along the way.

I heard his breath catch as I sashayed my naked ass through the bathroom door and shut it with a click, and I congratulated myself on making the best flounce in the history of flounces.

I wouldn't waste another second of my day thinking about Champ.

Quincy Taffet: 1, Percy Champion: 0.

But when I emerged from the bathroom a few minutes later, I realized my point-scoring had been a little premature.

"The man is either fucking diabolical or criminally negligent," I fumed. "How the hell am I supposed to aggressively not think about him now?"

The golden-brown fluffball in the middle of my hall runner cocked his head as if he were unsure also.

"Champ?" I yelled, though I could tell instinctively that I was the only human in the house.

Damn it. This was the second time this week Champ had left Hercules behind when he ran out the door in the morning.

The poodle jumped to his feet and spun around, barking happily the second his owner's name was called.

"Poor Herc. He's trying his best not to be in a relationship with you either, huh?" I knelt down to pat his soft, curly head. "Why do we put up with him? Is it that mischievous smile? Or the good neck rubs? Or that thing he does with his tongue that... er, never mind. You don't need to know about that. I'll get us some breakfast, and then you can be my assistant until your owner remembers you exist, okay?"

Hercules barked happily.

But on my way to the kitchen, I grabbed my phone and typed out an angry text.

Me: *Missing anything, Champion????*

For a man who was concerned about the symbolism of bringing me a fresh donut, he sure as hell left his pet behind all willy-nilly.

"Ah, crap. The Drakes-Dunwoody wedding party needs to move their initial consult up to ten o'clock," I told the dog as soon as I opened my laptop. Hercules didn't seem nearly as perturbed by this turn of events as I was. He barely looked up from where he sat at my feet, chowing down a bowl of the organic dog food I'd bought him the *last* time Champ left him here. "That's in just forty minutes."

I scrolled through Marissa's long, apologetic email, down to her email signature. Beneath her title—Marketing Coordinator for Drakes Automotive—was a promotional picture of her father, Tommy Drakes, dressed in a red Speedo and carrying a rescue buoy like a Baywatch-era David Hasselhoff, captioned "I'm here to save you! Save you... thousands off the sticker price on your new car or truck!"

I winced, and Herc paused his eating to tilt his head up at me.

"Hey. I'm not judging," I informed him. "Those ads are paying my exorbitant fee, and some of us have to source our own kibble, buddy. Besides, Tommy Drakes does other stuff too. Manufacturing. And real estate. And... horse things."

Actually, based on my client research, the horse stuff seemed less about bringing in revenue and more about supporting his only daughter, Marissa, my potential client. She was an accomplished equestrian, and Tommy was a proud papa.

Carlotta Drakes, on the other hand, seemed the type to care more about the horse's pedigree or whether

her daughter was wearing couture while riding, but I was trying to reserve judgment on her too.

My phone buzzed, and I glanced down quickly, then just as quickly rolled my eyes.

Delusional McBossypants Champion: *Uh, yeah. Already told you I'm missing THREE shirts.*

I rolled my eyes.

That's what *he* thought. He was actually missing at least four, by my count. Though maybe he'd been too drunk that first night at the Tavern to remember that he'd been wearing a Captain America T-shirt under his button-down and that I'd teased him about it until he'd pushed me down on my bed and we'd…

"*Nope,*" I said aloud. I needed to delete those memories from my brain, not revel in them.

Delete, delete, delete.

I probably also needed to delete the collection of recently liberated T-shirts from the back of my linen closet before Champ got a warrant to search the place, like the badass security company owner he was.

I grumbled, and when Hercules looked up in confusion, I snapped his picture and sent it to Champ.

Me: *Never mind the shirts. I meant YOUR DOG. You left him again. I'm going to hold him for ransom.*

I clicked off my phone and scrambled to my feet. "Come on. Let's take a walk, and then you can charm my prospective clients, okay?"

I grabbed the dog's leash off the coatrack by the door—where Champ had left it last night specifically so he wouldn't leave Hercules behind again—and led him to the tiny strip of grass between my building and the street so he could do his business while I made some phone calls.

Talking to my clients and focusing on business centered me, as it always did.

I spoke to Marco Perlman about offsetting the carbon footprint of his spring wedding with locally sourced organic food options.

I talked Aurelia Evers down from her dress panic by assuring her that there was plenty of lace on her bodice—in fact, too much lace if you asked me, but brides rarely did. I was there to make *their* dreams come true, after all, so I made it my policy to never offer advice or opinions unless asked… and even then, I was cautious.

I was just pulling up Posy Martinez's phone number to respond to her "bouquet emergency" when a toddler's high-pitched cry pierced the air.

My head swiveled toward the noise, and I saw Parrish and Diesel Partridge leaving the doctor's office down the street with their little girl. I hadn't met any of them, but it was impossible to live in the Thicket without knowing who they were, even for an outsider like me.

Parrish, who was shorter than his heavily tattooed husband by at least a foot, was the one carrying the baby. He also had his arm braced around Diesel's waist.

"Vaccines are never fun, baby," Parrish said soothingly as they approached. "But you were so brave. I think you deserve a cookie from Annie's."

Okay, so I might not be down for relationships, but there was something about a guy saying such sweet things to his little girl—

"Thanks, Parrish," Diesel said in his gruff voice. "I don't mean to get upset. It's just so hard to see Marigold cry, you know?"

"I know. 'Cause you're a great dad."

Oh. Oh, damn. That was even cuter.

Parrish wouldn't balk at buying *Diesel* a donut or accuse him of wanting a relationship when he didn't, that was for sure.

Hercules yapped excitedly, and Diesel lifted a hand in greeting. "Hey there, Quinn."

Despite me knowing most people in town by name, it was still odd to think they knew who *I* was. I hadn't joined the Thicket social scene since I didn't plan to live in town long — just long enough to build up my business while living and working rent-free in the building that used to house Aunt Cherry's dressmaking shop — but Diesel and Parrish seemed really nice.

"Morning!" I returned.

"This your dog? Mind if I pet him? He's adorable." Diesel bent down to pet Herc after I nodded.

"Not mine, I'm afraid. I'm dog sitting." Against my will. "Hercules is great for business, though. Clients enjoy him."

"Of course." Diesel balanced his daughter on his knee, and she smiled as she watched Herc jump around.

"Diesel's an animal lover," Parrish said, looking down at his husband fondly. Then he glanced back at me, and his gaze narrowed. "Speaking of clients, how *is* your business going? Is your calendar... booked up, would you say?"

"Oh, um. Going well. I'm busy. On the road to Nashville a lot."

"Ah, that's rough. Long drive, especially in winter," Parrish said.

I shrugged. "Not unexpected, though. Not much need of my services around here." I chuckled at the idea of there being a big-budget event in the Thicket — and then remembered hearing that Parrish Partridge was the heir to the Nashville-based Partridge Pit BBQ restaurant chain. I cleared my throat. "Never too busy to squeeze in a hometown client, though! Were you... looking to plan a wedding?" I glanced down at his hand, which already sported a scuffed-up ring.

"Us?" Parrish laughed lightly. "Oh, no. We're not the wedding type."

"Nah. We're the marrying type," Diesel agreed.

"Oh-kay?" I gave him a wan smile, though I had no idea what he meant.

"We have a different kind of event in mind that you'd be perfect for, though!" Parrish said happily. "We'll be in touch soon, okay?"

Later, I'd remember that this almost sounded like a warning, but I was too busy preparing for my client meeting and *not* thinking of Champ to worry about it.

Fortunately, the bright, airy showroom was already pristine, just the way I'd left it the night before. I lit some candles, tweaked the flower arrangements, and plumped the cushions on the vintage green sofa that Aunt Cherry had reupholstered shortly before she'd retired and left me her shop. Then I headed to my office/storage room in the back of the shop to brew some coffee and put together the planning binder I'd started for Marissa Drakes.

I knew there were a lot of people—for example, my ex-boyfriend Scott—who thought I was crazy for moving all the way to Licking Thicket and taking over Cherry's shop, but it wasn't so bad. The space was perfect, really. I just wished it was located somewhere a little less... *nowhere.*

Besides, it was thanks to Scott—and his brand-new twenty-three-year-old soul mate, Onyx, and his "teeny cash flow situation" preventing him from buying out my share of the event business we'd started together — that I'd had to relocate in the first place, so who cared what he thought?

"All in all," I told the dog firmly as I leaned over to pull a client questionnaire from the bottom drawer of my filing cabinet, "I am *over* men and their ridiculous opinions."

"Not all men, I hope."

I whirled and jumped, hand over my heart. "Mr. Dunwoody! You startled me."

"Trey," the man said softly. He was dressed in head-to-toe Ralph Lauren and seemed equal parts nervous and determined. "M-my name's Trey. You said on the phone the other day that we should call you Quinn, so you should call me *Trey*."

"Right." I blinked. "Yes. Whatever sets you and Marissa at ease, *Trey*." I forced a smile and extended my hand for him to shake. "Nice to meet you in person. Can I get you a cup of—?"

"I like your office. It's real nice."

"Oh." I looked around the organized chaos of the storage area. "Thanks?"

Trey swallowed nervously and ran a hand over his hair, then took a step toward me.

Hercules barked, and the sound made Trey flinch.

"Hush, Herc. Well!" I said brightly. "Why don't we go wait in the showroom for your lovely fiancée and her—"

"I saw you online," Trey blurted. "On your website, I mean. Your picture was there. With the pictures of the weddings. *Gorgeous*."

My eyes widened. He meant the *weddings* were gorgeous, right? He must. I chose to believe he did.

"And you looked so understanding," he went on. "I said to Marissa, 'That's him. That's just the man we need.' And she called you."

"Wow. That's... thank you. I work hard to make all of my events spectacular," I said firmly, "just like I will for you and Marissa. And even though six months isn't a very long time to plan, and I know you're probably nervous about all the work involved, I want you to know that I'm a professional and you're in good hands. You can count on me to take care of everything, and it'll all work out. Okay?"

"Yes." Trey exhaled a relieved breath and bit his lip. "I just knew I could count on you." He shuffled his feet. "You see, when I asked Marissa to marry me at Christmas, I-I wasn't sure if I was doing the right thing. She's so beautiful. So bright and kind. And I love her so much. I didn't want to lose her." His eyes were shiny. "But I have so many questions."

"Well, of course you do!" I relaxed enough to smile. "Mr. Dunwoody—*Trey*—large-scale weddings like these are complex. Otherwise, I wouldn't have a job. But all you need to do is love your bride and plan a wonderful honeymoon! Leave all the details to me."

"But my question is... do I love Marissa enough to marry her? H-how can I tell?" His words came out in a rush.

My jaw dropped. "I... I have no idea," I admitted. "Maybe you need a counselor? Or to talk to a friend?"

"Maybe..." He took a step toward me while Herc barked his head off. "It's just..." He tripped over a box of votive candles on the floor next to my desk and lurched toward me. I grabbed him to try and keep us both upright, but we tumbled to the floor in a heap, half-hidden behind my desk.

Trey lifted his head up and stared at me. The warm breath from his frantic panting hit my face, and I could have sworn there was a semi-hard dick between us that was definitely not mine.

I tried to push him off me, but he reached up to cup my face. "Quinn…" For some crazy reason, I got the feeling he was going to kiss me, so I pushed against him.

"Get off me," I said. "Marissa's going to be here any minute, and I'm not interested in anything other than that."

"No, wait. I just want to—"

"You have precisely three seconds to get the fuck off of him," a deep, familiar—and really, really *welcome*—voice growled from the doorway.

Trey jumped away, eyes wide and panicked like a deer in headlights. "What? No! I was just… we were talking! About the wedding." He jumped up and swallowed hard. "And we fell. But it was just an accident! I'm his client. Right, Quinn?"

I hesitated.

"Not anymore you're not." Champ folded his enormous arms over his chest and his no-nonsense tone made me shiver.

Under other circumstances, that protectiveness would have worked for me in a maaaajor way—okay, fine, even under *these* circumstances it was working, as the half-boner in my pants would attest—but I also really needed well-connected clients in order to build my business, and I couldn't afford to turn them away over a single embarrassing misunderstanding.

In truth, I had no idea what was going on with Trey Dunwoody. Was he questioning his sexuality? Was he having cold feet? He wasn't my friend, and it wasn't my place to sort his shit. My job was to get my clients through the nerve-racking process of wedding planning and to see them walk down the aisle.

"Trey is right," I said firmly. "He really did trip over a box of candles. As long as we all remember our roles from now on and act *professionally*, we shouldn't have a problem."

Trey nodded furiously, his cheeks pink. "That's... yes. Professionally. Of course. Thank you. I'm sorry. I'll just..." He coughed lightly. "I'll just go wait for Marissa in the front room." He made a move toward the door, and when Champ didn't budge, he sidestepped around him. But before he left, he hesitated. "Um. Are you... do you... work for Mr. Taffet?" he asked Champ.

Champ glared down at him, and then his gaze flicked to me for one quick second and his scowl morphed into a smile that was, frankly, way more menacing. "No, I'm not Quinn's employee. I'm his fiancé." He leaned toward Trey until their faces were inches apart. "And if you touch him again, *Trey*, losing your wedding planner is going to be the least of your worries."

Oh. My. God.

2

CHAMP

I stood in the center of the construction zone that had once been my bedroom and stared down at the text on my phone in annoyance.

Quinn (Gorgeous, blue eyes, drinks Howling Turtles): *Missing anything?*

Was the man kidding?

Fuck yes, I was missing *several* somethings. My patience. A large part of my sanity. And *three* of my favorite shirts, which had required me to leave Quinn's wearing nothing but my windbreaker and stop by my house for a change of clothes when I should have been behind my desk at Champion Security already.

What the hell was the man doing with them? Mopping his floors? Making a doll of me that he could stick pins into? Or was he just trying to get under my skin?

If so, mission accomplished, because I couldn't imagine anything worse than having to start my day by dealing with Jericho Zachary, the world's shittiest contractor, who'd turned a simple kitchen fix-up into a whole-house remodel that was entering its second year.

And Quinn thought I owed *him* an apology? Hell no.

At least I'd found a clean shirt protected in dry-cleaning plastic on one of the wall hooks that served as a temporary closet. I threw the shirt down on my still-made bed and typed a response to Quinn.

Me: *Uh, yeah. Already told you I'm missing THREE shirts.*

After hitting Send, I pulled on the starched shirt and did up the buttons before shoving the shirttails into my trousers with a sigh. I had a meeting with a potential client later in the day, and it was probably a good thing to show up looking more professional than my usual cargo pants and T-shirt anyway.

After leaving the Marines, I'd been eager to start my own private security company, to get out on my own and be my own boss. I hadn't fully realized back then that running the show would mean as many early mornings, late nights, and starched shirts as I'd ever had in the military.

Still, Champion Security was my baby. I was proud of the company I'd built, doubly proud of our reputation for going the extra mile for our clients, and prouder still of the men I had working for me. There was nothing I wouldn't do to keep it safe.

The phone buzzed with a response text, but I was running too late to check it. I raced down the elaborate but shabby wooden staircase, being careful to avoid the two rotten steps—lesson learned the hard way—before coming to a sudden stop at the bottom when I spotted an unexpected man in my foyer.

"Well, well, well. Percival Champion. It's been a while."

Jesus.

Okay, I lied. There was something far, far worse than dealing with Jericho.

"What in the holy hell are *you* doing here?" I demanded of my very ex-boyfriend. As far as I knew, he should have been in DC, working for the DEA, a comfortable five hundred miles away.

"Manners, Percy," Vince chided, smoothing down the lapels of the bespoke suit no ordinary government employee could afford. No doubt he'd hooked himself another wealthy guy and was spending that guy's money the way he'd tried to spend mine. "What would Bunny say?"

"We are *not* talking about my mother." My mother and I didn't see eye to eye on many issues, including my career, my insistence on living in the Thicket rather than her gated country club community in Nashville, and the fact that Vince was still on her Christmas-and-birthday-card list. "Just tell me what the fuck you want and leave. I have a job to get to."

"We have that in common. I'm here for work also." Vince strolled around the foyer, running his hand over the smooth wood of the wainscoting… and then quickly brushing the plaster dust off his fingers. "Looks like your dream house is really coming along, hmm? I can see now why you refused to consider buying the new construction down in Franklin like I suggested. Who'd want a place with luxurious amenities when you could live in a house like this, in a hotbed like *Licking Thicket*?" He chuckled to himself.

I felt a burst of lightning-hot anger.

I didn't bother reminding him that when I'd bought this big, old, run-down house, I'd gotten it for both of us, along with the adorable poodle Vince had just had to have. At this point, I could no longer remember what I'd ever seen in the guy or how I'd ever found him attractive, and I was really fucking glad he'd left me to take his DEA job.

But I'd be damned if I listened to him make fun of my home. Yes, the town was ridiculous. Yes, the puns were ruthless and terrible. And fuck knew this house was going to bankrupt me one day. But the town and the house were *mine* to make fun of and roll my eyes at. Not his. Never his.

"The place is coming along just fine," I informed him. "Just reinforcing some beams in the—"

A puff of drywall dust shot through the open living room doorway, followed by a muffled curse. "My bad!" Jericho called.

"—ceiling." I bit back a curse. "Look, I'm late for an important meeting, Vince," I lied, moving past him to the front door. "I don't have time for... whatever the fuck this is."

Vince's whole vibe reminded me of what a condescending fuck he could be and why it was a good thing we weren't a thing anymore. Something about him screamed manipulative and deceptive, but I couldn't quite put my finger on what it would be this long after our relationship had ended.

And, weirdly, I couldn't help but recall my conversation with Quinn that morning. No matter how much the man infuriated me—and even though I could swear he did it on purpose—there wasn't a truly mean or secretive bone in his body. He was only a casual hookup, but from the first minute, I'd trusted him far more than I trusted Vince.

I folded my arms over my chest. "Talk about something that doesn't nauseate me," I clarified.

Vince sighed again. "I'm here working that case I called you about back in November. You remember the one where sensitive information about Cartel de la Luna was stolen from Gustavo Santiago's compound and smuggled into the United States on *your* private plane?"

Shit.

I fought to keep my face impassive as my heartbeat kicked up several notches. "I remember telling you to get fucked," I said easily. "Champion Security's mission in Venezuela was a hostage rescue situation. No stolen information, no smuggling. The DEA has my report."

He smirked. "Sure. Thrilling read. But I feel like you left out some details."

The back of my neck prickled.

That report had been almost entirely fiction with more holes than swiss cheese. But I was surprised Vince cared enough about this case to still be searching for leads nearly two months later. He'd never been great at follow-through, which meant there must be more at stake than I realized...

And that was very bad news for Champion Security.

"For example," Vince said, watching me carefully, "your report never mentioned that the tourist you rescued was a disgruntled former employee of your biggest client. Or that he was suspected to have sold the cartel backdoor access to the Horn of Glory game system so they could use the game's in-app purchases to launder money. Or that he left the cartel's compound carrying a handheld Horn of Glory gaming device that he stole from Gustavo Santiago. Or that he disappeared the minute you touched down on American soil."

I set my jaw and stuck my sweaty hands in my pockets. I had no idea how Vince had put all of that information together. Hell, my team had barely put all that together, and we had inside information.

"Talk about a thrilling tale," I said mildly. "Those are some pretty wild claims. Where's your proof?"

"Funny you should ask, because it's closer than you might think." He laughed lightly. "Literally. See, Buck Nutter's ex-girlfriend found the stolen Horn device in his storage unit and sold it, along with some other items, to a dealer at a nearby flea market... though she can't remember which one. Still, shouldn't be too hard to find. That's why I'm here."

"Good luck with that," I said in a strangled voice. "Finding one particular Horn in the Thicket is like finding a needle in a haystack. It's the most popular game in the world, and it all started right here in town. Every man, woman, child, and bovine in Tennessee has at least one—"

"It's a sparkly, peach, first-generation Horn." Vince studied his nails. "There are only three in existence. So."

Fucking fuck.

Vince officially knew too much.

And the way he'd laid out the facts for me explained exactly why this was a nightmare scenario.

HOG's former lead developer was suspected of working with a drug cartel.

A HOG device containing sensitive information had been stolen.

And, most damning of all, HOG's viral video game was being used to launder money.

If any of this came to light, Horn of Glory would be embroiled in a PR nightmare bigger than anything I could remember. Not only would I lose my biggest client and the reputation I'd worked so hard to build, but there was also a chance Champion Security could be implicated in a cover-up.

I wanted the DEA to have the info hidden on that Horn—of course I did. I wanted the cartel stopped.

I just needed to make that happen in a way that didn't involve HOG Corporate, or a Horn, or Buck Nutter. An anonymous tip, maybe. Or an untraceable email. Whatever Jasper Huxley, my tech guy, decided to cook up.

But first, I needed to get that Horn before Vince did.

My mind scrambled to put together a plan. Most flea markets near here sold rusty radio parts and half-used tubes of toothpaste. There was only one vendor I knew of that would deal with a rare, valuable Horn. And the good news for me was that Trixie Peppers would rather be dropped in boiling oil than voluntarily share information with "the damn government."

"I'm not sure why you're telling me all this, Vince," I said honestly. "It's none of my business."

"Percy." He laid a hand on my bicep imploringly. "I know things didn't end well for us—"

I snorted. Understatement.

"—but you're not my enemy. I want to *help* you. I came here to give you a chance to do the right thing. To work *with* me so we can get this information together. If you make an effort, that'll go a long way toward convincing my bosses that you were innocent—"

I laughed out loud. "Oh, shit. You want me to do your job for you, don't you? To use my connections so you can impress your bosses? Jesus." With my thumb and forefinger, I grasped his shirt cuff, lifted his hand away from me, and towed him toward the door. "That is *not* gonna happen. You're barking up the wrong tree. I—"

Shit.

Barking.

I closed my eyes and dropped my chin to my chest as I realized why Quinn had asked if I was missing something.

Christ. He was going to kick my ass. That should probably not have made me feel as weirdly excited as it did, but then again, nothing about my relationsh—er, *interactions*—with Quinn had been as straightforward as I'd imagined.

What did it say about me that I enjoyed riling the man up nearly as much as I enjoyed kissing him?

What did it say that, as stressed as I was about finding the missing Horn, kissing him still felt like a priority?

Nothing good, that was for damn sure.

I stepped out on the porch after Vince and firmly shut the door. "I've gotta go. Good luck at Trinket Town," I said, casually mentioning the thrift store least likely to have the Horn.

I got in the truck without waiting for a response and drove back toward town. I'd have to take Herc to the office, but he'd love it, and the team would be thrilled. On the short drive, I called Hux at the office.

Our resident hacker answered after the first ring. "Yeah, boss. What's up?"

"I need you to get a team out to Thrifty Thicket ASAP. Talk to Trixie Peppers, who runs an electronics booth there. She's the one with all kinds of tinfoil antennae around her stall, and you have to approach without a phone on you. Find out what she knows about a peach-colored first-gen Horn of Glory console. If she's got it, get it from her at any cost. If not, find out what she did with it."

I pulled into an open spot in front of Quinn's shop and parked the truck.

"You think it's a good lead?" Hux said.

"Unfortunately, yes," I said tersely. "I'll meet you at the office as soon as I can and explain everything, but the DEA is sniffing around, and there's no time to lose."

"The DEA as in…"

"Vince. Yeah."

"Fuck."

"Exactly."

I disconnected, then hopped out and strode into Taffet Events, preparing myself to do verbal battle with a particular short and sassy wedding planner.

A battle that would not involve sex. Not this time, and not anymore.

It was bad enough that I'd already started thinking about him when he wasn't around and finding excuses to show up at his door all the damn time. This morning, I'd actually started feeling shitty for reminding him once again that we were not in a relationship… even though I knew I was doing it for his own good.

Quinn said he wasn't into relationships, but I couldn't help feeling like we'd crash-landed ourselves in the middle of one anyway. The man knew every one of my erogenous zones and how to tease me until I lost control. He knew how I took my coffee and the kind of kibble my dog liked best. The other night we'd even talked about my hopes and dreams for Champion Security, for fuck's sake.

It was only a matter of time until the expectations began… and, immediately after that, would come the disappointment and hurt feelings.

Quinn was a great guy, but Champion Security was my priority, especially now that Vince was sniffing around, trying to fuck things up.

So it was time to get my T-shirts back and say goodbye.

Quinn and Hercules weren't in the front room, but I smelled fresh coffee coming from his office. I hung back in the hallway, not wanting to interrupt a client meeting if I didn't have to… and that was when I over-heard some asshole getting all up in Quinn's business.

"Get off me," Quinn said. "Marissa's going to be here any minute…"

The fuck?

Ordinarily, this would have been where I turned around and walked right back out. If Quinn wanted to get it on with some other guy, that was… that was great.

Awesome. Perfect. *Convenient.*

But I heard Hercules barking a sharp warning. And then I heard Quinn grunting in struggle.

I didn't know Quinn all that well. He was a one-night… or, fine, *twenty-six*-night stand. But what I *did* know was that Quinn didn't do fear. He gave as good as he got, always. And no one was allowed to fuck that up.

"You have precisely three seconds to get the fuck off of him," I warned before I'd even cleared the doorway. When I saw a strange man on top of Quinn on the floor, I had to hold myself back from beating the fucker to a pulp.

The asshole who'd gotten all up in Quinn's personal space jumped up and started whining, but I didn't look at him because I was busy assessing Quinn. He seemed uninjured and pissed off, which was excellent.

It wasn't that I had any particular protective feelings about Quinn, of course. That would be absurd. But I couldn't abide predators.

"I'm his client," the preppy idiot bleated. "Right, Quinn?"

Quinn hesitated.

"Not anymore you're not," I decided. Nobody needed to work with someone who made them feel unsafe.

But Quinn contradicted me— because the man freaking *lived* to contradict me.

"Trey is right," he said firmly. "He really did trip over a box of candles. As long as we all remember our roles from now on and act *professionally*, we shouldn't have a problem."

The look he gave me dared me to push the issue, and I rolled my eyes. Quinn clearly didn't understand the concept of self-preservation.

The guy—Trey—stammered some more and tried to sneak around me to leave the room, but before he did, he turned his beady little eyes up at me. "Are you... do you... work for Mr. Taffet?"

I snorted. "No, I'm not Quinn's employee. I—" I was what? His bodyguard? His friend? Neither of those options would keep this dude from putting his hands on Quinn. Instead, I went with the most outrageous claim I could think of.

"I'm his fiancé." I leaned toward him and almost gagged on the overpowering scent of Invictus cologne. "And if you touch him again, *Trey*, losing your wedding planner is going to be the least of your worries."

As soon as the word "fiancé" winged its merry way

out of my mouth, I tried so hard to suck it back in, I made a choking sound.

Quinn realized this, of course, because he was an observant fucker like that, and his eyes suddenly changed from shocked to sparkling with mischief. "Yes. *Yes*. Mr. Dunwoody, please excuse my *fiancé* as he gets emotional sometimes. Isn't that right, Snickerdoodle?"

Ugh. The man *knew* how I felt about pet names.

I opened my mouth to say something when a woman's voice squealed from behind me. I spun around and moved swiftly to block the newcomer from Quinn. How long had it been since someone had gotten the drop on me like that?

"Easy," Quinn said softly. His hand landed gently on my back.

"Quinn! I didn't know you were engaged too!" The young woman standing in the doorway was tall and made even taller by the high heels she wore. Her dark, wavy hair cascaded artfully down either side of her face, across her shoulders, and over her chest. She wore a tight beige dress and carried a designer purse over one forearm. "Trey, honey, did you hear? Quinn and I can be bridal buddies! We can have wedding-planning double dates! How fun will that be?"

Oh God.

What had I done?

"Marissa." Quinn stepped forward and plastered on a big smile. "So nice to meet you in person. You're even more beautiful than in your engagement photo."

She made a little wiggling gesture of excitement. "Introduce me to your fiancé. He's so cute!"

Cute? *Cute?* I was a fucking soldier. I ran a global security firm and protected high-value targets around the world. I'd infiltrated heavily armed compounds and set off incendiary devices in some of the worst hellscapes on earth. Cute?

I needed to get the hell out of here and meet up with my team to find the Horn. How did Quinn do this for a living? Sitting through a bridal consultation and dealing with enthusiastic brides was the absolute definition of hell as far as I was concerned. I'd almost rather have been back in Afghanistan.

"Isn't he the dreamiest?" Quinn said with the voice of a cheerleader. I couldn't tell if he was joking or not when he laced his arm through mine. "Marissa, this is Champ... Percy Champion. Puddin' Pop, this is Marissa Drakes. Her family lives in Nashville but also owns Drakes Farm out past Layfield Crossroads. Oh, and this is her fiancé, Trey Dunwoody."

I nodded politely at Marissa before turning to Trey with a warning glare. Quinn bumped me with his elbow.

"Right. Well. Nice to meet you. I should probably leave you to it, Pookie Pie—" I began, deciding I needed to fight fire with fire when it came to these names. I reached over to the hook on the wall where Herc's extra leash lived... er, where it was *temporarily* located.

"Yes, gosh, don't let us keep you," Trey said in a relieved rush that set my teeth on edge.

"You know what?" I put the leash back on the hook. There was no way in hell I was leaving Quinn here with this guy, especially when he seemed so unaware of his own safety. "Now that I think about it, I should sit in on this meeting. Quinn's always wanting me to take a more active role in the wedding plans, aren't you, Possum?"

Quinn no longer seemed amused. "No. Nope. That's

completely unnecessary, *Lovebug*. I know you have your own *very important work* to do, and so do we."

I did. I definitely did. I needed to get the hell out of there and get on with my day.

"You're so thoughtful, Kittycat." I leaned over and placed a kiss on the tip of his nose.

"Kittycat?" he grumbled.

"That one's gonna stick," I murmured back with a smile.

"I'm still waiting for my apology," Quinn muttered.

"Don't hold your breath," I said the same way. "Oops! Phone call. Let me just grab this really quickly, Sugar Bear."

While Quinn led Marissa and Trey to the front of the shop, I took the call from Hux.

"Sitrep," I demanded.

"You were right." Hux sounded out of breath. "Trixie had it but said she sold it to a collector from Nashville."

Fuck. "Any intel on who the collector is?"

"Not yet. Riggs is still sweet-talking her. And you weren't kidding about the paranoia level. They're right now discussing government surveillance mosquitos, and Riggs just shared his recipe for homemade insect repellent. I'm wondering if Riggs's boyfriend should be jealous."

I glanced through the doorway to the front of the wedding planning shop, where an older couple had just joined the party. The older man had the same dark, wavy hair the bride had.

He looked really familiar for some reason, but I couldn't place him.

But Trey had used their entry to sidle a little closer to Quinn.

"Told you," I said absently.

The bride was waving her hands happily in the air as she seemed to be explaining to her parents that Quinn was a bride too. "Well, not a bride, *obviously*, but like… a groom? Is that right? Wait…" She frowned. "We need a new name. A gride! Or a broom!"

Quinn's eyes widened, and his lips opened as if to explain why broom might not be the best choice. But then he bit his tongue and glanced over at me. My eyes were still frozen on his lips as I remembered all of the ways those lips had made me feel the night before.

Quinn Taffet had magic fucking lips.

"Boss?" Hux prompted.

I blinked. "Yeah." I cleared my throat. "Yeah, so… wait. Doesn't your friend Kev know any game collectors from Nashville? He used to live there, and he's as obsessed with the game as you are. Find out."

Hux hesitated. "First, Kev is not my friend. He's Riggs's boyfriend's cousin, and he's *insufferable*. And second… he and I are kind of still on the outs from when I accidentally commandeered his orc forces to storm the Forbidden Quagmires of Sod."

I hated when my team talked in gamer speak. Even though HOG Corporate was one of our biggest clients, I wasn't familiar enough with Horn of Glory to understand half the shit Hux and the others talked about.

It was kind of a point of pride.

"Dude, just… mend your fucking fences, throw Kev an orc or two, and get me some intel."

I ended the call and slid the phone into my pocket. I needed to get to the office and do some research before my client meeting, which meant I needed to leave… but when I peeked back out into the shop, I saw Trey eyeing the chair beside Quinn at the small conference table.

Without thinking, I strode out to the front room and shoved a chair between Quinn's and the one Trey had been eyeing.

What was I doing? Not a clue. But I was going to keep doing it.

"Pardon," I said, giving Trey my best eat-shit smile.

Quinn's eyes narrowed as I brushed shoulders with him. "Pumpkin Roll... I'm fairly sure you were adamant you were *running late* when you so *lovingly* left me earlier this morning. You should go to work."

I flashed him a big grin, which seemed to startle him. "Nonsense. I wouldn't miss a chance to watch you perform your magic. You know I'm a sucker for weddings." Quinn gaped at me. I couldn't blame him. "Marissa is right, Dumpling. You'll make a lovely broom."

He opened his mouth to say something—probably something really snarky that I shouldn't have been looking forward to hearing but *was*—when Trey spoke up.

"We should get on with this," he said listlessly. "I have some calls to make."

A tiny wrinkle formed between Marissa's eyebrows. "You promised to take the day off, Trey. Mother and Daddy have luncheon scheduled at the Prim, and we're choosing wedding favors."

"Nothing could be more important than that," Marissa's father said firmly.

Trey nodded quickly.

Quinn's face lit up. "I love eating at the Primrose. You must try their pimento cheese quiche and peach mojito fizz."

Marissa reached her manicured hand over and placed it on Quinn's forearm as she leaned closer. "Oh my gosh, right? And their Vidalia Hoops. To. Die. For."

This was a side of Quinn I'd never seen before. After as much time as I'd spent with him, mostly naked and sweaty, discovering he had a Southern socialite side was a surprise. Maybe it shouldn't have been. He was a wedding planner in Tennessee, after all, but it made me a little curious to find out what else I didn't know about him.

I mean... not that I cared overmuch. We weren't dating or anything. I was simply an information gatherer by nature. Besides, Quinn obviously needed protection, and protection was my specialty.

Marissa's father held out a hand to shake. "Tommy Drakes. This is my wife, Carlotta." He nodded to the petite bottle-blonde at his side. "And you are?"

"Percy Champion. Nice to meet you."

"Champion." Mrs. Drakes's eyes narrowed. "You're not Bunny's boy, are you? She and I play bridge together."

"One and the same," I admitted. "She's a shark, isn't she?"

Quinn put a hand on my shoulder and dug in with his finger claws. "Honeybear, you should—"

"Stay!" Carlotta cried happily.

"Sadly, he can't." Quinn's words were hard. "You know how you get when we start talking about vows and commitments, My Little Teacake." He locked eyes with Marissa, tilted his head in my direction, and mimed brushing away tears.

"Aww." Marissa clasped her hands over her heart, and despite this whole fucked-up morning and the very real danger my company might be in, I felt the strangest urge to laugh.

Right before I strangled Quinn.

I said nothing and didn't move, so he summoned a smile and turned back to his clients, dismissing me. He clapped his hands once.

"Okay, then. First things first. I took your preliminary information already, Marissa, but you mentioned some concerns that would impact everything from the venue to the menu—"

Mrs. Drakes rustled in her designer handbag and pulled out a turquoise leather portfolio with a fresh notepad inside. She slid the bejeweled pen from its clip and twisted the top before preparing to take notes. "Yes, indeed. There will be *many* VIPs on the guest list, and security will be a concern—"

Security? I sat forward, interested.

"Before we talk about that, let's nail down the critical details," Quinn interjected smoothly. "Date, location, and budget. Then we can talk about party size, venues, and things like security."

The "critical details" turned out to be criminally boring. I tried to pay attention, but that lasted about half a minute. I began leafing through the stack of bridal magazines Quinn had left out on the table, but that was nearly as bad. I checked my phone for messages, but it remained stubbornly silent.

I had just finished stifling my third yawn and was ready to give in and invent an excuse to leave when a sharp object jabbed me in the thigh, making me fumble my phone and knock my knee on the underside of the table.

"Hey!"

"Right? Champ's excited about the idea too!"

Quinn told Marissa excitedly. "I'd love to come to Nashville and tour your club, and I can bring some color swatches if you'd like."

"Come tomorrow!" Carlotta decreed. "Tommy, honey, you'll be free, won't you?"

Tommy-honey looked only slightly less bored than I was, but he clearly loved his family. "Sure."

"And you, Trey?" Marissa demanded.

Trey shrugged. "I can try?"

"And… Champ?" Carlotta wondered. "You're more than welcome."

Oh, Lord. When I learned the woman knew my mother, I should have known she was a social climber. Fuck knew I'd met enough. I'd even dated a few.

"I… uh. I…" What was the most polite way to state that I'd rather light myself on fire than sit through another planning meeting?

Thankfully, Hercules chose that moment to stand up from his spot atop Quinn's shoe and shake himself vigorously enough to catch Marissa's attention.

"Oh my gosh, how adorable! What's her name? Can I pet that wittle baby?"

"His name is Hercules," I said quickly, pushing my chair back and standing up. "And he needs to go out. I'll — *we'll* be right back."

Quinn waved his hand in the air without looking up from his notes. "He's already been walked. You're welcome."

"Oh. You, um… you didn't have to do that," I muttered.

Except… he kind of had since I'd dropped the ball.

"No worries, *baby*. Always happy to help my Corn Niblet." Quinn turned to Marissa and said confidingly, "You know, when we first met, I thought Champ was just a pretty face, and *then* I worried he'd be a giant blockhead who couldn't make up his mind how he felt about me and would behave in the most bizarre hot-and-cold way. I didn't think he was the kind of guy who'd want to bring me fresh Annie's donuts in bed. Can you imagine?"

Marissa blinked up at me and smiled. "Really? Aw. He seems so devoted! Clearly the kind of guy who's into relationships."

"Right?" Quinn smiled wickedly. "You can just *tell*, can't you?"

Alright, now the man was just being mean.

"This has been… truly informative." I laid my hands on the back of Quinn's chair. "But it's so overwhelming for a newbie like me."

Quinn glanced up at me. "No stamina. It happens to a lot of… grooms." He turned to Carlotta. "They always *say* they can last for hours, but you get them past the bachelor party discussion and they fizzle out." He lifted a hand and let it flop limply.

I moved my hands to Quinn's shoulders and pressed a little more firmly than necessary. "I'm holding my powder for planning *our* wedding, Sweet Potato. I'll show you my stamina."

Quinn made a gurgling noise of mingled lust and annoyance that filled me with glee. Baiting him was too fun.

It was not my smoothest exit, but it worked, and after driving like a bat out of hell, I pulled into the lot at work and parked the truck.

I opened the door and pretended not to notice the old man sleeping at the desk in the reception area. Our temporary receptionist the past few weeks was ninety years old if he was a day, hard of hearing, and slightly narcoleptic.

Today, he wore a vintage army camouflage jacket with a yellow-and-purple kilt, which would ensure he blended in precisely nowhere. Most days, he only made it to around 11:00 a.m. before having to knock off for a siesta, but today, he hadn't made it that long.

He was still better than most of the temps we'd had before him. Most of them hadn't lasted a day with my crew of brilliant, overgrown-adolescent badasses.

"Morning, Herman." I sorted through the pile of junk mail and flyers on the desk.

The man startled awake so hard, he jumped to his feet and gave me a jaunty salute. "Ready to mount the attack, sir!"

I nodded. I wasn't sure which war he thought we were in currently, but it was good to know we were prepared.

"Good man. Any messages?"

"Nope." Herman sat down heavily. "Plumber came by to fix the leaky faucet in the men's room. Not sure what took him three hours or why he says he's gotta come back with a part. Back in *my* day—"

I glanced down as my phone buzzed.

Quinn (Gorgeous, blue eyes, drinks Howling Turtles): *If I didn't know better, I'd think you want me to have your dog, asshole.*

Herc. I closed my eyes and breathed in and out before looking up at the ceiling. "Fuck."

"Well, no need to use that kind of language, soldier," Herman chided. "When the plumber comes back to finish the job, I'll give him what for, don't you worry. In the meantime, your boys were lookin' for ya."

"Right. Thanks."

I pocketed my phone as I entered the big open-floor-plan office space we affectionately called the mosh pit. It was a high-ceilinged, white-walled room with wood floors and exposed beams, dotted with back-to-back workstations where many of my employees kept their permanent desks even when they were mostly away from the office on assignment.

All of them were empty.

On the far left wall were four doorways that led to the small kitchen, the bathroom, my office, and our server room. Along the back wall, separated from the rest of the office by a soundproof glass wall, was the space we called the war room. It was Hux's domain, with enough monitors and high-tech gear to rival any spy movie and a giant conference table ringed with leather chairs. This was where I found several team members huddled around Hux while he worked.

"Boss," Hux called when he saw me approach. "Perfect timing. Riggs just got here."

Riggs gave me a firm you-can-count-on-me nod, clearly still trying his hardest to make up for the colossal fuckup back in Venezuela. "I learned so much about the Illuminati from Trixie that I might never sleep again, but I got you a name."

"Cry me a river." I leaned against Hux's desk. "Why do I feel like your doctor boyfriend will make sure you sleep just fine, Riggsy?"

The others laughed while Riggs's face morphed from hardened soldier to demented cow like it always did when he thought about Carter.

I rolled my eyes. "Well? Cough it up. We need to put together a dossier on this collector so we can come up with a plan to beg, borrow, or steal that Horn back."

And then I had to go retrieve my dog.

For what would probably be the final time, given how pissed Quinn had seemed.

"That's the best part." Riggs beamed and turned his tablet to show me a copy of the man's license. "You already know him. *He's gonna save you… save you thousands on the sticker price of your new car or truck.*"

Ah, shit.

That was why Tommy Drakes had looked so familiar. He was the man with the car dealerships… and the really impressive abs for a man his age.

"So let's buy the fucking thing back," I said. "Make Tommy an offer that's double the sticker price. He's a businessman."

"Way ahead of you, boss," Riggs said eagerly. "I called Carter's cousin Kev and had him check with his Horny friends—" He paused. "Er, the Hornies are a special online forum for people who are high rollers in Horn of Glory—"

I held up a hand and shook my head briefly. "I lived my whole life without knowing that, Riggs. I'd hoped to continue living a life where I didn't know that." I fucking hated puns, and I wasn't shy about saying so.

"Right. Sorry. Anyway, there's a buying-and-selling forum where all the members are pre-vetted. Serious offers only, you know? And I had him offer a truly obscene amount of money for a sparkly peach first-gen Horn, but no dice."

"Fucking amateurs," Hux sneered. "Why the hell did you get Kev the Civilian involved, Riggsy? *Jesus.* Any true fan of the game knows you don't just go around making offers for a man's Horn all willy-nilly. These forums are for true connoisseurs—people who understand that owning a precious Horn isn't about the money. It's about *love.* It's about—" He broke off with a cough when he realized the rest of us were staring at him. "Anyway, just sayin', I'm not surprised it didn't work."

I shook my head impatiently. "So, fine. We do things the old-fashioned way. We find it and liberate it, and then we can give it back. Where does the man keep his collection?"

"Unclear. He owns a farm just outside the Thicket," Hux informed me. "Along with a mansion outside Nashville, a corporate office, three car dealerships, and a manufacturing operation. That Horn could be a lot of different places. I'm not sure how we get close enough to him to figure out which one."

I was pretty sure I knew one way I could get close to Tommy Drakes…

My phone buzzed with another text.

Quinn (Gorgeous, blue eyes, drinks Howling Turtles): *Lose my number, Butter Bean. And don't bother coming back for your dog. You don't deserve him.*

… but it was going to take some serious convincing and possibly some honey-glazed donuts to make it happen.

3

———————

QUINN

"Shit! Watch out for the red truck!" warned the man in the passenger's seat of my Volkswagen Beetle.

I glanced out the driver's window, over the wide strip of grass dividing the highway, to where a rusted-out red pickup bounced sedately along in the opposite direction.

Then I looked right, at the enormous, sexy control freak dramatically clutching the oh-shit handle above the door like he thought I might go *Fast and Furious* on him and suddenly hit the noz.

"Champion, I know how to drive my car," I said as patiently as possible—which was not very patiently since he'd been pulling this shit since the moment I pulled out of the parking lot behind my shop twenty minutes before. "You're the one who wanted to tag along on this meeting so badly. No one's forcing you to come. Zip it."

He was silent for precisely one second.

"Should you even call this a car?" Champ muttered

darkly. "I think 'rattling, orange death wagon' would be more accurate."

I shot him a glare that he met head-on.

"I'm just saying! It's your meeting, you wanna drive, *fine*. But I didn't survive multiple tours in Afghanistan to die twisted up like a pretzel in this Disco Barbie Dream Bug, so please watch the road."

He shifted his long legs in the cramped space, and his knee whacked the console hard enough to make the bobbling daisy figurine on the dashboard dance and my morning coffee wobble in its cup holder.

"First, I'll have you know, this is a high-end custom paint shade called *Opalescent Citrine*. And the rattle is… soothing. Like a built-in massage at no extra charge."

"Right. And I suppose the strobe light effect every time you brake is an advanced safety feature?" Champ demanded. "Is that even legal?"

"They're called undercarriage lights, and of course they are." At least, I was pretty sure. Chuck at Platinum Used Motors assured me they were a value-add, just like the custom paint and the dancing daisy… which I'd discovered the previous owner had superglued to the dashboard. "This vehicle is *iconic*. My brides think it's quirky and adorable, which makes them think *I* am quirky and adorable, m'kay? It's part of my marketing."

"Watch out for the pedestrian!"

"Wait, what? Where?" I hit the brakes, making the green and yellow lights on the dashboard and the undercarriage flash, and swiveled my head, looking for some stranded human on the highway—

"Over there in Amos Nutter's field." Champ pointed to a spot in the distance. "Feeding the cows. Jesus, Quinn, you didn't even *see* him."

"Okay. That's it." I pulled over on the side of the highway and slammed the car into Park. "What is going on here?"

"What? Nothing's going on. You're driving—a little aggressively and with limited situational awareness, if you're asking my opinion—because you insisted on being the one to drive. And I'm… sitting here encouraging you."

I pursed my lips and nodded. "'Encouraging' is one word for it. But what I mean is, clearly this is not fun for you in any way. So why did you need to come today at all?"

"What do you mean *why*? I explained it when I came by the shop yesterday afternoon, remember? I'm here to play the part of your devoted sidekick because I felt bad about springing that whole 'fiancé' schtick on you on the spur of the moment yesterday and then running out due to my, um, work commitments."

"You mean due to you falling asleep sitting up."

"No! Jesus." He hesitated. "Yeah, okay. *Fuck*. Fine. I maybe nodded off. But I felt bad about that too, as I told you." He turned the brightness of his lopsided grin from stun to kill and dropped his voice to a low purr. "And if you need me to remind you about the *other* things I told you yesterday afternoon… or the things I *did* yesterday afternoon… you just let me know. It's been a while since I gave road head, but I think we could reenact—"

"Stop right there." I smacked his hand as he reached for me. "There will be no smexy times in this vehicle, Champion. Her name is Rebecca, and she's *pure and innocent*."

Champ paused with his hand in the air. "You… named your car."

"Obviously." I sniffed. "And I will not let you sweet-talk and sex-addle me like you did yesterday afternoon… and last night… and also early this morning."

I felt my face go hot at the memory.

Memories. Plural.

"This time, I want an actual answer. And do *not*," I hurried to add when he immediately opened his mouth to speak, "try to convince me that this is to make up for leaving suddenly or abandoning Hercules, because that's kind of your MO." I raised an eyebrow, daring him to argue that. "So this time, try telling the truth. Begin with the part where you walked in on Trey and me and started beating your chest, and go from there."

Champ shifted uncomfortably. "I wasn't chest-beating. I was sticking up for you the same way I'd do for anyone in that situation. And that's why I stayed for the meeting too. Protecting people is my job."

I rolled my eyes. "Please. I can protect myself from Trey Dunwoody. I didn't need you to—"

"But you weren't," he interrupted. "Protecting yourself, I mean. Because you can't punch him without losing him as a client. Whereas me playing your protective fiancé gives me a certain latitude. That's all it was about. And then I stayed, to… you know. To… drive the message home. To let him know that I'd be watching him," Champ said firmly.

"And then you left because you were bored."

Champ winced. "Look, you started talking about *vermillion* for the bridesmaids, and I thought it was a disease, not a color, okay? I was out of my depth."

I laughed. I couldn't help it. "Uh-huh. So then… what changed later on?"

"Changed?" Champ repeated.

I leaned against the door so I could face him more

fully. "You fled my showroom in a vermillion fog — leaving your dog behind yet again — and I told you to get lost. So what made you rush back with a bag of fresh *commitment pastries* a few hours later and beg me to let you in?"

"Those donuts weren't a commitment-anything. They were a peace offering." He spread his hands innocently. "That's all."

I snorted. Those donuts had set a new bar for peace offerings… and I was never going to eat one again without getting instantly hard.

When I was truly angry — which didn't happen often — I was pretty much immune to sweet talk. It took a lot more than a charming grin and a half-assed apology to talk me down. And it was safe to say that after Champ had invaded my meeting, lied to my client, and run out, leaving his dog with me for the second time that day, I had been well and truly angry.

But then he'd *apologized*.

I'd had reason to know how talented Percy Champion was with his tongue, but when he'd stood in my back room yesterday afternoon and said, "I'm genuinely sorry, Quinn. I didn't mean to fuck up your meeting. Let me make it up to you," then offered me the bag of sugary treats with a sheepish "I asked Annie to make these up for you, nice and fresh," I realized just how magical that mouth could be.

I'd melted.

Then he'd broken off a piece of donut, held it to my lips, and watched me chew it — was donut-foreplay a category on Pornhub? Asking for a friend — before pushing me against the very same bookcase where Trey had tried to corner me earlier and sliding his way down my body.

I'd been hard enough to rip a hole in my pants by the time he got to his knees, and the sight of his big body in front of me—that cocky smile and the starched button-down—had pinged every single Quinn Taffet fantasy.

The whole rest of the evening had been a blur.

Which was why it hadn't occurred to me until we'd gotten in the car that morning—until Champ had *jammed* himself into the passenger's seat of my tiny car, with only a token protest at not being the one to drive —that I'd broken through my sex haze to question why the hell he'd come back in the first place, when he'd vowed he wasn't going to apologize… and why he suddenly wanted to spend his daylight hours with me, when ordinarily that was Not a Thing We Did.

"I'm waiting," I prompted. "I still don't hear an explanation."

"An explanation," Champ repeated, frowning.

I narrowed my eyes. I wondered if he was aware that he had a bad habit of repeating words when he wanted time to think up a lie.

"While you're coming up with a plausible story, maybe also explain how the hell you thought you were going to pull off the whole 'Are you Bunny Champion's boy?' thing. These people know Bunny Champion, okay?" I fumed.

The more I thought about it, the angrier I got.

"It's bad enough that I'm going to have to wiggle out of wedding-planning fiancé double dates with Marissa since I don't have an actual fiancé. Now I'm also going to have to convince Carlotta that you're related to a *different* Bunny Champion, which is just too ridiculous—"

"I *am* related to Bunny Champion," he muttered.

"*The* Bunny Champion?"

Champ nodded shortly. "She's my mother."

I thought about the Bunny Champion I'd seen at various Nashville fundraisers over the years. The woman was five feet tall, if you took away her four-inch heels and her three inches of champagne-blonde hair, thin as a wisp, and wore a perpetually cranky, mulish expression—

Huh. Okay, maybe there *was* a resemblance, now that I thought about it.

"Your actual mother," I said stupidly. I looked Champ up and down, but there was nothing in his chinos and sport jacket that screamed "hidden wealth."

"We're not close." Champ shifted in his seat, clearly uncomfortable. "But it's the truth—you won't have to explain that away. And you won't have to explain your fiancé away either, because I'll be sticking around. See how this works?"

"Sure, you're here today. But what about next week—"

"I'll be there next week too," he assured me. "For all your wedding-planning double-date needs. I got you into this, so it's only fair for me to be your fiancé until the wheels come off. Or until we go down with the ship. However you put it in wedding-planner lingo."

I blinked at him. "You—the man who three nights ago insisted that we switch sides of the bed before we went to sleep so it wouldn't seem like we each had an 'official side of the bed,' which would 'imply a relationship'—are willing to be my fiancé for the next six months?"

"Six months?" he repeated, and this time it wasn't an attempt to cover up a lie but to hide his horror. "Wait, what?"

"How long do you think wedding planning takes, my little Pecan Cluster?" I asked scathingly. "At six months out, this is already a rush job. The most desirable venues are already booked, and if Tommy Drakes didn't have more money than God, we wouldn't be able to get it done at all."

"I was thinking a week. Ten days if you wanted to figure out matching outfits. What the fuck do you do for the next six months?"

"Please," I scoffed. "There won't be a dull moment. The whole thing is a carefully coordinated dance. Yesterday, we had the initial meeting. A vibe check, if you will. Today, we discuss guest list, wedding party, which venues are available in June, some cute fabric swatches I have in mind, and any ideas Marissa has for her decor. For example, Mediterranean elegance or minimalism or more of a laid-back, eclectic style. I'll take a week or so to mood-board it—probably only a rough sketch since time isn't our friend—and then we start contacting vendors for samples—"

"Sounds inefficient," Champ blurted. "My team could plan that shit in a matter of days. And really, why wait? Get those crazy kids wed before they think better of it, amirite?" He smashed his hands together. "Why not challenge ourselves to see how fast we can get this shit sorted!"

"Uh. Because it's not a race—"

"Question! Are all the meetings going to be at the Nashville house? Because I'm thinking maybe you'll want to see Marissa at work, you know? Less disruptive that way. We could meet her at Tommy's corporate office. Or at one of his dealerships—"

I lifted an eyebrow. "How did you know that Marissa works at Drakes Automotive?"

Champ went still. "Drakes Automotive?" he repeated.

I folded my arms over my chest.

"I recognized her dad from the Speedo commercial." He shrugged with an ease I knew had to be an act. "It stands to reason she'd work for him."

"Does it, though?" I tilted my head. "You, a former military guy who founded his own security company, just told me you're the offspring of Bunny Champion, who's made a career out of lunching at her club and slaying unsuspecting bridge partners. And yet you want me to believe your first thought upon realizing that Tommy Drakes was the Speedo-wearing car salesman was that his daughter *must* have joined the family business?" I shook my head and made a noise like a game-show buzzer. "*Nnnhhh.* Doesn't track. "

"Well, that's..." He scowled. "Maybe Marissa mentioned it yesterday."

Wedding planning was a nonstop, high-stakes course in reading people. It didn't mean that I never got fooled, of course—witness the time I caught Scott and Onyx *in flagrante* on my antique four-poster bed back in Nashville—but it definitely gave me an edge when it came to reading people.

What I was reading now was that Percy Champion was lying.

And, more fool me, I was *hurt* by it.

"She didn't," I said firmly. "So maybe you googled my client. Ran a background check on her. Whatever you call it in badass-security-person speak."

Champ's face remained impassive... which I was pretty sure meant I was correct.

"What I want to know is why." I leaned toward the center console, arms folded. "And you'd better start talking, or you're gonna get real-dumped by your fake fiancé, Sugar Pop, and you'll be walking back to town. I've put up with a lot of your crap—" Twenty-seven mornings' worth, by last count. "—but I will not let you fuck with Taffet Events. Not my clients and not my reputation."

Close to him as I was, I couldn't miss the way Champ's blue eyes flashed with... God, I didn't even know. Respect? Understanding? Commiseration? Maybe all of the above. I also couldn't ignore the commingled scents of musky vanilla and sawdust that wafted off him. I thought randomly that the folks at Thicket Scent Co. were totally missing the boat on serving up Eau de Champion as a cologne. I wanted to roll around in it.

"I'm not fucking with your business. I wouldn't do that," he said seriously. Then he licked his lips and glanced away. "I just... I, um..." He ran a hand over his blond hair. "This is hard for me to admit, Quinn, but I think you were right. I mean, maybe I *was* feeling protective of you. With the whole Troy thing."

"You mean Trey."

"Exactly," he agreed solemnly. "I hate thinking of him making you uncomfortable. And I... I do like you. I mean, obviously I enjoy your company. And I really *did* feel bad about pulling the fiancé thing yesterday. So I'm here today to support you. As a... you know... a person in your life."

I whistled low. "Are you saying we're in a relationship, Champion?"

A muscle twitched in his cheek, and he blinked aggressively. "Well... I... no. It's not... It's more of a friendly kind of... you know."

I tilted my head. "A friendly... what?"

"A friendly… *relationship*," he whispered, hanging his head slightly.

"Holy shit," I whispered. "This is more serious than I thought if you're willing to use the R-word to get what you want. So what's the real deal? Is Marissa a murderer? Or is it her dad? Slaying people with his low, low prices? Or is it—" I gasped. "Fuck, it's her mom, isn't it? I knew it. She asked me my zodiac sign and my 'birth path number' to see if I'd bring 'auspicious energy' to planning the wedding. Red fucking flag."

He exhaled heavily and rolled his eyes. "No one is a murderer, Quinn. Jesus."

"Oh, fuck. That's exactly what the murderer would say! Is it *you*? Are you trying to murder *them*?" I teased.

He did the arm-foldy thing, mirroring my posture… though I had to admit, his was way more effective. "The only person I'm likely to murder is *you*," he muttered.

"Yep. Right back atcha," I said, dropping my teasing tone. "Especially since I'm now officially running late for this extremely important meeting, and if Carlotta turns me away because I arrive at an inauspicious time, fair warning, I will make you regret it. In fact, if you don't start explaining *now*, I'll call Ernette at the police station and tell her a strange man is carjacking me. 'He kept growling at me, Ernette! And giving me a straight-up murder glare! I was afraid for my very life. And then he said he was likely to murder me!'" I clasped my hands under my chin and blinked my eyelashes with frantic innocence.

Champ snorted. "Please. I know Ernette better than you do."

"Then you'll know she's a sucker for drama. They'll let you out in a couple hours, but by then, I'll have told the Drakes that you've been... running a trace on them."

"That's not what it's cal— *Ughhhh*." I could almost hear the man's molars grinding. It was kind of a thrill. He glared at me and pursed his lips. "You're not cute, you know. You're fucking annoying."

"I'm both. I'm multifaceted that way."

One corner of his mouth pulled up in a smile before he ruthlessly suppressed it. "*Fuck*. Okay, fine. I am investigating a... *thing*... for a... a client." He glanced up at me. "I'm not divulging a name."

I nodded slowly.

"I got a tip yesterday afternoon that Tommy Drakes might have information on the whereabouts of the thing... or might even have it in his possession. It's a huge coincidence, because I swear I didn't know about this when I met him yesterday morning. The problem is..." He hesitated. "I can't just ask Tommy about the *thing*, because I'm not sure how he might have... acquired it. Or whether he even knows the true value of what he acquired. And he has no reason to cooperate with me."

"Tommy Drakes is a thief?" I demanded, reading between the lines.

"No! Shit. No. Not at all." He paused. "Or not in this, anyway. Though he does have some connections to certain people who... well. Let's just say that Speedo commercial wasn't the only questionable thing he's done in his career. But the point is that I don't believe he stole this thing. Other people might have, though, before he got ahold of it."

"I feel like I'm playing twenty questions," I huffed. "Okay, so you're saying Tommy bought or found something that someone else stole? And does he know it was stolen?"

Champ's jaw worked. "Maybe."

I took that as a yes, to both questions. "And you want to… what?" My eyes flared as I realized the answer to my own question. "You want to steal it from him!"

"No," Champ said firmly. "I told you, I don't know if he has it. I don't know where he keeps it, if he does have it. I'm not planning to steal anything today."

"*Today*. But when you invite yourself along to visit Marissa at the car dealerships and to tour Tommy Drakes's other properties…?" I gave an outraged half laugh. "The audacity! Not only no, but *fuck* no. No way. This is my livelihood—"

"I'm not that much of an asshole, Quinn. I wouldn't do anything that would blow back on you."

"Well, pardon me if I don't believe you," I fumed. "Since you haven't told me a single truthful thing in the last twenty-four hours. Those apology donuts were donuts of *betrayal*. And those blow jobs were blow jobs of *manipulation*. You were using me." When I'd sworn to myself I wouldn't leave myself and my *business* vulnerable to that shit again after the Scott debacle. "Fuck, I'm such an idiot."

"Quinn." Champ's voice was regretful—though I didn't know if I could even trust that anymore—and he stretched out a hand toward me but let it fall to the console, like he knew touching me right then would set me off. "Listen. I swear on the life of… of *Hercules*—"

I snorted. "The dog you keep abandoning? That's not saying much, Champion."

He scrubbed at his forehead. "Fine, then I swear on Champion Security, this is the truth: I'm not the only one who wants the… the thing. Multiple other people are searching too. And if they follow the same clues that I did and find out that Tommy might have the *thing*… they're going to get it back from him, and they might not be nice about it."

"Not nice? Like…" I swallowed back my horror. "Wait! Wait, wait, wait. Are there *actually* murderers involved here?"

"No. Or… I guess, maybe. I don't know for sure. But Quinn, I am serious. It won't blow back on you. You won't be harmed, and neither will your business—"

"I don't care about that right now! Are you fucking kidding?" I leaned over and smacked his arm hard for even considering it. "If someone could harm Marissa and her parents, we need to call the police! The FBI. The CIA. The… whoever."

"One of the groups that's looking for the thing *is* the… the government. And trust me when I tell you, nobody in their right mind—especially a person with a business to protect—wants to have this… *thing* found in their possession. Tommy would not take kindly to us calling the police and opening that can of worms."

There was a ring of truth in that too. Shit.

"So what do we do? Who *do* we call? Who can we trust—?"

"Me." Champ grabbed my hand mid-flail. "This is my job, Quinn. This is what I do. *Part* of what I do. So let me do it."

My nostrils flared. God, I wanted to believe him. Every instinct screamed for me to trust him, though I had no reason to. "What is the plan, then?" I demanded. "What exactly are you doing today?"

"While you're meeting with Marissa and her parents, I'm going to take a quick look around. Reconnaissance. My tech guy got me some specs on the house, but there's quite a bit of missing info. All I want to do is fill in the blanks. See what he has for security."

I rubbed at my pounding temples. "You're casing the place."

"I'm not—!" He sighed and began again more calmly. "I'm investigating, Quinn. And I'm going to have to do it one way or another. This is the way that will be least dangerous for me and safest for your clients. I swear."

I should say no. I should immediately and responsibly say no. I should kick him out of the car, out of my bed, out of my life.

"Please," Champ said sincerely, and fucking Christ, that was all it took to melt me.

"So you're going to sit and talk about vermillion lace gowns, then?" I said grudgingly. "You're going to be my silent partner? My very-junior wedding-planning assistant?"

His eyes lit up. "I am. Vermillion is my favorite shade of green."

"Red."

"Wait, red lace? For the bridesmaid dresses?" He wrinkled his nose. "That's fucking…"

I rolled my lips together and stared at him.

"Fucking *delightful!*" he managed. "What a, um… beautiful vision that will be! Unique."

"*Hmph.*" I turned to face forward and slid the car into Drive once more. "Don't make me regret allowing this. Remember, you're a silent partner, Champion. Emphasis on the silent."

He mimed zipping his lips and tossing the key out onto the side of the highway…

But I should have known the control freak fiancé I *wasn't* in a relationship with couldn't stay silent for long.

"Quinn and Percy!" Marissa cried in delight as she threw open the door to the Drakeses' palatial home. Her long brown hair hung in loose waves from a high ponytail, which skimmed the boat neck of her cashmere sweater dress. "My favorite wedding-planning buddies." She threw her arms around each of us in turn.

I glanced at Champ, who seemed a little taken aback. Presumably, most of his missions didn't involve getting squeezed to death by enthusiastic former debutantes.

I gave him a look that said, "*Sorry, not sorry. You asked for this, fucker.*"

His return glance said something like "*Watch and learn,*" which was a little concerning, honestly.

"Marissa!" he exclaimed warmly, setting down the cardboard box of supplies he'd carried so he could step into her embrace. "Great to see you. I felt *so* terrible that I had to leave yesterday, but I—"

"But you were overwhelmed, like you said," she supplied, her big eyes filled with sympathy. "I get it. Wedding planning is such an emotional thing. You know, I was thinking about you two a lot last night, and I decided I really want today to be about *both* of us, you know? You guys *and* me and Trey. Because I know you love your job, Quinn, but I don't want you to spend so much time on *me* that you're ignoring your sweet Percy." She wagged a playful finger at me.

I stifled a snort. "Oh, nothing could be more important than our *relationship*. Isn't that right, Butternut?" I leaned toward Marissa confidingly. "Words of affirmation are his love language." To Champ, I added, "You're doing *great*, baby. Awesome job carrying that box."

Marissa beamed as she led us into the large marble foyer. "*So sweet.*"

"Hey, Rissy? Where'd you want me to put these — oh." A tall, heavily muscled young man with dark hair falling over one eye strolled out of a room to the left of the doorway and paused when he saw us. "You're late."

"We are. Traffic was terrible," I said apologetically. I shot a fulminating look at Champ. "Pedestrian on the highway."

The guy made a disbelieving noise.

"Just leave the folders on the table," Marissa told him. Then she drew her arm through his and steered him toward us. "Levi, this is Quinn, my wedding planner." She smiled at me. "And that is his fiancé, Percy. Guys, this is my friend Levi. We kind of grew up together."

Levi gave me a chin-lift, but when his gaze landed on Champ, he turned speculative. "I'm not just a friend. I'm an employee," he corrected in a no-nonsense voice. "I work for Christianson Protective Services, and we handle security for Mr. Drakes." He gave Champ an up-down. "You know all about security, don't you, Mr. Champion?"

I felt a second of pure shocked panic. *We've been made! He had a bug in our car! Abort, abort!*

But Champ returned his icy look with a goofy, affable smile I'd never seen before. "Sure do! I own a security company too. Champion's not nearly as big as Christianson Protective, of course," he said admiringly. He rocked back and forth on his feet in a way I'd never seen him do either. "But at Champion Security, we're all former military. *Oooh-rah*, you know? You serve, Levi?"

Levi shook his head reluctantly. "My dad did."

"Ahhh." Champ nodded as though this explained many things. "Well, we do okay for ourselves. You been to the new mall out in Hemlock Valley? The Swan's Crossing? One of our contracts," he said proudly. "And we've installed alarm systems for a *bunch* of folks. You heard of HOG Corporate?"

Levi's eyes narrowed, and my palms began to sweat.

"Oh my God, Levi, *chill* with the death glare." Marissa rolled her eyes and smacked his abs with the back of her hand. "Who cares about boring old mall security? Champ is helping Quinn plan their wedding, and you'd best make him feel at home, understand? Lord knows Trey doesn't have an opinion on anything. It's nice that some fiancés do."

"Truth," Champ agreed. "My Little Stink Bug here has been dying to get me more involved." He nudged me in the side, then yanked me against him when I stumbled. "I usually don't make time, but last night Quinn begged me—"

"Exaggeration," I scoffed.

Champ's blue eyes met mine in challenge, and he touched the tip of his tongue to the corner of his mouth. "You don't remember begging me last night?"

Oh, fuck. Oh, Champ. Harder. Please, harder.

I felt my face go hot.

"He said, 'Please, Champ. You have such incredible taste. Come and show the people your skills.' So I agreed, of course. Can't say no to my Dollface."

The urge to roll my eyes was nearly overwhelming.

"Wait. You?" Levi asked Champ, giving him a suspicious glance from his beefy shoulders to his beefy chest to his equally beefy thighs, lovingly encased in his neatly pressed pants. "*You* know about planning weddings? Dresses and decorations and shit?"

"Oh, no. Not really. I leave all the piñatas and balloon animals to this guy." Champ ran a finger down my cheek, and it was *not* hot. *It was not.* "But Quinn says I have a natural eye for form and style." Champ shrugged modestly. "After all, I picked him, didn't I?"

Levi turned his speculative gaze to me, eyeing me from my oxfords to my lilac pocket square, as if wondering what the attraction might be. I blushed.

"Levi," Marissa said abruptly. "Stop being rude. Be a sweetie and tell Daddy that we're in the parlor?"

Levi hesitated, and Marissa set her hands on her hips. "Today, please? My mother's waiting. And Trey's gonna make an excuse to leave any minute."

Levi gave Champ a warning look, then turned without a word and strode away.

Marissa rolled her eyes. "I swear, that man is allergic to weddings," she said hotly. "Ever since Trey and I announced our engagement at Christmas, he's treated me like I have the plague, and I have no idea why."

Champ and I exchanged a glance. The longing look Levi had leveled at Marissa before he knew we were there suggested one possible explanation.

But I was sure as fuck not gonna speculate about that to my bride, who was engaged to someone else.

"Well. Some men are just scared of commitment," I said brightly. "Immature, but what can you do?"

"Or maybe he's been in a relationship before and it didn't work out," Champ suggested. "And he's smart to be cautious."

"Or maybe he's just being an asshole," she sighed.

"Christianson Protective Services is his dad's company, and his dad's worked for my dad *forever*. Levi grew up with his nose in my business. After the wedding, we probably won't see each other as much, though. Which is a good thing." She cast a troubled look down the hall where Levi had disappeared. "Anyway. Let's—"

"Marissa!" Trey lounged against the doorway of the room to the right of the foyer, looking put out. "What's taking so long?"

Marissa summoned a smile for her fiancé. "Sorry, Trey. We're just coming. Look who Quinn brought!" She held out a hand to Champ like a game-show hostess.

The look Trey gave my fake fiancé was a little bit deer-in-headlights, and he tried to avoid looking at me at *all*. It was probably wrong and barbaric, but it really worked for me in all kinds of pants-tightening ways.

Marissa caught up to Trey and led the way down the hall.

Champ grabbed the box from the entry where he'd dropped it, and the two of us followed.

"Your cheeks turn a lovely *vermillion* when you're aroused," he whispered conversationally.

I stood straighter. "What happened to you being a silent partner?" I demanded in a hiss. "Teach a man a single vocabulary word and suddenly he's telling people he's my wedding style guru? And what's with the 'aw, shucks, I'm a mall cop' thing?"

"Levi knows who I am and what I do. Clearly I'm not the only one *running a trace* on people." He chuckled to himself, no doubt at my ineptitude with badassery. "If I'd known I was going to be going in as your fake fiancé, I might have made up a different identity when I introduced myself yesterday, but I didn't. And actually, this is for the best. They were bound to check out anyone you brought along, and this way, my honesty makes it look like I've got nothing to hide. But just in case, let them think my business does rent-a-cop stuff and alarm installations. Maybe they won't look deeper."

Hmph. Okay, that actually sounded reasonably intelligent.

But… if Champion Security didn't do those things, what *did* they do?

Champ looked at my face and laughed. "What did I tell you? You take care of the crepe paper streamers, Honeysuckle. Leave the investigating to me."

He gave me a wild grin before stepping into the parlor, crying, "Carlotta! Darling, how is it possible that you look younger than yesterday?"

I shook my head and followed.

I was pretty sure my bodyguard slash fake fiancé needed a keeper. And it looked like it would have to be me.

4

———

CHAMP

Twenty minutes later, I'd decided that leafing through the bridal magazines hanging around Quinn's place had given me more than enough information to handle myself in a wedding-planning session, *thankyouverymuch*. Piece of cake.

"I've been organizing the wedding mood boards on Pinterest and Trello," Marissa began, pulling over a rose-gold laptop.

I ran those words back through my head, and they still didn't make a damn bit of sense. I nodded anyway. "Good, good," I murmured. "Love me a mood board, don't I, Pickle?"

Quinn side-eyed me before turning back to the bride and saying with a completely straight face, "Oh, yes. Champ prefers Asana. He decided he prefers the multimedia capability since he has the potential to integrate his future wedding-planning TikTok and Instagram accounts into his wedding mood boards. He also has mood boards for his actual moods, which has been *so* helpful to me in understanding the complex processes of that big brain of yours, hasn't it, Nilla Wafer?" He looked up at me soulfully.

What the fuck was he talking about?

Marissa's forehead wrinkled. "Like, what do you mean?"

Quinn leaned forward. "Oh, like Champ's 'sad' board has photos of all the things that make him happy when he's feeling blue. Teddy bears, fresh daisies in a jelly jar, puppy kisses, that song by Pharrell, and—"

I reached over and clapped a hand over his mouth. "No. That's... that's private, Pork Chop. Besides, Marissa and Trey aren't here for that. They're here to discuss their own big plans. Isn't that right?" I flashed my best smile at Marissa. "Tell me more about what you lovebirds are thinking!"

I felt someone stiffen behind me.

I turned to see Levi, the Drakeses' family bodyguard, standing in the entrance to the doorway. His eyes roved over Marissa before moving toward Tommy Drakes, who'd been sitting pretty stoically while Quinn, Marissa, and Carlotta planned ways to spend money, only occasionally flicking annoyed glances at Trey, who hadn't looked up from his phone since we'd sat down.

"Excuse me for interrupting," Levi said. "Mr. Drakes, there's someone at the door for you."

"We're busy, Levi." Tommy waved a hand.

"Yes, sir. But they're insisting."

Tommy glanced up, and whatever he saw on Levi's face had him swinging gracefully to his feet. "Back in a minute, sweetheart," he told Marissa.

Maybe this was my chance to do a little snooping. If Drakes and Levi were busy with someone at the front door and Mrs. Drakes, Marissa, and Trey were busy here with Quinn, I could poke around with less chance of discovery.

I pushed back my chair to follow them. "Would you mind pointing me in the direction of your restroom? I had too much coffee on the way here."

Levi flicked me a suspicious look, but he must've decided whoever was at the front door was more of a concern than I was. He pointed to a doorway down a side hall before following his boss toward the front of the house. I made my way into the bathroom before turning right back around and sneaking out again. I returned to the room I'd spotted on the way in that looked like Tommy Drakes's office.

Sure enough, the dark-paneled room was exactly what it looked like. A heavy wooden desk with gaudy carvings down the legs took up the far end of the room, while dark leather sofas and chairs made up a seating area by a fireplace. I turned around to look for things of interest, like a file cabinet or computer, when the light from a nearby window glinted off a display case mounted on the wall behind the desk, catching my eye.

I stood and stared. The case took up almost the entire wall, and it was filled with every kind of hand-held gaming device I could think of. I crept closer to it, my eyes searching the collection greedily. Finally, I saw it. A sparkly peach Horn of Glory was mounted front and center above an old pocket arcade game, looking exactly like the pictures Hux had shown me.

The display was locked, which wouldn't have been a problem, except I also noticed two very high-end and discreet motion sensors protecting the case. Instead of trying to get into the display, I quickly pulled out my phone to snap some photos of it for Hux.

Before I could even get a second shot, though, I

heard footsteps and voices coming close. There wasn't time to get out the door without being seen, so I needed to either hide or explain why I was snooping around. There was no way I would get away with acting stupid after Levi had shown me to the bathroom directly—especially not when they knew who I was and were already suspicious of me—so I quickly moved behind a heavy window curtain in the corner of the room and prayed the old movie trick actually worked.

The fabric was thick enough to muffle their words but not so thick I didn't recognize the one that didn't belong.

"We were hoping a known collector like yourself could help us with our investigation," Vince said in a false-friendly tone.

Well, fuck. That had happened faster than I'd anticipated. I wasn't sure how he'd gotten around Trixie Peppers, and I didn't want to know, but it wasn't a total shock. My ex was smart, which was one of the reasons I'd been attracted to him in the first place. I simply hadn't realized at the time he had an ego even larger than his brain and ambition even bigger than the two of them put together.

Tommy Drakes didn't even try to fake friendliness. "Investigation into what, exactly?" he demanded in a don't-waste-my-time tone.

"We have reason to believe that there is a corrupted virus file loaded onto a stolen gaming device you recently acquired. The source code of this virus might help us track down a ring of international hackers," Vince explained, smooth as butter.

This was a lie, of course. The Horn supposedly held the Cartel de la Luna's financial data as well as identifying information for high-level cartel members that could put a serious dent in the cartel's ability to do business if it ended up in the DEA's possession. In the meantime, whoever held this data might as well have been holding a ticking time bomb. When Gustavo Santiago tracked down the stolen Horn, he and his people wouldn't ask for it nicely. They'd leave a swath of bloodshed and violence in their wake.

If Tommy tried to access the data on the device, it would put him in even greater danger, so it made sense Vince used the virus story to discourage snooping.

"I'm afraid I don't understand why you think I have this information or this device," Tommy said. There was a long beat of silence in which I imagined everyone in the room staring at the giant wall of gaming devices.

Vince finally spoke carefully. "We only want to take the device long enough to extract the data. Of course, we'd be happy to return the device itself back to you when we're done processing it."

Translation: *you will get your Horn back approximately never.*

"I don't believe I have a *stolen* device, so I'm afraid this has been a waste of your time," Tommy said. "Levi, please show this man out."

I bit back a smile. Implying Drakes had stolen property had been Vince's critical error. I didn't believe for one second Tommy Drakes would have handed it over voluntarily, but Vince still shot himself in the foot by making him sound like he was harboring ill-gotten gains. If only Vince had done his homework on Tommy Drakes, he would have learned the man was into some shady shit. In addition to the car dealerships and other legit businesses everyone knew about, Hux had found that Drakes was also connected to a couple of suspected chop shops, a low-rent strip club out by the

Nashville airport, and a dry-cleaning business that had a suspiciously high number of weed-smoking high schoolers as customers.

I'd told Quinn the man wasn't a thief, and that was true... mostly. Certainly, no one had ever pinned anything on him. But he wasn't a choirboy either. And there was no way he was going to cooperate voluntarily with a government agent.

"I don't mean to imply you stole the device, Mr. Drakes," Vince said quickly, trying to recover his schmoozing efforts. "Of course not. We assume you acquired it under completely legitimate circumstances. Of course you would have had no way of knowing it was stolen."

Before he could continue his desperate attempt to get back on track with Tommy Drakes, Levi's voice cut in. "Come with me, sir. Right this way."

Vince wasn't going to give up that easily. Sure enough, he stayed right where he was and came at it from a different direction. "Mr. Drakes, I'm afraid I'm going to need to take that Horn device with me today. It's necessary to preserve national security and—"

Tommy Drakes's voice cut through the room like an icy draft down my back. "Well, why didn't you say something? If you came here with a warrant, I'm more than happy to comply."

The silence lasted for a beat before Vince had to admit the truth. "Surely a warrant isn't necessary in such a—"

"If you do not have a warrant, you are no longer welcome in my home. Levi will see you out."

I heard a faint scuffle before Levi and Vince left the room. Just when I was wondering if it was safe for me to come out of my hiding place, I heard the creak of a chair.

Fuck.

A minute later, Levi came back into the room. "He's gone."

"How the hell does he expect me to believe a DEA agent is here about a hacker?" Drakes sounded annoyed, but his implication that Vince wasn't the brightest bulb made me want to laugh.

"I got his card. I'll look into him. In the meantime, Mrs. Drakes is looking for you. Marissa's come to some decisions about the wedding." Levi spat *wedding* like the word disgusted him.

The sounds of the chair creaking and feet shuffling across the carpet encouraged me that I might actually be able to escape this stifling curtain.

"We need to move this thing. I don't want him sniffing around, and I sure as hell don't want him coming back with a warrant and taking something that belongs to me. I don't give a shit what kind of information he thinks is on the damned thing. I'll never get it back in one piece if the government gets their hands on it."

"You sure you want me to move it now?" Levi asked. "Maybe we need to wait until the security guy is out of the house."

"Not worried about that guy," Tommy scoffed. "What would he be looking at me for? Besides, he's a *Champion*. If I know his mother, the man's never worked a day in his life. He's too busy helping his fiancé order Rissy's invitations. Move the Horn now before the fed comes back."

"You got it, boss," Levi agreed.

I rolled my eyes. Being a Champion had always

been a blessing and a curse—once a thing I'd tried to live up to and then a thing I'd tried to live down—but if it meant that Tommy Drakes underestimated me, I'd happily take it.

Their voices faded as they exited the room, but I needed to know what their plan was. If they moved the Horn, it would be impossible for me to find it again.

I snuck out from behind the curtain and moved quickly to the doorway. I could barely hear them now, but I caught Drakes saying, "Take… farm," which was enough for me. Hux had mentioned that Drakes had a farm outside the Thicket.

It was Quinn's lucky day, because we weren't gonna have to do a tour of all Drakes's properties. But I was pretty sure he wouldn't see it that way, because Quinn was *so* not gonna like what I had to do next.

I needed to get out to that farm, and I needed to do it ASAP, which meant I was about to fuck his mood board to hell and back.

Taking care not to look furtive, I turned in the opposite direction and wandered through the house until I found the front door. I opened and closed it before heading back to the wedding meeting.

Hardly anyone noticed my arrival. Trey was scrolling through his phone as if being in that meeting was the most excruciating waste of his time ever, while Tommy glared at him. And meanwhile, Quinn was gushing about something that had his client and her mother totally enthralled.

He's really good at his job, I thought with something that felt weirdly like pride. If I had to be fake-engaged to someone for the purposes of this op, at least I'd had the good luck to tie myself to someone competent.

And that made me feel both better and worse about what I needed to do.

"Imagine those big, wide windows in the ballroom, overlooking the pond and the gardens at River Mead, with a wedding arch in front of it." Quinn sketched in the air with his hand. "Something a little rustic. A little asymmetrical, even. Gardenias. Spray roses. And then Trey in his tux and you in the magnificent simplicity of your dress—"

Quinn paused as I slipped into my seat. "Sorry about that. Got a phone call I had to take."

He gave me a fake-fond smile. "Ah. You and your urgent work, my Precious Pearl."

I resisted the urge to laugh. I wasn't sure which of us was winning this battle of the pet names, but the fact that I looked forward to seeing what he'd come up with next was just one more of the unsettling aspects of my rel—uh. My acquaintanceship with Quinn.

"No, Puddle Duck, that was one of *your* clients. Brailey." I name-dropped the famous supermodel I only knew about from having heard guys lust over her when I was still in the Marines. I'd seen her on the cover of one of Quinn's bridal magazines, so I hoped like hell she was planning a wedding and not already married.

Quinn blinked at me, then frowned.

"You probably shut your ringer off when we got here, which is why she called me for her wedding emergency." I rolled my eyes while smiling warmly, like I was used to dealing with brides and their eccentricities. "She and Danny want to scrap all their plans at the winery and go full-on farm wedding. Apparently, farms are *the* hot trend for next year, and they want to jump on it now. She said Esme Covington and Pilar Martinez are getting married at their own farm, but Brailey and

Danny don't have a farm, and all the farms in the area are booked for March, hence the emergency."

Quinn narrowed his eyes at me. "Well, then. We'll find her something for June. Thank you, Angel Muffin, but—"

"Oh, no, not June," I interrupted. "God, no. She was very insistent on March. She said the only people who get married in June are... how did she put it?" I tapped my lip thoughtfully. "'Blue hairs and the nouveau riche,' I think?"

Carlotta gasped.

Quinn's eyes went from narrowed to comically wide. His mouth opened as if to say something, but nothing came out.

Marissa looked back and forth between Quinn and me. "Wait! Quinn! Are you planning *Brailey Driscoll's* wedding?" Her voice became excitedly high-pitched. "Mama, you know she's marrying the heir to that pharmaceutical company—"

"Danny Neil," Trey and Tommy said in unison, which was kind of comical. At least they were paying some attention.

Quinn's jaw tightened the slightest bit before he turned his thousand-watt smile at her. "Oh dear. Champ spoke out of turn. I make it my policy to never discuss my clients with one another. My Meatball hasn't learned discretion. That's why he's supposed to be my *silent* partner. Remember?"

The look he aimed at me should have lit me on fire. Fortunately, I'd been born with asbestos skin.

"Oh, my gracious! You're so right. I..." I clapped a hand over my own mouth dramatically. "Please forget I said anything."

"Already forgotten," Quinn said in a hard voice.

"Now, as I was saying, Marissa, if we book the ball-room at River Mead—"

Carlotta forced a tinkling laugh and touched the ends of her perfectly styled blond bob. "Quinn, Quinn. Let's not be hasty! Perfection doesn't happen on a timeline!"

Quinn smiled harder. "Actually, Mrs. Drakes, I'm afraid it *does*. At least when you're talking about booking a wedding venue for less than six months from now! So..."

"But maybe... maybe we don't want a wedding venue." Marissa bit her lip and turned her shining, hopeful eyes on Quinn. "*We* have a farm. We could totally have a farm wedding. And Drakes Farm... it's one of my favorite places in the whole world, especially in the spring when there are wildflowers everywhere. I practically grew up out there—"

"I wouldn't go that far, darling," Carlotta chuckled pointedly. "Especially not where anyone can hear you. But you're right—unlike *some* people, we *do* have a farm of our own." She tried and failed to contain a gloating smile. "It seems silly not to use it, doesn't it, Tommy?"

Tommy looked up from his phone. "What? Oh... really? The farm? I don't think..."

Quinn didn't need to hear the rest to join the fray. "He's right. Don't forget the realities of a farm wedding. There are bugs and allergies. Also, it's just so far from your friends and family, which makes overnight accom-modations—"

"I want to get married at the farm," Marissa said firmly, deciding in the moment. "The happiest moments of my life have happened there."

Quinn's face remained fixed in a polite smile, though his hand tightened around his pen until his knuckles turned white. I expected him to shoot me an annoyed look, as he usually did. To roll his eyes and say something cutting, to call me his Frankfurter and force me to say the word *relationship* again for his own amusement, to remind me I was his *silent* partner.

But instead, he avoided so much as a glance in my direction, and the energy coming off him wasn't inconvenienced or annoyed. It was *angry*.

Why?

Sure, it meant a little extra work for him to switch gears, but I'd heard him handle actual emergency calls from his brides over the past month, and I knew this wouldn't be the first time he'd scrapped a whole plan and started over. Was it a money thing? Did he stand to lose cash if his bride had a farm wedding instead of a big-ass city do? For all I knew, he got kickbacks from the venues or caterers or some shit.

Well, that sucked, but I'd make it up to him. Maybe I could help bump the price of the farm wedding. I hadn't been kidding about making sure none of this blew back on him.

"You know, I think the key to making a farm wedding really *elegant*," I began, like I knew what the fuck I was talking about, "is making sure you've got all the lavish touches. You know? Make it a, um… a juxtaposition? Of… old and new, rustic and refined? So, like, farm-to-table fine dining. And horse-drawn carriages or even… Oh! *Sleigh rides.*"

Everyone stared at me, and I wondered if I'd bitten off more than I could chew.

But then Marissa whispered, *"Brilliant,"* in a stunned voice, and Carlotta said, "Percy, your mother must be so proud."

I glanced at Quinn to see if he would share the joke,

but he was still holding himself very still, and when he spoke, he spoke slowly like he thought I might need special help to understand. "This isn't Canada, Champion, it's Tennessee. We don't get snow on the ground in June."

"March," Carlotta countered.

"What?" Quinn, Trey, Tommy, and Marissa said at once in varying tones of surprise, panic, outrage, and worry.

"The more I think about it," Carlotta said, "the more it just makes sense to go for early spring! So much happiness in the air. So much…"

"Pollen?" Quinn suggested. "Mud? And even in March, there's almost definitely not going to be snow. Now, if we waited a whole year, we might be able to arrange a snow machine—"

"Nonsense," Carlotta said.

"No way," Trey muttered. "We're gonna do this fast. I agree. March is great. Heck, let's do February."

Funny to see that eagerness coming from a guy who'd wanted to get all up in my fiancé's—fake fiancé's—business the day before, but I wasn't going to argue. February suited my purposes even better than March.

"Grouse season," Tommy said thoughtfully. "Could put together a hunt for the guests."

"Maybe you could do it on Valentine's Day?" I ventured.

Marissa clapped her hands and grinned. "Perfect! The most romantic day of the year."

Quinn held up his hands. "Wait, wait. A cold winter wedding outside on a fallow farm in the Thicket? That we would have to plan in the next five weeks?" He laughed like it was a joke.

Marissa's gaze turned dreamy. "It's going to be amazing."

"It's going to be impossible," Quinn said firmly. "And isn't it a little overdone—?"

Mrs. Drakes piped up. "Benedict Cumberbatch and Salma Hayek got married on Valentine's Day. I've been studying up on celebrity weddings."

Now Quinn looked adorably confused. "Benedict Cumberbatch married Salma Hayek?"

Movement caught my attention behind the bride. Levi looked restless. "I agree with Quinn," he said, surprising everyone. His eyes darted to his boss. "I only mean, we'll need time to implement appropriate security precautions. Five weeks is… soon."

Tommy smirked slightly. "Tell your father I'll up the budget. You'd be surprised what can be done if you're willing to grease the wheels, and I am." He winked at his daughter. "Anything for Rissy."

Levi looked like he was swallowing a live toad as he nodded.

I could tell by Quinn's flaring nostrils that he wasn't going to come around quite as easily.

I reached for his hand. "You'll do okay, babe. I promise."

He gave me an overwhelmed, unhappy look before he caught himself and blanked his expression. He withdrew his hand from my grasp. "I suppose I'll have to." The unspoken *thanks to you* came through loud and clear.

I grabbed his hand again, more firmly this time, and squeezed it in reassurance. "I'll help," I promised.

"Ohhh, no. No. You've done enough already, My Flower. You don't know beans about floral inventory challenges around Valentine's Day or the markup on labor to move supplies—not to mention electricity—out to a *field*," he said firmly. "I think it's best that you return to your work, and I'll take care of mine."

Unfortunately for both of us, his work *was* my work, at least for the foreseeable future.

"And deny your clients the benefit of my talents?" I blinked at him in confusion. "I couldn't possibly, Lover. Besides, I have access to many muscular men," I reminded him softly.

"Braggart," he muttered before plastering on a pretty smile for the clients. "So, a farm wedding at Valentine's! Sounds divine. Let's talk about the guest list. Champ, My Lambkin, haven't you been studying up on wedding invitations? Why not tell the folks everything you know about wrappers and belly bands and reception cards. Leave *nothing* out."

I was going to kill him…. but first, I was going to prove his ass wrong.

"Well, according to the January issue of *Bride Beautiful*, there are Etsy sellers who make custom watercolor drawings for your invitation's directions insert," I began, sitting back in my chair a little smugly. "They'd capture the farm in all of its charming glory."

The shocked look on Quinn's face was worth all the minutes I'd spent killing time while letting him sleep.

Marissa sat up straighter. "Oh my gosh, I've heard of custom maps, but a watercolor would be beautiful! Champ! You and Quinn are just the *dream team*. I just can't thank y'all enough!"

Trey rolled his eyes, and Tommy went back to scrolling his phone. Mrs. Drakes flipped to a fresh page in her notebook, and Levi looked at Marissa with little cartoon hearts floating around his head. But Quinn continued to stare at me like he wasn't sure what species of person I was. Like he wasn't sure whether he wanted to kill me with his laser eyes or throw me down on the Persian rug and ride me until we were both cross-eyed.

I knew that expression well because I was pretty sure I wore it a lot when I looked at him.

Deep in my brain, a warning bell started to chime, telling me that I was getting a little too comfortable with all the cute names and spending my nights in Quinn's bed, but I ignored it.

Quinn Taffet was a means to an end, nothing more. And when things were over—which was gonna happen sooner rather than later—I was going to walk away, leaving him with a successful (and lucrative) wedding under his belt, and leaving *me* with the Horn I needed to protect my client and move on with my life.

5

QUINN

They say you never know what you're capable of until adversity stretches you to the limit, and I knew this for a fact.

But until that meeting at the Drakeses' house, I hadn't realized that the inverse was also true: you don't know for sure what you will *not* put up with until it bribes you with donuts, addles you with sexytimes, and turns the Nashville socialite wedding of the season—the evening of glittering opulence that was going to relaunch you into the event-planning stratosphere and leave your ex and his boy toy gaping in stunned envy—into some kind of down-home, mud-splattered rodeo.

"So," Champ said, all smug and smiley as I pulled my tiny car out of the Drakeses' impressive gated driveway. "That went well, huh? Marissa seems pleased, I think, which is great. Makes me really understand the whole motivation behind this wedding-planning business. We can't change the fact that her fiancé is a douchebag who was trying to kiss her wedding planner, and her mom still has the personality of wet cardboard in designer shoes, but we can give Marissa a damn good party, and that's—"

"No," I interrupted firmly and, I congratulated myself, with admirable calm.

Champ turned in his seat to look at me. "No? As in, no she wasn't pleased, or no we can't give her a damn good party? Or no, I'm misunderstanding what wedding planning is all about? Because I think—"

"No," I interrupted again, this time a little more firmly and a little less calmly. "As in, we are not going to do this now. Just… stop talking."

"Right. Okay," Champ said slowly. "Is this a *you* thing? Needing to decompress after an op? I knew guys like you in the service. I can respect that. I guess since you and I are going to be working together, it's probably good for me to know your— *Whoa*! Hey! What the fuck, Quinn? Watch the trees!"

I swung the car to the grassy verge of the wide, poplar-lined road and stopped so abruptly my tires squealed.

"What the fuck, *Quinn*?" I repeated. "No, the correct question is what the fuck, *Champion*. What happened to silent partners? What happened to just getting the lay of the land? *What happened to you not screwing around with my business*?"

I slapped my hand against the steering wheel hard. Too hard. "Damn it." I shook my stinging hand, feeling tears behind my eyes. "Fucking damn it."

Champ made a *tsk*ing noise and grabbed my wrist, smoothing his thumb over my injured palm. "I'm not messing up your business. I'm not. I know I fast-tracked the wedding, but I promise I'm going to help you. And when we pull this off, it'll just increase your reputation as a guy who can pull off impossible shit. Plus, Tommy seemed willing to pay—"

"It's not about the damn money!"

Champ leaned back so far his skull *thunked* against the window, which was how I came to realize that I was leaning over the center console, shouting my head off.

Percival Champion made it hard to retain my composure at the best of times, and this was not the best of times.

I cleared my throat and sat back in my seat, snatching my hand from his. "It's not about the money," I repeated more softly. "It's about my reputation—my *business's* reputation—which I've been building up for *months*, and which you've managed to send into a death spiral in half an hour. Lying about Brailey Driscoll? Are you out of your mind?"

"Hey," Champ soothed. "Chill."

"Don't you dare tell me to *chill* when *you* are the one who has dropped me in a pit of *fire*."

"Shhh." Champ's voice was low and calm, and he grasped my wrist again, stroking his fingers down my sore palm, forcing my fingers to uncurl. "Seriously, Quinn, calm down. Tell me what's going on. Yell at me if you have to. But don't hurt yourself, for fuck's sake."

He wanted to know what was going on? Fine, then.

"I need the Drakeses' contract," I ground out. "I don't just want it, I *need* it. I have worked months and months to get to the place where a bona fide Nashville socialite would hire me to coordinate her wedding. Do you know how hard that is to accomplish when your business is located in the back end of nowhere? Do you? Let me tell you, it's fucking hard. I've coordinated charity events for free and planned corporate events I barely made a profit on just to get my foot in the door. I've bent over backwards to give couples their perfect weddings. I've worked endless hours—late nights, early mornings, every single weekend. I don't have hobbies. I don't have friends anymore. I drove my last car into the ground and put thousands of miles on this one. I've learned how to sew beading onto a train and how to rearrange flowers when a bridesmaid accidentally sits on her bouquet. I can fix a cake and mediate family traumas better than Dr. Phil. I don't date. The closest I've come is the one night back in November, after an absolute wedding from hell, when I went to the Thicket Tavern to let off some steam, and look how *that* turned out." I thrust a hand in his direction. "The commitmentphobic asshole I picked up that night ended up sabotaging me for his own selfish ends, and now my *second* event-planning business is as ruined as the first."

"Hush." Champ moved one big hand to cup my cheek. "*Hush*. I don't understand what you're talking about, but nothing's ruined, Quinn. I promise. Whatever it is, we can fix it."

I squeezed my eyes shut. The whole situation was awful and mortifying, and if I couldn't be calm and rational about it, I at least wanted to be angry. But when Champ talked to me in that deep, tender voice, when he said my name like he actually cared about me, even though I knew better, I felt my emotions slipping from rage into desperate sadness like a landslide I couldn't control.

"It sure as fuck *is* ruined if I'm not planning a Nashville wedding. I'll be stuck out here in the sticks forever."

Champ was silent for a moment, his thumb stroking over my cheek, and then he shook his head. "Nope. I'm still not getting why the location matters. I think you're getting stressed over nothing. Farm weddings are an actual thing," he explained like I might not have ever heard of them or thrown a dozen of them in my time. "You can decorate the whole barn with, like, lights? And… I don't know. Paper flowers? Or… sparkles. Whatever Marissa wants."

Despite myself, I snickered. Paper flowers? Really?

"It matters because I used to have a business here in Nashville," I found myself saying. "With my boyfriend, Scott." My eyes flew to Champ's. "I mean *ex*-boyfriend. Very ex. In fact, he's one of the many reasons I have no interest in a relationship ever again, you get me?"

Champ nodded. "More than you know."

"Right. Well." I swallowed hard. "Scott decided we were done because he met someone younger and hotter, which… whatever. I'm over that. It's just how relationships go—"

"It is," Champ agreed with a nod. "There's always a hotter guy or a better job."

I found myself momentarily distracted by this. *Was* there a hotter guy than Champ? What weirdos had he been dating? This explained so much.

"Anyway." I sniffled a little, because it felt nice to be understood. "The thing that bothered me most was that Scott not only screwed another guy, he also screwed me out of my share of the business we ran together, and *that* is something I cannot forgive or get over. He hired his new boyfriend to work for the company. *Onyx*," I said bitterly.

"Scott's new guy is named Onyx?" Champ winced.

"Yeah." I huffed out a half laugh. "I don't blame Onyx for anything. Onyx's only crimes are being twenty-two and utterly brainless. But I also was not about to work with him every damn day, and I was very open about that. Scott said if that was my choice, *fine*, but he'd keep the company. He said he'd buy me out as soon as he had the cash on hand. And I... I agreed. Enthusiastically," I admitted shamefacedly. "I told him I was going to create a bigger, better company of my own. I may have said something about..." I cleared my throat. "Him ruing the day?"

"Ah, jeez."

"Exactly. Looking back, it was so clear that I played right into his tiny hands." I'd believed that, whatever happened in our relationship, Scott wouldn't fuck with my business.

In other words, I'd been a fool... and apparently, I hadn't learned my lesson.

I cleared my throat and deliberately turned away from Champ, setting both hands on the steering wheel.

"Let me guess, Scott hasn't ponied up any money?" Champ's eyes went cold and a little scary—which was more than a little thrilling. "Remind me, what did you say Scott's last name was? And where does he live?"

I shook my head. "I don't want revenge. Not the kind that comes with you beating him to a pulp, anyway. I want the kind that comes from me getting back what was mine. Showing him that I didn't need him in order to create a successful business. And I'm getting there. I moved to the Thicket because my aunt Cherry retired and left me her dress shop—"

"Which is now Taffet Events."

I nodded. "I saved a shit ton of money by moving, and I'm really fortunate that I had this option. I know that. But having a business in the Thicket... that's not the goal. The goal is to get back to where I was. This event—Marissa Drakes's wedding—was going to be my triumphant return to the Nashville scene. And now… it's going to be a country bumpkin hoedown on a barren farm in winter. The gossips will have a field day, Marissa will be crushed, and I'll be a laughingstock."

My hands flexed and released on the wheel as I envisioned a scene where I lost my company and ended up on the street while Scott and Onyx laughed —

Champ nodded once. "Right. Okay, then. So, we're not gonna let that happen."

"You just *made* it happen," I reminded him.

"No. I suggested a location. The location is a tactical consideration, Quinn. It's not a deal breaker. We take the location into consideration —"

"Uh-huh. Have your information people given you the lowdown on the Drakeses' farm?" I interrupted before I actually started buying into Champ's can-do, rah-rah bullshit. "It's wayyyy over on the west side of the Thicket, out past the elementary school and Diesel Partridge's junkyard."

He frowned. "There's nothing out past the junkyard but the Christmas tree lot and that giant… Oh."

"Oh," I agreed grimly. "The old Windy Pig farm."

"The one with the…"

"Big, rusted-out green silo from the '50s that still says 'Windy Pigs'? Yeah. Tommy Drakes's great-uncle on his mother's side was a Windy."

Champ shook his head. "I don't wanna know how you know that. If the wedding planning doesn't work out, I could use another background analyst."

I refused to be charmed. "That farm is a giant pork-filled mud patch. They still keep pigs, in addition to horses. The house is gorgeous, according to the pictures I've seen, but the rest of the place?" I shook my head. "Precisely how many burly men do you have at your disposal? Enough to paint an enormous silo? Move some livestock? I can only imagine Carlotta hasn't been out here in years and doesn't remember the state of the place, or she would have pitched a fit."

"Damn." Champ whistled. "I didn't know."

"I figured. But that didn't stop you from parachuting right into my carefully planned event and throwing out mental images of supermodels cavorting on picturesque farms like hand grenades, did it? God forbid Carlotta ever asks Brailey Driscoll who her wedding planner is, or I'm sunk." I sighed.

"That... is another tactical consideration," he agreed.

I rolled my eyes. "Right. Look, I'm gonna fix this. Somehow. I generally do. But you're fired as my fake wedding-planning assistant. I will not be providing you a reference. And also—please try to control your disappointment—I think it's time for us to consciously uncouple. Our engagement had a great run, buddy, but we wouldn't be the first folks who couldn't handle the trials of wedding planning. It's not you, it's me. Please remember to collect your dog before you leave for good."

I tried for a smile and failed miserably. I felt shaky and overwhelmed, and I wanted nothing more than to be home—*by myself*—where I could vent my anger and frustration, probably drink an entire bottle of wine, and remember why alone was always, always the safer bet.

I shifted the car into Drive and started to pull out onto the street.

"Wait, no!" Champ said in a panicked tone that made me stomp on the brake again. "Wait. Look, I really am sorry, Quinn. I had to make a decision on the fly without all the intel. I fucked up, but we can recover from this if we stick together. As a team."

"*Stick* together?" I snorted. "That would imply that we'd been working together in the past. But one of us — it was you, by the way — decided to go rogue and make unilateral decisions that got us into this situation. That's the opposite of teamwork. What would you do if one of your men did that?"

I saw that point hit home. Champ sucked in a breath. He stared at me for a long moment. Then he said, "You're right."

"Thank you." I nodded, pleased that he agreed, even if I was less than thrilled at what his agreement meant. "So, like I said, I think it's best if we —"

"Go out for a late lunch."

I blinked. "Um, *no*. The opposite, in fact. No more lunches. Or meals of any ki —"

"I'll take you to SATCO." He paused dramatically, waiting for my reaction.

He was gonna have to keep waiting. "What's a SATCO?"

"Are you serious? It's impossible that you lived in Nashville and never heard of San Antonio Taco Company. It's a Tex-Mex place near Vandy. It's world-famous. Or at least Nashville famous. Seriously, you've never been? Oh, God, I'm about to change your life. The tacos and enchiladas will make you cry, they're so delicious. If you thought my peace-offering donuts were good, wait until you try my peace-offering tacos."

That was exactly what I was afraid of. I was all kinds of weak-willed where Percy Champion was concerned.

I shook my head resolutely. "I have leftovers at home."

"Please, Quinn," he said softly. "It's the least I can do after this morning."

"You're not trying to make up for something. You're trying to con me into going along with your scheme so that you can have access to the farm and search for Tommy Drakes's... whatever the heck you're looking for, even though it's going to destroy my business. Hard pass."

"No! I'm trying to call a team meeting. Kinda."

I scowled. "A what?"

Champ spread his hands and regarded me earnestly. "Look, you asked what I would do if someone on my team had pulled the stunt I pulled on you this morning, right? Well, it *has* happened. Last November, as a matter of fact, on an op in South America. And like you, I was pissed immediately after the fact, with good reason. I made that fucker take so many classes on communication, he could get his own daytime TV show. I made the whole crew do team-building exercises until their eyes rolled back in their heads. But what I didn't do was get rid of the guy. I didn't say, 'Fuck it, I'm gonna do everything myself from now on.' Instead, I figured out where the issue was and fixed it. The guy felt bad about what went down, and now he's the hardest-working teammate I've got, and I can be that for you. Just let me fix this."

"Because you want to search Tommy's farm," I insisted.

Champ blew out a breath. "Yes. Obviously, yes, okay? But that's not all I want. I truly do wanna make this right. I'm not Scott. I promised you no blowback, and I meant it. Also..." Champ ducked his head to catch my eyes and grinned his devastating grin. "I'm fucking hungry, and now that I remembered I'm in the neighborhood of these tacos, I'm dying for some, because their freshly made salsa… *hngh*. Mouth orgasm."

I shook my head, amused against my will. "I am not in the mood to be charmed, damn it. Or bribed with any available carbohydrate." But I thought about fresh salsa, and my traitorous stomach growled like a ravenous beast.

"Your stomach's on board. And I only want one lunch." Champ's pleading was nearly irresistible. "Let me make my case, and then you can decide, okay?"

I could picture him going through some kind of hostage negotiation rule book and getting to the section entitled "Make the other person believe they're in control."

But also… Damn it, I was hungry. And he owed me a lot, but I would start with a taco.

"Fine," I sighed. "Direct me to this life-changing taco place, then."

Half an hour later, we pulled into the parking lot of a tiny place with neon signs in the windows and a rickety wooden porch out front that could *not* be up to code.

"Oh, delightful. Does every taco order come with a side of E. coli as a free gift?"

"*Bup bup bup.* Bite your tongue." Champ unfolded himself from the passenger's side with a stretch and a groan that went straight to my cock—because I was weak from hunger, obviously. "I told you: freshly made salsa. Trust and believe."

But I didn't want to trust him, and I wasn't sure I *could* believe him. Not after that disastrous meeting.

Champ led me up the wooden stairs to the porch, and I shivered when a chilly breeze blew through my button-down shirt and sweater vest. Inside, the place didn't look any fancier than it had from the outside. The black-and-white tile floor appeared clean but had to be older than I was. The place did smell incredible, though.

Off to one side of the restaurant was a counter with order pads and tiny golf pencils. "We fill out these forms with our orders. I bet you want..." He looked me up and down, tilting his head to one side like a carnival psychic. "Green chicken enchiladas."

My stomach growled again, happy to be understood on this fundamental level.

"Nope," I said primly. "Salad with grilled chicken."

For a second, I thought Champ would argue, but he didn't. He filled out our forms—he'd ordered enough food and beer for three people, of course—then had a long conversation with the woman at the counter, who greeted him by name like a long-lost friend and spoke to him in Spanish.

It was another layer to Champ's personality, and I found it hard to reconcile them all. The sweet guy who stopped by my place at night. The former military man who ran a security company where he could assign his employees to do team-building exercises. The asshole who left his dog behind when he ran out my door in the morning like a pack of wild relationship wolves were chasing him. The earnest man begging me to trust him. The guy who was Bunny Champion's offspring, which meant he had to be rich beyond belief, even though he never acted like any of the incredibly wealthy people I'd ever met. And now, this Spanish-speaking taco connoisseur.

It was fascinating, because I wanted to know all these parts of him… and fucking frustrating, because he didn't seem to want me to get to know him.

When our food tray was ready, I headed for a table, but Champ steered me outside to the seating area on the rickety porch, where enormous metal patio heaters blazed in a ring around a hodgepodge of tables and chairs.

"More privacy out here," he said, nodding toward the empty tables and chairs.

"That's because it's January," I cried.

Champ moved around me and chose a table next to one of the heaters. He set the tray in the center, spread out the food, and sat down. "Local-known pro tip in winter: sit in the sun *and* close to a heater." He patted the seat next to him. "You'll be fine. I'll warm you up."

Right. Like that was a thing we did in our non-relationship.

When I didn't immediately comply, he turned the full power of that hot, blue gaze on me and cocked his head to one side. "Problem?"

"No." But my stomach swooped as I dragged myself toward the table. I was so turned around after the chaotic morning that even just sitting next to him felt dangerous to my equilibrium.

I took a seat on the furthest edge of the bench he was sitting on and took a deep breath. The heaters gave off a faintly smoky smell that was homey and pleasant enough that I felt myself relaxing a tiny bit, despite my impending death from hypothermia.

I drew my salad in front of me and picked at it with a fork. It was very… green. And very boring.

"Oh mi gawww," Champ garbled around a mouthful of something. He fanned at his mouth with one hand and shoveled in a bite of food with the other. "Issss so haht, but ah can't stahp ee-ing ih."

I laughed out loud. Add *ridiculously silly* to the list of Percy Champion's personalities. It was, arguably, the most devastating one of all, at least when it came to keeping my distance from him.

And *ugh*, the smug, smirky, sexy-as-fuck smile he shot me when he caught me laughing was like a knockout punch to my already weak defenses. "You're regretting that salad right now, aren't you?"

I was regretting many things at that moment. Mostly the fact that I couldn't seem to quit myself of this man, even though I knew better, damn it.

"No," I said primly. "Salad is nutritious, and if I eat the salad now, I can have cookies later. Always do the hard thing first, that's what my Aunt Cherry says."

Champ paused with a giant bite of food halfway to his mouth and stared at me pityingly. "Or you could just get rid of your arbitrary rules and eat cookies whenever you fucking want them because life is short."

The wind kicked up, and I shivered.

I pushed my very cold salad away. "Enough chitchat. This is a team meeting, right? That's what you said? That's why we need privacy? Then… read me in. What is it of Tommy's that you're looking for, and how do you know it's at the farm? Is it a folder of papers? A hard drive? A computer chip? A briefcase full of cash? A shipment of weapons that look like car mufflers?"

Champ reached out and snagged the waistband of my pants to haul me firmly against his side. He took off his jacket and draped it—in all its Champ-scented glory —over my shoulders, despite my sputtered protests. And he grabbed one of his plates—a plate filled with something that looked a lot like green chicken enchi-ladas — and plunked it down in front of me where my salad should have been.

"It's a Horn," he said.

"It's a…" I looked at the enchilada. "Huh?"

"I mean the thing Tommy has. The thing I'm looking for. It's a Horn. Like, from Horn of Glory." When I only blinked up at him, he continued. "The video game. With squash and orcs and seeds? Huge gaming sensation currently sweeping the nation?"

"I know the game, *obviously*. What's that got to do with Tommy?"

"Remember how he had that whole case of sports memorabilia off to one side of the foyer?" Champ licked salsa off his thumb in a really sexily distracting sort of way. "Well, old baseballs aren't the only thing Tommy collects."

Champ filled me in on the story of how Tommy had acquired a particularly rare Horn at a flea market, which lined up perfectly with the story he'd told me in the car earlier.

"And Tommy doesn't care that the Horn was stolen because he wants it in his possession." I found myself taking a bite of chicken enchilada without thinking about it, quickly followed by another. Holy shit, these were good.

"Correct." Champ handed me a beer, a pleased smile on his lips as he nodded at my plate. "Knew you'd love 'em. See why being on a team is helpful?"

"Mmm. So what does Champion Security want with the Horn?"

I could practically see Champ's walls go up.

"Want?" he repeated.

I ground my teeth together. "Yeah, not sure this whole *team* thing is working for me," I informed him.

Champ grimaced. "We're retrieving the Horn on behalf of our client, who'd like the Horn returned to them without involving the authorities. They don't want to become embroiled in an investigation."

"In the car earlier, you said there was a government agency out to get the *thing* you wanted from Tommy." I forked up more enchilada, unable to resist it. "Why does the government want a Horn of Glory Horn? Sudden interest in the rabid orange bunnies that have been stampeding people's homesteads, eating the Shasta daisies they bought with the *entire* proceeds of their last rutabaga harvest?"

Champ blinked, and I shrugged.

"I've maybe gone on a quest a time or thrice," I admitted. "But why are my tax dollars being used to search for someone's stolen Horn if the rightful owner doesn't want the authorities involved? Unless... wait, your client *is* the Horn's rightful owner, yes?"

Champ hesitated.

"You're going to steal the Horn from Tommy and give it to someone who's *not* the rightful owner?" I hissed. "What the fuck, Champ?"

Champ blew out a breath. "Look, there are things I can't tell you. My client..."

"I have clients too!" I reminded him hotly. "Clients who are relying on me to give them a wedding they can be proud of. And yet, here I am, entertaining the idea of letting you screw us all over. Tell me what you know!"

"Fine. Fucking..." Champ muttered. "Just fucking *fine*. Look, I *do* want to get my hands on the Horn, yeah, not because my client wants the device itself, but because I need to access the... the data that's being stored on it so I can neutralize it," he admitted in a rush. "And *no*, Quinn, I'm not telling you more because I'd prefer you didn't get mixed up in this, okay?"

Champ pushed up from the table to pace the small space crowded with empty tables and chairs. He was angry—maybe angry at me for pushing, or angry at himself for giving in, or just angry that he was in this position in the first place— and for some reason, his anger... comforted me. An angry Champ was an honest Champ.

"Also? I don't just *want* to get this Horn back from Tommy. I *need it*," Champ fumed, quoting my words about the Drakeses' wedding from earlier, "because I have an ex-boyfriend too. But unlike you, my ex-boyfriend isn't just trying to ruin my business. He might arrest me if he can make a case against me for allowing the Horn and the information on it to be stolen in the first place—which is another thing I'd really rather not explain. Suffice it to say, he wouldn't hesitate to do that if it helped him make a name for himself."

"Your ex is a cop?" I asked softly.

"Vince is a DEA agent assigned to this case."

Vince. I filed that information away and bit my lip. "So we have a similar problem. We both need to succeed here to save our businesses," I said sadly.

"Yeah." Champ came to sit on the chair beside me, facing away from the table. He rested his elbows on his knees and stared down at the ground.

"That sucks. Because I don't see how both of us can get what we want."

"The thing is, I *do*." Champ turned to me, impaling me with his crystal-blue stare. "We can both win here, Quinn. Because yeah, I had my own goals in mind when I suggested the farm. I definitely did. But I would not have suggested the farm if I didn't truly believe that you could plan a standout wedding literally anywhere. I knew it was gonna be too fast, and I knew you weren't gonna like it. And..." He twisted his jaw to one side. "And *yes*, there were many factors I hadn't considered about just *how* difficult it would be."

"Understatement."

"But I still believe in you. I believe you can make this thing happen. And you'll have all of Champion Security's resources at your disposal. If I have to pull my team off surveillance jobs to paint the Windy Pig silo, I will. If we have to tear it down and build a new one, *we will*. And having me take that Horn is in Tommy's best interest, and Marissa's too. I know it feels like you're plotting against him, but I swear to you, Quinn, you're helping him. Because he doesn't know that the Horn he bought is more than just a Horn, and he doesn't understand the shitstorm that will be unleashed when more people find out he has it or how that could impact his whole family's reputation. No amount of running around in a Speedo could salvage it. Vince, my ex, I think he might have put the pieces together, so the clock is already running down."

"And if Tommy realizes that my supposed fiancé stole his beloved Horn?" I demanded. "What about *my* reputation?"

"He won't know. We'll get a fake. Or... I dunno, once we figure out where he's keeping it, we can try to steal it at a time when there's plenty of other folks around for plausible deniability. Maybe both."

I chewed at the inside of my cheek. "Maybe we could get your team to do it when Marissa is meeting with both of us so there's no reason to suspect our involvement."

"Perfect," Champ agreed. "See, you're thinking sneakily now. I like it."

I rolled my eyes. "That's not nearly as much of a compliment as you seem to think."

"Sure it is." Champ grinned. "So… what do you say?"

Shit, was I actually considering it? Had I officially lost my mind?

"If you do this for me, I'll find you a new Nashville socialite client," Champ blurted. "A way bigger name than the Drakes family."

I frowned. "Who?"

"Not sure. I have to see who I know that's getting married," he hedged. "But I'll get you the client before the Drakes wedding. Promise." He held his hand out for me to shake.

I stared at it.

Another socialite client… That would be a hell of an incentive. "Okay, if I agree to do this, you're going to be my very *silent* partner. For real this time."

"Sure."

I took his hand, only shivering slightly when our fingers slid together. "You're going to take some communication training, like your guy did, except you're going to learn how *not* to communicate when it involves wedding ideas and my clients."

"Deal."

I wasn't sure the handshake was an indication that I trusted the man, but it was sure as hell an indication that I couldn't walk away from him nearly as easily as I wished I could.

"You won't regret this," Champ assured me before turning around and applying himself to his tacos.

I clenched my hand into a fist, still feeling his

fingers sliding against mine while my heart beat out a crazy rhythm.

Oh, I was pretty sure I already regretted it…

And it only took a few days for me to confirm this beyond a shadow of a doubt.

6

CHAMP

It wasn't until I was driving us home from Nashville that I realized in convincing Quinn to go along with my plan, I might have overpromised a little.

Or a lot.

It wasn't that I was worried about having enough skilled labor to fix up the farm—most of my team would love the break from their usual work, and if worse came to worst, I could draw on the trust fund I hadn't touched since the day I started Champion Security and hire more people to make it happen.

No, the real issue was finding a Nashville socialite who needed a wedding planner so I could replace the glitzy city wedding Quinn was hoping for.

I'd happily severed almost all my ties to the Nashville social circle the minute I'd left home for college. And while my mother would know the names of literally every person in Nashville society who was engaged —she probably had whole gossip dossiers on them—I would rather be forced to spend a solid hour playing fucking Horn of Glory than owe my mom a favor, which was exactly what would happen if I asked her for help.

"So..." I cleared my throat. "What about a minor league baseball player instead of a socialite? Would that work?"

I braced myself for yelling and flailing. When none came—in fact, when Quinn didn't reply at all—I glanced over at the passenger's seat and found him sacked out, with his dark head pressed against the glass and my jacket wrapped around his trim form like a large blanket.

My mouth twitched up before I could stop it. When I'd fed him beer at lunch, I'd completely forgotten how much smaller he was. It wasn't at all the same as sharing a couple of beers at lunch with the bulked-up folks I worked with. Quinn wasn't exactly slurring when we'd left the taco place, but he'd had a soft quality to his speech that had necessitated my taking his keys from him and trying to shove myself behind the wheel of his clown car.

God, the man was handsome. With his face relaxed in sleep, he looked even younger than he usually did, and I had to fight the urge to trace the Cupid's bow of his mouth with my fin—

Whoa. Okay, *no*.

I caught my wandering thoughts, and my brain made a sound like a record scratch. What the *fuck* was wrong with me? What had they put in those tacos?

Quinn was good-looking, no doubt. Fun to fuck. Even fun to talk to. But I was getting all kinds of confused if I was starting to think poetical fucking thoughts about the shape of the man's lips.

Getting the Horn was my priority—my *only* priority. The easiest way to accomplish that was to be around Quinn, but the man was still nothing more than my twenty-seven-night stand. And the sooner we could be done with this mission and get our rela—our *arrangement*—back on track, the better.

Hell, maybe if I found the Horn quickly, we could end the mission before the farm wedding ever had to take place, which would make Quinn all kinds of happy. I imagined him telling Marissa that we'd broken up, so the whole farm wedding concept was tainted by his broken dreams or some shit.

I chuckled to myself and glanced over at him again. The man would probably pull it off convincingly too. I'd been pleasantly surprised at how well he'd pivoted when it came to keeping up with our charade. I hadn't expected him to keep up with me outside the bedroom too.

And if I couldn't find the Horn quickly enough and the farm wedding had to go on… well, then I was going to keep my promises, even if that meant finding a fucking socialite and bribing them to hire Quinn. Not because I had feelings for the man, but because I wasn't the sort of guy to fuck over someone who did me a favor.

Unlike certain people in his life.

My hands flexed on the steering wheel so hard the plastic creaked as I thought of Quinn's ex, and I had to throttle back my rush of protective anger. As soon as I dropped Quinn off at his place, I was gonna get Hux to get me a full rundown on Scott the Onyx-fucker, and then I was going to schedule us a little chat. One Quinn never had to know about. One that would involve a large sum of cash landing in Quinn's account.

When I got to Taffet Events, though, the man was still deep asleep, despite the afternoon sunlight beating down on his face. I ended up pulling Quinn out of the tiny car, wrapping an arm around his waist, and half carrying him up the stairs to his apartment. *Platonically.*

After stripping him down to a sexy-as-fuck pair of tiny boxer briefs and putting him in bed—again, *platonically*—I forced myself to give Hercules some attention with a short walk to a nearby park. While Herc was busy running off his pent-up energy, I called the office to check in.

"Hey!" Riggs answered on the first ring. "How'd it go in Nashville?"

I filled Riggs in on the details of the morning, including our new critical mission of acting as undercover landscapers and silo painters. Then I asked him how his day went.

"Fucking awful," he said glumly. "You remember how I had to set up surveillance at that diner across the street from Carter's medical practice? Well, I hadn't realized that Carter's cousin Kev was acting as his receptionist this week. So, I set up the diversion out in the street to distract the staff while I sent a team in the back entrance, which is standard procedure. But as soon as the music started, Kev—"

Riggsy went on, and I knew I should have paid attention, especially as it concerned another Champion Security contract, but my brain had flipped a switch the second he mentioned his boyfriend.

His rich, Nashville-born-and-bred cardiologist boyfriend.

"…and so now Kev is fucking *traumatized* and vowing to get vengeance against me, and Carter's pissed and not talking to me, and—"

"Riggs," I interrupted. "Remember that time you

were sunburned on that op and I loaned you my hat, and you said you owed me a favor?"

Riggs was silent for a long, suspicious moment. "I remember it was seven years ago," he said warily. "And you've brought it up every time you needed a favor since then. What's up?"

"Your boyfriend is a socialite."

I could sense his surprise over the line. "Uh. I guess? I mean, Carter doesn't give a shit about any of it and only schmoozes when he has to for the Rogers Foundation, which is really more about pleasing his grandfather, so I don't know if—"

"Yeah, yeah. Carter's got all kinds of hidden depths. Total renaissance man. But he's connected to the highest levels of Nashville society."

"So what if he is?" Riggs was definitely wary now. "I'm not getting him involved in a mission. Not again. Last time—"

"Last time he got *himself* involved when he took a contract with Doctors Across Continents and ended up kidnapped," I pointed out. "My favor involves no danger whatsoever."

Mostly.

"Oh. Well, then—"

"I need you two to plan a big Nashville wedding and hire Quinn Taffet to manage it."

The squawking sound on the other end of the line was loud enough to get Herc's attention. The dog tilted his head at me, and I shrugged in return. "The man is a commitment-phobe," I whispered to my dog. "Tragic."

"Dude, I'm not even engaged," Riggs hissed. "And this is a very not-good time to bring *that* up, thank you very much. But you want me to plan a wedding big enough to need professional help?"

"Why aren't you and Carter engaged yet? You have the man's name tattooed on your—"

"*How do you even know that?*"

"Listen, I need you to get on it," I explained, gathering Herc for the walk back to Quinn's place. "You've got five weeks. Propose to Carter like we both know you want to, then have him hire this guy to plan a big to-do. The Rogers name carries a lot of weight in Nashville social circles, and I promised Quinn—"

"Okay, wait. Using Carter's social pull in Nashville to impress the Howling Turtle dude seems a little over-the-top," Riggs said.

I stopped in the street and nearly choked Herc when the leash went taut. "I'm not trying to impress anyone. This is business. It's all about the *op*."

"Mmhm. Sure. Since when do you care so much about inconveniencing assets?"

I opened my mouth to snap that Quinn Taffet was not an *asset* when I suddenly realized Riggs was right, damn it. "Since *always* because I'm not an asshole, Riggs. And that's not how Champion Security does business. So stop dicking around, put a ring on it, and make an appointment with Quinn. Five weeks, understood?"

"But—"

"Now, grab a pen because I've got a name I need Hux to run for me. First name Scott, last name... unknown at this time. He's a wedding planner in Nashville. Used to be affiliated with Quinn. Run some business records, and find me his current address."

"This is still 'all about the op,' right?" Riggs asked way too smugly. "Just checking."

Nosy fucker.

"Riggs, do we need to revisit the communication

classes and the team-building exercises? Because I can make that happen for you—"

Riggs cleared his throat. "I'll get this information to Huxley immediately, boss! You have a wonderful evening!"

"Much better," I told him. I ended the call and let myself into Quinn's shop, locking up behind me and letting Herc off the leash. I found Quinn still curled up in bed, sleeping off the lunchtime beer.

He's an asset. Nothing more.

The late-afternoon sun laid a warm golden stripe over his shoulder and down one arm, illuminating a smattering of freckles. An errant lock of hair curled the wrong way over one ear, and a faint pink imprint of his fingers showed on one cheek from where he must have been lying on his hand.

He was the most beautiful man I'd ever met.

My heart rate went from command-level steady to a funky kind of disjointed thumping as I watched him and cataloged all of the small injuries on his body.

A ragged and torn fingernail from where he'd gnawed on it a few nights before when Herc had slipped his leash on a late-night walk and chased a squirrel down a side street and into the dark night. Two small scratches above his wrist from when I'd accidentally scared him while he was trying to retrieve a lost fork in the bottom of the dishwasher. A yellow-green bruise on his exposed shin from where he'd tripped over my boots on a midnight bathroom visit a week earlier.

It was a habit to catalog small injuries like these on the men under my command, to evaluate the health and wellness of my team. But with Quinn, it was different. These little signs weren't indicators of operation readiness but indicators of how absurdly naive I was about how much time we'd been spending together lately.

I needed to leave.

And I would. I would leave.

In a minute.

After stripping off my own clothes, I slid into bed next to him and reached out to twist the little errant curl around my finger. Quinn's eyes fluttered open and caught me staring. The bridge of his nose crinkled in confusion, so I leaned forward to smooth it with my lips.

He smelled warm and soft with sleep. The faint scent of his high-end hair gel lingered on the pillow beneath his head, and for a split second, I imagined burying my face in it simply to inhale as deeply as I could.

"You're still here," he murmured. I brushed his lips with mine, stopping him before he could say anything else, before he could remind me of all the reasons I shouldn't still be here.

The sleepy hum he let out as I deepened the kiss went straight to my dick. I wanted him with the kind of hunger that was bone-deep, like a thirst that hadn't been quenched, despite all the times I'd had him just like this.

I knew that Quinn believed I showed up on his doorstep because he was convenient or, like last night's front-hall blow job, because I wanted to sweeten him up. The truth was… Well, I didn't know what the truth was, exactly, but it was way more complicated. Way harder to control.

The ex-soldier and the fussy wedding planner should have been the punchline to a joke. The Universe's way of getting back at me for giving Riggs so much shit when he'd fallen for his blue-blooded doctor. But looking at Quinn in that moment, the feelings that swamped me were anything but funny... and the absolute opposite of convenient.

In fact, the desperation I felt to get back inside his body and bury myself there was all-consuming and the closest I'd come to terrified in a very long time.

Want you. Need you.

My hands skated across every inch of his sleep-warmed skin. I heard the hitched intake of breath when my fingers reached his nipples and felt the warm breath against my lips as he exhaled.

I moved my mouth down his throat to the dip at the base and then licked my way down the center of his chest with small, open-mouthed kisses and bites. His heart thundered in his chest, and his legs came up to wrap around my back. I looked up at him and caught his half-lidded eyes for a beat.

You take my breath away.

They were words I would never say out loud to him, but they floated through my mind nonetheless. He was stunning. Despite his tendency to talk back to me and argue every little point, he never failed to make himself vulnerable in bed with me. When we were together like this, touching and sharing, there were no walls between us on either side.

Had I taken the time to stop and think about it, there would have been a Champ-shaped hole in the door of his apartment and a cloud of dust in my wake.

But he was addictive. And once I started touching him... and tasting him... I couldn't stop for anything.

Quinn let out a long groan of pleasure as I ran my chin down his cotton-covered cock and nuzzled my cheek against it. I peeled his shorts off and licked along the length of him before pulling him into my mouth for several long sucks. The curved and dark-haired muscles of his thighs tensed under my palms, and I gripped him tighter to keep him still while I worked him over with my mouth.

His small whimpering sounds and the hush of shifting sheets joined together to fill the room. I took my time kissing my way back up his chest to his nipples, his earlobes, and finally, his full lips. While we kissed, I yanked my own shorts off and fumbled in the bedside drawer for supplies. His body language was eager and willing. His muscles were tense with anticipation, and his eyes were bright with need.

Almost, baby. Almost time.

I covered my cock and slicked it up before reaching between his legs to prep him. We didn't speak, only shared moments of eye contact that were intense enough to make my jaw ache with all the words left unspoken between us. Promises I couldn't make. Plans I didn't dare consider. Tender words of affection that had no place in this… whatever it was between us.

Neither of us wanted this to turn into something serious, but somehow, my heart didn't seem to be on board. It wanted to fling itself out of my chest and into his in a way that would make this messy and impossible.

I pressed inside of him with a groan of relief and pleasure. Quinn's fingers grabbed my hair in tight fists as he held me close until our foreheads and noses touched.

His body was everything. Tight and hot and *mine*.

I reached under his back and around to cup his shoulders before increasing the pace of my thrusts. Instead of saying something I'd regret, I kissed him hard on the mouth and invaded his space until I was as much a part of him as I could possibly be.

We clung to each other with a breathless determination until each of us gasped through our own release and began to return to nothing more than a sweaty, jizz-slick heap.

Eventually, when we'd both caught our breath, I led him to the shower, where I spent many long minutes washing him with the diligence of a Marine preparing for his first boot camp inspection. No crevice remained unaccounted for in my ministrations.

By the time I finished, he was a shower-warmed puddle of goo. I dried him off and put him back in bed, where Herc and I snuggled him like particularly lazy sentinels.

I simply needed a little longer with him.

And then I would go.

7

QUINN

I woke up in the morning to the sound of the shop door closing downstairs with a firm *clack*, followed by the *thud-thud-thud* of heavy, booted feet on the front steps.

I was alone—again—because Champ had left without saying goodbye—again.

I sighed and flopped onto my back, and Hercules gave an answering sigh from the floor.

Because naturally, the dog was still here… again.

My ass still throbbed pleasantly from the night before, and my muscles twinged with the good kind of ache that came from a long, deep sleep, but there was a dull, empty feeling in my chest too. A feeling that was becoming way too familiar… and I didn't like it.

"You'd think this whole *Groundhog Day* scenario of him hurrying out the door in the morning wouldn't bug me after the first twenty-seven times," I told the dog matter-of-factly, looking over the edge of the bed. I pushed my messy hair off my forehead and frowned in thought. "Wait. Is it twenty-eight times? Twenty-nine?"

I sat up in a panic. "It hasn't been thirty, has it? I'd definitely remember if it was thirty."

Wouldn't I?

Hercules cocked his head like he wanted to help but didn't have enough toe beans to count that high.

"Who cares, right? The exact number doesn't matter."

Except it *did*. Somehow failing to keep an accurate count of precisely how many nights Champ had spent in my bed seemed really problematic. Like his presence was something I'd almost come to expect. Which maybe explained why I hated when he left without saying goodbye.

Fuck.

I swung around so my feet were on the floor.

"Okay, clearly the stress of the secret-mission thing is getting to me," I told the dog. "That's the variable that's changed in all this. I was meant to plan weddings, not to infiltrate pig farms for semi-nefarious purposes."

I scratched behind Herc's ears, and his whole body shivered with uncomplicated happiness.

"Champ needs me to cooperate, so he's being extra nice, what with all the tacos and the information sharing. I'm buying into it because the constant adrenaline rush of, you know, potentially watching my business go up in flames has made me susceptible. All those chemicals flying around my brain have caused this to feel real when it's not. Science is to blame here, not *feelings*."

But this logical explanation didn't get rid of my genuine disappointment... or how uneasy that disappointment made me.

"This is why Aunt Cherry has a rule about never bringing a man home more than three times. Shit starts getting confused," I informed the dog. "Also, three is a really easy number to keep track of."

I wished I'd kept in better touch with my friends after leaving Nashville. I could have used someone to talk to about all these things or to take my mind off them. But, like my apartment and all the stuff Scott and I acquired when we were together, I'd decided it would make for a cleaner break if I left those relationships behind.

Instead, I threw on a pair of sweats and some shoes. "How about a nice *long* walk for once, Herc?" I suggested. "I need exercise to clear some cobwebs."

The morning was cold when we first stepped outside, but by the time Herc and I had walked almost all the way down Walnut Street to the community events barn, the temperature had warmed, and I was feeling much better.

To be fair, that might have been less about the exercise and more about the people I met.

It seemed like every three feet, someone waved or called my name, like they'd been waiting for the opportunity to say hi, or reintroduce themselves, or ask about Aunt Cherry.

Lurlene Jackson had promised to make me a batch of the chocolate icebox cookies I'd liked back in the day.

Pete Timms reminded me of the Fourth of July weenie roast when I was fourteen, where I'd stared at gorgeous Colin Kearns all night but never got up the courage to ask him out. Then he'd laughed at my shock when he told me Colin still lived in town... with his husband and kids.

It was a little weird, and a little wonderful, and exactly the distraction I needed.

I took deep breaths of fresh, crisp air as Herc and I strolled the last couple of blocks home. The Thicket in winter smelled like coffee and woodsmoke. It was a happy, comfortable scent that reminded me of Champ. Or maybe Champ reminded me of the Thicket—

And just like that, that stomach-flipping, nervous-excited-vomity feeling was back in my stomach.

This was seriously concerning.

I was scheduled to meet Marissa out at the farm in a couple of hours for our first walk-through of the venue. Since Champ had hightailed it without a word, I could only assume I'd be going alone, which was great. Perfect. The last thing I needed was for him to tag along and suggest more ridiculous wedding stuff to further his investigation—*"All the best weddings are finger-printing guests for fun these days, Marissa!"*—that would require us to spend even more time together.

Five weeks might be impossibly short for wedding-planning purposes, but it was also way too long for me to spend impersonating Percy Champion's fiancé without losing my sanity. The more time we spent together, the harder it was to remember where the actual boundaries of our relationship were. The sooner it was over, the better.

At the last minute, I detoured across the street to Annie's bakery for some coffee and donut fortification. But the second I put my foot on the sidewalk, a tiny blond child raced out of the bakery. He only got five paces down the sidewalk before he rocked to a stop in front of me and Hercules, making Herc bark excitedly.

The boy popped the finger he'd been sucking out of his mouth and pointed at the dog. *"Canis familiaris,"* he whispered, wide-eyed.

Uh. "Pardon?"

"Beau? Beau!" A pretty blonde woman with a baby in her arms chased the little boy out of the bakery. "Oh, good Lord, I'm so sorry. He's fascinated with dogs, and his father insists on teaching him Latin words, because apparently being a mother of three little ones wasn't enough of a challenge." She sighed and ran a hand over the boy's hair. "Beauregard Siegel, what have I told you about running off without me?"

"Um." The boy wrinkled his nose. "'No running, Beau'?"

"Exactly," she said severely.

"But, Mama, I din' run." He blinked up at her angelically. "I jes… walked fast." He smiled at his mother with such irresistible charm and confidence in his own logic that I had to bite my lip to keep from laughing.

The woman bit her lip, also, like she was fighting the same urge. "It's bad enough that he's as sassy as I was at his age, but nobody told me he'd be as smart as my husband too. I'm sunk."

I didn't know the first thing about having children… but I remembered being one that no one quite knew how to handle.

I squatted down and addressed the boy. "His name is Hercules. You can pet him if you'd like."

Herc was straining at his leash like he really wanted to slobber his friendship all over the little boy.

The boy reached out a hesitant hand… and then giggled when Herc licked it.

The woman grinned as I stood back up. "Quinn Taffet, you are every bit as *delightful* as I've heard!"

I fought the urge to look behind me for a more delightful Quinn. "I… am?"

A familiar-looking older lady hurried out of the

bakery with a baby in her arms, puffing slightly. "Ava, honey? Oh!" She stopped short when she saw me, and her face broke out in a grin at least as wide as the blonde's. "Well, hey there, Quinn! Isn't this a treat?"

I blinked. Even after my morning walk, I was never *not* going to find it weird when people I didn't know seemed to know me. "Uh… hey."

"I'm Cindy Ann Johnson," the older woman said, pressing a hand to her chest. "You might recognize me from here and there since my Red's been the mayor of Licking Thicket since you came here on your summer breaks, back when you were a teenager."

"Right, yeah." I nodded. "I remember now."

"And this here is Ava," she went on. "My almost-daughter-in-law. Well, I mean… she once dated my oldest son, and then she also dated the man that my oldest son fell in love with, so she's as close to being my daughter-in-law as you can get without actual, you know, *law*. You understand?"

Weirdly, I was pretty sure I did.

"Cindy Ann, I think you're scaring Quinn." Ava laughed lightly. "We're harmless, I promise. We've just been meaning to come over to your lovely, *lovely* shop for the longest while and introduce ourselves."

"You have?"

"Ever since you moved in," Cindy Ann agreed. "Those window displays of yours are gorgeous. Wish I had such artistic flair."

"Oh. Well." I felt my cheeks go hot. I took a lot of pride in those window-scapes. "Thank you."

"And *event planning*," Ava said, swaying a little when the baby in her arms began to fuss. "I've always been so fascinated by that career. Takes not only great taste but also real leadership skills. You've gotta be a people person."

"I... I mean, yes. I like to think so," I agreed.

"D'you know, Quinn, your aunt Cherry and I go way back," Cindy Ann said. "I talk to her every month or two without fail. Plus, she made my wedding dress, *and* she was a member of the Beautification Corps before she retired. That practically makes you and me family."

What the heck was happening here?

"I feel like I've been remiss in waiting so long to come and pay you a call," Cindy Ann continued. "See how you're settling in. Making new friends. All that."

"Oh. Um. I've been busy," I said apologetically. "My business keeps me on the road to Nashville, so—"

"But I know Quinn's made at least one friend," Ava interjected. "Just this morning, Vivian Phelan told me Lurlene Jackson told *her* that Vienna Goodley saw Champ sneak out of Quinn's place early in the morning at least twenty-eight times in the last couple months."

Damn it, I knew it had been more than twenty-seven.

Wait.

"Someone saw Champ sneak—er, *leave*—my house in the morning?" I demanded. "All those mornings?"

"Sure." Cindy Ann blinked like she couldn't imagine why I was surprised. "Ever since Tucker let her move in to the apartment above his medical office—" She pointed across the street at a diagonal, to the big old house on the same block as Taffet Events. "—Vienna Goodley's been keeping an eye on the Main Street for us. To keep us safe."

"Safe," I repeated faintly. Strangely enough,

knowing someone was watching me made me feel *less* safe.

"But I'm so excited you and Champ are an item!" Cindy Ann exclaimed. "He's always seemed so sweet, hasn't he, Ava? His mother, Bunny—well, she was Isobel Henderson back then, of course—went to school with me before she married Champ's father and moved to Nashville. After Champ's father died, she and Champ didn't come back to visit much, but I always liked— *Beau*! Stop right there, mister, while I clean you up. Do *not* put that dog-slobber-covered hand in your mouth."

"You always liked… what?" I prompted fake-casually. Champ never volunteered anything about his past, and I couldn't deny I was thirsty for details.

But then Cindy Ann thrust a small, pink-clad baby at me, and I forgot about everything else as I scrambled to hold her securely under the armpits while Cindy Ann attacked the little boy with a wet wipe.

"*Heyyy.* Hey, there, baby girl." The baby stared up at me with big blue eyes, looking just as uncertain as I felt.

I'd never held a baby before, and I couldn't say I recommended the experience.

"So, Quinn, are you and Champ thinking about kids?" Ava went on.

"Oh, God, no. See, the thing is, we're not actually in a relationship. We're, uh…" I glanced down at the little boy. "We're *friends*." I gave Ava a significant look. "Friends who do sleepovers."

Cindy Ann glanced up from her cleaning job and wrinkled her nose in confusion. "Aren't you boys a little old for sleepovers?"

My cheeks flamed. I had not had enough caffeine to deal with this maturely.

"He means they're friends with benefits, Cindy Ann," Ava explained. "They're dating casually."

"Oh. Well, in that case…" Cindy Ann stood with an eager smile. "You might be interested to know that there are nearly two hundred out-and-proud gay and bisexual men in the greater Thicket-Nuthatch area, in case you're looking to upgrade to something more serious."

"What? God, no. That's—"

"It's true," Ava confirmed proudly, still swaying with her baby. "And the Thicket is also home to a well-respected charitable organization called Rainbows Over Tennessee, which helps support LGBTQIA+ youth, especially those who don't have appropriate support at home."

This speech sounded well rehearsed, which was confusing, but with the baby in my hands, it was hard to think clearly. "Okay?"

"Our own Tucker Johnson—that's Cindy Ann's son-in-law—founded the organization, and they do incredible work in our community and beyond. So incredible, in fact, that this year the Thicket Beautification Corps has decided to donate the proceeds of our annual SnoBall Fundraiser Dance to benefit Rainbows."

"That sounds great, but I don't understand what—?"

"—you need to do in order to get involved?" Cindy Ann beamed. "Oh, I hoped you'd feel that way. Parrish assured us you were the person for the job. You're hired!" she announced excitedly.

"Hired?" I shook my head. "I'm sorry, as what?"

"As our event planner, sweetheart. That's what you do for a living," Cindy Ann said gently, like she worried maybe I'd forgotten.

She took the baby back from me at last.

"I don't follow," I said weakly. But I was very much afraid I did. And if I was being asked to produce a giant charity dance *pro bono*, with only three weeks to plan, there was literally no chance of it happening.

"Obviously, we'd never actually ask you to plan the event," Ava explained, like she was inside my mind, hearing my thoughts. "Not this close to the date. But Lorraine Peevey, the lady who's run the SnoBall committee for years, has… erm. Taken ill."

Cindy Ann rolled her eyes. "Don't make it sound dramatic, Ava honey. Truth is, Quinn, she went down to the Villages in Florida to visit her sister a couple weeks ago, and you know how it goes in those retirement communities. Swingers every-dang-where. Lorraine got herself a little too much *free* love, and now she's on some *expensive* antibiotics."

Cindy Ann snorted at her own joke, and damn if that didn't make me like her even more.

"So, you'd just need me to…?" I trailed off.

"To coordinate vendors on the night and make sure there are no last-minute snafus," Cindy Ann said. "And to keep us on schedule. If the dance floor's not clear by the time the first SnoBall is thrown out, chaos ensues."

"There are… there are actual balls being thrown?"

"Mmhmm. That's the fundraising portion of the evening," she explained, though her explanation only made things *less* clear. "We'll go over everything Thursday. Seven p.m. sharp, Thicket Tavern. Okay?"

I rubbed my forehead. I really did *not* want another thing to be in charge of. But it seemed like most of the work was already done… and hadn't I *just* been thinking how much I needed a distraction from Champ?

"I'll be there," I agreed.

Ava reached over and gave me an impulsive hug. "I'm *so* glad, Quinn. You and I are going to be friends, I just know it."

My cheeks had to be violent red. I could feel them heating the air around me. "That would… that would be great."

"And listen, sweetie," Cindy Ann said kindly, "If Champ doesn't come up to scratch and you need a plus-one, you just let me know. I've got connections."

"A plus-one?" I frowned. "No, I don't think—" I stopped myself. After five minutes of conversation, I already knew that Cindy Ann would not take kindly to me saying I'd go alone. "I'll take care of it, I promise."

"Good enough." She patted my cheek maternally. "See you Thursday. And please tell your aunt Cherry I'll phone her soon," she threatened—I mean, *called*—over her shoulder as she walked away.

Oh, *fuck*.

I could just imagine Cindy Ann telling Cherry the tale of Champ and the Twenty-Eight Walks of Shame, embellishing every already embarrassing detail.

"Change of plans," I told Hercules, who was still staring after little Beau Siegel like his one true love had left him. "No time for donuts. You and I are going home."

The second we got inside, I hit Aunt Cherry's number, and while Hercules wisely curled up in his bed by the front window, I paced the length of the show-room as the phone rang.

"Hello," Cherry whispered. Her voice was hoarse,

and instant worry made my stomach flip. Aunt Cherry was normally hale and hearty. I'd never known her to be sick for even a day.

"Cherry? Are you sick?"

"Quinn!" Cherry exclaimed softly, sounding marginally more alive. "Hey, honey. No, I'm great. I—"

A deeper voice rumbled in the background, too low for me to really hear.

"Holy crap! Is that Mrs. Ambrose?" I asked. "She sounds worse than you."

For a long moment, Aunt Cherry didn't answer. I heard only the rustle of fabric followed by the *thunk* of a door shutting. Finally, she said, "That wasn't Marianne, honey. She stayed behind in Louisiana to visit with family. That was Terrance. You remember me telling you about him last time I called? He owns a bar here in St. Pete, but his son's mostly taken the place over now. He took me swing dancing last week."

"Um." I frowned. "No? I remember you mentioning a guy in Rancho Mirage a while back who liked high-stakes gambling, but I don't think you mentioned his name."

"Oh, *that* guy." Cherry snorted. "No, not him."

"The biker in Sturgis with the beard down to his navel?"

"Laws, no. I'm no man's old lady, Quinn."

"Right. Is Terrance one of the brothers in Ohio with the cheetah-print carpet on the walls of their bedroom—?"

"Oof. I told you about them, eh?" Cherry's wince was almost audible.

"Of course you did. You tell me about all your dates. Cautionary tales, you call them."

"Right." Cherry cleared her throat. "I guess I have called them that. But honey, Terrance is—"

"Listen, I can't wait to hear this story," I told her, "because I'm sure this dude is as ridiculous as all your others have been, and I could use a laugh, but before we get to that, I have to tell you before you hear from one of your friends that…" I took a deep breath. "I've been seeing someone."

Cherry gasped. "What? Oh, Quinn, that's—"

"I know. You're disappointed. But I promise, it's not serious, no matter what you might hear. It's just sex. I mean, high-quality sex. Really *frequent* high-quality sex. But that's all it is, okay?"

Aunt Cherry was silent for a second. "Quinn, you know it's okay to—" She broke off with a frustrated sound. "You're on your way to work now, aren't you? Honey, we need to catch up soon, okay? Thursday night. Or Friday."

I snorted. "I can't Thursday." I explained how Cindy Ann and Ava had finessed me into running the SnoBall… and how I was weirdly looking forward to it.

"Aww," Cherry said. "They're adopting you! I'm so glad. You always fit so well in the Thicket."

Did I? Huh. "I fit with *you*," I countered. "In your big-ass house, with all the window seats."

She chuckled. "Have you been by the old place? I'm curious what the new owners are doing with it. Probably tore it down and rebuilt the whole thing."

"Probably," I agreed softly. Which was exactly why I hadn't been able to make myself drive by, not in all the months I'd lived over the shop. I'd *loved* that place. As glad as I'd been to take over Cherry's shop, it was her house I'd really considered a home. I didn't want to see someone make it their own.

"Everything in life's temporary, honey," Cherry reminded me. "Buildings. People. Seasons. If you hold on too tight, you won't be ready for the next great thing that comes along."

"Yeah, I know." I'd taken that lesson on board and lived it my whole life. It was why I'd been only a tiny bit devastated when Scott and I broke up and why I hadn't fought him about keeping the business.

But looking around the Thicket, a place that was the epitome of "permanent," with people who remembered me even decades later, I couldn't help but think maybe Cherry was wrong about this one thing. Not everything had to be temporary.

Maybe there was a time and a place to fight for the things you wanted... once you'd figured out what they were.

As I drove myself out to the Drakeses' farm, past the big, green silo and down their long, rutted driveway, I decided I'd take the—what had Champ called it? —the *tactical consideration* of the location and use it as a personal challenge. I would make this wedding so spectacular, so glorious, so fun, and so memorable that next spring's issue of *Bride Beautiful* would be all about the hot new Rusty Crusty Pig Farm Wedding trend.

I would get my client married off, she and her parents would be thrilled, and I would not waste another minute feeling anxious about things I couldn't control, namely—

I came to a sudden stop at the top of the driveway, when the trees opened up to reveal a sprawling, two-story white farmhouse with a wraparound porch... and a familiar pickup truck parked front and center next to Marissa's Audi.

Delusional McBossypants Champion had crashed my wedding-planning meeting… again.

8

CHAMP

Seeing Quinn so angry shouldn't have made me hard, but it did. He grabbed his tablet out of the back seat, slammed the door to his little rattletrap, and came striding over to me with smoke coming out of his ears. "What the hell are you doing here?"

"Being your assistant, obvs." I handed over the coffee I'd picked up from Annie's for him. "I've been running errands all morning, boss. And frankly, I think I deserve a raise."

Quinn's scowl softened for a split second as he took a hungry sip, but as soon as the caffeine slid down his throat, the scowl returned. "Would've been nice if you'd informed me of your plan this morning. I wasn't sure you'd even be here."

"Awww, and you were missing me already, weren't you, Pookie? Look at that face. So much love. So much adoration." I reached out and ruffled his hair for good measure.

The resulting red streaks on Quinn's cheeks and neck were somewhat comical and somewhat worrying.

"Remember, you owe me a wedding," he growled in a low voice while he tried to finger-comb his hair back into place. "A good one. A *fancy* one."

"As if I could forget. This morning I had to harass a couple of my people at Champion Security for overdue expense reports and put the fear of God into whichever one of those fuckers keeps messing up the bathroom sink since I'm not paying a plumber to come out a third time. Then I needed to talk to a client—"

This was code for quietly grinding my teeth while Jacob Horn, the entitled jerk who was CEO of HOG Corporate, cursed me out about Champion Security's inability to lay hands on Gustavo Santiago's Horn and disarm HOG's PR nightmare before it went nuclear.

"—but I also made time to acquire *this*." I held up Carter's business card between two fingers.

Quinn snatched it away and stared down at it.

"Carter Rogers, M.D.?" he read. "Who's that?"

I spotted Marissa and Levi, her pit bull of a security guard, walking out of the front door, and I gently urged Quinn toward them as I answered.

"That is your society wedding. Carter's a well-known cardiologist from Vanderbilt. He practices near the Thicket now, but his family is as Nashville blue-blooded as they come. He and his groom are still in the early stages of planning. Still gathering intel, you might say."

"Huh." Quinn looked up at me with a wrinkled brow. "But they're ready to hire me to plan their wedding? You're sure?"

I shrugged. If Riggs knew what was good for him, they fucking would be. "Positive."

Quinn clutched the card in his palm. "Thanks, Champ," he said softly, and no lie, somehow all my shitty morning was a little less bad when he gave me a little smile.

I cleared my throat and faced our intended targets. "Whatever. No big," I said gruffly. "Deal's a deal. So, what I was thinking we'd do was—"

Before I could finish sketching out my plan, a horrible squealing sound came from behind Marissa and Levi. Quinn froze in his tracks before inching forward slowly.

I smelled the hogs before I saw them.

"No," Quinn hissed. His nostrils flared in anger. "Oh, God. I thought I could do this, but I cannot. This is not a *tactical consideration*, Champion—this is absurd. This is unhygienic and disgusting. This is… Oh, hello!" His face lit into a big bright smile as if we weren't in spitting distance from a great tonnage of pork flesh. "How's the bride on this… lovely day?"

The four of us looked around at the cold and over-cast sky before Marissa returned Quinn's smile. "That's one of the things I love about you! Your positive outlook. Trey felt like you had good energy right from the start!"

"Your energy wasn't the only thing he was inter-ested in feeling," I said under my breath.

Quinn stepped on my foot in retaliation. "And where is your handsome groom today?"

"Oh, working!" Marissa said airily. "Trey's a very hard worker. My mother was disappointed that she couldn't tag along to see you work your magic, but she's got so many luncheons and meetings, she couldn't be away from town for the whole day. I told her I'd tell her all your ideas when I got back tonight. I'm sure you'll have tons!"

"Tons," Quinn said, looking around with a tiny bit

of desperation, as if elegance would suddenly jump out from behind an old broken-down tractor and declare shabby pig farms the hot new thing.

"Quinn's the best at turning lemons into lemonade," I said, trying to think of an example. "One time our Chinese food was delivered without chopsticks, and he found... uh... he found us a set of pencils to use instead."

Quinn slow-panned to me and shot me a now-familiar *what the fuck* expression. I shrugged again.

Levi looked confused. "Why didn't you just use forks?"

Quinn crossed his arms in front of his chest. "Yeah, Love Chunk. Why was that, again? Something about your delicate—"

I cut him off quickly. "Also, he once planned a wedding at a venue that had been deliberately double-booked by one of his competitors. When the other wedding party showed up at the club, Quinn managed to move his own entire party onto the putting green, and it was so wonderful that people buzzed about it for months!"

Quinn's eyes narrowed like he couldn't believe I remembered that, and I rolled my eyes in response because how could I not? I'd heard him talk to his clients plenty of times in the past few weeks because, just like mine, they tended to call at all hours with emergencies. The only difference was Quinn was able to take his calls in front of me.

After hearing about his asshole ex the day before, though, that story took on new significance.

"You know, Popkin, you never told me who the other wedding planner was." I tried to sound casual.

"Unimportant," Quinn said just as casually, but the

look on his face confirmed what I already suspected. Fucking *Scott*.

I reached out absently to hold Quinn's hand. His fingers tangled with mine automatically, as if we'd been holding hands on and off for years. It felt nice. Really fucking nice. So nice, I couldn't manage to convince myself that it had been for Marissa's benefit.

"My point is," I went on, "this man is very talented. You couldn't be in better hands. I'm sure this lovely… ah… pastoral venue has… hidden magic. Somewhere."

Marissa clapped her hands and bounced on her feet, which set the little golden puffball on her winter hat bobbing. "Then let's get started so we can find the magic. I'm so excited to show you around." She threaded her arm through Levi's and began walking toward a distant gate in the fence line, fortunately well away from the pigs we'd seen.

Quinn and I exchanged a look at their easy familiarity.

"And we can take pictures for Trey," Quinn said meaningfully. "And maybe he can come next time."

"Maybe," she agreed. "Though, honestly, with our virginity pact, it's easier this way. The more time we spend apart, the easier it is to stay chaste, you know? So I was thinking— Ohmigosh, Levi, are you okay?"

Levi stumbled, scattering pebbles under his boots, before he righted himself. "Yeah, fine. Sorry."

"Um. Pardon," Quinn said politely, though I knew him well enough to know this had turned his nosymeter up to ten thousand. "Your… what kind of pact?"

"Virginity. Well, more like re-virginity. See, when Trey proposed at Christmas, we decided to stop having sex until the wedding. That way, it'll make our wedding night even more special. It won't be our technical first time, but it'll be our first time since committing ourselves to one another. Isn't that so romantic?"

Quinn lifted his eyebrows at me. "So. So romantic. And… unexpected. Especially since you believed the wedding planning would take six months. Trey certainly is…"

"Gay?" I suggested under my breath.

Quinn cleared his throat and elbowed me. "Thoughtful."

"Pretty sure it's the first one," I muttered.

Levi piped up. "I, for one, think that's amazing. You deserve to be treated like the treasure you are. He should be grateful to have such a lovely br…" He looked around as if suddenly realizing he wasn't alone. "Bride," he finished softly before reaching for the gate.

We followed them around to the back side of the sprawling farmhouse to a small outdoor shed in the back.

"We're going to put on muck boots since it's a little wet out here today," Marissa said happily, pointing to row after row of muddy rain and work boots. "Pick a pair that fits. We've got a ton."

Quinn's face lost a little color as he contemplated putting on someone else's nasty boots. "I… oh. Well, I guess if…" He looked up at me with a desperate plea for help in his eyes. I couldn't help but lean over and kiss the edge of his lips.

"Toughen up, buttercup. We're doing this," I murmured against his warm skin.

He huffed and pulled back to examine the boots for the least offensive pair in his general size. They happened to be purple with giant white daisies on them.

"Let me help you," Levi offered to Marissa, guiding her onto a nearby bench and picking a specific pair of boots off the shelf for her. He guided the boots onto her feet one at a time while looking up at her with stars in his eyes. Marissa's cheeks flushed light pink. "I know how upset you get when you mess up your nails."

"Thanks," she said with a sweet smile.

"Shit," Quinn murmured.

"Mmhm," I agreed softly. "Gonna need to keep an eye on that if you want this wedding to happen."

"It's happening," he said, recapturing his usual determination.

I grinned, making him automatically scowl.

"What? Why are you doing that with your face?"

"That's the Quinn I know and lo… lick," I said, scrambling to correct myself before poisoning the air between us with stupid L-words. "You're a fighter. You're going to kick ass."

He seemed to stand a little taller. "That's right. I am."

Once everyone was properly shod, we went back out into the weak winter light and trekked all over hell and back, trying to find a spot—any spot—we could turn into an elegant wedding venue.

It wasn't easy.

"If only the goats didn't need that pasture," Levi said with a sigh. "And you know how your dad feels about crop rotation."

Marissa squinted at him. "Not really, no?"

"Well, let's just say, the three pastures over there are off-limits." He pointed to fields of what looked like marijuana. "Your dad read an article about hemp cultivation, and now he's obsessed. You know, maybe you should find a different place. Or wait a year, until the crops are—"

"What about the overlook?" Marissa suggested.

Levi froze for a second, then turned toward her. "You wanna marry Trey at the overlook?"

Marissa lifted her chin just slightly. "Why not?"

Levi opened his mouth like he wanted to say something. Then he flicked a glance at me and Quinn and shut it firmly again. "No reason." He set his jaw. "No reason at all." He marched ahead, leading us up a gravel path.

As soon as we climbed over the rise of a hill, I felt Quinn's entire body language change. "Holy... *yes*. That's it," he said reverently. "It's gorgeous."

Levi glanced at Marissa, but she was too busy gazing out at the view next to Quinn to notice. "Isn't it amazing?" she whispered.

Quinn sighed happily. "It's the most beautiful spot in the county, I'm sure of it. Look how far you can see."

Marissa pointed to the large river snaking through the valley in the distance. "That's the Big South Fork of the Harriman River."

"You can see it even better since the trees aren't in bloom," Quinn agreed. "And—oh my word! Look at that rock formation over there!" He squeezed Marissa's arm excitedly. "Does that, or does that not, look like..."

"A *heart*!" he and Marissa finished together, wearing identical grins.

"That's Emmaline Proud-Nutter's land across the valley there," Marissa said. "I bet she'd let us decorate around it."

"This is the most gorgeous spot ever." Quinn sounded blissed-out, a tone I'd only ever heard when he was close to orgasm, and I had to turn away because the urge to wrap my arms around him was so strong.

"I had my first kiss right here," Levi said so quietly, I almost didn't catch it.

At the same time, Marissa sighed and told Quinn, "I had my very first kiss here."

Quinn and I made significant eye contact. *Oh hell.*

"Great," Quinn said with a loud hand clap. Three of us startled at the sound. "That's a sign this wedding was meant to happen right here. So romantic. The most romantic spot on the entire farm. We'll get a huge event tent set up with gas heaters and fairy lights everywhere. We'll have a fleet of horse-drawn carriages to bring guests out here from the house, and they'll be decked out in greenery and floral headpieces. I have pictures of what I'm thinking of. We'll put them on the design board."

As he continued to spell out his vision for the hilltop wedding reception, Marissa stood spellbound. I didn't blame her at all. Quinn was charming and magnetic. It was clear he was good at what he did, and I hoped like hell he would get the reputation he wanted in the industry.

While I stared at the moody spitfire in front of me, Levi stared at the bride. Someone *else's* bride.

This was going to be a major problem, but it wasn't one that was in my wheelhouse. I needed to keep my focus on *my* mission—finding the Horn, retrieving the smuggled data, saving my client, and keeping Champion Security's lucrative contract with HOG Corporate.

The faster I did all those things, the easier it would be for Quinn to get his job done. So I needed to do some recon.

"Marissa, would you mind if I head back to the house and use the bathroom?" I asked, flashing her a smile. "Shouldn't have gotten the large coffee on the way here."

She barely glanced away from the view. "Make yourself at home. If you go in the front door, there's a powder room down the hall to the right."

I thanked her and began walking toward the house. Within a few steps, I realized I wasn't alone. Levi trailed me like a pesky shadow.

"I'm sure I can find it on my own," I joked, hoping he wasn't following me for security purposes.

"We don't let anyone into Mr. Drakes's house unattended. I'm sure you understand."

I didn't respond. Instead, I used the trip across the field to try and figure out how to get time away from him. After a minute, I tried the obvious. "I would have thought you'd be tasked with watching Marissa."

"Rissy? No," he said with a snort. "She wouldn't stand for it. But I taught her to defend herself a long time ago. She's almost a better shot than me, and she's got a hell of a right hook."

A sharpshooter brawling bride who was afraid to mess up her manicure. Only Quinn could find a client like that.

"Still," I said, not giving up. "This is a big property with lots of workmen hanging around. You sure you've vetted them all well enough?" I nodded toward a particularly rough-looking man using a pitchfork to commit violent homicide on a nearby hay bale.

"Old Jimbo?" he scoffed. "The man kissed Marissa's skinned knees a time or two back in the day. Naw. Folks around here won't betray Mr. Drakes if they know what's good for 'em. But for damn sure, no one here's gonna betray Marissa, because they love her to pieces. You get me?"

What I got was that Levi was still suspicious of me. *Terrific.*

"Sure," I agreed easily. "She seems like a great person." We reached the house and turned down the hallway to the bathroom. "Thanks for showing me the way," I said. "I'll meet you back out front in a few minutes."

"I'll wait so you don't get lost on your way back." Levi narrowed his eyes at me. "You know, you sure do use the bathroom a lot. First at the Nashville house and now—"

"Does that revirgination plan seem odd to you?" I blurted, trying to distract him from his train of thought.

"Huh?"

"Marissa saying she and Trey weren't sleeping together until the wedding. I've never heard of such a thing. Have you?"

"Well… I guess I've never thought about it. But I think it's smart. And if that's what Marissa wants, Trey should respect it."

I tried looking around while he spoke, but it was impossible to see anything while standing in a farmhouse hallway. There was nothing but wooden plaques on the wall with phrases like *Live, Laugh, Love* and *Make Hay While the Sun Shines… No, Really.*

"I suppose you're right." I forced a laugh. "But God, could *you* go that long?"

"You'd be surprised what you can do when you love someone," Levi said starkly. He nodded at the bathroom behind me. "Did you change your mind?"

"Huh? Oh. No." After an awkward pause, I disappeared into the bathroom and shut the door. Then I braced my hands on the vanity and tried to think.

Levi was not going to just let me waltz around this place on my own during these wedding-planning meetings. If he was right about the staff who worked here—

and I got the sense he was—they were loyal to Tommy and utterly devoted to Marissa, so trying to bribe them would likely backfire. Five weeks wasn't long enough to earn Levi's trust. So I needed more Levi-free time here at the farm.

I could handle subcontractors for Quinn every day, which would give me more access *and* earn me points with the sexy man, but the farm's staff would still be a problem. I could also get some of my team in here as painters and landscapers, but I'd have to wait for Hux to provide them with some kind of background cover first since I was pretty sure Levi would want to run down every contractor Quinn hired.

As I flushed the toilet and washed my hands in the sink, I brainstormed ways to make myself useful while also getting unhindered access to the property, but I kept coming up blank.

Thankfully, Quinn was way ahead of me. It turned out, he'd zeroed in on the perfect solution without even realizing it… he just needed me to helpfully point it out.

9

QUINN

"This is going to work *perfectly*," I told Marissa, doing a small pirouette around the giant, cavernous bunkhouse out of sheer relief.

I'd been expecting hogs and mud, and yes, there were exponentially more of both than I would have preferred. But there was also the prettiest vista in Licking Thicket and this big, empty room right near the ceremony location, which was just *dying* to be turned into a prep area once we removed the bunk beds and old furniture.

I'd done a lot more with a lot less.

"I'm envisioning setting aside a room in the house for Trey and his groomsmen while you and your court get ready here," I said excitedly. "This area—" I waved around at the walls. "—I'm thinking we'll do a cream wash, decorate with plenty of greenery and copper fairy lights, and clean up these hardwoods while leaving them rustic and beautiful. We'll do a light renovation of the powder room, of course, but have a salon chair and nail station set up in here for you and the bridesmaids.

When it's time for the ceremony, your carriage will ascend the hill, creating the most beautiful fairy-tale aesthetic, and then you'll be married right in front of that view."

"Yes. *Yes.*" Marissa nodded excitedly. "I swear when you say this stuff, it's like you're painting a picture in my head, Quinn! So are you thinking tables and chairs, or…"

"Maybe we go more informal," I suggested. "You said a sunset ceremony, right? So maybe we go for homey and warm." I winked. "Something very *you.*"

"Aww." Marissa's eyes went soft and shiny. "You think?"

"Definitely. Because, honey, if we're committing to a farm wedding, we're going full-on *farm wedding.* We are leaning in," I proclaimed, squeezing her forearm briefly. "It's gonna be magnificent."

"I believe you," she said softly. She clasped her hands under her chin and bit her lip as she glanced around the empty room, like she was envisioning it packed with her family and friends. "Honestly, Quinn, I can't thank you enough. The country club wedding was about pleasing my mom. And I'm sure it would have been amazing, but *this*… Gosh, this is the wedding I was meant to have." She pressed a hand to her stomach. "It just feels right. And I would never have been able to ask for it if you and Champ hadn't suggested it. I feel like you two are the only ones in this whole wedding business who are looking out for *me*, and that means so much."

I clutched my tablet to my chest to hide my guilty squirm. "Well, to be fair, it was Champ's doing—"

"I guess, but you two are a package deal now. A team. That's how marriage works, right?"

"Ha. Yes. I suppose so." If by "team" you meant one person who ran out on another after a night of epic lovemaking.

Not that my feelings were still hurt, obviously.

Much.

"You complement each other so well," she continued. "Like, I could tell you weren't a hundred percent on board with the farm wedding idea when Champ first mentioned Brailey's farm wedding—"

"Yes, I definitely wished he hadn't said anything about that," I agreed.

"But then it was pretty clear that Champ was really excited about the idea for some reason. So, despite your hesitation, you backed him up. You went with it. You supported him."

"Well, actually I…" I frowned. I guessed I *had*, if you looked at the situation in a certain way. "Huh."

"And it was obvious, too, that you are the more experienced one of the pair of you." Marissa smiled indulgently. "Champ's probably like Levi. All about getting things done efficiently but with no real understanding of how the business works."

I laughed. "Spot-on."

"But it was clear that he knew he didn't *have* to know, because he trusted you to make it happen, and sure enough… here you are, leaning in, coming up with this gorgeous vision, surprising even yourself with all this stuff. Right?"

I felt my lips twitch and took a sip of my mostly cold coffee. "Right."

She sighed. "That's why you two are total couple goals. Such a great example of how real love works."

My coffee slid down my windpipe, and I choked.

Marissa pounded my back firmly. "I hope someday Trey and I can get to that place."

"Sure you will," I croaked, wiping my streaming eyes. "You're going to be married. He's going to be your partner in life."

Or at least, that was the dream I'd built my business on… even though I knew it rarely worked that way.

"Yeah," she agreed. She strolled around the room, trailing her hand over the back of a sagging couch and the worn-smooth wood of a bunk bed. "You know, Levi and I used to come out here all the time as kids? He's two years older than me, but his dad was out here all the time working with my dad, so Levi tagged along and we'd play. We used this place as our fort, because we could see any enemies approaching from down the valley, and he had a tree branch sword he was gonna use to fight off anyone who wanted to get me."

Uh-oh.

"How adorable!" I said, overly enthusiastic. "He was your protector even then! But that was so long ago—"

"No way." She snorted. "I wouldn't let him be my protector. I made him teach me to do things for myself. He taught me how to ride a horse and how to swim. How to do long division. Convinced my dad to teach me how to shoot when I was ten so I could go along on hunting trips with him and the Christiansons. Sat perfectly still while I painted a billion portraits of him when we were teenagers. Said I wasn't crazy for dreaming about running an arts program for underprivileged children someday, even though my parents preferred that I work for the family business. He's not my protector. He's my…"

Her voice trailed off, and I stared up at her, but she didn't notice. Her voice had a faraway quality.

Oh, sweet mother of fuck. This was *so* much worse than I'd thought.

Marissa *loved* the man… or something close to love, anyway. I could recognize the symptoms the same way I could recognize poison ivy and other toxic things I wanted to avoid.

But if she loved him, why the heck was she marrying Trey?

None of your damn business, Taffet, I reminded myself. *You are not her life coach. Your business is to get the couple to the altar.*

The *right* couple.

Which was to say, the couple whose names were on the dang invitations that needed to be approved and sent to the printer that very morning.

"He's your big brother!" I finished for her. "Gosh, how special for you to have someone who's basically the nearest thing to a *blood relation* that a *platonic friend* could be. And of course, he's very lucky to have you as his precious, beloved *baby sister*."

Marissa laughed lightly, and her cheeks pinkened. "I mean… it wasn't like that. Not back then, at least. I had a huge crush on him back in the day, and we… well. There was a time when I thought he had feelings for me too. You know, when I pictured my wedding day here on the farm as a little girl, Levi was the guy I sort of pictured waiting for me at the end of the aisle."

Fuck. Super fuck.

"Too funny!" I laughed a little desperately. "When *I* was a sweet baby Quinn, I had a crush on Prince Phillip—not the British one, the one from *Sleeping Beauty*. I think we would have been an absolutely *tragic* couple in real life, though. I mean, who wants to shack up with a guy who goes around kissing maidens without permish. But that's the thing about young love! It's usually shortsighted and *super* foolish. Anyway." I swallowed against the sticky lump of guilt in my throat and lied, "It's pretty clear that he treats you like a little sister *now*, which is really lovely."

She blinked at me. "You think he has brotherly feelings towards me?"

Sweet, merciful Jesus.

"Of course?" The words came out like a question, though I meant to say them with conviction. "I mean, the way he's out here helping to make sure your wedding goes off without a hitch tells the tale, doesn't it?"

One side of her mouth quirked up in a smile. "You know, I guess it does," she said softly.

Ugh. I felt lower than pond scum.

But I reminded myself that just because she might have some leftover feelings for her childhood crush, that didn't mean she didn't have even *more* passionate feelings about her actual fiancé, did it?

"Enough about Levi! Tell me more about Trey," I insisted avidly. "How did you two meet?"

"Oh. Um. We've known each other for a while too, I guess. His mom and mine are friends. We weren't close at all growing up, but then last spring, we both had our mixed doubles partners cancel at the last minute, right before the annual charity tennis tournament at our country club, and we ended up playing together. He was really encouraging. I'm not a great player, but he kept saying things like, 'Nice volley, Marissa!' Which made the afternoon not so bad, you know?" Marissa smiled shyly. "Then he asked me to go see a musical with him the following weekend, and things just… happened from there. Turns out, we had a bunch of stuff in common. Like, we both love wine tastings. And, um, he likes to cook, which is great because I like to eat. And he understands that I need space, so if we don't see each other for a day or two… or even *ten*, he's totally fine with it. Not jealous in the slightest."

"That's… uh…" I couldn't think of a way to end my sentence that wasn't a lie. The way Marissa described it, she had as much in common with her fiancé as I did with Annie at the bakery. "Great?" I finally said.

"Right? Yeah. I think so too." Marissa smiled. "Plus, our parents are ecstatic at the match. When Trey asked me to marry him over Christmas, I don't think I've ever seen my mom as purely happy. She told him yes before I had a chance to!" She giggled. "Apparently, our star charts align perfectly, and our enneagram types are very compatible. Oh, and I told you about the whole virginity pact?" She lowered her voice though there was no one else around to overhear. "That was actually *Trey's* idea. Isn't that sweet?"

"The… very sweetest," I agreed, while in my head, I heard Champ's voice saying, *"Gay. The man is gay."*

"He wants to show that he respects me."

"Uh-huh. It's so…" Once again, I was stumped. What was a word that meant "shady" but sounded positive? "Respectful," I agreed.

"Yeah." Marissa sounded a little less confident. "I don't suppose you and Champ ever considered making a pact like that?"

"A no-sex pact?" I snorted before I could control myself. "No." Little did she know, if you took the sex away from our relationship, there'd be no relationship.

None at all. Zero. *Bupkis*.

But then I thought of all the talking we'd done *around* the sex--of all the nights we'd stared up at my darkened ceiling while I told him things about my past I would never have said in the light of day, or laughed about how he found most children's stories horrifying, or heard the cocky confidence disappear from his voice for a moment when he talked about frustrations at work — and wondered if that was strictly true.

Not that it mattered, really. I couldn't imagine Champ showing up every evening just to *talk*. Lord knew the man never stuck around after daybreak.

"Anyway!" I pasted on a bright smile and tapped my tablet to bring it back to life so I could take notes. "Enough chitchat when we have the world's most epic wedding to plan, right? As I was saying. Coat of paint in here. Redo the bathroom. And outside…" I opened the front door of the cabin and stepped outside. "Looks like we'll need some boards replaced. Definitely some cleaning. But I can already imagine the casual shots of the groomsmen sitting out there, propped against the railings, can't you?"

She trailed after me, eyes wide. "I can, but…"

"You said the interior of the main house is in great shape, so that should be all set. But we're going to need lots of landscaping work over there and here." I circled my hand in the air.

"Okay…"

"And we're gonna need gravel," I warned. "Like, all the gravel in Tennessee, just to make some paths up to the parking area near the main house. Not to mention the carriages. How many draft horses do you have here? Never mind, it's probably not enough, but we can get those too."

"Whoa," Marissa whispered. "Quinn, are you sure

you can get this done in time? I know I was joking earlier about you leaning in and getting problems solved, but if we only have a few weeks—"

"It's a lot," I told her honestly, "but Champ knows some talented guys."

At least, he'd promised me he did. And in this area, I really did believe him.

Marissa nodded mechanically, but she still looked worried.

At that moment, a little car that looked like a four-wheel-drive golf cart came bumping over the rise, with Levi at the wheel and Champ hanging on to the oh-shit bar and looking decidedly unhappy.

At least it wasn't only *my* driving that put that look on his face. Poor, overgrown control freak. I wondered if he'd shouted at Levi to "Mind the hogs!" and I couldn't help laughing, which of course Champ noticed.

It was a sad commentary on my level of attraction to the man that even when he looked ready to murder me, the sight of him still made my heart thump faster and my stomach contract with want.

Levi pulled the cart to a stop right beside the front porch steps and made a beeline for Marissa. "Riss? What's got you looking so upset?" He darted an accusing glance at me, like maybe I'd upset her.

Which… I mean, I suppose I sort of had, accidentally.

"There's just a lot of work to do before the wedding," Marissa said. "I mean, I knew there would be, but I don't think I really *knew it*-knew it until Quinn and I started making a list."

Champ got out of the cart and stalked toward me. "Problem?"

"Nothing we can't handle," I assured him. In a

much lower voice, I asked, "Is a few minutes in the golf cart of doom enough to make you long for a ride in my rattling, orange, glow-in-the-dark death wagon? Because if so, Rebecca expects an apology."

Champ made a rude noise. "The day I apologize to your car—"

"Rissy, it's gonna be fine." Levi draped a comforting (and concerningly non-fraternal) arm over Marissa's shoulder and pulled her against his side. "You need a hug?"

Champ and I exchanged a glance, our amusement gone.

"No, I know," Marissa agreed. "Quinn's got people, and they'll get things done. I just... can't help worrying." She laid her head on Levi's shoulder. "I want everything to be perfect."

"I know, babe," Levi said softly, tucking back a tendril of hair that had escaped her sunshiny hat.

Champ flared his eyes at this development, like he wanted me to *do something*. But what did he expect me to do, rip them apart bodily?

He squeezed my hand. "I have an idea. Go with me, okay?" he murmured.

Was he kidding? The man was plotting something, but I didn't know what. *"Nope."*

"Quinn..."

"Ugh. Fine. But don't make any—" *Promises*, I wanted to say.

But Champ was already strolling away, approaching Marissa with a bright smile and both hands outstretched. "Marissa, honey, I can't imagine how much stress you're under." He clucked sympathetically. "Quinn and I both want to do as much as we possibly can to make this easier on you. Don't we, Pop-Tart?"

"Of course," I agreed, though my brain was still stuck on the fact that Champ was capable of clucking sympathetically. "You're our—*my*—priority."

"It's understandable that you'd be nervous about having all this happening while you're back in Nashville!" he continued. "You probably want to be more hands-on. Lots of brides do. Which is why Quinn and I think it would be best for your peace of mind if you move out to the farm until the wedding."

We do?

"You do?" Marissa gasped, eyes shining.

"Absolutely! And the best part is… we'll move out here with you! We'll keep you company in the evening and be on hand all day to oversee the landscapers and construction crews."

We will?

"You will?" Marissa clasped her hands under her chin.

"No, you damn well won't," Levi said firmly, and for once, I was totally Team Levi, because *what the fuck was Champ thinking?* "Rissy, your father will never allow it. Remember they had a break-in attempt at the Nashville house just last night."

Champ stiffened.

Marissa lifted her chin and cut Levi off. "Someone tried to get into the *garage* because they wanted one of Dad's classic cars. That has nothing to do with this. Dad will be fine with it, as long as you don't fill his head with a bunch of stupid conspiracy theory nonsense. I'm not eight years old, Levi, and there are no enemies coming through the valley. I don't need you to protect me. I have never wanted your *protection*."

"Riss, stop and think—" Levi threw out a hand toward Champ.

"No, *you* stop and think. You're not my big brother!" Marissa's cheeks flamed red. "And this is not *your* wedding, is it?"

Levi ground his teeth together so hard I thought his molars would crack. "No."

"*No.* So that means I'm in charge. And I say Quinn and Champ are going to move out here to the farm. And so am I. And if you try to sabotage that, I'll… I'll… never speak to you again." She nodded resolutely, hands on her hips. "And you know I mean it."

"Marissa." Levi sounded appalled and anguished. "I'm just trying to…" He blew out a frustrated breath. "You don't even know these guys. Your *dad* doesn't know them. You can't let them just wander around—"

"I know that they're gonna help me plan my wedding and not be all… *negative* about it." Marissa took a step in Levi's direction and poked him in the center of the chest with one perfectly manicured finger. "All you've been doing lately is telling me I'm wrong about this and wrong about that. Wrong for letting my mom convince me to take a few weeks off until the wedding. Wrong for letting Trey's mom railroad me about the bridal shower. Wrong for wanting the wedding here at the farm. Wrong for trusting Quinn and Champ. Since when d'you think I'm incompetent, huh? What the heck is your problem?"

Levi looked like he'd swallowed something sour. "Nothing! That's not… this is different, Riss."

"Is it? Because it feels like more of the same thing. I don't need a keeper, Levi. At least Trey thinks I can take care of myself. Trey thinks I'm perfectly capable of handling wedding plans."

"I never said… I didn't mean…" He ran both hands through his dark hair. "*Fuck,*" he whispered under his breath. "Fine, then." He lifted his hands and let them drop. "You wanna move out here, we'll make that happen."

"That's exactly what I want," Marissa said primly. "Thank you." Then she turned to me. "Great! That's settled. So what's next?"

"Uh." I glanced down at my tablet so I wouldn't have to see her brittle smile. "Invitations. Those need to go to the printer today as a rush job. We're already pushing it with timing."

"Right. Okay. Let's do it." She headed for the little golf cart, only realizing it wasn't big enough for the four of us when she stood beside it. "Oh! I can walk back—"

"Nonsense. You and Levi go on ahead in the cart," I insisted. "My Afternoon Delight and I will walk down and meet you. We need to have a quick chat about logistics anyway."

"You mean you want to have a moment alone with your sweetheart." Marissa winked. "So cute. Don't take *too* long, okay?"

I forced a smile and managed to wait until the cart had turned and headed down the hill before I rounded on Percy Champion and let loose.

"I am going to get the definition of *silent partner* tattooed on the inside of your eyelids, because you keep fucking forgetting."

"I know. I know! I'm sorry. I should *not* have signed you up for that without talking to you first—"

"You really shouldn't! Especially—"

"Especially not after I signed you up for the farm wedding without talking to you, yeah," he went on, taking the wind out of my sails.

"Exactly," I rallied. "*And* after—"

"After I signed myself up as your fiancé without asking you first. I get it. But when I tried to check the house, Levi wouldn't let me out of his sight. He practically offered to come in the bathroom and hold my dick while I peed. And then we got up here, and suddenly, Levi was a step away from pledging his love —"

"No shit. And it's way worse than I thought the other day because I'm pretty sure Marissa has feelings too. But I need this wedding to happen, Champ."

"Same. Which is why I had to do something drastic, and I didn't think there was time to talk to you first. I'm sorry."

I narrowed my eyes. "You're voluntarily admitting that you should have talked to me first? Are you feverish?"

"I figured I'd go for disarming honesty and a charming smile since you don't like it when I'm high-handed and bossy." Champ touched the tip of his tongue to the center of his top lip, then ran his teeth over his bottom lip before grinning a grin so devastating there should have been Geneva Convention rules about it. "How's it working?"

Too well. Though, frankly, the bossy thing worked for me also. In fact, there wasn't much about Champ that didn't work for me... which was kind of a problem.

I ruthlessly suppressed an answering smile of my own and told my dick to stand down. "It's not working at all. Did you stop to consider any other plans I might have? Other clients?"

"Of course. I know you're not going to be here 24/7. I don't expect you to be. I'll handle all the contractors who need to be handled."

I gripped my tablet harder and turned toward the

main house. "And search for the Horn every free moment of the day."

He nodded as he fell in step beside me. "Well, yeah. But the staff will be way less vigilant about locking things down with Marissa staying there. So at night, you can distract her with wedding plans and face masks while I concentrate on *my* work."

"No I will not. I have a client meeting on Tuesday evening about an anniversary party, Thursday I have the SnoBall Committee, and next Saturday, I have a vow renewal in Nashville that's gonna run late. So I guess *you'll* be in charge of facials and wedding plans."

"What the heck is a snowball committee?"

"Not *a* snowball, *the* SnoBall," I scoffed as though *everyone* should know about the SnoBall… conveniently forgetting that I'd only learned about it hours before. "It's a Licking Thicket *tradition*, Champion. It's a charity dance sponsored by the Beautification Corps. I'm running the event this year," I informed him. "And I can't do it from a pig farm."

Champ ran a hand through his hair, scattering the blond waves. "Okay, then. All the more reason for you to trust me to handle things out here while you do your work. See? Teamwork."

I looked into Champ's blue eyes for a long moment, and he stared back guilelessly. I rolled my eyes.

"And what about *your* other clients?" I demanded.

"Until I get my hands on the Horn, this is my single most important job." He grabbed my free hand and threaded our fingers together, swinging them as we walked. I wasn't even sure he realized that he'd done it, but I was very aware of the butterflies in my stomach. "You should have heard Jac—uh. My client. On the phone earlier today."

"Yeah? Angry?"

"Jesus. Fucking understatement."

"So annoying when you know you're doing the best anybody could under the circumstances. I always figured running my own business meant being my own boss, but the truth is I have dozens of bosses now, I just call them clients."

He snorted. "Exactly." He pulled me to a stop when we reached the bottom of the gravel path just beside the house and tugged me in so our bodies were aligned. I lifted my hands to his neck for, you know, lack of anything better to do with them.

"Thanks for listening," he said softly. "It's nice to have someone who gets it."

It really was.

"So, how about dinner tonight?" Champ asked.

"D-dinner?"

Champ's gaze was warm and amused. "Yeah, dinner. You know, the evening meal we sometimes get delivered to your place and eat with chopsticks in your bed?"

"Oh." He was right, of course. We'd eaten together many times before. But it was usually a spur-of-the-moment thing. A "hey I picked this up on my way over" kind of thing. Or a fuel-for-round-two kind of thing. Or a "you and I are both in the car near the Nashville taco place" kind of thing. This premeditated dinner scheduling was unprecedented.

Less hookup and more... date.

I tried hard not to show how much it threw me. Or how much I wanted it.

"Yeah," I agreed, because I was incapable of saying anything else. "I could eat."

"Good." Champ's hands slotted into place over my

hips, and he pulled me against his body with the easy familiarity of a person who'd held me exactly that way dozens and dozens of times before… because he had.

The realization made me a little breathless and a whole lot nervous.

When had this become a thing we did?

How had I come to like it so much?

How much was it going to hurt when this fiancé thing ended in a few weeks?

How the *hell* was I going to keep any distance from him when we were living together officially?

"House is over here!" Levi called from the porch. "In case you got lost."

"Levi!" Marissa whisper-scolded. "Leave them be! Just because *you* don't believe in love doesn't mean everyone has to be miserable."

Champ and I broke apart, and the second he let me go, I moved away from him. My heart was beating double time, and my hands were oddly shaky.

"No, no, Levi's right." I pressed a hand to my stomach. "No time for dillydallying with these invitations to get out. Let me grab the samples from my trunk."

"Marissa, if you'll get me a key to the house," Champ said, "I'll go home and start packing now. That way, we can move our stuff in immediately. Oh, and I should have asked earlier. You don't mind if I bring my dog, do you?"

"Not at all!" Marissa said happily. "I—"

"Tomorrow afternoon is plenty soon enough, Mr. Champion," Levi interrupted, like the giant wet blanket he was. "We'll all move in tomorrow."

"All?" Marissa repeated, squinting up at him. "I don't recall inviting you."

"I'm here as your security," Levi countered. "Ask your father."

"You went to my dad?" Outrage made her voice a high-pitched screech. "After I specifically said—"

"I didn't tell him about my other concerns, or he would have put a stop to the whole thing." He shot a look at me and then at Champ. "But I told him I wanted to be out here to keep you safe. And I don't regret it."

"I thought you weren't assigned to protect Marissa," Champ said mildly.

"I wasn't," Levi shot back. "But with all these unvetted contractors around, out here, far from town? Mr. Drakes agreed, it's a risk."

"God forbid I get to make my own choices and take normal risks like a normal person," Marissa muttered. "Whatever. I'll ask the staff to prepare *three* rooms." She rolled her eyes like this was the biggest inconvenience she could imagine.

"Actually, make that four," I blurted as an absolutely brilliant plan occurred to me—a plan that would not only help us achieve the goal of keeping Marissa and Levi apart but give me a snowball's chance in hell of actually managing to keep my sanity around Percival Champion.

"Four?" three voices repeated.

"Marissa, you were so convincing when you talked about your, um, virginity pact until the wedding that, ah…" I swallowed past a lump in my throat. "I decided that Champ and I should do the same. For *romance*." I met Champ's confused blue eyes and announced, "Sorry, Cornflower. No nookie until the wedding. I knew you'd understand."

Champ's eyes flared in surprise and something like hurt before cooling into a challenging look that seared right through me. "Of course, Butter Buns. Aren't you the sweetest, always trying to improve our relationship? I agree."

Oh, fuck. Why did his agreement make my stomach swoop nearly as much as his closeness a moment ago had?

His smile was the most mischievous, teasing thing I'd ever seen in my life, but Marissa and Levi were looking at us—her with an encouraging smile and him with outright suspicion—so I let Champ pull me into a brief, supportive side-hug. He leaned down and pressed a chaste kiss to my cheek.

"What the fuck was that?" he muttered as he nuzzled my neck.

"I made an executive decision for the good of the mission. *Go with it*," I whispered, quoting his words from earlier. Served him right to be on the receiving end of someone else's monkey wrench for once.

"Oh, I will," he promised. "No nookie until you ask for it, Shortcake." Then he whispered in my ear, low and hot enough to make me shiver, "Until you *beg* for it."

10

CHAMP

I left the farm in a dangerous mood while Quinn was still busy with Marissa.

Things weren't going my way with this investigation, which usually meant I needed to dig deeper and work harder. I needed to fucking think, and in order for me to think, I needed to purge my brain of Quinn for at least five damned minutes, which should have been easy but instead proved impossible.

Why the hell had I asked him to dinner? I had no need to share dinner with that man. *None*.

And what the fuck was that revirgination stunt? It wasn't like we were actually together. If he wanted to stop fucking, he just had to say so.

My hands clenched on the steering wheel as I thought of the way his eyes turned cloudy when we —

Nope.

What I needed to do was focus on the job. I had to learn more about the break-in attempt at Tommy Drakes's house that Levi had mentioned. It might have been a simple coincidence, but it could also mean that the cartel had put the pieces together like Vince had, knew Tommy Drakes had the Horn, and were trying to test his security.

Frankly, it was what I would have done.

That was why, instead of going home to pack my things, I drove to the office first to check in with the team and give them an update.

When I yanked the front door open, Herman startled awake like a sleepy basset hound and jumped to his feet. He'd traded his kilt today for a floral-print shirt, baggy khaki shorts, and Birkenstocks. "Cream, two sugars!"

I rolled my eyes. "Morning, Herman. Sitrep?"

"All's quiet, sir. That plumber hasn't come back," he said sourly. "But when he does, I'm gonna give him a piece of my mind."

"Excellent. At least someone around here is working hard." I stepped back into the mosh pit and found Hux yelling at someone through his headset, Elvo picking his teeth with an unbent paperclip, and Riggs cleaning his gun... on top of some very official-looking documents.

"Tell me one of you idiots has eyes on Drakes Farm," I said, storming into Hux's war room. Elvo straightened up so fast he knocked his chair over and tumbled to the floor. Riggs slammed his ammo clip home and holstered his weapon before raising an eyebrow at me. And Hux continued to call someone something that sounded suspiciously like a Space Chicken Provocateur. He didn't even look up when I spoke.

Elvo was the first to respond. "We have drone footage and elevation maps with heat signatures. Hux was trying to hack the existing alarm system to get eyes on the inside through motion-sensor cameras, but when he tried, something went funky."

"Explain," I said, pulling out a chair and sinking into it. Once I settled down, I noticed the large monitors on the wall had the images and feeds he'd mentioned. Good. They hadn't been completely slacking off.

Hux threw off his headset with a muttered curse. "Fucking Kev. I swear to God. He thinks our systems have a security vulnerability. Like I'd let our systems have a *security vulnerability*. The man is a professional couch potato, and he has the audacity to imply I—a man who was trained in cybersecurity by the United States government—know less about—"

I pinched the bridge of my nose and tried not to shout. "Skip to the point."

"Anyway," Hux continued, typing a few keys while he spoke. "I had to reboot after one of my process daemons froze, but we're up and running now."

One of the screens showed several images I recognized as views inside the farmhouse. No people were visible, and the place was still and quiet.

I sighed. Okay. Good. Now that we had eyes on the inside, we'd be able to see Drakes or Levi access hidden areas.

We'd also know if anyone else tried to access the house.

More views popped up as the screen shuffled between the cameras. I looked more closely and then stood up to walk toward the monitor on the wall. "What's that one? The study."

Hux's typing clacked while he selected the feed I wanted and expanded it to fit the screen. It was a similar office to the one Drakes had in Nashville, only less formal. Two windows were set into built-in cabinetry high on the wall.

"You think that's a basement room?" I wondered out loud.

Hux typed some more, and a different monitor showed floor plans of the old farmhouse. He zeroed in on a room on the bottom level. "Yeah. Looks like it's this room in the basement on the north side of the house."

I blew out a breath. Now we were getting somewhere. "Good. That's where I'll start looking when I move in."

Everyone around the table shot me a look of surprise. "Move in?" Riggs asked. "To the target's residence?"

Elvo's eyes widened in wonder. "This is why you're the boss. You have magical shit going on up there." He gestured vaguely to my face.

I explained how the topic of Marissa staying at the farmhouse had come up and how I'd quickly inserted myself into the plan. I also filled them in on what I'd overheard about the break-in at the Drakeses' house.

"I need to run home and pack some stuff. We're moving in tomorrow."

"We?" Yolanda said, wandering in to hand me a stack of checks to sign. "You… and the wedding planner?"

"Me and my cover, yeah," I said gruffly, daring her to make something of it. Fortunately, she caught the look Riggs sent her way and was smart enough to keep her mouth shut.

We spent the next hour and a half pulling together some surveillance tech for me to take with me. Small listening devices and cameras, as well as a motion-sensor alert for the entry gate so we'd be able to track who entered the property.

By the time I left to head back to my ramshackle excuse of a house, I was feeling better about the status of our mission. Surely once I was living on-site, I'd be able to get my hands on Drakes's Horn.

When I pulled up to the old Victorian, Jericho's truck was parked out front. It was beyond time for me to sit the man down and ask what was going on with the renovation—specifically, how much more I could expect it to cost—and I was in the perfect mood to lay down the law.

But when I got out of my truck, I heard country music coming from inside the house. And as soon as I placed my boot on the first step, a pane of glass in an upper-floor window gave up its grasp on life and fell listlessly to the ground a few feet away.

I clenched my hands into fists and closed my eyes. *Nope.* I did not have the patience for this today. At least Herc wasn't here to get hurt on the…

Herc.

Fuck.

After racing into the house just long enough to fill a duffle with clothes and toiletries, I shouted a greeting and goodbye to Jericho and ran back out to the truck.

Quinn was going to kill me for leaving Hercules with him once again. What was it about Quinn Taffet that made me lose my ever-loving mind?

Or did he do this on purpose? Did he deliberately set out to steal Herc when I wasn't paying attention?

I entered his apartment hell-bent on giving him a piece of my mind, but when I took the first steps up the stairs, I heard him singing the lyrics to "Teenage Dirt-bag," except… he was changing them slightly.

"'Cause I'm just a *poodle* dirtbag baby, yeah I'm just a *poodle* dirtbag baby, listen to Lady Gaga, baby…"

I came to a stop outside the open bathroom door and stared at the sight in front of me.

Both of them were soaking wet and covered in splotches of mud, but Hercules looked like the happiest dog on the planet with his big doggie grin and eyes only for his favorite human on earth.

Quinn Taffet was elbow-deep in dog mud.

For me.

Well… for Hercules. But it was kind of the same thing, wasn't it?

My chest suddenly felt like it was being constricted by a heavy band. This wasn't… this wasn't what was supposed to happen. How could a man covered in muddy dog water make me want to plaster myself against his naked body and fuck him into the wall? It didn't. This was simply my…

I racked my brain to think of a plausible excuse for my feelings toward Quinn. My go-to reason was simple thirst, but I could hardly claim a recent dry spell after thirty-something nights inside Quinn's body.

There was always the lust excuse. Quinn was a hot little package and incredibly responsive in bed. Who wouldn't want to fuck him?

And then there was the possibility I was using him to avoid going to my own place.

I'd bought a money pit of a house that only reminded me every time I laid eyes on it that I was never going to have the long-term relationship and white picket fence I'd always wanted. All the years I'd spent deployed had been full of naive daydreams about moving back home and settling down with someone. Finally resting after years of active duty. I'd wanted the elusive American dream.

Instead, I'd gotten a house even the Property Brothers wouldn't have touched, a dog who preferred almost anyone over me, and an ex who was currently most interested in fucking up my career.

But when I was with Quinn... none of that seemed to matter. Real life didn't press on me during those magical hours, and I felt completely sheltered from my troubles.

So. I was using him to avoid my real life. Seemed legit. I wanted to fuck Quinn into the wall because it made me feel good. Did it need to be any more complicated than that?

"Take off your clothes," I said in a low voice.

Quinn turned around in surprise. "What are you doing here?"

"Right now? I'm preparing to have sex with you," I explained before pulling my shirt over my head and tossing it behind me into the hallway.

Quinn's eyes narrowed suspiciously. "What about dinner? What about the revirgination plan?"

I gave him my most charming smile. "Dinner can wait. And the revirgination doesn't start until we get to the farm, silly man. Besides, in order for you to *re*virginate," I said, moving closer to him so I could begin peeling his clothes off, "someone's gonna need to pop your cherry first."

He tried to hide the smile, but I recognized it anyway. "I see. And just so we're clear... this is *you* begging *me* for said cherry-popping."

I pulled his wet shirt off and dropped it on the tile floor. "Definitely not."

"I'm not sure I should give you my maidenhead," he said with a delicate sniff. "It's very precious."

I yanked the button open on his pants. "That wasn't the word I would have picked, but okay."

"I'm annoyed at you," Quinn said as I shoved his pants to the floor.

He rested his hands on my bare shoulders to keep from falling over. I loved when he did that.

"That's okay. You can be annoyed at me while I fuck you." I kissed the inside of his thigh, right where the muscle curved and the hair thinned. He smelled amazing.

"Don't worry, I will... *hnghh*." Quinn's fingers dug into my skin as I wrapped my lips around his dick and began to suck him off. I fumbled my hand around behind him until I felt the recognizable shape of the lube bottle I'd spotted in the shower basket on the floor.

Once I had the lube in hand, I gathered some on my fingers and teased his hole, relishing every squeak and moan that came out of his mouth. How many times had I fucked him in this tiny bathroom? Enough that this was no longer the original lube bottle he kept in here.

While I continued to suck him off, I prepped him with long, possessive fingers until his knees began to buckle.

"Uh-uh," I warned, popping off his dick and standing up. As soon as I shucked off the rest of my clothes, I fished a condom out of the shower basket and suited up. "Not on the floor. Here."

I turned him and shoved him against the wall until his face was buried in the bathrobe that hung on a high hook. His body was pliant and went where I put him, so I grabbed his arms and stretched them high above his head to the row of hooks bolted to the wall. "Hold this," I grumbled behind his ear.

His breathing hitched as I moved one of his legs up and held it under his knee. I began to murmur dirty thoughts about popping his cherry, fucking him for the first time, as if we hadn't done this many, many times already. As if I hadn't been balls-deep inside of him enough to become addicted to the feel of him around my dick.

"You want me inside you? You want to feel stretched wide open on my cock? It's gonna hurt the first time, baby. But you'll be good for me, won't you?"

"Shut up," he tried to hiss. But it came out more like a whimper, like a hushed plea.

"You're so fucking sexy. You tempt me until I can't help but want to fuck you like this. Shove you up against the wall wherever we are and take you whether you're ready or not. Strip you naked and fill your virgin ass, show you what it's like to feel full, to want more."

They were just words. But they filled the air with heavy heat until we were both panting. Damp tendrils of hair curled on his neck. I nosed them aside before kissing him there, tasting the familiar salty warmth of him.

Quinn Taffet was dangerous. He threatened my well-being in more ways than I could count. I was sick and tired of pretending this... *whatever it was*... between us was purely physical. It wasn't. It was like a barbed hook that had gotten tangled up in my fucking psyche and wouldn't let go.

As I thrust inside his tight channel, I closed my eyes and gritted my teeth. *This*. This was where I wanted to be. Every fucking second of every fucking day. Wrapped up in him. Plastered as close as I could get with my arms tightly around him so I would know he was safe. He was mine.

It was the kind of obsession I'd only ever had before for missions at work. I'd never felt this way about another human being, not even Vince, and he'd been someone I'd planned on spending the rest of my life with. The knowledge of these intense feelings toward Quinn scared the piss out of me and kept me up at night.

Because I knew better. I knew better than to fall for someone again, especially someone so different from me. It would never work.

Besides, Quinn's goal in life was to recoup his reputation in Nashville society so he could eventually move back there and reign over the wedding scene in the city. He was meant for bigger things, and I wasn't going to uproot my business from the Thicket, especially when my largest client was here.

So I did what I always did. I took as much of Quinn as I dared in the time I had with him and tried to make it enough.

When I reached down to shuttle a slick hand over his shaft, his release was almost immediate.

"Fuck!" he shouted hoarsely into the bathrobe, taking one hand off the hooks long enough to bang a fist against the wall in front of him. "Fuck," he said again in a whimper.

I thrust in and out of him a couple more times until my balls drew up, and I felt my muscles contract a split second before the orgasm washed over me. I pressed my face into the side of his neck and breathed him in as he let go of the hooks and began to collapse to the ground. "Shh," I murmured, holding him tightly around the middle. "I got you. Hold on."

I turned to move him out of the bathroom and locked eyes with Hercules. He sat in the bathtub, still fully wet and very, *very* annoyed.

"Shit," I sighed. "The dog."

Quinn snorted lightly and moved out of my arms to help Herc. "You're the worst dog parent I've ever met."

It's you, I wanted to say in exasperation. *You make me fucking crazy.*

But I stayed quiet and helped him finish cleaning the dog before helping him clean himself. Very thoroughly.

By the time I followed him into bed, we were both worn-out, and Herc wanted nothing to do with either one of us.

"Not sure the sex was worth it," Quinn said, blowing out a breath.

"Liar."

"Well… I guess I don't have anything to compare it to since I was a virgin before that. It seemed fine, I guess."

I reached under the covers and pinched his bare ass. He laugh-yelped and moved away from me, but I grabbed him and pulled him back against my chest. "Be still."

I like this, I thought, not realizing I'd said the words out loud.

"Me too."

I thought back to my earlier mindfuck, wondering if I was somehow using him. "I don't want you to feel used," I said, probably making him question my sanity. I tried to clarify. "I mean… I like you. I want to be with you. I don't want you to think this is some kind of… that I'm just…"

"Why, Percival Champion, as I live and breathe," he

said in an exaggerated Southern accent. "Are you proposing to go steady with me?"

I sighed. "I just mean… never mind."

Quinn's fingers ran lightly up and down my arm. "I like you too."

I exhaled.

"But I don't want to marry you," he snickered.

"Jesus, no. *Fuck.*"

"But this is nice. Having someone to talk to and fuck on a regular basis. It's… convenient."

"And to think, I used to really believe being a wedding planner meant you were a romantic," I teased.

"Nope. I'm practical. Marriage—most relationships, really—are a sham. People are always looking for something bigger and better, and when they find it, they walk away. But I respect that other people are romantic and hopeful. That's why I'm committed to my job. *Forever* might not really happen, but that doesn't mean it's wrong to enjoy what you have while you have it." He looked up at me. "Sappy, right?"

"No. Your dedication to your career is one of the things I like about you," I admitted. "It's one of the things we have in common. You go above and beyond for your clients, just like I do. Hell, we're both relocating to a pig farm to do our jobs."

Quinn snickered. He turned around in my arms and leaned back a little so he could see my eyes. "I know you keep shit close to the vest, but this sneaking around and lying… I'm not used to it. It's hard for me. And I'm trying to trust you here—I *do* trust you, even though you keep getting me involved in shit without my consent—but it would really help me to know what the heck is on that Horn. I promise, I won't tell a soul—"

I didn't let him finish, because he was right. He

deserved to know more than I'd told him, if only so he'd take things seriously and keep himself safe. He'd backed my plays time and time and time again, and he'd earned my loyalty. "Yeah, Okay."

He scooted further back and propped his head on his hand with his elbow bent on the bed below. I tried to determine what information I could share with him without putting him in a precarious position.

"You already know I'm looking for a Horn of Glory device that contains sensitive information, and we think it might be in Tommy Drakes's possession."

"Right, but what kind of information?"

I hesitated, only because the idea of Quinn having enough information to make him a target of the Cartel de Luna made me physically ill. "Financial and possibly identifying information about drug cartel members."

"A cartel in Tennessee?" His eyes bugged out of his head.

"No. A South American cartel full of incredibly dangerous people."

Quinn's eyebrows shot up in surprise. "Marissa's dad bought a Horn containing *drug cartel information*?"

"Marissa's dad bought a *stolen* Horn—an incredibly rare, easily identifiable Horn—that happened to contain drug cartel information, yeah," I agreed grimly. "The other day when we were at the Nashville house and Tommy got called away? It was because my ex-boyfriend, the DEA agent, was at the door, asking for information on that Horn."

"Vince was there?" Quinn demanded. Then after a beat, "Wait, why don't we want the authorities to get the cartel information so they can stop them?"

Now came the tricky part. I didn't want Quinn to

think I was skirting the law… even though I was skirting the law.

"My client is HOG Corporate, the makers of Horn of Glory. To cut an incredibly long story short, they don't want their game or one of their Horn devices associated with a giant drug cartel investigation. Their stock prices would tank, and so would my reputation when it came out that I hadn't been able to protect them."

Quinn chewed this over for a moment. I expected questions and arguments about the morality of it, but all he said was "Fuck. So Vince knows for sure that Tommy has the Horn? Now we're in a race to find it?"

I appreciated his use of the word "we" more than he knew.

"Not exactly. If Vince knew for sure, he'd get a warrant, and that would be that. He must not have enough proof to get one."

Which was kind of weird when I thought about it, because he knew a fuck of a lot about the situation. How was he unable to prove any of it? I couldn't care too much, though, because that very much worked in my favor.

"But Vince isn't the only person looking for the Horn," I continued solemnly. "I'm concerned that if Vince put the pieces together, other concerned parties might have too."

Quinn was quick on the uptake. "You think the drug cartel knows Tommy has the Horn?" he gasped. "We need to warn them. Marissa is—"

"Marissa is fine. She's got a bodyguard," I reminded him. "And Tommy's homes are secure. But there was an attempted break-in at the Nashville place yesterday. It could be a coincidence—"

"But you don't think it was."

"No. My gut tells me it's connected."

He burrowed deeper into my arms. "I know this probably sounds naive, but... why doesn't Vince just ask to see it? Explain the situation about the data he doesn't know is hidden on the device, and maybe Tommy will just hand it over. For that matter, why don't *you* do that?"

His innocence made me want to laugh but also kiss him breathless. It was a stark reminder he didn't live in the same world I did.

"First off, Tommy's not the trusting type. Long before his Speedo commercial days, he made his first stake running chop shops and other small-time stuff. He thinks like a criminal, and he's savvy like a criminal. That's why, once he knew the DEA was sniffing around for the Horn, he sent Levi here to the Thicket to hide it at the farm. Once they get their hands on it, it'll become evidence, and there's no way Tommy will get it back. Furthermore, if Tommy admits to owning *one* stolen item, you'd better believe Vince will get a warrant to search the rest of Tommy's properties faster than you can say *probable cause*. Since I'm willing to bet big money the Horn isn't the only thing of, ah... *questionable provenance*... in Tommy's possession, that would be a very big problem."

"Right," Quinn sighed, rubbing a hand over his face.

"And as for me telling him... well, Tommy doesn't have any reason to trust me. Not to mention, I have a tiny concern that if I told Tommy what was on the Horn, he might simply decide to sell it back to the cartel or to someone else and turn a profit."

"He wouldn't," Quinn said firmly, leaning up slightly.

I shook my head. "You don't know that. You don't think like a criminal—"

"No, I think like a wedding planner. I've seen the way he looks at his daughter. She's his whole world. He'd never put Marissa in jeopardy to turn a profit. Trust me. I'm good at reading people."

"And if you were wrong and that information got into the wrong hands? You willing to take that chance?"

Quinn hesitated, sighed, and fell back onto the pillow. "Maybe not. Okay, so what *are* you going to do?"

"The idea is for me to find the Horn and get my tech guy on the case. Huxley is the best in the business. He'll get the information off the device, then turn the information—*without the Horn*—over to the government either anonymously or in a way that gives us some leverage or protection. Tommy will be left with a perfectly safe, very rare Horn, and once all the players know the government has the information, nobody will bother Tommy again, and our client will be kept out of it."

Quinn wasn't stupid, and sure enough, he narrowed his eyes at me. "That's if it all goes right. If you get caught...?"

"If I get caught, it's not much worse than if Vince gets his hands on the Horn. Possible legal consequences. Devastating consequences for Champion Security. Either way, Quinn, you knew nothing about any of this. No blowback on you," I said sincerely.

"I don't like it," he whispered.

I couldn't resist reaching out to run my fingers

through his messy, damp hair. "I know. It's not ideal. But I'm good at what I do, and I trust the men *under me.*" I rolled slightly until I was on top of him, then kissed him, pressing him down into the bed until we were both breathless.

When I pulled back, Quinn rolled his eyes... even as his hand lightly grasped my hardening dick. "I won't be under you for long, what with the new revirgination plan."

I stared at him in disbelief. "That... that was just a joke. We're not really going to— For *five weeks*?"

Quinn blinked up at me solemnly. "Don't worry, Angel Soft. You'll probably be too busy doing your nails with Marissa to worry about... not nailing anyone."

For some reason, my dick got even more excited by his teasing. I ground my cock into his hip. Then I leaned over and brushed my lips against his earlobe.

"Oh, I'm not worried about *me*, Piglet," I murmured in a low voice. "I like touching myself. I like thinking up scenarios in which I fuck unsuspecting wedding planners against the wall and make them weak in the knees. It makes me hard. It makes me *want*. And when I come all over myself thinking about it, I like to—"

Quinn clapped a hand over my mouth, and his voice came out pitchy and stuttered. "Good grief. For a person who can't say the word 'relationship' without turning blue, Champion, a startling number of your sexual fantasies concern *me*. Are you *sure* you'll be able to make it five whole weeks at Camp Stink-Ass without this ass?" He wiggled the ass in question in a way that made my eyes cross.

"Way easier than you will without my cock," I challenged, because... *fuck*, five weeks was going to suck, but I'd be damned if I gave in before he did. "I'll hardly even miss it."

But when Quinn snorted and wrapped his legs around me, I made the kind of executive decision that had made me a top operative in my field.

I rolled so he was on top, and then I pulled him down to kiss him. "Starting tomorrow," I whispered. "For tonight, I want to watch you ride me."

11

———————

QUINN

"Kiss me, Champion," I begged without caring how needy I sounded or worrying about trivial things like how I'd come to be pushed up against the wall in the bunkhouse at Drakes Farm, despite being in the middle of a five-week revirgination pact.

"Gonna do more than kiss you," Champ growled over my shoulder. He slid one big hand up my chest, pulling my back against his hard chest, while the other traveled south to mold my dick through my pants.

We groaned simultaneously.

Champ tilted his head down so he could whisper against my ear, "You know how I feel about you. I—" A loud beeping sound startled us both. "Wait, what's that?"

"Dunno. Finish your statement."

"Is that... Do you have an appointment now?"

"Maybe? Who cares! If you're not gonna talk, at least fuck me," I begged. "Do it now. Do it fast!"

"Just admit you want it," Champ purred. "Fight for it. You can have anything if you want it bad enough, Quinn. Quinn? Quinn—"

"Quinn? Hey, Quinn?"

"Gahhhh!" I jerked awake, so disoriented I nearly fell off my chair and brained myself on my desk.

"Whoa, hey!" Ava held up her two hands in a gesture of innocence, and her long, blonde ponytail swayed. "Just your friendly neighborhood Beautification Corps representative, coming to drop off Mrs. Peevey's Binder of Doom for you." She set down a large leather folio on the desk. "I didn't mean to disturb you, but I heard your phone alarm beeping, and I wanted to make sure you were okay."

"Yeah, sorry. Thank you." I ran a hand over my face and grabbed my phone to turn off my 30-minutes-to-meeting warning alarm. "Dang. I sat down to prep for my new clients, and I guess I conked out."

"No kidding. You were groaning like you were being tortured by an evil villain in your sleep."

That's because I was. Only not just in my sleep.

And not by just any evil villain but by Percival Fucking Champion.

And not regular old torture but two weeks of extreme sexual deprivation, the likes of which I'd never known.

I forced a smile. "How weird! No, I think I'm just stressed because I'm planning a wedding for Tommy Drakes's daughter, Marissa, and it's down to the wire. Only a few weeks to go."

"Ah. Stress dreams." She nodded in understanding. "I had those before my own wedding. Not getting enough sleep at night?"

"Tossing and turning for hours," I confirmed. Also, jerking off to the mental image of the tall, gorgeous blond on the opposite side of my bedroom wall spread out naked on his own bed, thinking thoughts of *me*.

It turned out the only thing more exhausting than

being dicked down almost nightly by a man with the stamina of an athlete was being *not* dicked down by that man after my damn treacherous body had spent thirty-something—yes, I'd officially lost count, and yes, that was very concerning—nights getting used to having him around.

Sometimes I held my breath to see if I could hear the sound of his soft snores through the wall. Sometimes I imagined I could *smell* him. I'd even cracked and dug my purloined T-shirts from the back of my linen closet, just so I could feel like I was sleeping in Champ's embrace.

And it didn't help that Champ was a giant tease who was determined to make me crack before he did.

Every morning, he slid past me in the hall on the way to the kitchen, all shower-damp and irresistible, and gave me a chaste kiss along with a "Sleep well, Gobble Muffin?" even though no one else was around to hear his ridiculous pet names.

He'd lean over my shoulder when I was calculating cost projections at the kitchen table as if the price of passed hors d'oeuvres fascinated him.

And every night, as soon as I shut my bedroom light off, he'd call me to ask an "emergency" question about what Marissa might have said during our pedicure night or to re-re-re-confirm my schedule for the following day, like he knew his voice in my ear would leave me wanting more of him… which it did.

Champ seemed to be enduring the dry spell just fine, but being so close without touching him was killing me. I should have been planning to capitalize on the new clients I'd signed and strategizing my triumphant return to Nashville, but instead, I was distracted at work and impatient with clients.

In short, I would have ended this fucking revirgination a week and a half ago…

Except I also knew this torment was only a taste of what I'd be in for when our fake-fiancé thing was over.

I was officially addicted to the man, and I had no idea what to do about that.

"If I can help with anything, just let me know," Ava offered, and I gave her a warm smile, because honestly, she was *so* sweet.

Unfortunately, I was pretty sure there was only one person who could help me, and I was trying my damnedest to stop craving him.

"Thanks, but I've got things pretty well in hand in terms of wedding prep. We've got a couple crews out at Drakes Farm, and they're doing a phenomenal job." Partly thanks to Champ's constant, hands-on supervision.

"I meant to help *you*, Quinn." Ava's smile softened. "You know, if you need to vent? Or if you need a pep talk?"

"Oh." I blinked at her in surprise… just as my fail-safe meeting alarm went off. "I can't today, but another time, that would be awesome. Thank you."

"Offer's open, babe. See you Thursday night. Don't forget it's your turn to bring snacks. Oh, and don't forget to find yourself an escort for the dance too, or else Cindy Ann is gonna take it upon herself, and I heard Jimbo Garvey from the Feed and Seed has been asking after you." She winked and sailed out the door.

I snorted and scrubbed a hand over my forehead. It was a strange truth that the SnoBall meetings had become a highlight of my week these days. I was never gonna get used to this town, but there was never a dull moment.

The bell over the front door chimed, and I heard Ava greet someone on her way out. "Quinn! Your next meeting is here!" she called.

Twenty minutes early? *Shit.*

"Please take a seat! I'll be right with you," I called. I jumped out of my chair and grabbed my tablet, only pausing to pinch my cheeks and smooth my hair—

And then a body pressed up against me from behind, just like in my dream, while a pair of strong arms wrapped around me.

"Take your time. I'll help myself," Champ whispered into my neck.

Oh, fuck, that felt good.

Without conscious thought, I tilted my head, giving him better access. "I thought you were supposed to be supervising at the farm this morning."

Champ made a noise of agreement. "I left a couple of my people in charge out there. Levi had to drive up to Nashville this morning because Marissa has some kind of dress fitting, and Tommy sent not one but *four* of his other goons to take Levi's place. I can't move out there today without bumping into one of them. Besides, Hercules missed you."

Hercules barked excitedly, announcing his presence near my ankles.

"Hush," Champ told him. "Go find your bed." Without giving me room to move away, he bent down and unclipped the dog's leash. Herc trotted off to the front room with a jangle of tags.

Champ straightened and wrapped his arms around me once again. He gripped one end of the leash in either hand and jerked the material flat against my stomach.

"Afraid I'll try to run away?" I asked breathlessly.

"Maybe a little." His tongue traced the edge of my ear, and I moaned. "*Mmm.* You smell good. Warm and sleepy. Were you napping?"

"No." He nipped at my earlobe, and I squeaked. "Maybe."

"No fair, sneaking in town to nap." Champ's grip on me tightened. "I haven't slept well in days."

"That's awful," I said breathlessly. "Any particular reason?"

Champ huffed out a laugh, and his thumbs hooked into my waistband—so close but so far from where I wanted them. "Say the word, Quinn, and this revirgination is over."

Ugh. I wanted that so, so badly.

But it would make me feel so much better if he'd say it first.

"The only word I'll be saying right now is *goodbye*," I said tartly, "since I have work to do, and so do you."

Champ backed up a pace, giving me just enough room to turn around... though he still had the damn leash wrapped around me. From this close, I could see that his eyes looked tired. And despite his cocky grin, there was tension in his shoulders that I hated to see.

I brushed a strand of hair off his forehead. "Still no luck with the search?"

He shook his head once. "I'm convinced Tommy keeps his collection in the basement, but I haven't figured out how to get at it. And it feels like every damn time I open my bedroom door to go searching, I find fucking Levi in the hall, waiting for me." He cracked his neck from side to side and blew out a breath. "Pretty sure he's a vampire."

"And your tech guy hasn't found any blueprints that show that room?"

Champ shook his head. "Not uncommon if this was designed as a kind of panic room or secret vault. Which is great for Tommy, not so much for *me*."

"At least there's nothing new from your ex. Or anything at all from the cartel."

"That we know of," he reminded me. For the first time since the start of this "mission," Champ sounded a little defeated.

"We still have three weeks to the wedding." I patted his chest lightly. "You'll figure it out. I have faith in you."

Champ stared at me, and I pulled back immediately, feeling my face go hot.

That comment had been *way* too sincere. In the absence of sex, my mind had apparently turned into a huge pool of *sap*, and now I was drowning in it.

"I-I mean—" I tried desperately to think of a way to pass it off as a joke.

Champ ignored my rambling. "I have so much riding on this," he said softly. "My client's reputation. All the people I employ. I can't afford to fail. Champion Security is—"

"Your first priority," I guessed when he trailed off.

Just like building Taffet Events was for me.

"It's the only thing I have that's *mine*," Champ said unexpectedly. "My money pit of a house... that's a relic from a future I thought I was gonna have but didn't. My family name is about something I was born into and rejected. Hell, even my dog is yours more than mine at this point. But I built Champion Security from the ground up, based on a reputation I earned when I was in the service, and the people who work for me... we're a family. I can't let them down."

How the hell was I supposed to keep up any

defenses against this man when he said sweet shit like that?

"Look, if things get bad enough, *I'll* help you find the Horn. I know you'll be embarrassed when my plan works better than yours, though, so we'll keep that in our pockets, m'kay?"

Champ threw his head back and laughed out loud, and I watched the whole show from the front row. When he looked at me again, his expression had lightened.

"I get why you're so good at your job. There is some kind of fucking magic about you, Quinn Taffet. You always know what to say."

I was glad one of us thought so. I felt like I'd come perilously close to showing that I was starting to have very real feelings for the guy, but apparently, I'd dodged that bullet.

"Well! Let's hope my next meeting thinks so," I said lightly, pushing out of his arms. "I'm having my initial meeting with your client in about ten minutes."

"With *my* client?" He frowned. "Who?"

"Dr. Carter Rogers and his fiancé, obviously. Have you sent so many Nashville socialite clients my way that you can't remember them all?" I teased.

The truth was, I owed Champ a huge thank-you. I'd googled them the day after Champ gave me Carter's card two weeks ago, and it turned out the Rogers family was as blue-blooded as you could get in Tennessee. Having Carter as a client would more than make up for having Marissa Drakes's wedding ruined...

Though seeing how much progress we'd made, I was pretty sure it wasn't going to be ruined at *all*, and in fact, it might just be the highlight of my portfolio.

Champ froze. "Carter and his fiancé are coming here today?" he demanded. "Really?"

"Why do you sound surprised? I called his business number a couple weeks back and spoke to his receptionist — a sweet guy named Kev —"

"Kev," Champ repeated. "You spoke to… Kev."

"Yep. He's Carter's cousin, but he was filling in for the week. Said he was so excited to hear from me that he was putting this appointment right on Carter's calendar. He must've told me, 'This is the best thing *ever*,' like three or four times, and he said his cousin's fiancé was going to be overjoyed at the prospect of wedding planning with me, so that's fun." I narrowed my eyes when I clocked Champ's deer-in-headlights expression. "What's that look mean? Is there a problem?"

"Problem," Champ echoed, and I narrowed my eyes. He was doing the repeating thing again. "No! No problem at all. I didn't realize there'd be such a… a rush, that's all. I figured you'd wait until Marissa's wedding was over to plan the next one. I figured there'd be five weeks instead of two."

I tilted my head to the side. "I told you it usually takes a year to plan a wedding, right? The sooner we get started, the more options they'll have, especially if they want to get married in the city."

"Right. You're right. And, uh… did you call to confirm the appointment? Carter's a doctor," he explained. "He has emergencies sometimes."

"As a matter of fact, yes. I called him at home earlier this morning and spoke to his fiancé. I think he said his name was William something —"

"Riggs," Champ said in a choked voice. "William Riggs."

"Yeah, that's it. He seemed surprised but agreed

that they'd be here." I hesitated for a second before admitting, "He didn't sound very overjoyed, though, to be honest. He muttered something about Kev and... vengeance?"

"Oh, that's just gamer speak," Champ explained quickly. He waved a hand. "They're really into Horn of Glory, and that's how they talk. I'm sure Riggs will be *incredibly* overjoyed. So, ah... I'm gonna go." He hooked his thumb in the direction of the front door. "Gotta make some... phone calls real quick."

"Are you gonna take your—*mmmph*." Champ cut me off with a kiss that was scorching hot and somehow soothing at the same time, like rain after a drought. I gripped his t-shirt with two hands, digging my fingers into his chest, and poured two weeks' worth of longing and frustration into kissing him back.

He pulled away a minute later to rub his thumb over my bottom lip. "Later."

"Oh. Okay. Y-yeah," I agreed, licking my lips and savoring the taste of him. "Thanks for stopping by!"

Thanks for stopping by? What the hell was wrong with me?

The door jangled as he left, and I attempted to pull myself together—or at least to rearrange my dick so my pants lay flat—when I realized that *no*, he had not taken his damn dog.

I shook my head, even as I grinned at the golden-brown puffball. "Your owner is so weird, buddy. Come on, let's get ready for this meeting."

Hercules darted ahead of me to the front room just as the door opened for the third time that morning.

I expected Herc to start barking his head off the way he usually did with strangers, but instead, he walked up to the pair expectantly, almost like he knew them.

Odd. I hadn't known Champ was that close with Carter.

"Good morning!" I said sunnily. "I'm Quinn Taffet. You must be… Dr. Rogers?" I asked the slightly older and handsomer of the two men. He was blond, like Champ, but wore chinos and a cashmere sweater over a button-down shirt.

"Please, call me Carter." The man glared at his fiancé and folded his arms over his chest. "At least I *assume* that's the name I'll be using."

Uh-oh. Clearly they'd been in the middle of a spat on the way over, maybe about changing names after the wedding? No matter. It wouldn't be the first time I played referee.

"Uh… Great!" I enthused. "Carter." I turned to the younger, taller, much more muscular of the pair. "And you're William?"

"William Riggs." He smiled confidently. "But everyone calls me Riggs."

"Riggs," I agreed, thinking that sounded familiar. Didn't Champ have a teammate named Riggs? Maybe that was how he knew them. "And here you two are, ready to declare your love to the world!"

"*That* remains to be seen," Carter muttered under his breath.

Riggs winced.

"Alright, let's get the hard part out of the way first. I'll take down the details of your…" I looked around for my tablet and realized I'd left it out back. "Shoot. Actually, let me grab my tablet so we can get down to business. Can I bring y'all some coffee? No? Please have a seat." I tilted my chin toward the planning table as I scurried away.

The moment I was out of sight, I heard Riggs rumble softly, "Baby, please—"

"Do *not* 'baby' me, Riggs. How many times do I have to tell you? You don't propose for an op! *Asshole.*"

Wait… *what*? I paused in the hallway.

"I didn't propose!" Riggs insisted. "This was all a… a misunderstanding."

"No shit."

"Carter." Riggs sounded a little desperate. "How many times do I have to apologize? I forgot Champ asked me to do this meeting until Mr. Taffet called this morning to remind me. I couldn't say no, baby! It's for *Champ*. I owe him. And all we have to do is play along, okay? I know the timing wasn't the greatest, coming after that thing a couple weeks ago—"

"*Thing*? You hired a bunch of singing fruits and vegetables to accost me and my cousin outside my place of work, Riggs!"

"They were a flash mob," Riggs explained in the tone of a person who had already explained this multiple times but was prepared to continue explaining it for the rest of his existence. "It was supposed to be a distraction so the team could get into the restaurant across the street from your office to plant some cameras—"

"I don't care! You *knew* Kev was filling in as my receptionist that week! And you *know* he lost almost the entire crop of citrus fruits at our homestead during the last Horn of Glory blight!" Carter said furiously. "When the lemons started dancing, Kev started sobbing right there in my doorway. Scared my patients to death. Mr. Lampman thought he was hallucinating and began moaning that the end-times had come."

"That was a regrettable oversight," Riggs admitted. "But—"

"Was the part where they were singing 'Marry You' also an oversight?" Carter interrupted. "Hmm?"

"Well. I mean…" I could practically hear Riggs's mental wheels spinning. "Sort of? The dance troupe Hux found only knew a few songs. It was 'Marry You,' or 'Happy Birthday,' or 'Feliz Navidad.' We felt this was the best option."

"We," Carter said witheringly. "You mean you, Champ, and the other brilliant minds at Champion Security."

Oh, fuck. Riggs *was* one of Champ's people.

I sucked in a breath as hurt and fury warred in my stomach. I was going to kill the man.

"*Shhhh,*" Riggs insisted. "Quinn will hear you! Look, I didn't expect Kev would take pictures. Or send them to Vienna Goodley. Or that Vienna would post them on the Thicket Happenings Facebook page—"

"Uh-huh."

"And I really hadn't expected the Beautification Corps to throw us that surprise party."

I bit my lip and restrained a snort. Ava and Cindy Ann got around, man. But *Jesus*. Poor Carter.

"A surprise party," Carter shot back, not even bothering to be quiet, "to celebrate a nonexistent engagement, based on a question that you didn't ask, thus making me the first human to suffer through the world's most ridiculous marriage proposal dance number only to *not be proposed to.*"

The silence after he spoke was louder than his shouting had been.

"Wait," Riggs said. "Wait. Did you… I mean, you didn't actually… *want* me to propose. Did you?"

"No," Carter scoffed. "Obviously not. We've only been together a few months. You've never had a relationship that lasted longer than a few nights. You're not the proposing type."

I wasn't sure who he was trying to convince, but I was pretty sure it wasn't working on any of us.

Riggs was silent again for a long moment. I grabbed my tablet and snuck back to the doorway to catch a glimpse of his face, but I couldn't. I envied Herc's spot on the floor.

Finally, Riggs said, "Carter? I love you. I mean, I *really* love you."

"Yeah," Carter said instantly. "I know. Just… let's drop it. Whatever the fuck we're doing here, let's just do it and leave. I have patients."

"I assumed you'd want to wait a year or two before getting engaged. Make sure you really like living so far away from Nashville in that giant mansion your grandfather bought. Make sure you like living with *me*."

"Good. Great," Carter insisted more desperately. "I didn't think for a minute that you were actually serious. Obviously. I… I wasn't fooled."

Riggs's voice warmed. Gentled. "I also figured you'd want something fancy. Something a fuckton more memorable than a singing banana—"

"Lemons," Carter corrected. Then he cleared his throat, clearly mortified, and yelled, "Excuse me? Mr. Taffet? Could we start? I need to get back to work!"

Riggs sighed.

"Yes! Coming!" I called. I tucked my tablet under my arm.

On impulse, I darted back and grabbed a binder

stuffed with samples from one of my previous clients, along with a giant black Sharpie.

"Sorry about that. Here we are!" I took a seat at the table, and the other two did the same.

Riggs watched Carter with puppy dog intensity, but Carter refused to meet his eyes.

I understood Carter's position on a deep, deep level. Riggs seemed like a nice guy, and his love for Carter was clear, but there was nothing like being used for an op to remind you of where you fit in a man's priority list.

The men of Champion Security needed to be taught a lesson, starting immediately.

I clapped my hands once. "Before we start, I have to tell you, I've been in this business a long time, and I thought I'd seen it all, but hearing Champ speak about your love for your fiancé has been so inspiring, Mr. Riggs."

Riggs blinked. "It… has?"

"Oh, yes. He tells me you're a true romantic. Not many men are as eager for commitment as you are. You're a lucky man, Dr. Rogers."

Carter lifted one eyebrow. "Aren't I just?"

Riggs's booted heel tapped the carpet anxiously. "You know, Mr. Taffet, about the wedding… Carter and I have decided to wai—"

I held up a hand. "No worries. Champ has already shared your entire vision with me."

"He did?" Riggs's eyes widened. "But—"

"I admit the initial planning was a bit challenging, though." I beamed and leaned toward him confidingly. "First tattoo ceremony."

"First…?" Riggs shot Carter a nervous look. "No, I think there must've been a misunderstanding. I already have a tattoo. Several, in fact."

"Oh, I didn't mean *your* first, Mr. Riggs." I laughed indulgently. "Obviously. I meant, the first time *I'd* be in charge of planning a ceremony where one groom"—I extended a hand toward Carter—"would tattoo the other in front of the guests." I shifted my hand toward Riggs.

Riggs's mouth fell open. So did Carter's, but his eyes lit with unholy glee too.

"You look surprised, but I assure you, it's true. Tattoo weddings are a rarity in Tennessee." I shook my head. "I can't imagine why, though! This is the twenty-first century, and neck tattoos are quite accepted. Not to mention, Dr. Carter is a medical professional and probably quite steady-handed."

"Steady..." Riggs paled and swallowed. "Aren't there laws about that?"

"You'd think, but no!" I lied. In point of fact, I was confident there were tons of regulations prohibiting the whole thing... but it seemed Mr. Riggs didn't know that.

I opened up the binder from Posy Martinez's second wedding—to a heavily tatted, fifty-something rock star—and pointed triumphantly to the enormous tattoo on the groom's neck.

Carter's eyes flew to mine in confusion, and I tilted my head significantly. He grinned.

"Is that a..." Riggs squinted. "A platypus giving birth?"

"Nonsense. It's a fierce dragon breathing fire," I said with dignity. I paused and pursed my lips, staring at the bright green blob. "It's the best she could do, given the awkward angle. And anyway, it's the thought that counts, isn't it, Dr. Rogers?"

Carter clapped a hand to his mouth, but an evil snicker escaped anyway. "Oh, yes, Mr. Taffet. I couldn't agree more."

I began to hand him the Sharpie I'd swiped from the supply shelf. "Why don't you do a practice version now?" I suggested, flicking my fingers toward Riggs's neck. "I'll take a picture of this first attempt for your wedding scrapbook."

"Actually." Riggs made a choking noise and grabbed for the marker. "I don't think that's necessary."

I ignored him and slapped the marker in Carter's outstretched palm. "Don't be afraid to go bigger than you think," I advised. "You want your design to be visible from a distance. Were you thinking of a unicorn, perhaps?"

Carter tapped the marker against his lips. "I was thinking… capybara? But I could just go with letters. Property of Carter Rogers has a ring to it. Does 'property' have one *i* or two?"

I laughed. Carter's eyes twinkled at me.

Riggs did not seem to find us funny.

He stood and planted himself behind his chair. "You know, I think it's important to remember that we don't need to decide *everything* today—"

"No, of course not. That's why you'll rehearse." I smiled benevolently.

"Remember it's for *Champ*." Carter wiggled his eyebrows and beckoned Riggs closer. "You can't say no, baby. *You owe him*."

"Don't be nervous. Sit down, Mr. Rogers," I instructed.

"Mr. Riggs," he corrected, eyeing the marker in Carter's hand mistrustfully.

"But." I cocked my head, all innocence. "I thought Champ said you'd be taking Dr. Rogers's name?"

"Well, yeah, I will eventually," he agreed distractedly, though his full attention remained on the marker Carter held. "Carter, baby, let's not be hasty. Remember that big Thicket dance thing is coming up. Remember revenge is beneath you, okay?"

"Wait." Carter blinked, and his smile fell away. "Are you serious?" he whispered.

"Uh." Riggs looked confused. "Serious about the SnoBall? Or about not letting you at me with that marker? Because I'm pretty sure I'm serious about both."

Carter's eyes went shiny. "Riggs."

"Ah, shit." Riggs sat back down and took Carter's hand. "Don't be upset, baby. If it'll make you feel better, go ahead and ink me. It'll wash off. I think." He leaned toward Carter and tilted his head back, literally exposing his jugular.

And yeah, okay, my shriveled, pragmatic, unromantic little heart maybe grew three sizes at the gesture.

"I meant taking my name," Carter said softly. "Were you serious about that?"

"Oh, that." Riggs straightened in his chair. "Yeah, of course. I'd love for us to have the same name once we're married. I mean, you've already made me part of your ridiculous family, right?"

Carter nodded.

Riggs shrugged. "I wanna share everything with you."

"Really?"

"Baby." Riggs shook his head. "After all we've been

through, how could you doubt it? I want to be with you forever, Carter Rogers."

Carter bit his lip. Then he stood, threw the marker so that it landed close to Hercules, and launched himself into Riggs's arms to kiss him passionately.

I rolled my eyes at the dog. Herc sighed in reply.

They really were a cute couple. Riggs just needed to get better friends.

"Quinn, I'm sorry," Carter said breathlessly when they finally broke apart, "but we have to go. Riggs and I will be back after we... ah... you know."

"Actually get engaged?" I ventured.

Riggs's gaze swung to me. "You knew?"

"Not until I overheard you two talking. Your voices carry like you would not believe." I waved a hand toward the back room, where I'd been listening. "So I'll put the tattoo ceremony on hiatus, then? Just as well. I might be in jail for murder once I find your boss."

"Champ wasn't trying to bait and switch you," Riggs said quickly. "I think in his own fucked-up way, he was trying to move things along between Carter and me. Champ genuinely wanted me to propose and for you to plan the wedding. And we really will keep you in mind to do that just as soon as we're ready, right, Carter?"

"Hell, no!" Carter winked at me. "Quinn, I like you. And the next time I—or my grandfather—need a party planned, I will absolutely call you. But the next time this guy proposes?" He patted Riggs's chest a little more firmly than necessary. "He'd better have a minister in tow, or a capybara neck tattoo will be the least of his worries."

Riggs squeezed Carter against him. "Baby, have I

ever told you how hot you are when you threaten me with bodily harm?"

Carter snickered, but the second their gazes met, the air thickened with tension, and they began eye-fucking each other right there in the showroom.

"I think maybe you look a little flushed, Doctor," Riggs suggested. "Maybe you need to cancel your patients for the day and get someone to take your temperature."

Carter turned beet red and hurried Riggs out the door, but it looked like he was very much on board with that plan.

I couldn't help but think of Champ and wish… well, I didn't know exactly what I wished where he was concerned. But after I kicked his ass for lying to me about Carter and Riggs, I was pretty sure I was done with the revirgination thing. It clearly wasn't working. It might even be making things worse.

"How about we cut off early and go read your owner the riot act, hmm?" I suggested. Herc yapped in agreement.

But before I could lock the showroom door, it opened for the billionth time that morning and a stranger walked in.

"Good morning! Mr. Taffet?" The man's smile was disarmingly polite, and his suit was Tom Ford, if I wasn't mistaken.

"Yes. Can I help you?"

He pulled out a badge, and his whole demeanor suddenly seemed a little more menacing. "Agent Vincent Parler, DEA. I'd like to ask you a few questions."

Champ's ex-boyfriend. *Shit. Be cool, Quinn.*

But I couldn't.

Was there a word for people who became incredibly anxious around men with badges? Because whatever that disease was, I had it. My palms went sweat-slick instantly, and I was suddenly, irrationally sure that I'd not only killed someone that morning and forgotten about it, but I probably also still had the gun on my person.

"I want you to know, I've paid my taxes appropriately," I babbled. "And that light herbal refreshment I partook in that one time in college? I haven't done that since freshman year."

He frowned at me, and I caved.

"Okay, maybe a couple of times since!" I admitted frantically. "But I haven't rolled the devil's lettuce for years, I promise. And those speed limit signs weren't well marked! I'd like an attorney."

"Mr. Taffet," the man said impatiently, dropping his friendly mien, "I'm here to ask you about your relationship with Thomas Drakes."

"Thomas Drakes?" Damn. Champ's repeating thing was contagious.

"A little over two weeks ago, you were seen leaving Mr. Drakes's Nashville home. You were also recently spotted at his farm in Licking Thicket. And we have bank records showing large sums of money transferred from his personal account to yours." He lifted an eyebrow. "Are you saying you don't know him?"

"No, of course I know him. I'm planning his wedding. I mean, not *Tommy's* wedding." I tittered nervously. "His daughter, Marissa, is my bride. I mean, not *my* bride, but *a* bride. Whose wedding I'm planning."

Oh, God, this was terrible. Debilitating.

"Your story is that Drakes is your client?" He

looked around my shop, his eyes resting on the floral arrangements and the collection of bridal veils hanging by the dressmaker's dais.

"Well… yes. Because he is. The money was for vendor deposits. I can show you receipts, if you'd like. I don't think Mr. Drakes would mind."

There. That was easy enough. *Just stick to the truth, Quinn.*

"And what about your relationship with Percival Champion?" Vince asked, switching tacks.

"Champ? Uh. He and I…" My whole body broke out in a fresh round of sweat, because when it came to Champ, I couldn't stick to the truth. I wasn't sure what the truth *was* anymore.

I was so not cut out for this shit. I was way too nervous to lie to the DEA agent and tell him Champ and I were engaged… but also, this was Champ's ex. I wasn't going to admit that Champ was a fuck buddy I was fairly certain I'd developed complicated, unwanted feelings for.

My anxiety must've communicated itself somehow, because a deep, menacing growl came from the floor at my feet as a little golden-brown ball of canine prepared to defend me from the nearest threat. Vince actually backed up a pace as Hercules bared his teeth.

"Sorry." I squatted down to grab the dog's collar. "Calm down, Herc. Everything's okay," I soothed.

Vince blinked down at the dog for a moment in surprise, and then his expression cleared.

"Hercules! Remember me?" He squatted down beside me and reached out a hand to the dog but snatched it back when Herc snapped at him. "Ah, poor boy. You never quite forgave Daddy for leaving, did you?"

"Daddy?" I looked from him to the dog.

"Oh, didn't Percy tell you? We adopted Herc together once upon a time. We were practically engaged," he said, managing to sound both smug and wistful.

"Huh. No, Champ never mentioned that."

His smile turned pitying. "Well. Percy was never very good at sharing information, especially when it comes to important things. Trust is not his strong suit."

Ew. I couldn't believe this was the guy Champ had been planning to spend his life with. He'd seen Champ's *house*. Had co-owned Champ's dog. This explained so much of Champ's current attitude, but also… *ew*.

I hated more than anything that Vince was right — Champ played everything close to the vest, and despite all the information he'd already shared with me, I knew there was more he wasn't saying.

"Let me guess," Vince continued. "You two are sleeping together. You care about him deeply, because Percy's easy to fall for, but you're frustrated because he's holding back. He'll give you his cock, and he'll lend you his dog, he'll spend lots of money on you, but anything more than that…" He made a *tsk*ing noise.

He'd spend money on me? *Ew.* But the rest was pretty close to true, so I bit my tongue and said nothing.

"It's okay. I get it. I've been where you are, Quinn. It's not just you. Percy can be… difficult. He's not a man who knows how to love. Everything is about his business, his career. I got tired of the secrets and lies. Coming in second all the time." He spread his hands in a helpless gesture. "I just wanted to be loved. I wanted *romance*. You understand, don't you?"

What I understood was that Vince wanted something, and he was trying to manipulate the fuck out of me. But it was still terrifying to have someone rip the deepest fears out of your chest and hold them in front of your face.

I was not a person who believed in romance or relationships. I *knew* better.

But I was very afraid I was falling for Champ anyway.

"Quinn—can I call you Quinn?" Vince said. "I truly hate to tell you this, because you seem… really nice. But I'm afraid Percy's been using you. Trying to exploit your connection to Tommy Drakes so he can gather information for one of his investigations."

"W-why would he do that?" I forced myself to say. I didn't have to fake my breathless voice. Vince really *did* know Champ.

"Because his career will always come first." Vince sighed. "It's almost an obsession with him."

In my mind, I replayed Champ saying, "Champion Security is the only thing I have that's *mine*…"

"Look, Percy doesn't trust me anymore because I finally walked away from him to protect my heart. But deep down, I still care about him. I still want to help him. If he gets caught stealing from Tommy Drakes… well, if he doesn't end up *dead*, he's for sure going to end up prosecuted. If you want to prevent that from happening, you need to make sure I get access to Drakes Farm before he does. Champ won't save himself, Quinn. He doesn't know how. But *you* could save him."

I swallowed hard and tried to think. "Tell me more. What *exactly* would you need me to do?"

12

CHAMP

I'd spent the day at the office putting out several fires for other clients and teleconferencing with a couple of prospective new clients in Atlanta and Miami. Riggs had been off-grid for most of the day, and I hadn't gotten to follow up about his meeting. Hux had finally gotten me an update on Scott Morganstern, the only ex-boyfriend shitty enough to rival my own, and his copious financial troubles. Yolanda and Sasha had gotten in a minor fender bender in one of our company vehicles, and I had to take care of the paperwork. By the end of the day, my head was low-key throbbing, and all I wanted to do was set my eyes on Quinn Taffet to absorb whatever-the-fuck magic he had that helped me relax.

As soon as I entered the farmhouse kitchen that evening and saw his expression, though, I knew there would be no relaxation in my near future. In addition to sporting an angry face, he was also chopping vegetables violently with a knife that seemed comically large for the job.

It didn't take an intel operative to determine something was up.

"Hello, Percival," he said with the same kind of peevish emphasis on my name Vince had enjoyed using.

"Uh, hi?"

"You owe me a half hour of my life back." He chopped frantically. "Make that a whole hour."

I opened the fridge to help myself to one of the beer bottles I'd stashed in there earlier in the week. "That's probably beyond my abilities, but I'll see what I can do," I promised. I opened the bottle and took a long, cold slug before glancing around the kitchen. "What happened? And should we be talking about this out in the open? Where are Marissa and Levi?"

"Still in Nashville at a dress fitting, and before you ask, I saw Levi's goons head to the bunkhouse with a stack of pizza boxes." He gestured wildly through the air with the knife as he spoke. "As for what happened, where do I even begin? Your pals Riggs and Carter are delightful — by which I mean delightfully not-engaged."

Fuck.

"But they're gonna be engaged any minute," I said in what I hoped was a convincing tone. "It's seriously more of a technicality that they haven't sealed the deal. And since this really smart and sexy wedding planner I know keeps telling me it takes a year to plan a wedding, I figured… why not just start planning Carter and Riggs's do, and then it'll be all set by the time they're ready?"

"That is the most ass-backwards — *ugh*. You are not charming!" He chopped so hard tiny vegetable pieces flew through the air like confetti. "Also? Another one of your besties — that's my sarcastic voice, by the way — thought it would be *totes adorbs* to stop by the shop and threaten me." He stopped ranting for a minute and crinkled his face. "I was positive he was gonna lock me up for speeding tickets, or weapons charges, or tax evasion. Possibly murder. And do you *realize* how awful I look in prison orange?"

The man was impossibly sexy when he was ranting wildly, but fortunately, I knew a surefire way to calm him down, at least long enough to make sense of what he was saying.

I lunged forward and neutralized his weapon before slamming my mouth on his. He gave an aborted little *meep* sound before it turned into a moan of pleasure. He let me go for it until his brain reminded him he was mad at me.

"Good God! No. Off, you mongrel!" He pulled back from me, quickly lurched forward for one more kiss, then pulled back again. "I'm mad at you, remember? Jeez. Have a little respect."

"Mad at me for what, exactly?" I asked at the same time my brain helpfully put the pieces of the puzzle together. Someone I knew threatened to lock him up? "Vince went to your place? *Fuck*."

Quinn's eyes narrowed accusingly. "Yes. Pretty much my thought exactly."

I felt a twist of anger and unease in my gut. I didn't want Vince Parler anywhere near Quinn Taffet. Quinn was off-limits.

"What did he say to you?"

Quinn picked the knife back up from where I'd placed it on the counter and returned to his chopping. "He said if I didn't help him find the Horn, you were going to be hanged in the town square at high noon."

"Be serious." I clenched my hands into fists to keep from grabbing him and shaking him. I needed every single detail of their conversation, and I needed it now. "Tell me everything."

Quinn looked up at me and sighed. "First of all, calm down. Take a breath. That vein in your head is going to burst, and then I really will need to find the Horn myself."

"This isn't funny, Quinn. What did he say? I can't believe he got you involved in this. That motherfucker."

Quinn studied me for a minute. "You want to know exactly what he said? Every single word?"

"Yes!"

"Then agree to my terms."

I threw my hands up. "Terms? What possible terms could you—"

"I need a date to the SnoBall dance next week," he blurted.

We stared at each other. Neither of us had ever used the D-word before.

He recovered quickly. "Not a date-date. Just a… date. An escort. To keep the town matchmakers off my back, okay? Cindy Ann Johnson and her List of Potential Dates scare the crap out of me. Do this for me and I'll tell you everything Vince said."

I stepped closer to him and noticed his breathing hitch. "You're going to tell me everything he said regardless," I said in a low voice.

Quinn swallowed. "Yes, obviously. But… I still need a date to this thing. It's important. There are a *shocking* number of well-connected people who live around here and are planning to attend. And now that there won't be a Carter Rogers society wedding on my roster—"

"I'll go," I said before he had to ask me again. "Of course I'll go if you need me to."

The sentiment behind my words, that I would do whatever he needed of me, floated around me like a comforting fog. It felt right. Offering to meet his needs fed that part of me that wanted to protect people. Protect *him*.

I cleared my throat. "What did Vince say?"

While he told me about my smarmy ex trying to intimidate him, I did my best to keep breathing steadily when all I really wanted to do was murder a particular DEA agent.

"He's lying," I said when Quinn finally took a break from talking to throw the vegetables into a large soup pot and add several spices. "Or else he's completely delusional about the cause of our breakup. I wasn't the one obsessed with my job—*he* was. He didn't start out like that, but somewhere along the way, he let this… career competition take over. He wants to be the best, get to the top the fastest, impress people. When we first met, he said he wanted to settle down. We adopted Herc. I bought my place here in the Thicket. Then he decided at the spur of the moment to take a big job in DC. That was when I couldn't keep pretending we wanted the same things. But I still can't really figure out if he was lying about wanting to settle down or if he changed his mind once he saw how much more was out there for him."

I reached over to steal a piece of carrot left on the cutting board and pop it in my mouth. "It doesn't really matter, but it does explain why he's so rabid about this case. He's obviously using it to try and make a name for himself there."

Quinn stirred the big pot before turning to me. "He wants me to wear a wire or something and ask Tommy to show me his Horn collection."

I rolled my eyes. "Vince is an idiot. How does he expect you to explain your interest in this one particular *hidden* Horn to Marissa's dad? Because that one isn't with all the others."

He shrugged. "Alternatively, Vince wants me to get him access to the property while Levi isn't around. Let him search the place himself."

Alarm bells went off in my head. "He said that? That he wanted to search the place without the homeowner's knowledge?" What the hell was Vince thinking? Would he truly risk his job just to prove he could solve this case?

Quinn nodded. "It wasn't that shocking. Isn't that what you're doing too?"

"Yeah, but I don't work for the government. Chain of custody and illegal search and seizure aren't concerns for me. Not to mention, I have permission to be here by the homeowner." If Vince had truly suggested an unauthorized search of the premises, that changed everything. I needed to talk to the team. "What did you tell him? How did you leave it?"

"I let him believe I was mostly convinced, then told him I had to think about it. I left it open so I could talk to you and see what you wanted me to do."

I was floored by his trust and faith in me. For as feisty and independent as Quinn Taffet was, he was actually deferring to me on this.

There had to be a catch.

"You're really good at this teamwork thing, Taffet," I said softly. "But stay the fuck away from Vince, you hear me? If he's on a quest for glory, he won't think twice about dragging you down with him."

Quinn shook his head. "I'm not worried about *me*—"

"Well, I fucking am. I want you to avoid him completely, okay? Put him off. Tell him you're too scared to get involved. Tell him to get a warrant. Better yet, just don't take his calls."

I hated the idea of Quinn even hearing Vince's voice, letting Vince's manipulation poison his brain.

His jaw set mulishly. "What happened to you not being bossy anymore?"

"I just don't—"

Before I could press him on it, Marissa came into the kitchen talking a mile a minute at Levi about something having to do with goats.

"Nubians' milk is higher in butterfat, but Toggs lactate for longer," Marissa said, making Quinn turn around in slow motion with a funny look on his face.

Levi nodded. "But Nubians are loud as hell, Rissy. You don't want that shit in your ears all night. Now, I know you don't like their small ears, but La Manchas are the better dairy breed, all in all."

"Agree to disagree," Marissa replied in a singsong voice. "It's mooch anyway because Daddy prefers the pigs."

"Moot," Quinn murmured under his breath. "*Moot.*"

"It's mooch because you live in the city," Levi corrected. "And you're not a goat farmer."

"Rancher," Quinn murmured. "For the love of the English language, people…"

"Whatcha making?" Marissa asked, moving over to the pot to inhale the fragrant steam.

"Pasta fag-ee-olee," he said with a straight face. "It's an old recipe that originated at an old-timey restaurant in Orlando, I believe."

I closed my eyes and mouth to keep from snorting. When I opened them, Quinn winked at me.

The bloom of warmth in my chest stayed there all through dinner, and it wasn't until hours later, when I'd waited for the house to go to sleep, that I realized my headache had disappeared. Hanging out with Quinn was easy, even when there was no sex involved—hell, even when my fucking *ex* was involved—and I had to admit that Levi and Marissa were easy to be around also. I almost felt bad about sneaking around behind their backs.

Almost.

But I had a job to do, and now that Vince had set his sights on Quinn, I needed to find where Levi had stashed Tommy's Horn more than ever.

I crept way down the stairs to the finished basement. After two weeks of adding additional surveillance tech to the house and sneaking around the property at night, I'd determined the Horn had to be down here. None of the other buildings had the proper HVAC system to support a valuable electronics collection. It was too humid in Tennessee to store them in an outbuilding with no air-conditioning.

I was turning the corner to head back toward Tommy Drakes's study when I heard a noise. I flattened myself against the wall and listened.

A low voice muttered a curse from the direction of the study. I took a few more steps as silently as I could before turning to peek through the doorway when a body bolted out of the study and slammed into me. We both tumbled to the ground in the carpeted hallway until I was flat on my back and the intruder lay on top of me.

"Fuck, *shit.*"

Before I recognized Quinn's voice, my hands recognized the familiar feel of his body. The body that had been off-limits to me for two long weeks.

"What are you doing?" I hissed.

"You really need to squeeze my ass when you ask me that?" he hissed back.

"Helps me think," I said, smiling big now that Quinn Taffet was back in my arms. "What are you doing down here?"

"What do you think? I'm looking for the Horn. Same as you."

My smile dropped away, and my arms tightened around him involuntarily. "No. No way. Was I not clear earlier? You will not involve yourself in this. Do you understand?"

I could hear the eye roll in his voice even though it was too dark to see it. "Was *I* not clear earlier? You are not the boss of me. Also? I'm already involved, remember? Your boyfriend involved me."

"He's not my boyfriend," I growled. I didn't add, *You are*, but it was a near thing.

Quinn shifted on top of me, rubbing a hip across my dick and waking up all of my senses. I let out a little groan.

"Stop that," he warned, rubbing his hip across me again on purpose. I squeezed my eyes closed. "We're not having sex, remember?"

"Why?" I asked in an embarrassing whimper.

"Because apparently you want to win our little contest more than you want to fuck me." Quinn sounded angry. I opened my eyes again but still couldn't make out his facial expression.

"No. No fucking way. I have wanted to fuck you every single day since I met you. Do not pin the revirgination bullshit on me when it was *your* idea." I may have snuck my hands under his shirt to feel his warm, bare skin.

"What?" Now he was the one who sounded squeaky. "You haven't missed this at all. And you've been deliberately teasing me for two fucking weeks!"

"Teasing you?" I barked. "I've been stretching my ears for any sound of you through the wall at night while jacking off imagining your mouth around my cock. Are you telling me — ?"

Quinn's mouth slammed into mine in a desperate kiss. His urgency mirrored my own, and we grappled at each other's clothes until we were naked and humping on the floor like wild animals.

I wasn't sure if this was angry sex or something a little more cordial, but I honestly didn't care. Either way, I needed to come with him, inside him, against him, on him, under him... any of the above.

"Suck my cock," he said against my lips. "Want you. Need it. Please."

I spun him around until my mouth was on him and my nose was pressed against his balls. A vague corner of my brain worried about where the Champ Security surveillance cameras were in this hallway, but I was too hungry for Quinn to do anything about it.

Quinn grabbed me and forced my body to bend until we found ourselves in a dirty, panting sixty-nine on the carpet outside of Tommy Drakes's basement office.

"Fucking fuck, I wanted this," Quinn mumbled before sucking me. It was a hot, heavenly clasp. I tried to give him the same pleasure he gave me, but it was a losing battle. Two weeks of pent-up lust had put me on a hair trigger.

"Baby, coming," I warned through gritted teeth. I

pulled off and jacked his slick cock until I felt his warm release hit my face. It was hot as fuck and pushed me over the edge into a mind-blowing orgasm.

When we both finished, I moved around to face him, grabbing my T-shirt to clean us both up before kissing the hell out of him. "God, I missed you," I said against his lips.

"Why didn't you say something if you wanted this?"

"Why didn't *you*?" I demanded.

He sighed and snuggled into my chest. "I don't know. Part of me wanted things to cool off between us, but…" He let out a little laugh. "I honestly never thought you'd go along with a stupid revirgination plan."

I pulled back and grasped both sides of his face. My eyes had adjusted enough to make out his semi-sheepish expression. "Revirgination stops here," I said firmly. "It's done. Your cherry has been well and truly popped. *Again.* Come to my bed because I'm not done with you."

Thankfully, my bossiness didn't seem to be an issue for him postorgasm because he obeyed my order and followed me back to my room.

"I know you think I'm being high-handed," I said when he climbed under the covers and snuggled up beside me. "But I really don't want you involved in this investigation. I don't want you involved with Vince."

"You're worried about me?" Quinn teased. "Aw, Nutter Butter. So loving."

I wished the man would take me seriously. "I promised you no blowback, remember? But I can't keep that promise if Vince is involved." I fucking hated that fact.

"I hear what you're saying," he promised. "I'm not

gonna take any unnecessary risks. I was today years old when I learned that I really don't like authority figures."

I grunted. "Please. I could have told you that weeks ago. Though you seem to like it well enough under certain circumstances."

Quinn rolled on top of me, and his grin lit up the darkness… while the sweet weight of him against me lit up all sorts of other things. "Know what else I learned today?"

"Hmm?"

"Your taste in men has *vastly* improved in recent weeks, Percy."

I laughed out loud and then moaned when Quinn leaned down to take my mouth with his.

My concerns about Vince were long forgotten. Until the following week, when they all came rushing back.

13

QUINN

"And then my aunt Bertie did her duck-lip disapproval face—you know the one?—and said she thought my dress was pretty but a bit... *plain*. At the final fitting! Can you even imagine?" Marissa fumed. She jabbed a stem of dried pampas grass into a tiny bud vase with excessive force.

"Mmm." I watched Marissa carefully from across the bundles of dried flowers and vases laid out on the table in my showroom—ground zero for wedding favor assembly this week.

Before she and Levi had taken their trip to Nashville for her dress fitting the week before, I'd have said Marissa was holding up just fine under the stress of wedding preparations. The farm had been a bustling hive of activity that had only ramped up in the last week, but she seemed to take it all in stride, like something about the rolling hills and wide-open skies soothed her. She'd been pink-cheeked and happy... or so I'd thought.

Now, though, she suddenly showed all the signs of a bride who was ready to explode. I wasn't sure what had changed. And I felt a bit guilty that maybe I'd been too busy obsessing about Percy Champion and hadn't been paying attention.

"Pay your aunt no mind," I advised. "It's *your* wedding, girl. Your dress. Your decision."

"Is it, though?" Marissa attacked a clump of starflowers, ripping them apart so violently that the dried petals swirled in the air around us like hot pink snowflakes and landed on her greasy ponytail.

Oookay.

"What happened?" I demanded, setting down my own miniature dried flower bouquet and leaning my hands on the table. "Spill it all."

Marissa shook her head, her eyes shining with unshed tears. "Nothing to spill. Doesn't matter anyway. My mother—" She jammed a willow branch into the vase so hard the stem broke and tiny white buds hung drunkenly over the edge. "—paid the seamstress extra to embellish the dress as a rush job. They'll deliver it today."

"Embellish it." I ran a hand over my mouth.

I hadn't been involved in Marissa's dress selection, but the one she'd chosen was exactly perfect for her. A formfitting, winter-white, off-the-shoulder, long-sleeved mermaid silhouette with a sweep train that highlighted her lovely figure and natural beauty. It was the sort of dress that would have looked perfectly elegant had Marissa opted for the Nashville wedding I'd originally concepted but was versatile enough to work well with the understated boho chic of the farm wedding she'd preferred. In fact, the only thing that could possibly ruin that dress would be... embellishment.

"Crystals." Marissa sniffled. "Seed pearls. It's costing my dad a fortune. I'm so… *blessed.*"

"Oh, honey." I leaned across the table to grasp her forearm. "Come sit down. I've got cookies—"

"Can't. They're also taking in the dress by an extra two inches around the waist. Apparently, my rushed wedding is fueling rumors that I've got a bun in this oven." She laid a hand on her flat stomach. "When the truth is, I haven't seen my fiancé in *weeks*, and I can't even get him to return my calls." She picked up a dried globe thistle by the business end and gasped. "Mother*fucker.*"

"Okay, enough. Come and tell Dr. Quinn all about it. Is this just about the dress? Because we can pick those crystals right off again." I gently pulled her away from the disaster of a flower arrangement and sat her down on the green velvet sofa.

"It's about *everything*," she sniffed. "Trey's mom was at the fitting, and she told me she and my mom have been working with a real estate agent to find us a house as a wedding gift. I said I'd like to help pick it out, and Aunt Bertie called me ungrateful. I mentioned that I want to go back to school next fall to study music therapy for kids, and my mom said it was time for me to grow up. Trey's mom said if I want to work with children, I can just have some of my own, because she can't wait to be a grandmother, but I don't want kids for another few *years* at least."

"Oh, sweetheart." I patted her back gently.

"And I don't know when things veered so out of control, but it's too late to change, you know? I'm already committed to Trey. To this wedding. Everyone's worked so h-h-hard." As Marissa spun her engagement ring around her finger, the giant diamond flashed rainbows around us from the sunlight through the window. "And then there's Levi…"

"What about Levi?" I demanded.

"Levi says I shouldn't settle. If I'm not happy with Trey, all I have to do is say so. But that's easy for him to say, isn't it? He never does *anything* he doesn't want to do…" She swallowed and looked away. "…even if I ask him to."

Danger, danger, danger.

"Have you… asked him to do something?" I asked fake-casually.

She spun her diamond more aggressively but didn't answer.

"You said you and Levi were close in the past."

"Yeah," she whispered. "I thought I was in love with him once, if you can believe that. He was the first boy I ever kissed. The first boy I ever… *you know*… one summer night up at the overlook." Her cheeks turned pink, and her eyelashes fluttered closed for a beat.

My eyes widened. Marissa lost her virginity to Levi at the overlook… where she was now planning to marry a different guy while Levi watched?

When had this become a telenovela?

"Wow," I managed.

"But then I went to college, and he started working for his dad, which meant protecting *my* dad, and… well, it turned out our feelings were just kid stuff. We grew apart because we wanted different things. Which is *fine*, of course. Of course it's fine."

Fucking hell.

I tried not to picture my big wedding client disappearing in a puff of Levi-shaped smoke. When I'd first noticed the tension between Levi and Marissa, I'd chalked it up to an old childhood crush. But if she was still thinking about it and talking about it in the final lead-up to her wedding to another man… that was a problem.

But, I reminded myself, it wasn't *my* problem. Not yet anyway. If she wanted to call off her wedding to be with another man, so be it. But I didn't need to be the one to help her get to that point by encouraging her.

"So! Are you excited about the SnoBall?" I asked, plastering on my best pageant smile with the blatant change of subject. "I've gotten a kind of behind-the-scenes the last few weeks. It's going to be amazing!"

She scraped her teeth against her bottom lip before giving me a tremulous smile. "Yeah." She took a breath and then smiled bigger. "Yeah, actually, Trey is coming in for it and told me he's bringing his dad's '55 Cadillac so we can arrive in style."

After a few minutes of idle local gossip and excitement about the SnoBall, Marissa seemed almost completely recovered from her earlier stress.

She patted my leg before standing up. "I'd better get back to the farm and take a shower. Mama's coming for the dance, and she's bringing a hairstylist from Nashville for an updo. Will I see you at home before the fun?"

She was such a kind person, and her inquiry made me feel tender affection for her. Maybe I *did* need to talk to her about the Levi thing, but I certainly couldn't do it right now when I'd promised Ava I'd stop by her place to go over some last-minute details before the party tonight.

After sending Marissa off, I walked Herc to Ava's house and entered her happy chaos. I'd been to her place a couple of times in the past two weeks to talk to her—or, rather, get her polite commands—about the SnoBall. It seemed poor Mrs. Peevey, despite her dubious dating choices, had organized everything well. I truly would only need to worry about dealing with any little fires that popped up during the night itself.

"Flippin' biscuits, if my babysitter doesn't show up soon, I'm going to lose my ever-loving…" She glanced at little Beau, who clung to her leg, while balancing a baby on each hip. "*Patience.*"

I bit my lip against a smile while I thanked my stars that I had not been born with a uterus. "I'll be out of your hair in a hot minute. I just needed to pick up the gratuity envelopes you wanted me to manage for the band and catering staff."

She lifted her chin in the direction of a leather day planner on the counter. "They're in my planner. Are you all set with a date for the dance? Because if not, Cindy Ann and I can get—"

"No!" I barked, recognizing the fake-casual voice of a Southern matchmaker. I cleared my throat. "No, thank you. I'm all set."

Her eyes danced. "So you found yourself a date, then?"

Little Beau transferred his sticky hands onto my own designer jeans. I glanced down at him, wondering if a good feral hiss would do the trick to avoid a trip to the dry cleaners. "Champ is taking me." The words were out before I realized the toddler had most likely been in on a deliberate distraction operation. I bit back a curse. "Just as friends," I added quickly. "We're, ah, just… you know."

"Friends?" she teased. "The sleepover kind? Or the *sleepover* kind?"

"I'm afraid I don't know what you mean," I said primly.

"So you're not..." She glanced down at the sticky-handed menace before looking back at me with a raised eyebrow. "Plowing his fields?"

It took me a minute to figure out what the hell she was trying to ask, and then I deliberately misunderstood her. "He doesn't have any fields. He lives in town."

I quickly grabbed the envelopes from the planner and moved toward the door. She stalked after me.

"You two aren't participating in... amorous congress?"

I winced. "I don't know much about politics."

Her jaw tightened. I could see the hungry small-town gossipmonger in her eyes. "Quinn Taffet. You know what I'm asking."

I blinked at her. "No, ma'am. But I need to run and get ready for the dance." I slithered out of the door and bolted toward the car.

"Are either of you bringing an al dente noodle to the spaghetti house?" she called after me with clear laughter in her voice.

My face heated, and I refused to look back. "No. But we are sucking and fucking!" I called over my shoulder.

As I backed out of the driveway, I saw her close her eyes in frustration as her little boy started asking questions.

Served her right.

The next few hours flew by as I showered and dressed, helped calm Marissa down after she learned Trey would be late arriving from Nashville, and finally made my way downstairs, where Champ was waiting for me in the front hall of the farmhouse.

The man wore a tux like it had been invented solely for him to do it justice.

"Dear God," I breathed.

His eyes darkened, and he pulled a hand out from behind him to reveal a small plastic box. "For you."

I stepped closer. The familiar scent of his woodsy cologne was endearing. It reminded me he wasn't the kind of person to suddenly use a fancier scent for a formal night out. Champ was Champ regardless of where he came from or how he dressed.

When I realized what was in the box, my heart betrayed me with a little Victorian-era swoon. "You got me a boutonniere?"

He opened the box and removed the small cluster of flowers. When he stepped forward to put it on my lapel, his lips eased into a grin. "I'm Bunny Champion's son. Emily Post was practically my nanny."

I snorted. The faint scent of pine wafted up from the fresh sprig of it mixed with the baby's breath in the flower cluster, but it didn't hold a candle to the scent of Champ himself standing so close to me.

"I want to lick your face," I admitted under my breath.

His grin grew even wider. "Maybe later. And I'm only saying that because Herc got there first, and I know how you feel about sharing me with others."

I elbowed him and stepped away, trying my hardest to remove myself from the dizzying effect his nearness seemed to have on me. "Let's go. I need to get there early."

"The truck's already been warming up for ten minutes," Champ said, holding out his arm to escort me through the front door. Formal dance Champ was a dangerous Champ.

On the short drive back through town to the community events barn, I thought about his "sharing" joke. We'd obviously never said anything about being exclusive, but I had to admit to being uneasy at the thought of him hooking up with anyone else.

Uneasy is a massive understatement. Try stark-raving insane with jealousy.

I cleared my throat. Champ turned to look at me with a furrowed brow. "You nervous?"

"No. Not at all. I love this stuff."

He looked back at the road but reached across the center console to take my hand in his. It was warm and strong. I pulled it up to my lips and kissed it without thinking. "Thanks for coming with me," I said.

"We made a deal, right? I'm just holding up my end of it." He flashed me a smile that was probably meant to be reassuring, but my stomach dropped.

I knew he probably wasn't coming because of the silly Vince-intel agreement... but why *was* he here? What were the boundaries of this non-relationship relationship?

I wanted to ask him, but I was scared. If he told me I'd been deluding myself, or —*fuck* —if he looked at me with pity, how would I continue working beside him, pretending to be his fiancé, until Marissa's wedding?

"Yeah," I said, forcing a smile. "Of course."

He squeezed my hand and continued to hold it. After a few more minutes, I forced myself to take a breath and stop overreacting. I was working tonight. The date was a side benefit. That was all.

So I did what I always did when I was a little mixed up and started talking. "At the last SnoBall meeting, everyone was talking about this funny song they play—What is it? Like 'Ice Ice Baby' or 'Funky Cold Medina,' something cheesy like that—and everyone dances to it with their date. And I just don't want to be standing on the sidelines like a doofus when it happens, you know? I mean, if you're okay with that? You don't even have to really know how to dance. It's just for fun, they said. But everyone gets out there and—"

"It's 'Oh, What a Night' by the Four Seasons," he said, turning to me with a face so fucking attractive, I wanted to smack it. "And of course I'll dance it with you. You're my date. It's the date dance."

I swallowed and looked out the side window at the clear night air. "How did you know that?"

"My mom was born and raised in the Thicket—though she'd like to pretend she was created in an Hermès showroom—so I've been to many a SnoBall over the years, especially back when my grandparents were alive." He looked over at me again before focusing on the final turn. "But I've never danced the date dance with anyone."

"I should have gotten you a boutonniere," I blurted. "Shit. Fuck. Gah! What kind of date am I? What kind of *event planner* am I? Fucking hell."

His laughter filled the cab of the truck. "You know I don't care, right?"

Once he pulled into the large gravel parking area beside the giant weathered-wood barn, I hopped out and raced over to the edge of the lot to scramble in the scraggly bushes. I found some greenery of indeterminate ancestry and plucked it away from its source before making my way back to him and fastening it to his lapel using a hairpin from the event emergency stash in my pocket.

"Did you know Americans use the word 'bouton-niere' to refer to the actual floral cluster, while in Europe, that's the name for the lapel buttonhole itself?"

Champ's hands settled on my hips. "I see what you mean about wanting to lick people's faces," he murmured. His warm breath brushed my forehead half a second before his lips followed, pressing soft kisses on my forehead and eyebrows. His eyes reflected the thousands of twinkle lights decorating the outside of the event, and the sight was utterly dazzling. "I didn't tell you how incredibly sexy you look in this tux."

I accidentally let out a little groan. "Don't start something right now. I beg you."

His hands roamed under my jacket to my ass and squeezed. "I'm not. I swear. It's way too chilly out here. Besides, this wedding planner I know tells me it's better to do the difficult thing first."

I melted into him just long enough to taste the side of his neck with a few open-mouthed kisses. "Mmhm. Okay."

We started kissing for real... until a tiny scrap of a woman with a perfectly coiffed blonde bob barked out, "Percival Champion! Kissing in public? How *gauche*."

Champ jumped away from me, and I turned away to catch my breath and will my erection to subside.

Oh, shit. That was so unprofessional of me. The only thing that could make it worse was if—

Champ reached for my hand and pulled me closer to his side. "Mother? What in the world are you doing here? I thought you were in Florida."

Yup. That would do it.

Oh, God. I couldn't meet Bunny Champion this way. I'd already been caught making out *gauchely* in the parking lot. I couldn't do a meet-the-fucking-parents right then. Not on Emily Post's life.

But as I started pulling away, Champ's hand tightened around mine like a vise. The expression on his face never changed despite the bone-crushing pressure in his grip.

"I love to support local charitable endeavors, as you well know." Bunny paused and sniffed delicately. "Or at least as you *would* know if you ever returned my calls."

"In person?" Champ asked dubiously. "When's the last time you were in the Thicket?"

"That's neither here nor there." She lifted her chin. "I heard the strangest rumor from none other than Carlotta Drakes that my son was engaged. *'Engaged?'* I cried. 'Carlotta, darling, that's not possible!' But she assured me that she'd heard it herself and even met my son's affianced groom! And then that above-her-station *harridan* forced me to endure her fake sympathy noises about how the younger generation is terribly flighty— though not *her* daughter, of course." Bunny smoothed a finger over her blonde helmet. "Honestly, Percival, whatever sins I have committed as a mother, I did not deserve *that*."

A beat of silence passed, during which I struggled not to laugh.

Then Champ said, "Mother, I'd like you to meet Quinn Taffet of Taffet Events. He's Licking Thicket's premier event planner and will be overseeing this evening's arrangements. Quinn, this is my mother. Bunny Champion."

She narrowed her eyes at me, and I was glad that I'd worn my one-and-only designer tux for tonight.

"What happened to Lorraine Peevey? She's overseen this event for years."

I opened my mouth to mention the Villages all up in her lady bits, but Champ beat me to it. "Unfortunately, she fell ill while visiting friends. Quinn was chosen to take over."

Mrs. Champion sniffed. "It's probably for the best. She's getting a little long in the tooth if you want to know my opinion." She gave me an intrusive once-over. "Any relation to Cherry Taffet?"

This felt like a very strange reversal of what Champ probably went through every time he introduced himself, and I felt a pang of sympathy for him.

"Yes, ma'am. Cherry is my aunt."

A reluctant smile appeared on her judgmental face. "Cherry and I grew up together. I haven't seen her in ages, but she's good people."

I blew out a breath. "She is. Thank you for saying so."

"Well. You and I will catch up more soon, but for now, you'd better get in there before all hell breaks loose." She gestured toward the main entrance to the barn, where a line of attendees was already stepping through a dusting of fake snow and into the glittering winter wonderland the committee and I had created inside. "This event has been known to go off the rails from time to time."

Thankfully, it didn't go off the rails on my watch.

As soon as we entered the hall, time seemed to speed up the way it always did when I managed a live event. As the guests arrived and the band started, little fires popped up here and there, but nothing out of the ordinary. In fact, it was the most fun event I could ever remember attending, let alone working… and a huge part of that was thanks to my date.

Champ helped me solve a minor crisis involving a burnt-out fuse, made sure I always had a glass of sparkling water in my hand, and was able to help me clear the dance floor in plenty of time before the giant silver-and-white "snowball" drop—one glittery balloon for every three dollars donated to the fundraiser—that showed just how much money Ava's group had raked in. Best of all was sensing Champ's eyes on me throughout the night, watching him fight an eye roll while he danced with his mother, and letting myself sink into the feeling of what he and I might be like if we really were a couple.

When the evening was more than half-over, I got myself a plate of truffles and leaned contentedly against a pillar by the dessert table as I watched Tommy Drakes lead Marissa out on the floor. I believed Champ when he said that Tommy had some criminal connections, but I didn't care. I'd heard Tommy bragging about his "beautiful, intelligent daughter" more than once over the course of the night, and I was pretty sure Marissa had too. Hopefully, that would make up for the fact that her asshole fiancé still hadn't shown up.

"Sweet girl. Even if she does have terrible taste in mothers."

I straightened as Bunny Champion parked herself against the other side of my pillar and watched Marissa alongside me. "Ma'am—"

"Oh, calm yourself." She waved one hand imperiously while sipping from a martini glass with the other. "I'm not here to be impressed. I'm here to take a load off. I forgot how tiring these events can be." She turned her gaze—which was really absurdly like Champ's gaze

—on me. "You seem to be handling the excitement just fine, though. I've been watching you off and on all night. You haven't broken a sweat. And I've heard several people say this was the most fun SnoBall in years." She reached over and grabbed a caramel truffle from my plate.

"Oh, well." I shrugged and tried not to blush. "I can't take credit for that. Mrs. Peevey did the hard part. I'm only playing the part of coordinator for the evening. Though I do have a few notes about things I — I mean, *Mrs. Peevey*—could do a bit differently next year."

She snorted. "I'm sure you do. But I wouldn't count myself off the hook for next year just yet. If I know Lorraine Peevey, she'll be more than happy to retire as coordinator and let you take charge. In fact, that might've been her aim in getting you to step in tonight."

I frowned. I hadn't considered that, and I wasn't sure what I thought about it. "I'm not sure where I'll be next year. I… I'm from Nashville originally. I plan to move back there once I've built my business up."

"You and Percival, in Nashville?" She raised her eyebrows. "After he swore he'd never live there again? You must be some kind of miracle worker."

"Er, not quite. You see, I…" I rubbed the back of my neck. I couldn't lie to the man's *mother*. "I'm not sure what will be happening with Champ and me. The news of our engagement was, um…" I glanced around to make sure there were no Drakes in the vicinity. "A bit premature."

She narrowed her eyes.

"As in, we're not engaged," I explained.

Her expression didn't change.

"Not even dating," I elaborated. And when she still

didn't reply, I said a bit desperately, "We're not in love. No feelings. Understand?" I licked my lips nervously. "Although, if you could just keep that to yourself for a couple of weeks, I'd appreciate —"

"Horse puckey," Bunny said in a perfectly posh accent.

Oh, fuck. Did that mean she wouldn't keep the secret? Champ would kill me for blabbing.

"No, seriously, ma'am, I can't stress enough how important it is —"

"I meant, there is no way that you and my son don't have feelings for one another. He's never kissed another man in public to my knowledge, not even Vincent, and they dated for years. And he would never hold your hand if you weren't something special to him." She waved her hand imperiously again. "The rest will sort itself out. With you at the helm, I have no doubt."

I wasn't sure if I should feel complimented or concerned. Maybe a little of both.

"But why do you want to move back to the city anyway?" Bunny asked.

"To get back what I had," I said immediately. What I'd had before fucking Scott had ruined it all.

Bunny lifted an eyebrow. "If what you had was really that great, why did you leave in the first place?"

I blinked at her in surprise. Something about her words hit me. I *hadn't* fought for what I wanted when Scott left. If it was really that wonderful, why hadn't I?

"Nashville's my home now, of course," she went on, "and I love it there—all three of my husbands loved it there—but honestly, Quinn, it's deathly dull, and you know it. Everyone knows everyone else, everyone's tired of seeing the same old things, everyone's *jaded*. I swear that's part of the reason Percy decided he could never live there. What Nashville folks really want is someone who can offer them something fresh and new. A little bit of Thicket reality and ingenuity we can import from time to time to spice things up."

I side-eyed her deeply. "The Thicket is spicy?"

"The Thicket is *different*," she countered. "And that makes it interesting. Not to mention, practically speaking, the city's a wasteland." She waved her hand, which I was coming to recognize as one of her habits—one I kind of enjoyed. "Why, just this week, I heard about a well-respected wedding-planning business that's supposed to be going under due to financial misman-agement, and their poor clients are fleeing like rats from a sinking ship! Far smarter to base yourself here in the Thicket," she said firmly. She gave me a saucy grin. "And if that keeps you close to Percy, so much the better."

I had no idea how to respond to that. Fortunately, I didn't have to because we were interrupted by a young woman I'd met earlier in the evening.

Anita Shelton came over and dropped into a chair next to my pillar. "Mind if I sit here? My feet are killing me in these shoes."

I offered her my truffle plate. "Have one of these. They'll cure everything, including high-heeled regrets."

Anita chuckled and reached for one of the truffles. I took the opportunity to introduce her to Bunny, who surprised me by leaning around me to engage with her. "Aren't you Diamond Shelton's oldest?"

Anita nodded. "Yes, ma'am."

Bunny looked between us before settling back on Anita. "I know your mother through the community garden project. She said you'd recently gotten engaged to Hubert and Jasmine's son."

Anita's face lit up. "Yes, ma'am. Elijah proposed on New Year's."

Bunny clasped my arm. "You simply *have* to hire Quinn here to plan the wedding. He's the absolute best in the Thicket. I was talking earlier to Susie Dalton about a wedding she went to in Nashville that Quinn planned, and she said it was miles above anything else she'd ever seen."

I stared at her in shock, but before I could ask her what the fuck, Anita wiggled excitedly in her chair and asked, "You've done big Nashville weddings?"

I nodded. "That's all I did for a long time before moving to the Thicket. Now I do weddings anywhere. Right now, I'm planning a wedding for Marissa Drakes and Trey Dunwoody here at Marissa's family farm. It's going to be gorgeous."

If it didn't get canceled by a little inconvenience named Levi.

"Oh my gosh! Mom told me she wanted to hold it here in the Thicket, but she was worried there wouldn't be a planner in Nashville willing to come this far. I've got to go tell her!"

"You do that!" Bunny called after her.

When Anita left, Bunny sank against the pillar again with a happy sigh.

"I… I don't know what to say," I began. I couldn't help but feel like she was helping me under false pretenses. "I was serious before, ma'am. Champ—erm, *Percy*—and I are only casual friends."

"Then I look forward to watching you both become enlightened. I feel like planning the SnoBall won't be the only temporary thing that becomes permanent." Then she winked—*Bunny Champion* winked—at me.

I flushed beet red, and Bunny laughed. "You're an utter delight, Quinn Taffet. And to think, I wasted so much time trying to reconcile myself to the last boy Percy dated! Come and see me in a few weeks, won't you? Once Carlotta's daughter's wedding kerfuffle is over. I'm planning a fundraising gala in the autumn, and I'd love to talk through a few ideas with you."

"A gala? With... *me*?" I whispered. That was bigger than a wedding. It was bigger than five weddings. "But..."

"Bring Percy if you'd like, or not if things don't work out." The smile dancing around her mouth suggested she didn't think that would be the case. "I have a lot of ground to make up where my son is concerned, but I'll start with this." She reached over with one finger and pushed up my chin, which had dropped open. "And Quinn? It's worth noting that I might not have *come here* to be impressed... but I am anyway." She straightened off the pillar with a sigh and resumed her usual intimidating mien. "You have a good night."

I stared at her in such absolute panicked shock that I didn't manage to whisper, "You too!" until the woman was halfway across the dance floor.

Dear. Sweet. Angel. Baby. Jesus.

Had that actually happened? Was this *real*?

I needed to tell Champ immediately—in fact, I was shocked he hadn't made a beeline for me when he saw me chatting with his mother—but for the first time all night, I couldn't see his blond head towering above the crowd.

When the strains of "Oh, What a Night" started, I waited for him to come and find me the way he had for the other two dances we'd danced together... but he didn't come. So I went searching.

I spotted Carter talking to a handsome man with

glasses and noticed Riggs wasn't with him. I moved in his direction. "Hey, sorry to interrupt, Carter. Have you seen Champ?"

Carter frowned and led me aside. "He left with Riggs and the others. Didn't he tell you?"

My breath caught—literally stuttered in my lungs like I'd forgotten how to inhale, of all ridiculous things. My arms began to tingle all the way down to my fingertips, and my stomach lurched like I was falling to Earth from a great height.

"No. He... no. Why did they leave? Was there an emergency?"

An asteroid headed toward the Thicket?

A random puddle of quicksand had appeared in the parking lot, and lives were on the line?

A litter of puppies needed good homes?

I wanted to hear something, *anything*, except...

"They're on the job," Carter confirmed. "So I guess it depends on what you consider an emergency." He leaned closer and lowered his voice. "Hux informed them of the obvious. There's no one at the farmhouse right now, so it seems the perfect night to do a more thorough search for the Horn."

Alarm bells replaced my disappointment again. "But there are advanced security systems in place out there," I hissed.

Carter studied me. "You know they're former Marine intelligence operatives, right? A farmhouse alarm system is nothing to them, especially with Hux doing his computer thing." He placed a hand on my arm comfortingly. "It'll be okay. They never fail a mission."

"Right." I nodded woodenly. "Of course they don't."

Because the mission always came first.

I gave Carter a half-smile and made a lame excuse, but as I walked away, I realized I should really have expected this. Hadn't everything with Champ been about the mission from the very beginning? He didn't have feelings for me. Fuck, no. He was sweet because he wanted my cooperation.

He was the motherfucking baby tiger Aunt Cherry had warned me about all those years ago, and I'd let myself get mauled.

I got the call from Hux while I was in the middle of the Spanish Inquisition with my mother. She'd already asked me twenty questions about Quinn, including how we'd met (certainly not a cheap pickup at a bar), what he did for a living (besides stealing people's T-shirts and dogs), and what my intentions were (to escape her clutches as soon as humanly possible).

"I have to admit to liking him more than I expected," she admitted in a softer voice. "He's obviously brilliant at his job. He appears quite dedicated."

Something about this statement got my back up. "He doesn't appear that way, he is that way. He genuinely cares about his clients."

"Hmm." She tapped one manicured finger to her lips. "You know, Percy, I do think Quinn suits you better than your last boyfriend did. Though I still think you could have tried harder with poor Vincent, of course."

I stared at her, wondering how I could possibly murder her for being oblivious to what had actually gone down between "poor" Vince and me. Thankfully, that's when my phone buzzed with Hux's call.

"I'm going to speak with Quinn," she decided. "Get to know him a bit better. See you later, darling."

The urge to follow her and protect Quinn from her machinations was strong, but I knew Hux would only be calling for something important. Besides, Quinn Taffet was a spitfire who could hold his own against any Nashville socialite, even my mother.

"Champion," I snapped after accepting the call.

"Did it occur to any of us that the target would be wide open for the taking tonight, boss?"

It took me a minute to understand what he was saying. My eyes jumped around the large event facility and landed on Marissa talking excitedly with Levi and Parrish Partridge, Tommy Drakes accepting a fresh cocktail from the cash bar, and his wife, Carlotta, holding court at one of the nearby tables full of society-type ladies I didn't recognize.

That left no one at the farmhouse except the perimeter guards, and they all knew me since I'd been living there. Hux could loop the camera feed inside the house and we'd be all set... as long as Tommy and Levi didn't walk in on us snooping and decide to take a closer look at the security tapes.

"Get over here and pick us up," I said before pulling my phone down to tap in a group text. How could I have missed this opportunity?

You were too busy drooling over a sexy man in a tux and trying to make sure his event went smoothly.

I bit back a curse and texted the team to meet out front. On my way out the door, I ran into Carter's cousin.

"Kev, can you do me a favor and find Quinn for

me? Tell him I had to go, but I'm leaving the key to my truck in the wheel well for him."

Kev's eyes widened when he saw Riggs and Elvo rush past me toward the door. "What's going on?"

"We have a lead on a situation and need to get out there right away. Can you please make sure Quinn gets the message?"

Kev nodded absently. His eyes moved past me to the open door, where Hux was waiting in the van.

"Thanks." I clapped a hand on his shoulder before following Riggs and Elvo.

"Carter's going to kill me," Riggs mumbled after Hux pulled away from the curb.

"Surely he understands the mission comes first." I yanked my bow tie off, unbuttoned the collar of my shirt, and removed my jacket.

There was silence for a beat before Riggs said, "I hate to tell you this, boss, but the mission absolutely does not come first for me anymore. Not by a long shot."

I turned to stare at him. "Excuse me?"

His face relaxed into his usual mischievous grin. "Just wait till you fall in love, Champ. There's life outside of work, believe it or not."

I frowned. "Of course there's life outside of work. I've never denied that."

For some reason, my brain unhelpfully flashed up an image of Quinn in his tux. Maybe if we made this quick, we'd finish in time for me to sneak back into the ball before it was over. I had plans tonight, and they involved removing that tuxedo from his body piece by piece.

"I'm just saying that accomplishing our mission is a lot more important—" I stopped.

I'd been about to say it was more important than Carter's feelings, but was that true? Our mission right then was to save a gaming software company from a public relations disaster. Hardly a life-and-death situation.

Back in the military, I'd trained myself to compartmentalize and put the mission first. Vince's bullshit had just reinforced that. But it had become so ingrained, I'd never stopped to consider the cost.

"Jordan confirms no movement on the security feeds, boss. They left the place wide open," Elvo confirmed.

I shook off my disordered thoughts. I didn't have time to consider the cost right then either because Horn of Glory was our biggest client, and I owed it to them — and to my team — to get us through this job successfully and safely.

"Good. Okay, we're going to do a full sweep of the basement. If we loop the security feeds, Yolanda won't be able to warn us if anyone's coming, so we all need to be on the alert. If any of the Drakes return early and find us there, I'll tell them I invited you back for a drink."

We spent the rest of the drive talking through details of how to get in and out of the place as quickly as possible. Time was running out to find this Horn. The wedding was in two weeks, but there would be rehearsals and welcome dinners beginning several days in advance. Once that happened, I'd no longer have the same access to Tommy Drakes's farm.

When we pulled up, I focused on the mission. We moved quickly through disarming all security measures and looping the camera feeds before making our way methodically through the house. This was the first time we'd been able to use additional tech in the search, so Hux and Elvo worked together to slide the borescope under locked closet doors and into locked drawers. Even Hercules seemed to understand the seriousness of the moment, because he scampered along after us but didn't bark or interfere.

As I suspected, we found nothing in the main areas of the house and soon found ourselves in Tommy Drakes's study in the basement.

"Why doesn't he have an office on the main floor?" Elvo asked, looking around at the unimpressive space. "This is… *Lord*." He noticed the garish framed poster of Tommy Drakes running down the beach in a Speedo.

"Can we focus, please?" I asked. "I managed to get into the closet, but there's nothing there."

Riggs ran his hands along the spines of the books in the built-in shelving unit along one wall. "I've never seen so many collectible handbooks in one place," he murmured. The books were interspersed with display cases holding various items of indeterminate value. Model cars, trains, and airplanes. Old wooden toys. Unique tobacco pipes and antique snuffboxes. It was a mishmash of stuff that screamed clutter to me but clearly meant something to Tommy Drakes.

It took my brain a minute to register footsteps in the hallway, but before I could alert the team, Kev came racing into the room, chest heaving and cheeks pink with exertion.

"Guys, *guys*!"

Riggs stared at him. "Kev, what the fuck? Why are you here?"

"They're coming back! Right after you left, I overheard that guy, the one from the commercial, say he had a headache and was going to head back to his farm. That's where we are, right?"

Elvo nodded. "Tommy Drakes. But fuck, Kev, how did you know where we were? And how'd you get here so fast?"

"Motorcycle."

The four of us stared at him, but it was Hux who asked the question. "You ride a motorcycle?"

Kev flapped his hand in the air like it was no big deal. He was still struggling to catch his breath. "Confederate B120 Wraith. Killer bike with kick-ass aesthetics. Kinda… steampunky?" He shrugged and leaned against the built-in, resting his elbows on the shelf behind him.

Hux blinked in disbelief. "*You* own a Wraith? That's a hundred-thousand-dollar bike."

Kev shrugged. When he shifted his weight, his elbow knocked over a pottery jar, which bumped into a metal puzzle toy and sent it skittering across the shelf. He turned with a sharp inhale and tried to set the items back to rights. In the clumsy attempt, he bumped a wooden bookend and sent two books tumbling to the floor.

"Oh God," he breathed, clearly panicking. We all lunged forward to help him just as he reached out to push the bookend closer to the remaining books. It didn't budge. In his confusion, he yanked it, which sent the entire shelving unit flying away from us…

Revealing an enormous hidden vault door that was, predictably, locked tight.

We all stood there and stared at it for a beat before Kev let out a whimper. "I didn't mean to."

Riggs squeezed his shoulder. "No, Kev. You did good. This is what we've been looking for. It has to be."

I snapped back into action and turned to Hux. "Quick, take video so we can get specs. Elvo, take still pics. Riggs, figure out how to get this shelf thing to close again. We have to get out of here before Drakes returns."

Hux muttered something about beginner's luck. Elvo shot a million photos. Hux took video footage, and Riggs finally discovered the opposite bookend was the key to getting the shelf closed again. We raced out to the van, forcing Hux headfirst into the cargo area when he paused to stare at Kev's killer bike for too long, and sped down the driveway after Kev as fast as we could.

We were only a hundred yards down the main road when we saw headlights approach and a blinker indicate someone was planning to turn into Drakes Farm.

"Fucking Christ," Riggs said on an exhale, sinking down further into the driver's seat.

"That was close," Elvo agreed.

"Take us to Champion Security," I said. "We need to figure out how to get into that safe."

Hux popped his head up from the back seat. "Who spends a hundred grand on a motorcycle?" he asked nobody in particular. "Does he have a death wish? That bike… that's the one everyone tries to get closer to get a picture of. People with that bike sell it because they fear for their fucking lives. He's *asking* to be hit by a damned car." He drew in a deep breath before muttering, "Fucking idiot."

"Dude," Elvo said, craning his neck to get a look even though it was too dark to see the motorcycle. "That shit is sex on wheels. Admit it."

"Mpfh," Hux grunted.

Elvo sucked his front tooth. "Whatever. I'd let him

take me for a ride, just sayin'." I could practically hear his eyebrows waggle.

"Hey." Hux shoved his shoulder. "No. Just... *no*. We don't do sexy-talk about Kev the Civilian, understand. He's practically Riggs's little brother."

Riggs shrugged, completely unconcerned. "I'm going to see if Kev'll let me take it out. I knew he had something in his second garage bay, but it's separate from mine."

Elvo thumped Riggs in the shoulder. "Are you even listening to yourself? You're talking about your new Richie Rich life now like it's no big deal that you each have multiple separate garages at your *estate*."

"It's not my estate. It's Carter's. And his grandfather purchased it for him as a gift."

Elvo cackled. Riggs defending the mansion he lived in always cracked Elvo up. "Poor baby. And you're forced to live there."

"We do share it with others," Riggs reminded him. "It's not just the two of us."

Elvo laughed even louder. "Kev lives in the basement, and the servants live in the guest house. Jesus, Riggsy. Listen to yourself."

Riggs turned to me, and I knew before he even said it what was going to come out of his mouth. I shot him a look, but he mouthed off anyway.

"Why don't you give Champ a hard time if you're going to piss on rich people? He's from obscene money."

Before I could remind him that I'd sunk most of my money into our business and my money pit of a house, Hux interrupted. "Wait, so you're saying Kev's grandfather bought him the bike?" He laughed scornfully. "Fucking figures. I need me a rich granddaddy."

Riggs laughed. "Uh, no. Their grandfather's old money. He invests in houses, not motorcycles. Not to mention, he'd probably have a heart attack if he saw that bike. He's the protective sort, you know? Especially about Kev."

Hux scowled. "So you're saying he bought it himself? How?"

"Kev made his own money from selling some kind of patents or something." Riggs shrugged. "I'm not really sure. He keeps that shit close to the vest."

Somehow, this seemed to make Hux even more pissed off.

I tried ignoring them so I could focus on the work we still needed to do tonight. Finding the vault was a huge step in the right direction, but that was half the battle. Now we needed to figure out a way to get inside it without alerting Tommy so that Quinn wouldn't fall under any suspicion.

As if I'd summoned him, my phone vibrated with a text, and I pulled it out to see Quinn's name on the screen.

My attention scattered again when I read the message.

Quinn (Gorgeous, blue eyes, drinks Howling Turtles): *FYI, you're an asshole.*

I ground my back teeth together to keep from biting out a curse.

Me: *I'm sorry I had to leave. We had to take advantage of an opportunity. I knew you'd understand.*

He knew how important my work was. How important Champion Security was. How important keeping the business afloat so I could take care of my team was.

Quinn (Gorgeous, blue eyes, drinks Howling Turtles): *Oh, I understand the mission comes first. Hopefully* *it'll keep you warm in bed tonight because I sure as fuck won't.*

My stomach pitched. Quinn was obviously pissed, but was it annoyance that I'd left early, or had I really hurt him?

I felt out of my depth, and I hated that.

Riggs yanked open the van door. "Alright, people. The faster we get this done, the faster we can get back to our lives."

I clenched my phone tighter.

I wasn't sure whether I *had* anything to get back to after I was done tonight. And for the first time in a while, I felt a tiny kernel of doubt, like I'd made the wrong call somewhere along the line.

"Champ?" Hux stuck his head back into the van. "You coming, or what?"

I took one last look at my phone before putting it to sleep and sliding it back into my pocket.

My doubts would have to wait. It was time to work.

15

QUINN

It wasn't easy keeping my pageant smile on while seething inside, but I was used to it. Event planners had to make it seem like things were perfectly wonderful even when the world turned to shit.

Thankfully, things were going just fine tonight — as long as you ignored the large crater in my chest, *which I was very much attempting to do* — so I'd managed to go through the motions of doing my job and making polite chitchat without anyone noticing that my heart wasn't in it.

During a quiet moment, I'd even taken a call from one of my favorite repeat brides, Posy, who was planning her fourth attempt at "forever" and was just as freaked-out as she'd been during the first.

"I can't have the apricot Juliet roses I wanted, Quinn, because Tarquin's mother looks hideous in apricot. But since everyone knows apricot Juliet roses are the only flower worth having, that means I simply cannot have *any* flora whatsoever, which leaves… *fauna.* I've decided I'll carry a whole bouquet of emu feathers

—from coral-colored emus dyed specifically to match my bridesmaid dresses, of course! Do you think if I pay extra, they can dye the *whole* emu? Because I was thinking... you know how some people release doves?"

For one heart-stopping moment, I envisioned a scenario where Posy released a flock of pissed-off coral emu into a crowd of socialites and the unholy carnage that would follow.

The vision was hella distracting, and while I gently redirected her to some non-emu-based options, I didn't think about Champ or racing out to Drakes Farm to confront the bastard about reneging on his promise at all.

Sadly, that only lasted four minutes.

I knew the best way to get over my anger and disappointment was to focus on work, as I'd done in the past. That should have been easy because Taffet Events was having a phenomenal night. Bunny, despite being utterly *blind* when it came to spotting a real relationship, was a beast when it came to sales, and she'd spent the last few hours of the SnoBall on some kind of campaign to drum up business for me. By the time the band played the last song, I'd been approached half a dozen times with inquiries about planning various events in and around the Thicket, as well as two more potential weddings in Nashville.

For the first time in my entire career, I had so many leads, I could pick and choose which events I most wanted to handle. It was a dream come true. The culmination of a ton of hard work. A moment I wanted to hold close and revel in... but it turned out that was really hard to do when the person you most wanted to revel with wasn't around to celebrate because the mission had to come first.

Logically, I knew Champ was making the smart choice. The choice I would have made even a few months ago. But I hadn't been acting smart for a long time where Champ was concerned, and it was a little humiliating to know that I was the only one.

As the caterers began cleaning up and the band put away their instruments, I said goodbye to the last few straggling guests.

"Quinn, you've gotta come to the Tavern with us for the after-party!" a slightly-tipsy Ava insisted. Her pretty blonde hair had tumbled from its updo, and she carried her strappy red shoes in her hand. "We want to toast you and your hard work!"

"Aw. That sounds like fun," I agreed half-heartedly. "But rain check, okay? I'm tired, and—"

"And your date's a dumbass, right?" she concluded. She took a step toward me and slung a slender arm around my shoulders. "I saw him duck out earlier with Kev and a couple of his guys." She rolled her eyes. "Which is it, a work issue, or are they headed for the bar?"

"I, uh…" I had no idea how to respond to that. I couldn't believe she'd noticed Champ and the others leave. When she was done running the Beautification Corps, I was pretty sure she could have a second career as an international spy.

"Either way, this was your special night, and he's been a *dick*. So come out with us and have a few drinks. We'll get you hopped up on moonshine and righteous indignation, and then you can go home and get all up in his grill. You'll feel better."

"Oh, *hayel* no. I'm not going anywhere near Champ's grill," I assured her. "And he's not getting up in mine either. That's what started this bullshit."

"Quinn." Ava tilted her head like I was the one being silly. "I meant *talk* to him. Don't be afraid to lay on the volume if you need to. Tell him *exactly* how you feel. It'll make you feel better and give him a chance to make it right."

I shook my head. "That's not how it works for us. We're not…" I lowered my voice. "We're not in a relationship. We just have sex. And sort of live together. And work together temporarily." I hesitated. "And occasionally have meals and deep conversations with one another. And casually, unofficially share custody of his dog."

"Oh." Ava nodded slowly. "Yeah, no, I can see how that's… a very different thing." She pursed her lips thoughtfully. "I still say, though, you need to have it out. Make up a list of the things you want to say. Write it all down so you can be cogent and clear. Then when you read it to him, erupt like an emotional volcano and bury him in lava."

"Bury him in—"

"Come to the bar and I'll help you! Oooh, and so will my friend Mal. He's the *best* at relationship lava."

"That's so sweet, but—" I broke off, unsure how to say "your friend sounds insane" in a positive way.

Fortunately, I was saved from having to explain at all, because my phone buzzed in my pocket.

"I've gotta get this. Probably another bridal emergency. You go on ahead," I told Ava, squeezing her hand in thanks. "I'll try to catch up."

We both knew I wouldn't.

"Fine, fine," she grumbled. "Just remember you've got friends who have your back. And if you change your mind, come find me."

As she turned away, I hesitated. Part of me wanted

nothing more than to leave with her and drown my sorrows. Another part wanted me to do exactly what she'd advised and give Champ a piece of my mind. But I knew neither of those options would make things better.

My phone continued ringing, and I finally dug it out of my pocket impatiently, ready to deal with another non-emergency emergency. When I saw who was calling, I stared at the screen, wondering if I was losing my mind.

"Aunt Cherry?" I answered, half expecting it to be a hallucination. "Did I summon you?"

Her warm, familiar laugh helped me let go of some of my tension. "You sure as hell did, indirectly at least. I must've gotten pinged by the Thicket grapevine a hundred times tonight, young man. Supposedly my nephew has landed himself a devoted, wealthy hunk of a man and is rumored to be soon planning his own Taffet wedding extravaganza! Why am I the last to know?"

The very idea of me and Champ married was so ridiculous, I barked out a laugh that bounced off the walls of the nearly empty space and startled the cleaning crew. I walked out the front entrance and down around the side of the building to get a little privacy.

The February night was freezing cold but clear, and the happy little white lights twinkled in the light breeze. I took in a deep breath of fresh air and let it out in a cloud of frosty white.

"First of all, tell me you're someplace warm and sunny," I said, deliberately ignoring the Thicket gossip.

"Sure am. We're in Florida."

I nodded politely to a young couple still lingering in

the parking lot. "Still? You and Mrs. Ambrose must really love it there."

"Actually... Marianne decided to stay in Baton Rouge permanently because her daughter-in-law's expecting twins. So it's just Terrance and me now."

"Terrance? Wait, the same guy you mentioned to me..." I counted on my fingers, then gasped in horror. "*Three weeks ago?*"

Cherry hesitated just a moment, but it was enough to warn me what was coming. "Yes, dear. We're... well, I guess you could say we're a thing."

"A thing?" I said a little more screechy than I'd intended. "What kind of thing? A friends-with-benefits thing? A help-me-drive-this-big-RV thing?"

"No, honey," she said patiently. "He's helping me drive a big something, but it's not—"

"Oh, God." I gagged. "*Spare me the details.*" My whole world seemed to tilt on its axis.

"It's a pickup truck," she finished with a chuckle. "Mind out of the gutter, Quinn. We're staying with some friends of his in St. Pete. It's beautiful here. I wish you could see it."

"And this guy... Terrance... he's... you're... Is it *serious?*"

"Very," she said almost shyly. "In fact, I'd kind of like for you to meet him when we head north this summer."

I didn't want to meet her Terrance. In fact, I didn't want to even acknowledge his existence during a phone conversation. "I don't understand," I muttered. "You don't believe in relationships."

"I didn't, it's true, because I'd never had one that worked out. It's a little like trying to convince someone that the ocean exists when they've only ever seen puddles." She sighed dreamily. "But the moment Terrance and I met, I knew he was different. We just... clicked. And I saw how wrong I'd been. He's my ocean."

I pulled the phone away from my ear to check that the caller ID was, in fact, showing the phone number of the sarcastic, pragmatic woman who'd been my role model all these years, because this poetry-spouting person sounded like a total stranger.

Someone had been force-feeding her Kool-Aid.

"Cherry. Cherry, listen to me," I whispered urgently. "He's not your ocean, okay? The ocean isn't real." I paused. "I mean, *oceans* are real, but Terrance isn't one. He's a baby tiger masquerading as an ocean! He's luring you in, making you think that there's the potential for more than sex and that he sees you as a teammate, but the second—and I mean, the fucking hot *second*—you lose your mind and start thinking relationships are a thing that could happen for you, he's gonna pounce and rip your heart out."

"Quinn, my sweetheart." Cherry sounded amused. "Have you been drinking?"

"What? No." I waved a hand impatiently. "I'm trying to tell you—"

"What I'd like you to tell me is why Cindy Ann Johnson, Bernadette Faulkner, and Bunny freakin' Champion all texted me tonight that you're in *love*!" she teased.

"I couldn't possibly say," I replied stiffly. "Percy Champion is the man I told you about weeks ago. The one I've been sleeping with. It's *not* a romance. He doesn't believe in relationships." I straightened my spine. "And neither do I."

"Really? Because these ladies sent photographic

evidence of you two dancing earlier, sweetheart, and the way you're looking at each other seems pretty serious… and pretty special."

"Well, it isn't," I insisted desperately. I needed this false hope like a hole in the head, especially after everything that went down earlier. "It's a one-night stand that got out of hand. And I really, really need people to stop trying to convince me it's something it's not. I needed a date, he was available. *I do not have feelings for Percy Champion!* And Percy Champion definitely, *definitely* does not have feelings for me."

I stood there for a long moment, letting the winter air freeze my balls off, struggling to control my breathing. It wasn't until my cheeks went numb that I realized my eyes had started tearing up.

Fuck. I never cried. What the heck was wrong with me tonight?

Cherry finally broke the silence. "Quinn." Her voice was filled with regret. "I—"

"I've gotta go," I said quickly. "Busy. Working. I'll call you soon, okay? Love you!"

I ended the call without waiting for her to say goodbye.

My hands were shaking in a way that had nothing to do with the cold as I stalked to the parking lot.

I was *livid.* So incandescent with anger, astronauts could probably see from outer space.

How the fuck had this happened?

How had I gotten to this place, where people thrust evidence of *feelings* and *relationships* in my face, and tried to tell me it was perfectly sane to throw your heart in a relationship meat grinder if the man you were dating was your *ocean?*

How dare Cherry say Champ looked at me like I

was *special* when the motherfucker had ditched me without a word, which was not a thing you did to a special person?

I had no clue how I'd gone so spectacularly wrong, but I knew exactly which gorgeous, bossy asshole to blame for it…

And I knew how to make it right.

I punched a number into my phone. "Ava? Yeah, I changed my mind. Save me a seat, okay? I'm on my way."

16

CHAMP

When we got to the office, I was determined to get the information we needed about the vault and make a plan to infiltrate it as quickly as possible so I could return to Quinn at the farm and beg his forgiveness.

I had no desire to go home to my half-broken house and sleep alone in a cold bed. The thought that Quinn was angry at me didn't sit well in my gut, and the idea that I'd hurt him made me feel even worse. I needed to explain myself and make him understand.

Our motley crew settled in at the conference table in the war room with our laptops, Riggs and I still wearing the remnants of our tuxedos. Elvo had ducked into the bathroom and changed into a spare set of sweats he kept at the office for working out. Jordan had already been here monitoring our surveillance feeds and had the coffee brewed and ready.

"Faucet's busted again, boss," they said cheerfully when they emerged. "Call the plumber back."

I grit my teeth. Owning Champion Security meant that the buck stopped with me, *always*, whether it meant working long hours or taking care of the stupid faucet these animals kept jacking up. But fuck if I didn't sometimes get tired of having to handle everything myself, even down to the sinks and faucets.

"I'm not paying that plumber to come back again. Elvo, I'm sending you the contact info for my contractor right now. Ask him to come in here ASAP and check it out."

He nodded. "Your contractor knows his shit?"

"Fuck no. He's terrible. But he's still better than whoever Herman hired. Huxley, where are we with the specs on the vault door?"

Hux was able to determine the make and model of the door fairly quickly, but that was the easy part; cracking the lock was going to be nearly impossible.

We'd actually broken into a vault very similar to this on a mission while still on active duty, but in that case, we'd been allowed to drill into it because we'd be long gone before the owner discovered the breach. That wouldn't be possible this time.

We had to find a way to get in there, remove the Horn's data, and get out without leaving evidence of the break-in, otherwise, Tommy Drakes would have a pretty good idea of who caused the problem. He wouldn't be able to legally prove it was us, so I wasn't worried about the fallout for my team, but he might take revenge by blacklisting Quinn, and no matter what Quinn thought of me, keeping him safe was a promise I would not break.

Elvo put out feelers to a couple of guys we'd known back in the day who'd gotten into slightly less-legal stuff after leaving the service. Riggs and Jordan worked their contacts to get us the exact same model of vault door delivered ASAP so we could run some simulations, even as Hux got busy enhancing photos, trying to nail down whether Tommy's unit had any redundancies we needed to factor in.

Two hours into our research, Riggs cracked.

"Boss." He leaned over in his chair and spoke softly enough that no one else could hear. "It's Saturday night. We've gotten as far as we can on this for now—"

He broke off when the front door opened and someone strode into the lobby.

"Which one of you failed to lock the fucking door?" I demanded.

"Pretty sure that was *you*, Champ," Elvo remarked.

Shit. I had a strong suspicion he was right. I was losing my mind, now, on top of everything.

Great.

"It's probably Kev," Hux muttered, assuming the guy had decided to join us again. "I'll deal with this."

But when the angry, tuxedo-clad man came storming into the back room, it wasn't Carter's cousin.

All heads swiveled to watch Quinn Taffet as he stalked through the empty mosh pit with fire in his eyes. No one said a word. Hux's fingers went silent on his keys.

The man was ten kinds of gorgeous, three sheets to the wind, and utterly focused on me—in other words, as irresistible as gravity—and no force on Earth could have prevented me from rising from my chair and throwing myself at his feet…

"Fuck you, Percival Champion," Quinn spat with a hitch in his voice. "Fuck you so fucking hard."

No force except that one, because when the weight of Quinn's rage hit me square in the chest, it kept me rooted to my seat, staring up at him.

His cheeks were bright red, and his eyes shone just

like they had that first night back in November, but his whole being radiated misery and anger.

"Quinn," I began, but he held up a hand to cut me off.

"This is not *your* speaky time, Percival. You could have spoken to me earlier, but you didn't. You left without saying a word." He swallowed hard. "So now you can listen."

I wanted to argue, to tell him that I'd asked Kev to pass him the message and Kev had gotten distracted, but my excuses sounded lame to my own ears.

I could have made the time to tell Quinn, but I hadn't. Because deep down, I'd known he'd be disappointed.

Quinn removed what looked like a bar napkin from his pocket. The thing was covered in tiny blue scribbles that crisscrossed the tissue in both directions like ancient hieroglyphics. He squinted down at it.

"Fuck you, Percival Champion! Fuck you so fucking hard." He paused. "Wait, sorry, I said that part. *Ahem.* You're an asshole, and I'm so angry with you I could shit... *spit.* I mean spit." Quinn glanced up. "Ava's writing is really fucking loopy."

I kept myself from blurting out how beautiful he was because I valued my life, and he was clearly on a roll.

He brought the napkin closer to his face, took a deep breath, and cleared his throat. "Champ, the whole time I've known you, I've tried to give you the benefit of the doubt. You lied to me, I forgave you. You used me, I went along with it. You talked to me about teamwork and trust, I believed you. You *made me* believe you. You fooled me into believing that our... our... *non-*

relationship... was something important. And special. And I fell for it."

My stomach pitched and swayed like a boat in chop.

"But when someone is your teammate—" He paused long enough to hiccup. "You don't leave them with no explanation like you did tonight. When someone is special, you don't *break oaths* to them like you did tonight. And I know we're not anything real—not dating, sure as fuck not engaged—but I'm a person, Champ. A human being. And I deserve better." He sniffed and swayed slightly, catching himself on the back of Jordan's chair. "So I came here tonight to bring you your dog—"

I glanced behind him but didn't see Herc anywhere.

He flipped the napkin over, squinted again to bring the writing into focus, and began reading from the other side. "—but now I have realized that Hercules also deserves better. He deserves someone who remembers he exists and doesn't treat him like an unwanted reminder of a dream that didn't come true."

I sucked in a breath. *Direct fucking hit.* Under other circumstances, I would have applauded. As it was, all I could do was stare at the drunk avenging angel in front of me and pity every person who'd ever underestimated him.

Including me.

"So Herc's mine now." He looked up at me with a drunken glare as if emphasizing the point. "A-and you'll just have to accept that. And, in addition," Quinn continued after another hiccup, "your mother is way cooler than you are, and I know she's probably not perfect, but neither are you, and she's just trying to love you in her own flawed way, and you don't deserve her either, so I'm keeping her too. And the prosecution rests."

The team sat frozen in shock around us. I was sure they'd never seen me get my ass chewed out by anyone before.

Quinn crumpled up his napkin and stuffed it back in his jacket pocket before looking up at me again.

He didn't move his head, but I saw his eyes suddenly jerk around the room to note the audience we had. He stood a little taller and puffed out his chest defiantly.

"So. Okay, then. That's all I came here to say." He nodded once, firmly. "Ava and her friend are waiting to drive me home. *Alone*. Without any lava! Because I sure as shit don't need lava. Even though it's really hot. Also? Goodbye."

He turned on his heel and stormed out. I stupidly stared after him.

"Oh my God," someone whispered.

"Champ has a boyfriend," someone else added.

"A boyfriend who's fierce as *fuck*," Jordan breathed.

"But he's sure as shit in the doghouse," another chimed in.

I turned to glare at them. "Do you mind?"

Riggs came closer and clasped my shoulder before meeting my eye. His brows were furrowed in concern. "No offense, boss, but you fucked that up pretty big time."

"No one asked you," I hissed.

Elvo stood up and moved closer. "Riggsy's right. What the fuck did you do, man?"

"Nothing. I… I maybe told him earlier tonight that I'd be there for the date dance, but then Hux called about the farmhouse being empty, and plans had to change."

"You broke your promise," Jordan said flatly. "Not cool."

Riggs held up a placating hand. "Not ideal, but sometimes it happens," Riggs said. "What did Quinn say when you told him you had to leave? Was he this angry even then?"

"I didn't… You know what? Fuck this. We have stuff to do—" I shifted my weight to stand, but Riggs set a hand on my shoulder to keep me in place.

"You didn't what?"

I shut my eyes briefly. "I didn't tell him, okay? I… We were in a hurry. I asked Kev to relay the message, but I guess he didn't because he overheard Tommy leaving. We don't need to talk about this right now," I gritted out through tight lips.

Hux sighed. "Oh yes we do. You need to fix this."

I ran my hands through my hair. "There's nothing to fix. It's not a big deal. For some reason, this guy's got me all twisted up, but it's not a big deal. I'll let him cool down, and I'll get my dog back, and then… it's not a big deal."

Riggs's lip turned up slightly. "You're repeating yourself."

I glared at him. "It's not a big deal," I said again, feeling acid in my throat.

Elvo nodded. "No, no, I get it. You're saying *Quinn's* not a big deal. That makes sense. I mean, who even is Quinn? Some silly wedding planner? No one, really."

I had him up against the wall with my hand around his throat before I even realized I was moving. "Get his fucking name out of your goddamned mouth," I growled in his face.

Elvo simply grinned like a fool. "Really? I thought he wasn't a big deal. Pretty sure that was the phrase you used."

"Several times," Jordan agreed.

Riggs was smiling just as big. "Hoo-boy. This is gonna be fun. The boss is whipped. I knew it. Didn't I call it?"

Hux groaned. "Riggs is going to be insufferable."

I let go of Elvo and clenched my hands into fists to keep from shoving him. Or worse. "Can we get back to work? Tiny matter of a fucking *vault* to break into."

Riggs stepped closer and grabbed my upper arms. "Boss. For real, though. This is good news. You deserve to have someone twisting you all up. It's about time. I fucking hated Vince, and you know that's the truth."

Elvo nodded. "Douche."

"Besides, take it from someone who never thought he was gonna get involved with anyone," Riggs said. "When shit on the job goes south, it's good to know you have someone who's there for *you*, not for the mission."

"I don't have time for distractions right now," I reminded him.

"Love is not a distraction." Riggs tilted his head aggressively. "It's the *point*. You and Quinn are stronger as a team, ever think of that?"

I had, more than once. But I was afraid to let myself believe it for real.

Hux tapped his chin. "Hey, does Quinn know what you did to his ex? Because if you need a way to get back in Quinn's good graces—"

I shot him a look.

"Fine, fine, shutting up now." Hux mimed zipping his lips. Then he unzipped them a fraction of a second later. "Except, just to say, you should probably loop

Quinn in before he hears it somewhere else." He zipped back up.

"Sorting out my... my *dating life* is not getting me into that fucking vault," I reminded them all.

I was barely keeping a handle on my temper, and I needed to get us focused back on the job before I went racing out after Quinn with my tail between my legs.

Riggs took his seat again. "Boss, I already told you, there's not much more to do right now. We can handle this ourselves while you go tell Quinn —"

"Jesus Christ, Riggs, find your balls and reattach them! *The mission comes first*," I snapped, hating the words even as I said them. "How many times do I have to tell you that?"

The teasing grin fell from Riggs's face and was replaced by a stone-cold stare. "How many times do *I* have to tell *you* that it really fucking doesn't? Respect-fully, sir, my partner comes first. Always. He happens to be a really patient person—thank fuck—which is why I'm still here at this hour on a Saturday night. Because if it came down to him or this job? Well, I love you all like my own brothers, and I'd miss working with you a *lot*, but there are a million clients out there, a million ways to serve. There is only *one* Carter Rogers. Only *one* man that I love." He narrowed his eyes and leaned closer to me. "Also, my balls have nothing to do with this job, so let me tell you where you can stow *that* toxic bullshit."

Jordan clapped silently.

"Don't you ever forget that the job won't love you back," Riggs said more quietly. "Keep putting the mission above the person you care about and you'll end up just like douchebag Vince. I'm sure the DEA isn't keeping him warm at night."

Before I could tell Riggs to shut the fuck up, he turned back to his computer and woke it up with an aggressive click of his mouse.

Hux didn't turn around to stare, but Jordan did. When they opened their mouth to share their own stupid wisdom, I shut them down. "Where is my fucking vault, Jordan? Not a word out of you until it's *here*. Understood?"

They sighed and nodded before settling back at their own workstation. Before long, the only sound in the room was the clicking of keys on keyboards and the silent screams of my gut begging me to go out to the farm as soon as possible to check on Quinn.

Riggs's final comment about Vince replayed in my head, reminding me that Vince had, in fact, chosen work over our relationship. And it had hurt like a bitch.

It's not the same at all because Quinn and I aren't in a relationship.

I remembered the look of betrayal and hurt on Quinn's face when he'd stormed in here tonight, the roil in my gut when I felt the wrongness of my actions, the recent realization I slept more soundly when tangled up with him in the same bed, the red-hot anger I'd felt when Trey fucking Dunwoody had come on to him in the back room of his shop.

We weren't in a relationship. We were simply forty-five days into the hottest, sweetest, most fulfilling one-night stand I'd ever known.

Which was why, when I finally made my way back to the farmhouse and found Quinn's bedroom door locked, I felt both like beating the hell out of myself for stupidly developing feelings for the man… and crying myself to sleep because I'd fucked it all up.

17

QUINN

I deliberately put earplugs in after getting home from the SnoBall so I wouldn't know whether or not Champ came knocking that night.

Okay, no, let's be honest—I put them in because I knew if I heard him knock, I'd cave. Angry as I was at him, I still wanted him in my bed. I still craved his arms around me and his gruff voice in my ear.

Fucking asshole.

Ava had solemnly promised me that venting my feelings would make me feel better, but she'd lied. After leaving Champ's office the night before, I'd felt nothing but mortified, drunk, and heartsick, and I'd lain awake for hours.

But after sleeping like crap, I woke up this morning determined to put Percival Champion behind me and focus on the wedding. Thanks to Bunny—who I really owed a lunch, or a dinner, or my firstborn child out of sheer gratitude—I'd landed a bucketful of potential new event clients, and Anita Shelton had already texted to ask if I could meet this morning at my office before she and her mom went back to Nashville.

My new mantra was *The Mission Comes First*, and I was beginning to embrace the concept. I'd actually enjoyed myself at the ball last night. Making my home permanently here in Licking Thicket was an attractive option. The people were friendly, the area was beautiful, the price was definitely right, and I could still have plenty of Nashville clients, which felt a lot like having my cake and eating it too.

After showering and dressing for the day, I stepped out of my room and almost body-slammed Levi sneaking out of Marissa's room right across from mine. He wore pajama pants and an old Christianson Protective Services T-shirt.

"Good… morning?" I asked, wondering what the hell he was doing on this level of the house when his bedroom was on the main floor.

Levi's face turned beet red, and he stammered out an excuse. "She… ah… she, um. Headache powder!"

I blinked at him. Headache powder? Were we back in the 1800s suddenly?

"Rissy had a lot to drink last night," he continued. "So I brought her a headache powder for her hangover. My granny's special trick."

"Hmm. Where's Trey?" I asked, crossing my arms in front of my chest as if I was a truant officer.

Levi's jaw tightened, and a flash of anger crossed his face. "The asshole never showed. She cried the whole way home."

"What the fuck? After promising to bring his dad's classic car and everything? What was his problem?"

Now Levi was the one crossing his arms. "First, he called and said he had an important work thing, so he was running really late. Fine. Then, when the dance was over, Riss called him to make sure he was okay, and the asshole was home asleep. I don't believe he had a work thing at all."

Neither did I, but I wasn't about to throw a wrench in the works of my largest wedding client right now.

"It's more important whether Marissa believed him," I suggested, raising my eyebrows.

Levi mumbled something under his breath and moved past me to the stairs. I followed him down, shooting daggers into his back with my eyes until he turned toward his bedroom, hopefully to shower, dress, and forget all about his childhood ladylove. This thing between Marissa and Levi was a problem that did not seem to be going away.

I walked into the kitchen, expecting it to be empty at this time on a Sunday, but Champ was already there, sitting at the long wooden table, nursing a cup of coffee.

Speaking of problems that weren't going away…

Fuck. Well, I had to deal with him sometime, right?

"Quinn—" Champ's voice was gravel-rough like he'd had as bad a night as I had, and my knees went weak.

"Busy! Breakfast time!" I called, and then I detoured hard left, into the walk-in pantry closet.

Yes, I had to deal with him sometime, but not right then.

Unsurprisingly, the sound of Champ's familiar footsteps followed me into the small space. I bit out a curse under my breath when he closed the door behind him.

"I don't want to talk about it," I snapped, not taking my eyes off the canned tomatoes. They needed attention. What, with their… labels and… whatever.

His big body pressed against mine, pushing my

chest into the edge of the shelves. "Good. I don't want to talk either." The low, sleepy rasp of his voice brought goose bumps up all over my skin. I closed my eyes and clenched my teeth.

I was strong enough to resist this man.

His hand moved around and slid under my shirt to the bare skin of my belly before moving down into my pants.

Okay, no, I was not strong enough to resist this man.

"We're—" My voice cracked, and I cleared my throat. "We're not doing this. We're done. Over. We're... mad at each other."

Way to go, big boy. You told him.

"Mmm. More like mad *about* you."

He didn't stop moving his hands across my skin. His big, strong, warm hands, hands that had spent hours bringing me pleasure. My mind was a highlight reel of memories of that pleasure, enough to make my heart thunder and my lungs desperate for more oxygen.

I needed to elbow him in the gut. Turn around and shove him off me. Tell him how angry I was. And I was going to. In just a minute.

"No, see..." I began weakly before sucking in a breath when his finger grazed my cock. *"Oh God."*

I tried to remember how I'd felt the night before. The pit in my stomach, the hole in my chest, how flat and joyless everything had seemed when he'd left me behind... but it was impossible to remember any of that when the ridge of his cock was lined up perfectly with the cleft of my ass, promising me so much pleasure.

And I deserved pleasure, dammit. Just because he was an unfeeling ass didn't mean I couldn't use him for my own sexual release. An orgasm would be just the thing to knock my headache out and loosen my limbs.

I would use him for sex. Just this once. Because of… medical reasons, really.

"I'm sorry," he murmured against the back of my ear. "About leaving you last night. You were right—you deserve so much better than that."

One of his knees slid between my legs and nudged them apart. His thumb flicked the button open on my pants before strumming down my shaft over the cotton of my underwear.

"I do," I breathed. "I really do."

"You deserve to be treated well," he said before grasping the shell of my ear between his lips. "*Pleasured* well."

I braced my hands against the shelf in front of me to keep from impaling myself on it. "Yes."

Champ's hand reached inside my boxer briefs and grasped my dick, squeezing just the right amount before moving his hand down to fondle my balls.

"Fucking Christ," I groaned. "Why… you… and the talking. Not good."

His mouth moved against my ear, and his voice was low enough to vibrate in my stomach. "No talking this time, sweetheart. Someone might hear."

My stomach rolled over deliciously at the sound of an honest-to-God real endearment out of his mouth.

I vaguely recollected that the house would be full of people this morning. Tommy and Carlotta had stayed overnight. Marissa and Levi. Presumably, Trey would show up at some point this morning to offer his apologies.

We couldn't have sex in the damned pantry.

My pants and underwear hit the floor while

Champ's mouth continued moving down the side of my face to my neck with open-mouthed kisses after pressing a finger into my mouth to get it wet.

"Oh God," I groaned again when the spit-slick finger reached my hole. I stood up on tiptoes before relaxing down against it and letting him in. "Oh fuck."

"That's it. But I need you to be quiet." His voice was mesmerizing.

"Uh-huh." I nodded and closed my eyes, dropping my chin to my chest when his finger pressed in deeper. The small space was getting uncomfortably warm. "More."

His free hand came up to cover my mouth in a tight grip. The feel of him silencing me was so hot, I felt my dick jerk.

"Shhh," he warned against my bare shoulder. When had he pulled off my shirt? I stood almost completely naked in Tommy Drakes's kitchen pantry.

During breakfast time.

A whine escaped my throat only to be muffled by his hand.

"Want to get inside you," he said under his breath, almost as if he was talking to himself. "Please."

I nodded against his hand, trying not to feel as desperate for him as I clearly was. Champ fumbled behind him before letting out a curse. "No wallet, no condom. *Fuck.*"

I let out another whimper and slumped back against him. His hand moved up to hold the front of my throat as his voice stayed low and warm in my gut. "Stay here while I go—"

"No," I blurted. "It's okay. It's… you can… we don't need…"

The tension between us vibrated with unspoken words. "We've never talked about going bare."

I let out a breath and reached behind me to hold the back of his head. "I've never... Not with anyone." I would have gone bare with Scott, but he'd been squeamish about the mess, which I'd later been grateful for. "Can we? Please? I haven't... I mean, I've tested since..." I cleared my throat. "It's only been you for a while now."

The hand on my throat tightened almost imperceptibly while his thumb grazed up under my jaw to angle my head. His lips moved to mine. "Same. It's only you."

We kissed, an intense moment unintentionally dividing our time together in two, before and after. Going bare together meant we could no longer pretend it was simply a months-long one-night stand, no matter how much I was fooling myself into thinking this was over.

His free hand moved to the shelf in front of me and grabbed a slender green bottle of olive oil. Within moments, his oil-slick fingers invaded me. I sucked in a breath and arched back, begging for more. It was quick and dirty, debauched and risky in so many ways.

We both knew someone could walk in at any moment. Tommy Drakes, father of the bride and suspected small-time criminal. Carlotta Drakes, society maven and gossip queen. Marissa Drakes, sweet, trusting client who deserved my professionalism. Levi, who was in charge of keeping the farmhouse free of bullshit like this. Possibly Trey Dunwoody, the sexually confused groom who would no doubt get his rocks off watching Champ's bare butt flexing as he drove his cock into me.

I should have cared deeply.

I didn't.

I begged him for more. Begged him to pound into me harder. I whimpered stupid truths about wanting him never to leave me again. All the while, my conscience pleaded for us to stop.

"Someone will hear us," I warned in a breathy voice.

"Let them," he growled.

"What if they… *oh fuck, just like that…* what if they walk in here?"

Champ smelled like sweat as he pressed even closer to me. "Then they'll see me fucking you against this wall."

"They'll fire us," I whimpered, clutching at his hip to make sure he didn't actually listen, to make sure he didn't actually pull out of me. "They'll make us go."

"Not. Until. I'm. Done." His voice was a hiss in my ear, his strong thrusting changed to slow undulations that punctuated each word and brushed past my gland with every stroke. "Listen to me, Quinn Taffet. I'm not leaving this body for anything. Do you understand? Not for anything."

I vaguely heard people moving around in the kitchen on the other side of the wall. Marissa's cheerful voice and Tommy's deeper one, but I let myself float away in a lust-filled haze. I trusted Champ to take care of us, of *me*. I knew nothing bad could happen to me while in his care and in his arms.

"Well, good God, would you look at that?"

Tommy Drakes's voice seemed to be only inches away, and my eyes flew open. Champ's hand tightened over my mouth.

"What is it, Daddy?"

"You remember that wedding planner you were

thinking of using initially, baby girl? Look at this article in the paper. Seems like Trey did us a favor by finding us Quinn."

"It's the only one he's done," Levi muttered.

"Where is Quinn this morning?" Marissa wondered. "I stopped by his room, but it was empty."

I sucked in a breath… at the same moment Champ tagged my prostate with expert perfection. Sweat ran down my temple and dripped onto Champ's muscular forearm, but I could no more have left that pantry than I could have sprouted wings and flown. I was exactly where I most wanted and needed to be.

Champ leaned over and licked the sweat before running the tip of his tongue along the edge of my hairline and groaning low in his chest as he moved his hand down to jack me off. It was all I needed to let go.

I sucked in a breath, but before I could let out a bellow, Champ clamped another strong hand over my mouth to muffle my orgasm. I screamed into his palm while he let out a soft chuckle that ended in a choked gasp. His body shuddered against my back as he pushed deep inside me and came.

We were a damp, sticky mess in a small space that now reeked of sex and sweat, but all I could think about was the tender caress of his thumb as it smoothed a damp piece of hair off my temple.

Champ's lips grazed the side of my throat. "I don't want to pull out," he admitted softly.

I didn't want him to either. I wanted him to stay inside me for as long as it took for him to become a different person, the kind who would consider more than stolen moments when it suited him. The kind who could admit when he wanted something more.

The kind who believed in something more than one-night stands.

He started to pull away from me, but I reached back and grabbed a handful of his hair. "Don't."

My voice came out ragged and scared, the opposite of something casual. I forced myself to let go and shrug him off, letting out a little laugh as if it was all some kind of joke.

"Just worried about the mess," I said, lying through my teeth.

Champ put a hand on my back. "Stay right here." He moved past me to grab a box of tissues off the shelf. After ripping them open, he pulled out a handful and used them to clean me off.

My face burned with embarrassment and discomfort. He'd always taken tender care of me after sex, but this was one of the times I wished he wouldn't. The last thing I needed was to like him more.

To want him more.

To want more *with him*.

I gritted my teeth and said what I should instead of what I wanted. "I need to get to work."

Champ looked up at me with furrowed brows. "So early on a Sunday?"

I moved away from him to yank my clothes back on. I could worry about a shower and a change of clothes when I got to the shop. "Yeah. Meeting with new prospective clients. Your mom, ah... your mom hooked me up with some killer referrals."

"She did?" He sounded shocked, like he wouldn't have expected her to help me.

"Yeah. She did," I said, trying to bite back the defensiveness I felt. "I also had plenty of time to work the room last night after you left."

I slipped my shoes back on and ran hands through my hair, hoping like hell I didn't look like the fuck toy I felt like.

"Quinn, I'm sorry. About last night, I shouldn't have—"

I held up a hand and plastered on a big smile. "It's fine. You apologized already. Have a good day, Champ."

After breezing out of the small space, I waved a quick hello-goodbye to the Drakes and rushed out to my car.

I was halfway to the office before I remembered what he'd said right before we had sex.

It's only you.

What the hell had he meant by that?

My mood was not improved when I saw the man waiting for me outside my shop.

"Agent Parler," I said with a polite nod before unlocking the door, stepping inside, and pushing it shut behind me.

Unfortunately, Vince didn't take the unwelcoming hint. He grabbed the door with his hand and let himself in. "I was actually coming to check on *you*, Mr. Taffet. Heard you had quite a night last night."

I glanced over my shoulder suspiciously. "Yes, the SnoBall was lovely. I can't take credit for any of it, though. I was just a last-minute substitute for Lorraine Peevey—"

Vince's mouth pinched in a pitying frown. "I'm not talking about that," he said softly. "I'm talking about Percy being… well, Percy. I heard that he abandoned you at the party."

I felt my face go hot. Fucking Thicket gossip mavens. Was I really sure I wanted to make my home in a place where my business was no longer my own damned business?

"I'm doing just fine," I assured him. I bumped up the heat on the thermostat and headed for the back room. "But I do have a client meeting, and I'm running late, so—"

"Mr. Taffet... *Quinn*... forgive me, but you don't look fine. You look..." His eyes ran up and down me, taking in my wrinkled shirt and pants, which probably looked a little worse for wear after being on the floor of the pantry. "A little heartbroken. And maybe hungover."

"Heartbroken?" I echoed. I turned around to face him, arms folded over my chest. There was no way that would have been in the Thicket gossip, not after the rumors of our engagement were flying here and there and everywhere. "Not at all."

"Forgive me. I know you and I aren't friends yet." He held up both hands innocently, and one corner of his mouth lifted in a hopeful smile. "But I hope we can be. After all, nobody understands what it feels like to be in love with Percy Champion quite like you and I do."

I blinked and frowned. "You're mistaken. I'm not—"

"No, I imagine after last night you're not feeling very loving at all. Honestly, I don't know what Percy was thinking." Vince made a disgusted noise. "A handsome, intelligent man like you should come first."

"I... yes," I agreed weakly. I shook my head to clear it. "Look, Agent Parler, now's not a good time—"

"Of course, of course. But have you given any more thought to what we discussed the other day? About you helping me?"

"Not really," I lied. I shrugged. "I've been focused on my work and the SnoBall—"

"And conflicted about what Percy will think?" Vince sighed. "I understand all too well. Which is why I hate to point this out to you, but you need to understand. Quinn, if Percy comes under investigation—and he will, if Tommy doesn't catch him first—what do you think are the chances that *your* involvement in this won't become front-page news? I would hate to see this affect your business."

My eyes widened. "Excuse me? I don't take kindly to threats—"

"Oh, for heaven's sake. It's not a threat!" He heaved a put-upon sigh. "I'm really tired of always playing the role of the mustache-twirling bad guy in Champ's narrative. He needs to make *me* the asshole so he can feel better about his own failings, just like he tells himself his mother is this evil social climber when she's actually quite nice. I'm trying to look out for you here. I might be the *only* one looking out for you."

I stared at Vince, wishing I could read his mind. He was right. Bunny wasn't nearly as bad as Champ had led me to believe. Was it possible Champ had been wrong about Vince also? Had he been trying to circumvent Vince all this time when he should've been trusting him and working with him? The only thing more impossible than figuring Champ out was figuring out his ex-boyfriend.

"Quinn, I respect you, but you're blind right now, just like I used to be. Percy Champion is never going to love you back, just like he'll never apologize for what he did to you last night. Just like he'll never make you his first priority." He patted me on the shoulder. "When you're ready to get real and protect yourself, call me."

Vince turned and walked out the door, and I stared after him, long after he'd turned and strolled up the street. I probably should have been considering the points he'd made and pondering how I could protect myself and my business.

But instead, all I could think was that Vince had been wrong. Champ *had* apologized to me this morning —it was the very first thing he'd whispered in my ear in the pantry, and just like every second of that fucking hot interaction, it was emblazoned on my brain.

And if Vince had been wrong about that... was it possible that he'd been wrong about other things too?

18

CHAMP

Quinn left the pantry so quickly, I felt dizzy. By the time I got myself cleaned up and put back together, he was long gone. I entered the kitchen to the stares of the entire Drakes family.

"Good morning," I said, flashing the smile I used to use back in the service when interacting with the brass.

Marissa looked past me toward the back hallway. "Were you...?"

"In the pantry?" Levi added.

"With Quinn?" Marissa finished, her eyes sparking with a knowing glint.

"He thought he saw a mouse," I said with a shrug. "We looked everywhere but couldn't find anything."

Tommy's eyes narrowed at me. "We don't have mice. I pay a service." Then he turned to Levi. "Call the pest people and get them out here. We will not have mice here with all our guests coming."

Carlotta blinked awake over her coffee mug. "Mice?"

"Like I said, we didn't find anything. No need to

call anyone," I said quickly. "Our search was very... thorough."

Carlotta put a hand on her chest. "I don't care. Get them out here. You can never be too careful with pests."

"We appreciate your diligence," Marissa said with a grin. "Although I thought you two had agreed not to... *hunt mice* again until after you were married."

Her father frowned at her. "What does that have to do with anyth—"

"Hello!" Trey said, waltzing into the kitchen from the front hall. "Good morning. So sorry I'm late, but I brought donuts!" He leaned over and kissed Marissa's cheek, and she flushed pink but didn't look particularly pleased.

Levi jerked, his knee bumping the underside of the table and making all of the drinks slosh.

Tommy's face darkened. "Where the hell were you last night?" he asked.

Since I didn't want to be caught in a Drakes family drama scene, I scooted around Trey to the front hall with a murmured goodbye, then collected Hercules and headed out. When I was almost to the front door, I heard Marissa telling Trey in a furious voice that she couldn't be bribed with donuts, especially when they weren't even Annie's donuts, which reminded me of Quinn again.

I was beginning to accept that almost every-damn-thing did these days.

Fuck, I really wished I knew where his head was at. I debated stopping by Taffet Events just to make sure he was okay, but Riggs stopped that plan with one simple text.

Riggs: *At the office. We have news. You coming in?*

I groaned. Who the hell had decided to have mandatory Sunday hours today?

Oh, right. Me.

Me: *Yeah. Be there in five. Or call me and fill me in.*

Riggs: *No can do. See you soon.*

No can do? I frowned down at my phone, picked up the dog, and jogged the rest of the way out to the truck.

When I got to the office, I nodded a greeting at our drowsing receptionist. "Herman."

"Not at all, sir!" He jumped to his feet with a cordial smile. "And Happy New Year to you too."

Well, that explained why he was here on a Sunday.

I bit back a sigh and continued past him toward the group assembled in front of Riggs's desk when Herman's voice called out, "Hold up, boss. Message for you from your roommate." He held out a large sheet of yellow legal pad paper. "I wrote it down to make sure I got it right, just like he asked me."

My heart leapt when I pictured Quinn calling to talk to me, but the message wasn't from Quinn.

In shaky scrawl, the note read: *Jericho says you have bugs. Call him ASAP.*

Great. The Drakes may not have had mice in the pantry, but apparently, I had bugs at my house. Sometimes I hated living in Tennessee.

I glanced up at Herman with a sigh. "Jericho's my contractor, not my roommate," I explained. "He's doing work at my house."

Herman's jowls dropped, and he leaned toward me slightly. "Yes, sir, but he was here earlier. That's when he…" His eyes got big as he finished the sentence by mouthing the words *found the bugs*.

I frowned, then remembered I'd asked the team to call Jericho over to fix the faucet in the bathroom the night before. Figured the world's slowest contractor had done this one thing fast.

"Got it. Thanks, Herman." I'd have to have Hux source me the best pest company in Tennessee. I was tired of dealing with contractors who didn't do things properly.

When I got into the back room, I came to a stop and stared at the chaos surrounding me. Hux and Elvo were dismantling Hux's computer setup. Jordan and Casey were inventorying our small weapons cache. Yolanda and Riggs were boxing large stacks of folders. "What the fuck is going on?"

Riggs gave me a slight but firm shake of the head. "Look, I know you're obsessed with this case, but it's Elvo's birthday. Remember I told you Carter would have his cook make us a big spread to celebrate? We can work *later*."

I opened my mouth to remind him that Elvo's birthday had been back in December and we'd celebrated it by playing an epic twelve-hour video game at Carter and Riggs's house. It was one of the few times Kev had allowed us into his special gaming room. But I closed my mouth when I met Riggs's eyes. It had been a while since I'd seen that look.

Something's up. Act normal.

I nodded. "Fine. But if you think I'm day drinking again like we did for your birthday, you're mistaken."

He let out a breath and rolled his eyes. We both knew Riggs's last birthday had been spent ankle-deep in goat shit while we barely got an executive hostage away from a local rebel group in Uganda. He'd never let us live it down.

I joined them in gathering up the critical equipment we needed before moving out to our vehicles. It wasn't until I got out to the parking lot that I put two and two together.

Bugs.

Fucking Christ. Someone had put listening devices in our office? Someone had *infiltrated our security company*? It was unacceptable. The very thought made me rage inside.

Who would do this? It couldn't be Vince. He worked for a government agency, and I could not believe that he had enough information to obtain a warrant to plant a device like that. There was Tommy Drakes, but he had no idea we were looking for something of his, because there was no way he'd let me and Quinn stay in his house if he suspected.

Could it be the cartel?

Fuck. That made the most sense. I hadn't heard any more about any attempted break-ins at Tommy's Nashville place or any of his business locations, but that didn't mean they hadn't happened. Or maybe they'd gotten cautious and backed off. Knowing we handled security for HOG Corporate, maybe they'd backed off and let us do the work for them, hoping we could lead them to the missing Horn... or even to Buck Nutter, the man who'd stolen the device from Gustavo Santiago's compound in the first place.

"You're doing a lot of thinking over there, boss," Elvo said from my passenger seat as we began the drive toward Carter and Riggs's house.

"Yeah. Let me keep thinking until we get there."

Until we got to someplace where we couldn't be fucking overheard.

Unfortunately, the drive was too short. Before I had come to any helpful conclusions, we'd pulled up outside of the giant mansion Carter's grandfather had procured on the edge of Licking Thicket for his grandsons.

I waved everyone over to my vehicle and had everyone toss their electronics in the back before we reconvened in the side yard.

"What the fuck is going on?" I demanded of Hux, specifically.

He kicked at the dead grass below his feet, looking nauseated. "It's on me, boss. I run anti-surveillance checks monthly. I figured that was enough since the office is always staffed and our alarm system has, like, fifty-seven redundancies. But I guess I should've been doing them more often, because somebody got in."

"How, Hux? How the fuck could this happen?" I couldn't even imagine a stranger getting access to our inner offices. The idea made me want to punch something. "And how long could someone have been listening to us?"

Hux met my eye. "Max twenty-six days. My last sweep was thorough. As soon as Jericho alerted me to what he found, I scanned through our video footage. The only people who've been in the office unaccompanied who aren't regular staff are Herman, the plumber who worked on the bathroom sink, and Jericho."

"If it's Herman, I'm retiring today." There was simply no way. The man was ancient and trustworthy.

"Agreed," Hux said. "And Jericho was the one who alerted us to the bug—without dismantling it, either, so we wouldn't tip off whoever was listening."

"How the hell did he know to do that?" I demanded.

"Not sure. Spy movies, maybe? And I mean, I guess it could've been some kind of double play on his part, but… damn it, I just don't think so. What do we know about the plumber?"

I scowled. "Don't ask me. I didn't hire him. Riggsy did."

"Me? Definitely not," Riggs said. "Hux did."

"Ah, fuck," Hux sighed. "No. Not me."

I ran a hand over my forehead. "So you're telling me that we run one of the best security firms in Tennessee, that we intentionally keep our crew small and highly vetted in order to maintain that security, and that we've been infiltrated by the most pitifully simple social engineering attack I've ever heard of?"

Riggs nodded grimly. "The plumber came multiple times and shut the entire bathroom for an hour on one of those occasions. In addition to the listening devices in the bathroom, he could've planted them in the drop ceilings. Hell, maybe he even hacked into our servers."

"The systems too?" I demanded. "Hux, is that possible?"

I could tell how upset Hux was, but now wasn't the time to be defensive, and he knew it. "It's possible. Remember when I told you one of my process daemons froze up a couple of weeks ago and I had to reboot?"

None of us knew what the fuck he was talking about, so I made a rolling hand gesture to get him to skip the technical jargon and give us the gist.

Hux huffed out a breath. "Long story short, *yes*. That could indicate an attempt to place surveillance in our computer systems. It's highly unlikely they succeeded. It'll take time for me to check, though. I'm only one person."

Elvo's forehead crinkled. "Can't Carter's cousin help? He's technical, right? And we trust him."

Hux scoffed. "Kev? Run cybersecurity scans? *Pfft.* Please."

Riggs frowned. "You know he's a genius—"

He was cut off by a disembodied voice that sounded like it was coming from a nearby tree. "I could out scan you anytime, anyplace, Huxley."

We stared at the tree.

Hux hissed, "Please tell me you all heard that too, or I'm going to have to admit Kev has finally made me lose my mind."

Elvo stepped closer and inspected the tree to see if he could find the speaker.

Kev's voice came from the tree again, making Elvo jump. "This house is secure. Anti-surveillance scanning complete. You may enter and continue your useless prattle away from the winter chill. Besides, Mrs. Clayborn made cheesecake brownies, and they're not going to eat themselves."

Elvo immediately turned and started walking toward the house. Riggs jogged to catch up with him. "She makes the best desserts."

Before following them, I glared at Hux. "Put your stupid gaming feud aside. We need Kev's help, and you know it."

Hux's jaw flexed. "Fine. But he works for *me.* He does what *I* say."

The tree laughed.

I rolled my eyes and turned toward the house. "Yeah. Good luck with that."

He followed me toward the promise of snacks and security, muttering the whole way about nosy egotistical gamer imposters who fancied themselves real-world cybersecurity experts.

I didn't pay much attention to him. I was too busy

trying to figure out how worried we needed to be that the Cartel de la Luna was deep in our business on the hunt for the Horn.

I needed to contact Jacob Horn, and Jesus fuck I didn't want to. I knew that Champion Security was already on thin ice with them, and this might be the last straw. But I also knew that we would need to bring in additional personnel if the cartel was definitely involved, including personal security for each of the company executives, as well.

Once we got inside, we set up around Carter and Riggs's huge kitchen table... with Hux still protesting every step of the way.

"Kev, we need to be in the lair, for fuck's sake. We need access to your dedicated internet. This system out here is practically a dial-up."

"Only a poor craftsman blames his tools, Huxley." Kev sniffed and studied his nails. "Besides, my lair wouldn't be my lair if I let every Tom, Dick, and Huxley down there, now would it? May the odds be ever in your favor." He grabbed a cheesecake brownie and prepared to depart.

"Kev." I grabbed his elbow and pulled him into a front sitting room. "Let's not be hasty. We need your help. What if I were to offer you a contract job?" I explained what was going on and the resulting need to assess the security of our computer systems. "Hux can only do so much himself," I said.

Kev dipped his chin and let out a long-suffering sigh. "Especially with his... limitations."

I bit my tongue against a laugh. He'd always made veiled comments about Hux's slightly lower IQ even though both of them probably qualified for MENSA.

"Can you help us?"

Kev pursed his lips and finally nodded. "I could. But Hux works for *me*. He does what *I* say."

I coughed to cover a laugh. "I can't do that. He's the one with longer-running knowledge of our systems."

He tapped his foot on the floor. "Then we're equals. I will not report to that... egotistical orc-hoarder for all the pips in Hornlandia."

I blinked at him. "I don't know what that means, but you've made your point. You're equals."

With that sorted, I returned to the kitchen to tackle our other problems.

I called Jacob Horn at home, which was every bit as ball-shriveling as I'd imagined it would be. After quickly calling some friends at other security companies to see if I could borrow some reinforcements for the next couple of weeks, we made a plan to protect the HOG executives and were finally able to get back to the business of trying to get into Tommy Drakes's vault... which was going to be even more complex now that we would need to set up our operation here at Riggs and Carter's place.

After a few frustrating hours in which it felt like we were making negative progress, I decided to take a break and check in with Jericho at my house. I had a lot of questions for him, starting with how a civilian would recognize a listening device when he found one.

"I'm headed out," I told the team. "Carter, Kev, and Riggs have agreed to let us work from here for the time being. Don't be afraid to source whatever you need and use the company card."

Riggs waved his hand over his shoulder. "Vault should be here this afternoon. Got a hold of the delivery driver, and they'll bring it here."

I blew out a breath and stretched my arms over my head as I walked out into the winter sun with Hercules. The drive to my old Victorian was short enough to make me reconsider selling the old thing once the renovations were done. But the house was meant for a family, not a single workaholic.

Quinn's accusations the night before had been spot-on: the house, like Herc, was a reminder of a fantasy life I was never going to have. Unlike Herc, I didn't have any responsibility to keep the house. I'd be better off with an apartment in town like Quinn had.

When I stepped out of the truck at the house, I noticed the front yard was clear of construction debris. New wooden shutters hung neatly next to each window, and the glass panes were all intact for once. The exterior still needed a paint job, but at least the house didn't look quite as haunted and dangerous now as it had only a couple of weeks ago.

"Jericho?" I called as I stepped into the front hall.

"Back here," a voice replied from the kitchen. I made my way down the hall and ran a hand along the freshly sanded banister. The smooth wood curved under my fingers, and the scent of sawdust tickled my nose. It really was starting to come together. The trim work looked amazing, and the hardwood floors were sanded and ready to stain. I could finally imagine what it would look like when it was done.

I came around the corner and stopped. The marble countertops had been installed, and the cabinetry was primed and waiting for paint. "Holy shit," I breathed. "It looks so different."

Jericho stood up from where he'd been putting the top on a large bucket of primer. "It's coming together alright," he said in his drawl. "You get my message about your surveillance issue?"

"Yeah. You really did us a solid. Thank you. We've relocated somewhere else while we figure out what the hell is going on. How'd you know what you were looking at?"

Jericho wiped his hands on a paint-stained bandana before meeting my eyes with a knowing smirk. "I worked for the State Department for fifteen years."

I let out a laugh. My cowpoke contractor had been in the CIA? "I didn't see that coming."

He dipped his chin in acknowledgment. "That's the point, isn't it?"

After studying him for a beat, I said, "You looking for work?"

He gestured around us at the half-finished kitchen. "Got all I need right here."

"That's not the kind of work I mean."

Jericho shrugged. "It's the kind I want right now. Sometimes the job starts to own you instead of the other way around and you need a hard reset. That's where I'm at."

"Well, if you ever change your mind, come find me. I always have work for people with intelligence experience. Although… I can't say I'd want to lose you here at the house until you're done. The place looks incredible."

Jericho smiled and dipped his head again. "Rocky start, but the finish should be smooth. I'd say another two weeks and you'll be able to bring your new husband home."

I choked on my breath. "New husband?"

"Word around town is you're engaged to the wedding planner. That not right?" Jericho leaned down to grab the dirty paintbrush and tray. I couldn't tell if he was deliberately acting casual or if he was simply making conversation. Either way, warning lights flashed in my head.

I tried to figure out how to tell him the truth without fucking things up with the Drakes. Gossip in the Thicket was aggressively active, like the wisteria vines on the trees behind my house.

I swallowed. "I'm not sure what the living situation will be once the house is done," I said carefully. "He may want to continue living above the shop."

Both of those things were true. I exhaled.

Jericho chuckled. "I thought maybe the whole thing was a rumor. Surely if you were engaged, you would have brought him here to see the house before now."

"And give him tetanus? No, thanks. Besides, he'd be full of opinions, and it would take even longer to get this done than it already is."

I turned to go upstairs when Jericho stopped me in my tracks. "Not that it's any of my business, but why is the US government spying on you?"

I spun around to face him. "The US government? What makes you think it's the government?"

"That tech is specific to the US alphabet agencies, far as I know. We came across it at an embassy in a country that shall remain nameless. Found out the DEA had decided to surveil some lower-level targets without the courtesy of informing us ahead of time." He crossed his arms in front of his chest. "Got our asses chewed for destroying the tech when we found it because it costs a shit ton of money."

I wondered out loud. "In this case, it looks like the DEA's enemies got their hands on some of it. Probably found it like you did and repurposed it for their own ends."

"You mean a drug boss found it in his mansion and then used it to spy on someone else? Nah. It's not that simple. Ask Hux. Having the cameras and listening devices aren't enough. You have to have access to the back-end software, and that shit is locked down tight."

I stared at him for a minute, possibilities swirling through my mind.

Jericho studied me. "Tell me a square like you is in trouble with the DEA. I'll laugh my ass off."

"Not officially, no. But we've got an agent breathing down our necks regardless. He wants something related to a client of ours, and he thinks we have information we're not sharing—"

Jericho frowned. "Yeah, but if your agent had probable cause to install surveillance equipment, he'd have probable cause to get a warrant to search your computer systems or bring you in for questioning. That doesn't play."

He was right. *Fuck*. So it was the cartel's MO but the DEA's technology? Where did that leave us?

"So... do you?" Jericho asked.

"Hmm?"

"Do you have information you're not sharing?" he teased.

I realized just how little I knew about Jericho. There was a strong possibility he was in this up to his ears. It was time to stop being so trusting.

"A 'square' like me? Nah." I shrugged. "Anyway, thanks for the heads-up and all the incredible work on the house."

It wasn't until later, after I'd gathered a few fresh T-shirts from upstairs—T-shirt-related thefts were definitely on the rise in the Thicket — and was driving back to Riggs and Carter's place that I cringed as I recalled Jericho's words about Quinn.

It was true I hadn't brought Quinn to the house, and I knew he'd noticed it. He'd mentioned it more than once, especially back in the beginning. But why would I have brought him to a construction site when his place was so comfortable and tidy? It wasn't important to have him over just for the sake of it, and surely Quinn understood that...

I nearly stopped short on Walnut Street, and Elmira Byrd waved to me from her front porch.

Hadn't I had nearly the same thought about Quinn last night in the van on the way to search the farmhouse? That surely Quinn understood that my business was important?

Maybe the issue wasn't that Quinn didn't understand how important my business was or how unimportant my house was. Maybe the issue was that I hadn't been clear about how important *he* was.

I didn't know exactly what we were — Sleeping together? Dating? Friends with benefits? — but I knew I wanted him around. And the thought of not having him in my life filled me with anxiety. *Lots* of anxiety. Which was a new concept for me.

I'd meant what I'd said to my team. Quinn had me twisted up inside. I had a new kind of nervous feeling when I was away from him, something I'd never felt when I was with Vince. It made me want to stay with Quinn or at least know where he was and whether he was safe and happy at all times.

He'd made it clear many times that he wasn't a relationship guy, and fuck knew I'd made it abundantly clear that I wasn't either. Both of us had really good reason to feel that way.

But the way Quinn had come to Champion Security last night to yell at me—that was not the action of a man with no skin in the game. And the way I was obsessing about him right now… well, that suggested that shit had changed for me too. So maybe that meant…

Maybe it meant that I needed to fucking talk to Quinn instead of deciding things myself for once.

When I parked the truck, I realized I hadn't, in fact, returned to Riggs's place to work. I was parked outside of Quinn's showroom, exactly where I wanted to be.

Taffet Events was a hive of activity. Two women exited the front door, happily chatting and carrying a white paper gift bag I recognized as Quinn's new-client welcome pack. I'd helped him put his logo stickers on the front of them one night after an epic round of sex on the antique chaise in his front room.

I got Herc out of the truck, then stepped onto the sidewalk and peered inside. The plate glass window was clean and crystal clear, providing an excellent view of this week's tablescape. Every week, he put together a different theme to draw in clients—always full of color and life, always in perfect taste just like Quinn himself —and more than once, I'd seen Thicketeers stand and stare at the arrangements with a combination of delight and envy. The man was incredibly talented.

Had I ever told him so?

When I opened the door, Quinn looked up from his spot at the small desk where he was typing on a laptop. The look on his face turned from open and welcoming to strangely guarded.

I hated that. I'd been messing up on so many fronts

lately because I'd made stupid assumptions, and I was through with that.

"Hey," I said, looking around. A young man and woman were at the round conference table, flipping through magazines, and an older lady I recognized from the flower shop moved around me toward the back room with fresh floral arrangements to store in the fridge.

"Hey. I thought you were at Carter's place." Quinn bent down to pat Hercules, who'd clearly missed Quinn in the few hours they'd spent apart… probably almost as much as I had. He glanced around and lowered his voice to a whisper. "He stopped by a little while ago and told me what happened. Can't say I'm thrilled to know someone overheard me yelling at you last night."

I dropped into one of the chairs in front of his desk when what I really wanted to do was snatch him up and take him upstairs for a naked coffee break. I looked around again at the people keeping me from being able to do just that.

"If someone overheard you telling me off for being an idiot, that's the least of my concerns. We're going to work at Carter and Riggs's place for a while until we figure out who's been monitoring Champion Security and why." I felt as awkward as I sounded. I hadn't come here to talk to him about work or to rehash what had happened the night before. To be honest, I hadn't come here purposefully at all.

I'd been running on instinct.

"Um, good?" Quinn said, furrowing his brows as he studied me slumped forward in the chair. "You okay? I'm sure it freaked you out when you discovered—" He darted another look around the room. "—that whole situation. And I don't want to upset you more, but I need to tell you about—"

"Have dinner with me tonight," I blurted. My voice came out rough and too loud. The couple at the nearby table glanced over, and the florist stopped in her tracks to stare at me. I cleared my throat and lowered my voice. "At a restaurant. Like... like a..."

Quinn's eyes went huge, but the edges of his lips turned up. Instead of finishing my sentence, or better yet, ignoring it, he sat in silence. Like a man who knew what he deserved and was willing to wait for it.

He was enjoying this.

I felt my own smile tugging at my mouth, even as my heart thundered and sweat poured out of every square inch of my skin. "Fine. Yes. Like a..." I ran a hand through my hair and looked at the ceiling. "Date," I pushed out.

Quinn stood up and walked around the desk until he was standing right in front of me. When I leaned back in the chair to look up at him, he shocked the hell out of me by seating himself directly across my lap. His arms snaked around my neck, and his lips brushed my ear.

"Why, Percival Champion, as I live and breathe... of course I'll go out on a date with you. Thought you'd never ask." He pulled back enough for me to see his knowing smirk. "And since we're engaged to be married, can I just say *it's about time*?"

I rolled my eyes and pinched his ass. "Brat. Get off me. I need to get back to work, and clearly, you need to do the same."

His laugh made my chest open up so I could breathe easier. Was there anything that sound wouldn't cure?

Before climbing off my lap, Quinn leaned in and pressed a kiss to my lips. It was slow and serious, tender and full of so much meaning, I nearly fell off the chair. I wanted him desperately, in my bed, in my arms, in my life.

And it turned out it wasn't so hard to make time for both Quinn *and* my job. In fact, I felt newly energized and clearheaded enough to tackle all of the questions in front of me.

I stood up abruptly and held him away from me. "Gotta go. Pick you up here at six."

"You gonna keep your promise this time?" Quinn asked. His voice was teasing, but there was a hint of seriousness there too.

"Come hell or high water," I vowed. "Even if Tommy Drakes comes knocking on my door with the Horn in his hand, I'd just—" I hesitated. It seemed wrong to *lie*. "Okay, I'd probably snatch the Horn and then come pick you up."

Quinn laughed out loud. "Or, and this is just a thought, you could *call me* and *explain*. I don't ever want you to not do what you need to do for your business. I just want to have a heads-up. That's all I ask. Okay?"

"Yeah. I can do that." I gave him one more kiss because I couldn't help it, then headed out. "You wanna keep Herc with you?"

Quinn's lopsided grin nearly stopped my heart. "We *ask* now? Who are you, and what have you done with Percival Champion?"

I rolled my eyes. "I'm a man who's learned his lesson. Or who's trying to learn, anyway. Six o'clock," I reminded him.

As I pushed open the shop's front door, I heard the young woman ask Quinn, "Who was that?"

His soft laughter made me slow my steps.

"My one-night stand," he sighed. "The kind that doesn't ever seem to leave. Can't say I mind it. Look at the man, for God's sake."

My face heated, and I refused to acknowledge hearing the compliment. But I caught myself grinning like an asshole the entire drive back to Carter and Riggs's place.

19

QUINN

Despite feeling nervous and awkward, I managed to get my shit together by the time Champ showed up for our date.

I had mixed feelings about accepting his dinner offer, but it hadn't mattered in the end since my mouth had decided to accept him regardless.

Now here we were, digging into an appetizer sampler plate at the Steak 'n Bait, the Thicket's premier fine-dining experience, surrounded by other couples.

I twisted my napkin nervously. "I… I meant to tell you earlier. Vince came by today." I filled him in on nearly everything Vince had said, except the part about Champ never loving me. I wasn't nearly masochistic enough to bring up *that* little fact.

Champ blew out a breath, but it was clear that he was struggling to keep his temper. "Maybe, *possibly*, he has a point about my mom. But the rest? No way."

"I know, but—"

"He's a manipulative ass. If he can't make you

betray me because you care about me, he'll try to make you question me."

"I know, but—"

"He is *not* looking out for you."

"Yes, I *know*." I placed a hand over Champ's on top of the table. "Look, I believe you, okay? He was convincing… he really got me for a minute there. But what I wanna know is *why*? Why is he so obsessed with this?"

"Vince has always been like this to some extent. Obsessed with the job and proving himself." Champ sounded bewildered. "I don't know, really. It makes me realize that maybe I *never* knew him as well as I thought I did." His gaze refocused on me. "But what I do know is that I didn't ask you out on a date so we could talk about my asshole ex. Pretty sure that's not date talk."

"Fair enough." I popped a tater tot in my mouth and gave him a teasing grin. "I haven't been on a date in so long I might've forgotten. And the last time I went out to eat with a man, we shared a chef salad. Scott was obsessed with calorie-counting, and he wanted me to be too."

"I don't wanna talk about *your* asshole ex either." Champ eyed me over his beer bottle and grinned at me lasciviously. "But I don't mind telling you how fucking amazing your body is. Strong legs. Perfect fucking ass. I've never figured out how you manage to eat like a horse and still look like that."

"Lucky genes," I said. "And I go for a run most afternoons when the shop is slow." I gave him a once-over, giving particular attention to his broad shoulders and the biceps straining the fabric of his shirt. "You must find time to squeeze in workouts somehow, but I don't know when."

"We have a gym at the office," he admitted. "Good place to take out my frustrations when shit isn't going right on a job."

"Will you still use it while you're working from Carter and Riggs's place?"

Champ's eyes met mine with unexpected intensity. "Was hoping to find other ways of working out in the meantime."

The breath escaped my lungs in a ragged exhale. "Oh."

He made a low noise in his throat that went straight to my dick. I reached for my cocktail but fumbled it, sending vodka cranberry splashing over the edge of the glass. Champ's growl turned to a low laugh, which didn't help matters.

"What's taking them so long with the food?" I wondered aloud.

"You in a hurry, Chicken Nugget?" he teased.

I met his eye again. "My pants are too tight."

His laugh brought out a dimple on his face that was doing a serious number on my equilibrium. "I can help take them off later." He took a slow sip of his beer. My eyes followed his lips as they wrapped around the bottle. "With my teeth," he added with a grin.

I raised my hand and tried to get our server's attention. "Check, please." Champ's laugh was loud as he grabbed my arm and pulled my hand down to kiss it.

"Patience, baby. You're going to need your energy, so we might as well wait for our food."

Once again, the casual and sincere "baby" went straight to my gut, which didn't help the pants situation at all.

We passed the rest of the meal in a comfortable kind of flirt-fest. It had been a long time since I'd enjoyed dinner out with someone as much as I did with Champ. He was good company: smart, funny, engaging. He told me stories about various deployments with his team, and I shared several wedding disaster stories to lighten the mood. Unlike my ex, Champ was attentive. He seemed to enjoy the stories I told, even when they overflowed with minute detail and went off on unintended tangents.

I babbled my way through several vodka cranberries until I was happily chirping at him the whole drive back to the farm.

"This isn't the farm," I said stupidly when Champ parked the truck behind my shop.

"No, babe. It's not."

I followed him out of the vehicle and to the back door, remembering Herc was here. "Oh my God, you remembered the dog for the second time today! It's a miracle."

"Herc's here?" he asked. I opened my mouth to ask if he was serious when I noticed him wink at me. "That's not the only reason we're here."

Champ unlocked the door and stepped inside, greeting Herc with pets before reaching for his leash. It took me a minute to realize my keys were still in my pocket.

"How did you get the door open? Did I forget to lock it?" The idea of accidentally leaving both the shop and apartment vulnerable to break-ins sobered me up quickly.

He clipped the leash to Herc's collar and stepped past me to take him out back. "Nope. I used my key."

I followed him to the large patch of grass on the far side of the parking area. "Your key? *Your* key?"

"No. Hercules is a poodle."

It took my alcohol-soaked brain a minute to get the joke, and I quickly realized he was trying to distract me from the revelation that he'd had my key copied.

"Boundaries, Champion," I growled at him.

The streetlamp above him lit up his blond hair and sent shadows moving across his face. Despite the strange lighting, he was still gorgeous, even when his smile faded and his eyebrows furrowed.

"Remember when you had the flu before Christmas and you could barely get out of bed for a couple of days?"

"How did you even know about that? I told you I was out of town for a job." I hadn't wanted him to see me red-nosed and bleary-eyed, sounding like a hundred-year-old chain-smoker.

He stepped closer and cupped my cheek with his big hand. The warmth of his touch reminded me how cold it was outside.

I nuzzled into it.

"I'm an intelligence operative, sweetheart," he said softly. "And you needed someone to take care of you."

I stared up at him. "I had… I had… delivery."

He leaned in and pressed a kiss to my forehead before turning back to urge Hercules back inside. "You had homemade chicken soup from Thelma's Sandwich Shack, organic throat lozenges from that bougie Summer Honey store, and Triple Chocolate Cake from Annie's."

Champ grabbed my hand and yanked me along like I was another animal he needed to corral. My brain spun with a new reality. "You brought that stuff to me? I thought I'd ordered it in a fever state."

"You did, sort of. You called *me*. And I couldn't just

ignore you. I mean, protecting people is kind of my job, so."

I dug my heels in so he couldn't pull me further. "Hold up. You're telling me that you answered my delirious phone call, then delivered me organic food and throat drops from three different stores because you're a professional bodyguard? Really."

Champ's face turned beet red.

"I'm not your client, Champ," I said softly. "Not now. Not then."

"No," he agreed just as softly. "But I think…" He sucked in a deep breath, and his whole body went tense, much the way it had when he'd tried to say "date" earlier. "I think even back then I knew you were *mine*. Mine to take care of. Mine to protect."

I gasped. Literally gasped. "But you don't… and *I* don't… And you never *said*! You never fucking said a word!"

"Well, no. I wasn't ready to admit it even to myself." Champ rubbed the back of his neck, making his biceps bulge against his shirt. "I, ah… I had to break in to this place the first time, with the soup, because you were too sick to answer when I knocked. And then I had to change the locks, obviously, which I realized after the fact was kind of… a lot." He cleared his throat, more adorably flustered than I'd ever seen him. "As in, *stalker* level a lot. And I realized you might have opinions about that, or maybe make assumptions. So I replaced your key to the old lock with your key to the new lock without saying anything and then kept the spare in case you needed something else."

I was too stunned to speak. All I could do was shake my head wordlessly, overwhelmed and… really turned on.

"I know." Champ's throat worked. "I know it's an invasion of privacy and whatnot. I never used the key again after you recovered, I swear. And knowing what I know now, I think it was probably beneficial, given that you'd had a nasty breakup with fucking *Scott* not too long before. But, ah… I can't claim that had any bearing on what I was doing at the time, so."

Holy shit. I had no idea what I was supposed to feel, hearing this. Weirded out, maybe? Angry that he'd been so overbearing and high-handed and, yes, *secretive*?

But I wasn't.

I simply couldn't work up a single iota of righteous indignation. And since on any given day half my body weight was comprised of righteous indignation, this was a big deal.

Instead, all I felt was… wanted. Protected. Sunshine-warmed, all the way down to my toes.

I was an independent person, and most of the time, I didn't *need* to be cared for. But that didn't mean that I didn't want to be sometimes.

And the knowledge that Champ *wanted* to care for me so much that he was willing to step in and do it even when he thought it might make me angry? That made me feel special and precious.

It wasn't logical at all. Aunt Cherry would probably tell me…

Actually, I had no idea what Aunt Cherry would tell me anymore, because maybe I hadn't understood Cherry as well as I thought either.

"You're not saying anything," Champ pointed out a little nervously. "Go ahead and rant at me. I can take it."

"Scott wouldn't bother stalking me," I said softly. "Especially not with Onyx to entertain him."

"Scott is a fucking idiot," he said dismissively. "We've established this. Not only did he cheat on you, he took out half a million dollars in loans against the business so he could finance a big-ass car, a fancy vacation, and the down payment on a new condo. Really, the way his clients are deserting him is his own fault."

I blinked up at him, my mind replaying something I'd overheard Bunny say during the SnoBall, and even something I'd overheard when Champ and I had been in the pantry earlier.

"Oh my God. Did you ruin Scott's business?" I demanded.

"No! Scott ruined Scott's business." Champ hesitated. "I just might have encouraged some society contacts I had to spread the word, that's all. As a public service."

The idea of that should not have made me as gleeful as it did.

"Scott would never have done something like that. Just like he'd never have broken my locks to bring me soup."

Champ's shoulders slumped. "Yeah, well. I guess it's pretty obvious why I haven't tried a long-term relationship since Vince, then, huh? My boundaries are kind of all or nothing." He firmed his jaw. "But I'm not sorry. Asshole had it coming."

"No. Champ, listen." I cupped his cheek and tilted his gaze up to mine because it was important that he understood. "Scott wouldn't have broken my locks to bring me soup... because he never cared about me that way. That's how I know he wouldn't bother stalking me. And back when he and I were together, I thought that was good. *Smart.* Because relationships were for suckers, and I never wanted to become dependent. But the truth is, I just never wanted to depend on someone like *Scott.* But you… you took care of me, and I…"

I couldn't make myself continue. There was vulnerable, and then there was *vulnerable*, and there were so many things left unsaid between us.

"Let's take Herc back inside, Quinn." Champ's voice was deep and sure. "Let me show you how well I can take care of you, baby."

I swallowed. "Aren't we going back to the farm?"

He shook his head. "We're staying here tonight." His hand landed on my lower back, and his lips brushed against my hair. "So I can fuck you until you scream. And this time, I won't have to stop you."

"Oh," I squeaked. "Oh. Sure. M'kay. Yeah."

So on board for that plan.

I raced up the stairs to my apartment, shucking my clothes as quickly as I could. By the time I dove onto the bed, I was buck naked and stroking myself.

Champ took his sweet time, but when he arrived, there was a noticeable bulge in the front of his trousers. Just seeing him like that got me hotter. "C'mere," I said.

He shook his head and crossed his arms before leaning idly against the doorjamb. "Want to watch you for a minute."

His eyes were dark and piercing. He had a way of looking at me that made my stomach clench and my heart rate spike.

I spread my legs open and moved my stroking hand down to cup my balls while I used my other hand to stroke across my chest. "Maybe I'll pleasure myself if you're going to stay all the way over there," I teased.

His eyes darkened. "I'd like to see that."

We both knew I was full of shit. I'd waited all day to get his bare cock back inside me. Just the thought of it had made me hard on and off for hours. But I wasn't going to make it easy for him, so I called his bluff by reaching over to the bedside table, fishing out a bottle of lube, and fingering myself in front of him.

Out of the corner of my eyes, I saw his chest rise and fall more rapidly as he watched me. "Fuck," he rumbled. "Get yourself ready for me."

"I'm getting myself ready for something," I said in a croaky voice. "Gonna have to get out the dildo in a minute if you don't get over here."

He didn't move from the doorway. "I'd like to see that."

We'd done it before. One night after Champ had been out of town for a three-day work trip, he'd shown up desperate and hungry. He'd found the toy sitting on my bedside table, where I'd left it on a towel to dry after washing it the night before. "Been missing my cock?" he'd asked before spending the next two hours edging me with everything *but* his cock.

Tonight I didn't want a toy. I wanted him. And only him.

"Champ," I breathed, hoping it would be enough for him to understand my need. If I started truly begging, it would get ugly.

"Do you have any idea how sexy you are?" he said, unfolding his arms and stepping into the room. His eyes stayed on mine. "How much you turn me on? I can't even fucking think straight anymore with you in my head, but I'm through trying to fight it."

My heart tripped over itself, but I didn't dare speak. I moved my slick fingers up to stroke my shaft again.

"Earlier today, in that closet, when you said you hadn't been with anyone else since me…" His voice sounded husky and raw. "I wanted to pound my fucking chest. Don't get with anyone else, Quinn. Do you hear me? No one else."

Air sawed in and out of my lungs as I tried not to pass out. Was he saying he wanted this to be a thing? An official, exclusive… thing? The R-word needled at the back of my brain, but I didn't want to speak it.

"Champ," I said again. My voice sounded needy and wrong. Thin and scared. What if this was just something he was saying in the heat of the moment?

His hands fisted to his sides. "You don't get with anyone else," he repeated. "Because you're mine."

I stared at him, frozen. "Yours to… to protect?"

"To protect. To take care of. To tease. To worship. Tell me you're mine, Quinn. Say the words to me."

My head spun, and my vision sparked. "Champ." Was that the only word I was capable of speaking anymore? And if so, was it any surprise? He filled my entire world, and I was overwhelmed by it.

He finally got to the bed and leaned over me with one hand on either side of my head. His nose brushed mine, and his voice dropped to a whisper. "Say it."

I squeezed my eyes closed and felt a hot tear slide down my temple. It was followed by the warm press of his tongue tracing the same route.

"Champ," I whimpered. "Yours. Yes. *Please*."

"No one else," he said, almost to himself. "Just us."

I nodded, feeling the familiar warmth of his breath and inhaling the familiar scent of his cologne. "Yes," I said again. "Need you. Want you. Want this. Us."

It was the most vulnerable I'd made myself with him since meeting him several months before, but in spite of everything we'd been through—or maybe because of it—I trusted him. The man was so aggressively anti-relationship that if he was saying these words to me, he had to have thought about them ahead of time. If anything, I knew he believed what he was saying. That he was ready to try.

Whether or not he was capable of following through with the promise was another thing entirely, but in that moment, I didn't care because I simply needed him, as much of him as I could possibly get.

Champ's hand cradled the side of my head while he pressed soft kisses along the other side of my face. "You're so fucking beautiful. And smart." He punctuated each adjective with kisses. "And funny. And strong."

I pulled him fully on top of me and wrapped my arms and legs around him, even though he was still fully clothed. We kissed and touched and reveled in each other's bodies until he was as naked as I was and pressing the tip of his slick cock against my hole.

"You feel so good," I groaned. My hands grasped the swell of his biceps before moving up to his wide shoulders. He was strong and heavy and didn't hesitate to put me where he wanted me.

Champ moved his arms behind my legs to hold them up. The divot of concentration between his eyebrows made me want to laugh. No matter how frantic our lovemaking was, no matter how bossy and demanding he got, he always made sure that he wasn't hurting me... and that I was into it every bit as much as he was.

When he pushed inside me, I blew out a breath of relief. I'd been reliving this feeling all day, and now that he was back inside me where he belonged, I realized my memory hadn't done it justice.

"Just like that," I murmured when he brushed my gland. He pulled back and pushed forward again until I let out a deep, debauched groan and tilted my head back on the pillow. Sex with Champ was the best I'd ever had, and knowing he was bare, that there were no barriers between us, made it even hotter.

Champ's lips tugged gently on the skin over my collarbone until he changed his tactic and sucked a mark into my skin. Between sucks and bites, he murmured to me in that mesmerizing voice of his.

"You tie me in knots... Swear to fucking God, you have me under a spell... I'll do anything... just... Christ, sweetheart, you feel so... Quinn, fuck... Don't... don't stop letting me in your bed... I need..." He thrust deep inside and let out a groan. "I need you. I need..."

His hand reached between us to wrap around my dick. I wasn't even sure it was necessary since his words and that fat cock of his had brought me to the edge already. But as soon as he took hold of me and pulled back enough to meet my eyes, it was over. I was so fucking gone for him.

His words washed over me as my orgasm hit. "That's it, baby. Let go. Let me hear you. When you come, you're gonna take me with you." I arched against him, grasping wildly at his sweat-slick skin as he continued to pound into me and jack me at the same time.

I shouted his name in a choking plea as my muscles contracted around him and my body fell into the sweetest kind of release—the kind that seemed only to come when Champ was with me.

My brain continued to float as he withdrew and pushed one of my knees up. I opened my eyes to catch him staring at my hole. Just when I was ready to pull away from him out of embarrassment at my wrecked ass, he reached down and used his fingers to gently press some of his escaping cum back inside me.

I let out a low noise as his heated eyes snapped up to meet mine. Time slowed as the truth became clear.

He thought it was hot. He wanted his release on me, *inside* me. Champ was marking me as his.

I opened my mouth to say something, but no words came. His eyes stayed on mine as he kissed the inside of my knee, my bare hip, the center of my chest, the side of my neck, and finally, my lips.

I wrapped my arms around him and held on tight as he continued to kiss me slowly.

It turned out, no words were needed. We slept wrapped up in each other's bodies the rest of the night.

Even when we moved back to the farm the following day, we continued sleeping together like that.

Neither of us was ready to say the words out loud that would name this new and precious thing between us, but it didn't matter because we both felt it and reveled in it.

For two whole weeks, I floated along in this new reality—the one where Champ and I were together for real. The one where I was an accepted part of the Thicket with a thriving business, with clients coming out of my ears. The one where Marissa Drakes's farm wedding was going to be a gorgeous spectacle that was talked of for all the right reasons.

But if there was one thing I'd learned since becoming an event planner, it was that nothing ever went entirely smoothly. Emergencies cropped up when you least expected them.

In this case, the emergency looked a lot like Levi Christianson sneaking out of Marissa's bedroom again in the predawn hours of a Friday morning that just so happened to be the morning before Marissa's wedding day.

"What the fuck?" I hissed at Levi, closing my own door softly behind me before Champ could wake up.

After trying and dismissing a million different potential ways to get into the vault in the Drakeses' basement, Champ's crew had finally decided that the only way to get the Horn was to drill the lock. Since this was going to be noisy and impossible to conceal, his team was going to go in during the wedding itself, while Tommy and his staff were busy enjoying the festivities and Champ and I had wedding-planning alibis.

If Champ woke up to find Levi in the hallway, I wouldn't put it past him to whisk the man off to an undisclosed location until Marissa was safely married.

Levi's eyes went from wide and guilty to narrowed in accusation. "Don't act like you and Champ haven't been having sex too!"

I gasped and clutched my throat. "You're having *sex*?" I cried like someone's maiden aunt. "Might I remind you that Champ and I are..." The word got stuck in my throat until I forced it out. "Dating? Neither of us is *marrying someone else tomorrow*," I whispered furiously.

"I thought you were engaged?" Levi folded his arms over his chest.

"Irrelevant!" I shot back. "We're talking about *you* right now and your... *Marissa*... who is someone else's fiancée! Is this some kind of wild-oat sowing on her part, or are you two…" I couldn't even say it. I could only imagine the look on Tommy Drakes's face when he discovered his precious baby girl had been schtupping the very man who was supposed to have been protecting her.

"I'm in love with her," he whispered back. He looked as miserable as he sounded when admitting the truth. "We're in love with each other."

I threw my hands up. "Then why is she marrying someone else?"

My brain helpfully substituted Levi for the image of the groom at the wedding. I wondered if it was as simple as—

"I'm not good enough for her. Obviously."

I stared at him. He was good-looking, in a Licking Thicket hoedown kind of way. And I knew from living with him for the past month that he was thoughtful and kind, especially to Marissa. Levi wasn't a terrible catch. Was he?

"Your dad owns a large security firm," I began, as if trying to sell him on himself. "You're decently employed, well respected, competent, good-looking, fit, and surprisingly good at identifying obscure country-music songs on the radio…"

"I didn't even go to college. Trey… he's all the shit I'll never be. Fancy degree. Fancy job in suits. Country club memberships. Hell, the only thing I ever did with a golf club was take out Pixie Denton's mailbox after she called Marissa a whore at the homecoming dance."

Dear God. I was living in a teen drama.

"Have you talked to her about it?" I asked, trying not to clench my teeth so hard I'd wind up with a headache before the day even started.

"And ruin her wedding when I have nothing to offer her? I wouldn't do that."

I shot a look past him to the bedroom door he'd just come out of dressed in nothing but a pair of boxer shorts. "Yeah, fucking her the day before she's set to marry another guy probs won't ruin anything. You're a real prince," I muttered before walking past him to the stairs. "Tommy and Carlotta arrive today, asshole, but I guess that's none of my business. Remember to bring Marissa by my office later this morning so we can go over the rehearsal dinner stuff for tonight."

Until someone canceled this wedding, I had a job to do.

I stormed downstairs, shoved a Pop-Tart into my mouth angrily, and hate-poured coffee into a travel mug before taking out poor Rebecca's undercarriage on the country road to work.

My fuck-it attitude lasted all of four hours before I caved and called the one person I could ask for advice without causing some kind of Licking Thicket security breach.

"Quinny!" Aunt Cherry exclaimed. "Baby cakes, how are you? I've been meaning to call you. I felt so bad about the way we left things after the SnoBall—"

Oh, right. Shoot. "No, that was… that was all on me. I'm sorry, Aunt Cherry. I was in a mood. But things are better now."

"Better… as in you and the man you've been romantically not-romantic with have patched things up? That's a relief, I have to say, sweetness, since Bernie sent me a picture of you and Champ canoodling at Annie's the other morning. I'm pretty sure when you've been with your one-night stand for forty days and forty nights, you can't claim it's any kind of *stand* anymore."

I sighed. I did not want to know where she got her information.

"We've patched things up," I agreed. "In fact…" I hesitated, because speaking the words out loud seemed like bad luck somehow. "I think we have decided to be… cautiously romantic."

"So much better than romantically cautious," she said happily. "I'll tell Terrance it's time to gas up the truck."

"But Cherry, that's not why I'm calling. I need advice. *Not* about my, um… affairs."

"Okay," she agreed cautiously. "Shoot."

I filled her in as much as I could on Marissa's situation without tying it to Champ's investigation… which was almost impossible when not wanting to let Champ down was my primary motivation for not telling Marissa to head to Vegas immediately.

"So, let me understand," Cherry said when I was done. "This woman—your bride—is marrying an ass who tried to kiss you before your first meeting?"

"Well. Yes. I think he might be a little closeted, and I don't know his whole story, but—"

"Quinn, I'm sympathetic, but you don't get a free pass to cheat on your partner because you're questioning your sexuality. You talk to your partner about the situation, and *then* you see what's what."

I closed my eyes. "No, I know."

"And you're saying the other man—Levi the bodyguard—is in love with her but won't make a move?"

"He doesn't think he's good enough for her," I confirmed. "She'd have to give him an engraved invitation."

"And would she? Is your client in love with her bodyguard?"

I sighed miserably. "Definitely. She's been in love with him for decades, and he's been pulling away from her just as long because he doesn't think he has enough to offer."

"Oh, Lordy. Would she even listen to you if you told her?"

I hesitated, then admitted, "Marissa wouldn't hesitate to listen if I told her this. She'd jump in Levi's arms and have him on a plane to Vegas by sunset. The only reason she hasn't done that already is because she doesn't think Levi loves her that way."

"Oh, honey. And you're hesitating to talk to her… why?" Cherry asked plainly. "Please tell me this isn't about you wanting to lose a contract."

"No! Not that exactly. It's just… my job is to plan the wedding, not to offer her life advice. My business reputation—"

"Your business reputation ain't worth shit, pardon my French, if you don't have your integrity," she said firmly. "Do you know how many of my own brides I had to dissuade from buying the absolute wrong gown for their body type, even if it meant losing their business altogether? I can't tell you how many thousands of dollars I might've lost, sweetie, but I can tell you I always managed to sleep at night. Besides, didn't Bunny Champion set you up with a dozen or more new clients? She said she did. Said she hoped she'd gotten you to realize that life in Nashville won't hold a candle to life in the Thicket."

"Well, yes, but…"

"Setting up shop in the Thicket was plenty good for me all those years. I got plenty of Nashville brides, if you'll recall, and I never had a dry spell for clients. Not in forty years! Besides which, it was always nice to be able to give the personal touch—"

"It is. I agree. I'm planning to stay in the Thicket, but—"

"Honey, go talk to your client—"

"But there's nothing more useless than tying yourself to a man," I said desperately. "You told me that a million times. Wouldn't it be silly to encourage Marissa to cancel this wedding and run off with Levi when she'd really only be tying herself to a *different* sort of man?"

Cherry was silent for a long moment. "Sweetheart, there's something I should've told you a while ago. Did you know that I was engaged, once upon a time?"

"You were? To who? I don't remember—"

"No, you wouldn't remember him. Fred jilted me at the altar before you were born," she said quietly. "But he took my heart with him. Or at least I thought he did."

"Wait, really? Oh, Cherry—"

"For the longest time, I believed I was protecting myself by never letting myself get involved with someone seriously again. Told myself that working with my brides was the closest I was ever meant to get to the altar. I spent a lot of lonely years. And I can't entirely regret it because it means that I'm able to be with Terrance now, but... I hadn't realized until the other night just how much of my own anger and pain I'd passed on to you unintentionally. And for that, I'm truly sorry."

"You don't owe me an apology—"

"Hush. I *do*. Because now I see a lot of things clearly. Like how relationships are meant to work. And

how being honest and up-front about your feelings —
with your man, with your clients, with *yourself* — is the
only way to truly be happy. So you tell me, Quinny:
Are you gonna be happy if you let Marissa marry this
idiot when she could have someone who looks at her
the same way you look at Percy Champion?"

Fuck. She was absolutely right. I couldn't do it.

"If it's *real*, Quinn, if it's meant to be, it's gonna
happen at some point anyway, but you'd be saving her
years of heartbreak and pain if you intervene. Trust
your gut, sweetheart. Have faith that things will work
out the way they're supposed to. And don't be afraid to
lean on your man too. He'd want to support you in
doing what you know is right."

I hung up but stared at the phone in my hand for a
long while.

I wanted to believe that Champ would support me.
Under any other circumstances, I was sure he would.

But I also knew that being honest with Marissa
meant that Champ was going to have to come up with a
new plan with only hours to go, and he was going to be
incredibly, incredibly angry.

Possibly angry enough to end our non-relationship
relationship.

Did I really have enough trust in him, in *us*, to risk
that?

"Morning, Quinn!" Marissa called as she sailed in
the door, ready for her appointment. "Ready for the
rehearsal dinner?"

"Marissa, honey." I blew out a breath and forced a
smile. "We need to talk."

20

CHAMP

With one day to go until the wedding, my job had become a total fiasco.

Despite two weeks of trying with our own vault door and multiple consultations with experts ranging from vault manufacturers to an imprisoned art thief named Le Chaton, we *still* hadn't found a way into the safe without making a hell of a lot of noise and leaving an obvious hole in the damned thing to announce our theft. Unless a solution fell into our laps, we'd have to go in during the wedding reception and stage a burglary, which was the most inelegant solution I could have imagined for a group of trained professionals.

Jacob Horn was breathing down my neck about getting this resolved "one way or another," reminding me that our contract was up in just five months, and complaining nonstop about the additional protection coverage I'd put in place for their executives at my own personal expense.

On top of that, Vince had not only talked to Quinn after the SnoBall—a fact which enraged me to no end

—but he'd also ambushed me when I was leaving Annie's Bakery the other morning with Quinn's donuts and threatened me right out in the middle of the fucking street to get him the missing Horn or he'd put me in federal prison for interfering in an investigation.

It had been all I could do not to confront him then and there about the surveillance equipment in my office, but I hadn't wanted to play that card yet. I wasn't sure if we'd been infiltrated by the DEA, the cartel, or some third factor I hadn't even accounted for on my mental chessboard, and telling Vince would narrow my options.

In fact, the only redeeming thing about the past two weeks was that this was almost over... and that when the wedding was done, for better or worse, I'd still have Quinn by my side.

I sat back from my laptop at Carter and Riggs's big kitchen table and rubbed my face with my hands. This shit was getting on my last nerve. If I didn't care so much about retaining the Thicket's largest corporation as my client, I'd let them go just to have it be over once and for all. I was sick and tired of hearing about Horn of Glory.

"So of course I let him tinker with my bobbetts," Kev said, talking to anyone who would listen, which was approximately no one as far as I could tell. "I mean, wouldn't you? Anomaly451 decimated the swarming audacious volt-hornets that were en route to my Fern Fairie camps, easy as you please, with his laser volt-revokers and spin traps. It was like... well, it was like a knight riding in on a danged pegicorn." He bent down to pet Hercules.

Hux clapped his hands over his ears and cried,

"Boss, tell Kev to shut up. This is killing me. It's… it's workplace harassment or something."

"I can't harass you by talking about the video game created by Champion Security's biggest client," Kev said smugly. "I can talk about my Horn all day. And maybe I will."

"Kev, please try to contain yourself, okay?" I demanded impatiently. "And Huxley, do your fucking job."

"But who gives a shit about any of Kev's Fern Fairie camps? If the volt-hornets had destroyed them, you could have purchased new ones at the solstice market-place next week. Jesus."

Kev shot him a hateful glare. "Anyone can *buy* a win, Huxley. The truly honorable player wins with nothing but hard work and the might of his Horn. Not that I'd expect *you* to know that." He sniffed. "You're just jealous because Anomaly451 likes me better than you. Did I mention he gave me his crystal jade? *Because he did.* I'm going to mount it on a scepter and get plus ten royalty every time I wave the damned thing. And I'm going to wave it at your shithole tambor-oxen hovel every time I pass it on my air-speeder!"

Hux sighed. "It's an air scooter. In case you don't recall, your creepy Horn-flirt downgraded your air-speeder when he tinkered with your bobbetts."

"*It was a mistake!*" Kev shouted. "I already told you he apologized."

Hux shrugged and made a big production of putting his headset on.

Kev turned to me. "Champ, I cannot tolerate these working conditions—"

"Great. Same. Trace the source of that surveillance equipment, and we'll get out of your hair."

Thankfully, their squabbling was interrupted by the arrival of Riggs and Carter.

"We come bearing coffee," Riggs said, handing out the drinks.

"And gossip," Carter added with a glance at me. I closed my laptop and took a sip of my drink.

"What kind of gossip?"

He took the seat across from me at the table. "The kind I'm not sure if we should be concerned about or not? I had lunch with Tucker Johnson earlier. When I stopped by his office to pick him up, I overheard Vienna Goodley talking to Lurlene Jackson about seeing someone suspicious outside Taffet Events last night."

I shoved my chair back and stood up, leaning my hands on the table. "Someone was at Quinn's place? Riggsy, go talk to her and find out exactly what she saw."

Riggs took the seat next to Carter and lifted a placating hand. "Already done. I spoke to her right after Carter called me about it. She said she saw a man around six feet tall dressed in dark clothing and a dark wool cap looking in the windows and trying the door. She called the cops when she saw him try the door, but they came out and didn't find any sign of a break-in. Between you and me, she probably makes enough false claims as to be on their special list of busybody wannabe witnesses."

I looked at my second-in-command. "But you believed her."

He nodded. "She said he came back after the cops were gone and snuck around back. She called the cops again, but they slow-rolled the response because of a scuffle out at the Devoted Dogs' roadhouse around the same time."

Elvo moved away from the safe he'd been focused on and clapped Riggs's shoulder. "What two-bit B&E perp comes back to try again after the cops arrive?"

Riggs shook his head. "None that I've ever known."

"Which means it wasn't a petty criminal." The idea that someone sent by the Cartel de la Luna might have been trying to get inside Quinn's workplace, his *home*, made me feel like vomiting.

"Okay, *maybe*. But boss, aren't you always the one telling us not to jump to conclusions? I agree, it's suspicious, so I asked Marlon Waters at Uncle Marlon's Tax Prep if he could get us copies of his security recordings from last night, just to see if the intruder might appear. He said he'd send them over. Why don't we wait, and—"

"Get on him again," I instructed, already halfway to the door. "Get that footage *now*. I've gotta go." I needed to find Quinn immediately. To set my eyes on him and confirm for myself that he was okay. And I didn't care how bossy it made me, Quinn wouldn't be working there anymore until after this case was closed and the Horn was no longer associated with him in any way.

Riggs scrambled out of his seat to follow. "Want me to come with you?"

I waved him off. "No. You stay here and keep trying to find us a way into that vault. And could you ask Mrs. Clayborn to take care of Hercules? I want to end this *tonight* if we can, before someone gets hurt."

Before *Quinn* got hurt.

When I got to the front door, I yanked it open and strode through the doorway, nearly knocking Quinn on his ass.

"Baby? Oh, thank fuck. I was just coming to get you." I grabbed the front of his jacket in my fist and pulled him into a tight embrace. "Jesus. I'm overreacting, I *know* I'm overreacting, but I—" I felt his uneven breathing and realized he was crying. I held him away from me by his shoulders. "Wait, are you okay? Did something happen? Are you hurt? Talk to me, dammit."

"I did something that's going to ruin your p-plans," Quinn wailed. "I'm s-so sorry. But Cherry said to do what I knew I could live with, and I just knew I couldn't l-live with myself if I didn't do it. Maybe I could have lived with it *before*. A few months ago—even a few weeks ago. Before I really knew how good it could feel to be with the right person. But now I do, and I couldn't let it go—I'm so sorry, Champ. Please believe me."

The noise of my men racing toward his sound of distress drowned out what he was saying, and I was halfway through visually inspecting him for injuries when his words caught up to me.

"Wait, what did you say?"

Quinn's breath hitched in a teary hiccup. "I… I told Marissa not to m-marry Trey. That she should marry for love. So she and Levi left for Vegas on her friend's private plane. They already took off."

I felt my team's stares from behind me, and my shock was probably much the same as theirs, even though I should have seen it coming. "You told your client to marry someone else? The day before her wedding?"

He held up his hands. "I know. I know. But I couldn't let her marry that guy. Not when she and Levi are meant to be together. It wasn't right to let them make such a big mistake."

"So the wedding is off?" Riggs asked, going into work mode. "If so, we need to move *now*. Otherwise, we'll lose access to the house. Quinn, do you know if Tommy and Carlotta have arrived in town yet? Who's at the farmhouse right now?"

Quinn didn't take his eyes off me. "They're already there, but they don't know the wedding is off yet. No one does except Trey." He reached for my hand. "Champ, I have an idea about how to get the Horn."

I opened my mouth to tell him he was sure as shit not getting more involved in the Horn op, but then I remembered what Riggs had said the night after the SnoBall.

You and Quinn are stronger as a team, ever think of that?

"Tell me your idea," I said, pulling him out of the cold and into the warmth of the huge house.

Once we were settled around the table with laptops and Elvo's favorite brainstorming whiteboard propped up on a deep windowsill, Quinn started laying it out.

"Listen, I know I've suggested this before and you've shut it down, but Tommy Drakes *loves* his daughter. *Adores* her. Dotes on her. You should have heard him the night of the SnoBall. He paraded her around to everyone and introduced her as his brilliant business partner, his strategic marketing expert, the heart of their family. He talked about how smart and funny she was, and he made sure Levi was always close enough to keep an eye on her for protection."

"Levi was doing more than protecting her," Elvo muttered as he wrote *Tommy proud of Marissa* on the whiteboard in red ink.

Quinn continued. "My point is, Tommy would do anything to protect her… including giving up something that is currently putting her in danger with a notorious drug cartel. I am *positive* this is so. I'd stake my reputation on it."

"You're suggesting that we ask Tommy directly," I said. "But baby, we've talked about this option. What happens if we're wrong? He could move the Horn to another location or sell that information back to the cartel himself."

"Besides," Riggs added, "Marissa's not in danger anymore if she's back in Nashville and the Horn remains here at the farm, or if Tommy moves it to some-place completely separate from where his daughter is..."

Quinn shook his head. "She *would* still be in danger because the cartel and the DEA won't *know* he moved it. The way this works is not only by asking him to help us, but by convincing him that giving the Horn to us will get both the cartel and DEA off his back completely."

"How do we do that?" I asked.

"We convince Tommy to give the Horn to the DEA. To Vince. Which would neutralize the cartel *and* the threat of an investigation."

I stared at him. "Quinn. You know we can't. That would leave our client completely exposed and connected to this. It would be a PR disaster if the infor-mation stored on that Horn is even half as incriminating as we think it is."

Carter set a tray of sandwiches in the center of the table. "You could always take the information off the Horn before you give it to Vince."

Hux shook his head. "It's tricky to make info like that disappear completely unless we reset the Horn, which would be really obvious."

Quinn's eyes flared wide and excited. "Okay, what

if we gave Vince a decoy Horn? Can HOG Corporate give us one that looks exactly like the missing one? Can we fool them?"

Hux laughed. "A sparkly peach first-gen? Are you kidding? No. Only three were created before the mold was broken, and no one's ever created a successful forgery. One belongs to a sultan in the Middle East, who shows it off at his lavish parties. The second was sold to an entity in South America we now know to be Gustavo Santiago, head of the Cartel de la Luna, and was subsequently stolen and sold at a flea market in Tennessee to Tommy Drakes, the Speedo guy." Hux's voice sounded pained at the indignity that this Horn had endured.

"And the third Horn?" Quinn asked.

Hux shrugged. "Some say Elon Musk sent it into space. Others say Warren Buffet keeps it in his subterranean hideout beneath the suburbs of Omaha. Personally, I like to think..." Hux's cheeks flushed, and his voice went hoarse. "I like to think a mysterious rich benefactor bought and hid it so that someday it'd be found by someone truly worthy of holding it. Kinda the way Excalibur found Arthur, you know?" He cleared his throat and wiped his eyes surreptitiously. "But in any case, we won't have it for this op."

"Wow. That's... a very moving tale," Kev said, picking the crust off a sandwich with unusual focus. "So I guess that's out. Darn."

Carter turned to glare at his cousin. "Tell them."

Now Kev's cheeks turned pink. "*Moi*? Tell them what? I'm not part of this, remember? You all keep making a point of how I'm not a team member and you don't need my help."

Carter sat down in the seat next to him and

squeezed his shoulder. His voice softened. "Kev. This is really important. You know it is, and you know I wouldn't ask you if it wasn't a matter of life and death."

Kev's eyes widened. "Life and death? I thought it was a public relations thing?"

I leaned forward so I could see him better around Elvo's wide shoulders. "That's what it is for our client, but the information we think is on there is protecting the identities of cartel members as well as their financial transactions. This information could potentially be used to stop an incredible amount of illegal drug production and movement. As soon as we distance our client from the source of the information, we'll turn it over to the DEA so they can take action on it. And beyond that, the lives of every single person associated with Champion Security could be at risk if the cartel gets desperate enough. They've proven that they can get close to us already. That's why we're here." I waved my hand in a circle to encompass the whole enormous house.

Riggs added, "The Cartel de Luna is responsible for importing seven metric tons of cocaine into the United States in the last four years and could be responsible for up to a hundred thousand drug overdose deaths in America alone."

Kev groaned. "Fine. *Fine*! I'm your mysterious rich benefactor."

Hux looked like he'd been shot. His face went slack and pale. "You…? No. Not *you*. Not this Horn."

"Yep. Me. With this Horn. Lo siento, *HogMasterHux*." Kev gave Hux a smirk that said he wasn't sorry at all. "Don't be too sad. You'd never be worthy of holding my Horn anyway."

Huxley opened his mouth to retort, but all that

came out was a sad puff of air. He clamped his mouth shut again so hard his teeth clacked.

Carter turned to me and gave a small, unnecessary nod. We all knew Kev had a big heart and would agree to anything that would help the greater good…

As long as it didn't involve Huxley.

"Thank you," I told Kev sincerely, and he nodded.

"Okay, so now that we have a decoy Horn…" I turned back to Quinn. "What's the best way to approach Tommy Drakes?"

21

QUINN

Everyone turned to me expecting me to have a plan fleshed out rather than just a vague idea of what we could do.

I realized that this experienced team, a group of smart, capable men headed by Champ, respected me enough to value my input, knowledge, and experience. My lungs expanded as I took in a deep, cleansing breath and relaxed.

Part of me felt like I'd finally found my home. Instead of breaking down into a heap of grateful tears, I forced myself to focus on the op.

"Okay, first… I need to show you this." I pulled a piece of paper from my back pocket and unfolded it onto the table. "It's a note from Vince — Agent Parler. I found it on my back door this afternoon when Marissa and Levi were leaving. I'm not sure when he could have left it — "

"Motherfucker," Champ swore, running a hand through his hair. "I might know. Vienna Goodley saw someone trying to break into Taffet Events earlier, which is why I was just a bit upset when you got here."

Holy shit. Vienna really *was* protecting the Thicket.

"Champ was just a tiny bit upset," Riggs reiterated. "Not close to a blind panic, no matter how it might have appeared."

Champ shot him a dark look. "We're trying to get security footage from the tax place next door to see if we can get an ID, but I thought it might be someone from the cartel poking around, not fucking *Vince*." He took the note off the table and scanned it quickly. "Holy shit. This sounds…"

"A little unhinged," I suggested. "Yeah. It freaked me out." Especially since I'd already been an emotional wreck over the Marissa thing.

Champ pulled my chair closer to his and casually dropped an arm over my shoulder, which felt incredibly nice and incredibly right.

"Mr. Taffet," Champ read. "It appears that my previous friendly warnings have gone unheeded, and you have decided to throw your lot in with Percy's. I wish I could say I'm surprised, but I'm not. Percy is good at inspiring devotion, even though he's terrible at returning it. Yet I can't help but urge you one last time to consider working with me. My colleagues and I can not only ensure you're not prosecuted as an accessory to any crimes Mr. Champion and his fellows might have committed, I can also offer you financial compensation. Name your price —"

"He's offering Quinn a *bribe*?" Elvo demanded. "Holy. Fucking. Shit."

"My exact thought," I agreed. "I'm no lawyer, but that doesn't seem… ethical."

"Or legal." Champ dropped the letter back to the

table and threaded his free hand with mine. "Shit. Is he *that* determined to get a promotion? Or is this personal for him?"

Several pairs of eyes wearing identical stunned expressions stared back at me.

"At the end of the letter, he says that he hopes I'll stop by his motel later today to discuss my terms," I told the others. "So I was thinking—"

Champ let out a humorless laugh. "Well, that's not happening. Over my dead body. A wedding planner is not a security operative."

I pulled away from Champ and tilted my head to look at him with one raised eyebrow. There was a difference between being lovingly protected and being told what to do. I appreciated the former, but I had *never* appreciated the latter, and that wasn't going to change.

At no time had I been planning to actually go to Vince's motel on my own without a plan, and yet suddenly, there was nothing I wanted more.

"Beg your pardon, Bossy Pants?" I asked between clenched teeth.

Champ looked around at his teammates as if they'd support him on his Neanderthal statement. "You're not going over there. Case closed."

"Okay, I can see there's been a teeny, tiny miscommunication," I fumed. "You and I might be together, but you are not the boss of me. I will make my own judgments and go where I want. If I want to go to Vince's motel after I leave here, I will damned well go to Vince's motel, and there's nothing you can do to stop me. So if you would like to offer a suggestion or an opinion, I would welcome that. But you can take your 'that's not happening' bullshit and stick it where the Horn don't shine. Understand?"

Carter leaned over to Riggs. "Is that how I sound when I'm arguing with you?"

Riggs nodded. "Mmhm."

Elvo sighed and grabbed another sandwich before leaning back to watch the show.

Champ stood up and loomed over me, resting his knuckles on the table so he could get in my face. "Vince is using you, Quinn. He's manipulating you to get what he wants. Surely you see that."

The reminder made me angry. "Of course I do! I've seen it from literally the first time he introduced himself, and I'm so fucking pissed, because that day he visited me after the SnoBall… Fuck. He talked such a good game, he almost had me fooled. But I'm even angrier that he's using *you* to do it. As if leaving you wasn't stupid enough, now he has to mess with your life like this? I'm so mad at him, I can't stand it. But you *still* don't get to tell me what I can and can't do. You can protect me, Champ. I want you to. But you don't get to manipulate me too!"

I could tell by the way his face fell that I'd scored a direct hit. My palms started to sweat. I didn't want to argue with him, but my mouth was used to fronting, and apparently, my brain couldn't stop it from going down this ridiculous road.

"Manipulate you? Me?" Champ demanded. "Why would I manipulate someone I love? Do you think so little of me that you'd actually think I'm trying to control you for my own entertainment? *I don't want you hurt.* Do you understand? I don't want you to die. Someone tried to break into your shop last night, and for a while there, I thought it might have been someone from the Cartel de la Luna. I was on my way out the door to find you, to protect you, when you arrived."

"Oh. My. God." I pushed to my feet and leaned into his space, too, so that our faces ended up inches apart. "So you're saying it would be okay for *you* to be out running around if the Cartel is involved? Fuck. That. You might be a trained protector, but that doesn't make you impervious to bullets. And if you think I'm going to let the most important person in my world put his life on the line while I sit back and make fucking flower arrangements, you're out of your fucking mind."

It wasn't until Riggs leaned over to Carter that I realized I'd missed something big. "Did we know they were actually in love?"

Carter shook his head. "I'm not sure *they* knew," he whispered back.

I blinked at Champ. His words played back in my memory. "You... you love me?" I breathed.

His forehead crinkled. "I tell you your life is in danger and that's what you're taking from this?"

I grabbed the front of his shirt and grinned. "You love me?" I repeated.

"Mpfh," he grunted, lowering back down into his chair.

I barked out a laugh. "Not good enough, Percival Champion. Say it."

His blue eyes met mine. "Already did. You say it."

I still held him by the shirt front and pulled him close again. "I love you so much it terrifies me," I admitted in a soft voice. Despite the table full of men, I felt like it was just the two of us in a bubble.

Champ's big hand came around to cup the back of my head. "I love you too. But it means I can't let anything happen to you. I can't, sweetheart. Please don't expect me to stop protecting you."

He tempered the statement with a kiss that was tender and loving. It wasn't the kiss of a sixty-four-night stand. It was the kiss of forever. The kiss of new beginnings.

It was Hux's voice that exploded our little bubble. "Can we get back to the op, please? Because this shit is awkward as fuck."

Kev sighed. "You're just jealous because you're the only person here who doesn't have someone in their life."

Hux huffed. "You're claiming your pissant Horn-flirt as a special someone now? Are you for real? They could be a fourteen-year-old girl or a sixty-year-old Russian oligarch. Jesus, Kev. Use your brain."

Kev's knowing smirk was new. "We've had video sex, moron. He's got a killer body."

The room went quiet for a beat before everyone started asking questions. Champ finally called a halt to it by shouting, "Back to work! We don't have any time left before Tommy Drakes finds out Marissa and Levi have flown the coop and this shit all goes FUBAR."

He turned back to me. "You know Vince wants you to get him into the farmhouse."

"Not if he has to get the Horn out of the vault himself," I countered. "What he'd really like, what he's been asking for all along, is for me to convince you to turn the Horn over to him. Alternatively, he'd probably like me to steal it from you and give it to him. And in a pinch, he'd love to know how *you're* gonna get the Horn so he can take it off you immediately afterwards."

"*Fuck.* That's Vince's MO, alright. Why do his own work when he can piggyback off someone else's?"

Champ looked around at his team. "And he knows how we work too. I shared too many stories with him when we were together. He'd probably expect us to go in during the wedding reception, and if we went with that plan, he might have caught us."

Elvo shook his head. "No, boss. Vince knows how we used to work. He doesn't know shit about how we work now. Improvise, adapt, and overcome."

"Oorah," the rest of the team barked.

"And," Riggs said, placing one huge hand on my shoulder, "they don't know about our secret weapon."

"True." Champ leaned over and snuck a quick kiss on my lips before turning back to the task at hand. "Okay, so first, we figure out a way to approach Tommy and get him to cooperate."

I nodded firmly.

"Then, we'll set it up so that, to all outside observers, Marissa's wedding is still happening. Might be too late to get Trey on board, but we can ask the Drakes not to tell their guests the wedding's off until the very last minute. We lure Vince to the farmhouse so he can steal the Horn right after we've supposedly stolen it, except it'll be Kev's Horn we'll be using as a decoy. We let him walk out with the decoy—no violence, nobody gets hurt, especially with the Drakes family still on-site. Agreed?"

Everyone nodded.

"Hux, are you ready to strip the data off that thing as soon as we get it?" Champ continued.

"Not a problem."

Champ reached for a sandwich. "What data do we put on the decoy? It has to be something believable."

Riggs asked Hux several questions about his ability to decrypt the data quickly once we had it and whether or not using any of it on the decoy would be an option.

Hux explained the various types of encryption it could have on it, and Kev piped up to add to the conversation. They completed each other's sentences in a way that proved their shared passion for the topic of cybersecurity. The two of them together were a sight to behold as long as they forgot they hated each other. I wondered if Champ had ever been tempted to offer Kev a job just to lock down his expertise.

I turned to Champ. "They can talk over options as much as they want, but until we actually get the Horn, we won't know for sure what's possible or what the data actually is, right?"

He made a sound of agreement.

"Okay," I said, grabbing his arm. "Then let's get this op started. I don't want Vince to get to the Horn before we do."

We ran through ideas with Elvo scribbling on the whiteboard and Hux tapping away at his laptop until we felt confident in the plan. Everyone agreed I was the best person to approach Tommy since he'd feel the least threatened by me.

Champ agreed. "He may be a small-time criminal, but he's not the kind of guy who's going to hurt you for asking to see his Horn."

Riggs turned to Elvo. "Getting the HOG Corporate account is the best thing that ever happened to us, if only so we get to hear him say shit like that. You'd never know he was a man who hates puns."

"Oh, no, you would," Elvo argued. "You can practically see the boss's blood pressure rising."

Champ ignored them. He put his hand on my chest and met my eyes. "We will be nearby if you need us, and I'll plan to 'come home' to the farmhouse not long after you get there. You won't be alone, okay?"

"I'm not worried about Tommy. The worst that can happen is him saying no to our request," I said with confidence, even though my stomach churned with nerves.

I wasn't worried about *Tommy*; it was Vince I was terrified of. The man set off my alarm bells like crazy, and I couldn't figure out if it was because of high-key jealousy since Champ had dreamed of a future with him or if it was because he was damned good at intimidation tactics.

Either way, I wasn't looking forward to talking to him.

We went through the plan one more time. I declined Hux and Champ's attempts at loading me up with surveillance tech. "Dude, I'm just going to talk to my client. It's fine." But I wouldn't have been surprised to learn that someone had slipped a tracking device in my pocket when Champ hugged me tight enough to cut off my circulation.

His blue eyes retained their familiar intensity, but his voice softened. "I meant what I said earlier, you know. I really love you."

My heart felt like a cage suddenly opened, expelling manic butterflies desperate to be free, and I wished I had the magical ability to transport us to an alternate reality with no Horns, no canceled weddings, and no weirdo ex-boyfriends to contend with, where I could listen to Champ repeating those words all night long.

But since that wasn't an option, I was willing to fight for our happily ever after in *this* reality, so I could hear him tell me again for the rest of our lives.

"I really love you too. And that's why I'm one

hundred percent going to do this. Because I want to protect what's mine too. Do you trust me?"

"Yeah, I do." Champ pressed a hard kiss to my mouth before pulling away and clearing his throat. "But if something happens to you..." He grasped my jaw with both hands and lowered his voice until it was even deeper than his usual baritone. "Just know that if anything happens to you, I will burn the world down to make it right." He leaned in and kissed me hard on the mouth before repeating his warnings against my lips. "You call me the minute your gut starts squawking, understand?"

I nodded, and I imagined my face must have shown just how much his words affected me because Champ stood a little straighter. "Okay," he said. "Let's do this."

I couldn't say I minded Champ's protectiveness when he kept his bossiness in check, not one little bit. It was seriously sweet and hella sexy. Who wouldn't want someone to look out for them while also trusting them to do what they felt they needed to do?

After finally hopping in my car, I drove down the long driveway and took a deep, cleansing breath. The idea of setting up Vince was fucking with my nerves, so I decided to do that part first and get it over with. The plan had assumed I'd get Tommy's buy-in first, but I was confident he'd help us in some way.

I wasn't as confident in my ability to fool Vince. Might as well try it and see.

I turned right toward Vince's motel instead of left toward Drakes Farm.

With Champ on my side, what was the worst that could happen?

22

———

CHAMP

As I watched Quinn's car head down the driveway, I replayed the last bits of our conversation. Quinn had asked me the dreaded question.

Do you trust me?

I'd felt my team's eyes burn the back of my neck.

"Yeah, I do," I'd said firmly. Because it was the truth.

But I'd meant what I'd told him too. I'd burn down the world if he was hurt. Hell, as wired as I felt at that moment, I'd burn it down if he was mildly inconvenienced. I had a whole new appreciation for what folks like Carter and Yolanda's wife went through when we were out on a dangerous op.

Once Quinn's car was gone, I'd barked at the team to get back to work. It took about half a second for them to start peppering me with questions.

"Was that such a good idea?" Kev asked, wringing his hands. "Quinn's kinda scrawny."

Hux, who was the shortest one of us by far, crossed

his muscular arms in front of his chest and glared at him. "Small doesn't mean you can't fuck a guy up."

Kev's cheeks turned pink, and his eyelashes fluttered.

Riggs nudged me with his elbow. "We loading up in the surveillance van? I know we said we'd let him go it alone, but…"

Everything inside of me screamed to go after him in the van, put as many eyes on him as possible, and be prepared with an arsenal in case things went south.

"No. He'll recognize the van and think we don't trust him."

Elvo shrugged. "Doesn't take a van to keep an eye on the guy. Not when Hux has loaded Quinn's phone up with the usual security suite."

I turned to pin Hux with a glare. "You hacked his phone?"

Hux firmed his jaw and opened his laptop without looking at me. "He's family, boss. I don't make the rules."

Out of the corner of my eye, I noticed Carter turn to Riggs with a questioning eyebrow raise. Apparently, my second-in-command had neglected to tell his man that we looked after our own, even when it involved a little bit of invasion of privacy. Riggs shook his head in a *not now* gesture.

I was torn between wanting to prove I trusted Quinn and wanting to keep him safe.

Ultimately, there was no question.

"Hux, pull up the feed. We're going to trust him to make this happen, but we're going to have his back too." I turned to Elvo. "Let's assume we'll still need to get into that vault our way. With the wedding off, we're gonna have to do a smash and grab if things go south."

"You got it." Elvo returned to the vault and his pile of tools to get back to work on our Plan B.

Meanwhile, Hux pulled up the tracking information for Quinn's phone. "Champ."

The team rarely called me something other than "boss." I stepped closer to look at his screen.

"What did you find?" On the screen, I noticed a tiny wedding cake icon approaching a red devil icon on a map of Licking Thicket. "What the fuck am I looking at?"

"Erm. The wedding cake is Quinn. And the devil icon… Let's just say it's possible that I neglected to deactivate the tracking device I put on Vince's phone a while ago."

Riggs stepped in to look over Hux's other shoulder. "He's not going to the farmhouse, boss. Quinn's at the motel where Vince is staying. The plan called for him to talk to Tommy first."

I stared at the red devil as my anger grew to resemble the same. "That fucking bastard," I murmured.

Riggs straightened up. "Okay, calm down. I'm sure Quinn doesn't intend to—"

"I don't mean Quinn," I gritted out. "He's probably tackling the hard part first. It's one of his things." One of the ridiculous quirks that had become so incredibly important to me somehow.

I clenched my hands into fists. "What I don't understand is why the fuck Vince cares about this so much. He used to be a total rule follower. Not the kind of guy to be skulking around trying to obtain a Horn without a warrant with the help of an untrained wedding planner. For damn sure not the kind to be leaving *written evidence* that he'd offered that wedding planner a bribe—"

"Marlon Waters sent over his security footage," Hux said as a notification chimed on his computer. "Sweet. Looks like he's got it set to record only when it senses motion. Saves me a shit ton of time."

Hux tapped a key, and a grainy image appeared on his screen, showing the dark alley behind Taffet Events… and an even darker blob jogging across it.

"Well, that's fucking anticlimactic," Elvo said. "Our intruder appears to be a kangaroo."

"I was thinking capybara," Carter commented. "Those fuckers are scary." Riggs shot him an amused, besotted glance and rubbed a spot on his chest.

"Have faith, people. Jesus." Hux froze the frame during the one instance where the blob appeared to be facing the camera and tapped several more keys in quick succession. The image resolved and brightened like magic until Vince's face appeared on the screen.

I shook my head. "Add this to the list of shit that doesn't make sense. It wasn't the fucking cartel breaking into Quinn's place. It was my overachieving ex-boyfriend?"

"Or," Hux said, dragging the word out. "What if it's… both?"

"Both," I repeated, not understanding… and then suddenly, I did. "You think Vince is working for the cartel?"

Hux shrugged, but I could see the fire in his eyes. He got that look often when he was on the right track. "I mean, do we think Vince is just going rogue for no particular reason? Is he really that desperate for a promotion? Or is it more likely that his taste for luxury caught up with him and he had to find an alternate source of revenue once he didn't have a rich boyfriend to buy his Rolexes—"

The silence in the room punctuated his point.

Hux cleared his throat and shifted uncomfortably. "Uh. Sorry, boss. I'm gonna go back to not jumping to conclusions now."

"Yeah, but..." Elvo ran his hands through his hair. "Boss, wasn't he the one who told you about the missing Horn all the way back in November? How'd he know about that?"

I nodded slowly. I was finding it hard not to jump to conclusions myself. "There have been a bunch of things he knew but shouldn't have known. Kev, can you take over the tracking surveillance so Hux can call his contact at the DEA? I want to find out what the official status of the Horn case is on their end. Maybe we've been going at this the wrong way from the beginning."

Kev nodded and reached for Hux's laptop. Hux stared at him with wide eyes. "Fuck that. You can pry this laptop from my cold, dead hands."

I passed my laptop over to Kev. "The surveillance app is on here too. Let Hux pull it up, and you can use this to keep an eye on Quinn. Thanks." I shot Hux a glare. "Be a team player, asshole."

I couldn't help but look over Kev's shoulder as he continued to monitor Quinn's location.

That wedding cake was everything I cared most about in the world. As soon as I admitted it to myself, it seemed so obvious I wasn't sure how I'd managed to stay in denial for so long... except that it felt so different from any emotion I'd ever experienced before that maybe I hadn't recognized it.

Vince and I had been puzzle pieces that didn't fit together, each trying to change the other into someone more compatible. I'd thought that if I just wanted us to work out badly enough, if I put in maximum effort on my own, I could make us work out, and when I'd failed, I'd decided to avoid commitment and attachment entirely so I wouldn't feel rejected again.

With Quinn, I'd tried to *avoid* fitting with him from the first day because I'd been scared shitless of what he could mean to me if I let him inside my walls, but it hadn't mattered. Every part of who he was spoke to me. Lit me up. Both challenged and soothed me. I felt known and unconditionally accepted—even for all the annoying, bossy, overbearing parts of me—but also motivated to become the best, least-overbearing version of myself so I could give Quinn what he needed.

I sat down hard in a chair beside Hux's station and stared blankly into space.

"You okay?" Riggs asked, pausing beside my chair.

I nodded without looking up.

"Just experiencing the gravitational shift of your personal universe beginning to revolve around a different star than Champion Security?"

I glanced up at him and nodded again.

Riggs smiled. "I'd try to comfort you by telling you this will actually make you *better* at your job—more careful, more decisive, less inclined to take stupid risks—but I know you won't believe me yet." He patted my shoulder. "But if you need me for anything, I'm here."

"Yeah," I gritted out. "Thanks."

When I'd put this team together after leaving the service, I'd chosen my teammates carefully. They needed to be men I trusted to do their jobs, trusted to have my back and each other's.

I hadn't realized I'd be creating a family… but that seemed to be exactly what I'd done.

I didn't breathe normally again until the wedding cake was at least a mile away from the red devil and

Quinn (Gorgeous, blue eyes, drinks Howling Turtles) appeared on my phone.

I stared fondly at his contact name. He was so much more to me now… but what was there was all still true.

"Babe," I said in a rush.

"I'm okay." His voice held a thread of amusement. "I told Vince your crew was going to use the wedding reception tomorrow as cover to get into the vault. I tried to sound like I was deliberately throwing him off the trail by telling him I didn't know where the vault was but that I'd caught you more than once in the outbuilding closest to the hog pen. He had that superior look in his eyes, you know the one? Like he knew more than I did, which I hope only means he knew the location of the vault wasn't in the hog pen and not anything else. Anyway, I'm glad that part's over, and I'll see you when I'm done talking to Tommy."

"Be safe," I said before ending the call.

I scrubbed a hand over my head. Vince knew the location of the vault? How the hell could he know that unless he'd…

Fuck.

I snapped my fingers at my crew. "Another fact to add into the mix? Jericho said the bug was government issue, possibly DEA. I dismissed that at the time, thinking there was no way the DEA would work that way. But we also couldn't figure out how the cartel was using it without access to the tracking software."

"But if Vince is working for the cartel," Elvo began.

"Then he has access to all the DEA's tools, with none of those pesky legal restrictions," Riggs finished. "He bugged our office. He tried to hack our computer system."

"Yeah," I said heavily. "Vince couldn't program a

remote control on his own. But who knows what kind of hackers the cartel might have on their payroll? I'm trying not to jump to conclusions here, but I think that's exactly what happened."

I still found it shocking, though. As much as I disliked Vince, I never would have thought him capable of this.

"Are there any leads on Buck Nutter's whereabouts? I can't decide if I want to find him or not," I admitted. "But it would be nice if he could tell us what the fuck the information on the Horn is and whether it's worth all this trouble. What happens when we finally get our hands on the Horn and it's full of someone's FarmVille harvest totals?"

"It's not *FarmVille*," Kev said with a withering sigh. "I can't believe you think this is anything like FarmVille."

Hux returned from the hallway where he'd gone to make the call to his contact at the DEA, and shot Kev a commiserating look. "Champ's never really understood. Just let it go. It's a generational thing."

"We're the same age," I growled. But I could tell by the look on Hux's face that he'd learned something. "What'd you find out?"

"According to official records, Vincent Parler has been on mandatory administrative leave since January first."

I stared at him. "That's not possible."

"Also, there is no record of this case in their systems. Nothing under Cartel de Luna that's associated with Tennessee, nothing with the name Buck Nutter, and nothing mentioning Horn of Glory."

My heart rate sped up the way it did when shit started to go down on a mission. "Holy shit."

Vince was the linchpin of this whole case. It felt like reality had upended itself. Fortunately, Riggs indirectly helped me settle myself again when he walked over to Kev and clapped him on the shoulder. "Focus on the red devil. Make sure he's not following Champ's cake."

Getting Quinn safe and putting this whole situation to rest were my priorities now. I could obsess over what the hell had happened to Vince later.

Thankfully, the red devil stayed at his hotel. By the time Elvo and I got to Drakes Farm, Quinn had already texted me that Tommy had agreed to consider his plan, precisely as Quinn had predicted. Turned out his wedding-planner instincts were on point.

Tommy had a lot of questions, which was to be expected, but he invited us to sit down with him and discuss it as long as his personal security team was there as well.

His personal bodyguard turned out to be Levi's father. When I met Rod Christianson, I wondered how the dynamic would change between the two alpha males now that their kids had run off to Vegas in a shocking elopement.

I had not expected Tommy to greet me with a handshake when we stepped into his home office, then offer me a celebratory cigar and a guest chair next to Quinn.

"Couldn't be prouder of my little girl." He leaned back in the leather desk chair behind his large wooden desk and puffed on his own cigar. "Levi's like the son I never had. He's the man I'd've chosen for her if anyone around here asked my opinion."

"Yep. Don't get me wrong, it woulda been nice if my boy'd been a little less dramatic about the thing." Rod rolled his eyes and leaned his elbows against the arms of his chair. "Heck, I've known how he felt about

Marissa since they were kids. Not sure why he had to wait until the last minute to tell her so. Buuuut, he pulled his head out of his ass eventually, so I guess that counts for something."

Tommy nodded. "Woulda been nice if they'd figured this out before we had to plan this whole shindig and paint over my dang silo. Carlotta's had to call an emergency consultation with her astrologer, her stylist, and her spiritual healer just to get over the shock. And Junior Dunwoody called me to express his outrage about my daughter dumping his son—"

"Asshole," Rod muttered.

"Yep," Tommy agreed. "Seems Trey flew off to Mexico with his best man the minute Marissa told him the wedding was off and left his parents to call their guests—"

"Second-generation asshole," Rod pronounced.

"So all in all, I'm glad to be clear of that family. Besides, Quinn said Marissa and Levi will be back in time to eat dinner and cake and celebrate her marrying the *right* guy, which is more than a lot of folks can say. And I s'pose I could get someone out here to paint me another pig."

Quinn and I stared at him blankly.

"You know, on the silo? I had a real soft spot for that Windy Pig."

I opened my mouth, then shut it again and nodded politely.

Tommy and Rod exchanged a look. Rod nodded once, and Tommy leaned forward in his chair to rest his forearms on his desk. "Alright. Enough socializing, boys. Tell me more about what you want with my Horn. Quinn explained a good bit, but I'm finding it all a little hard to believe. Drug cartels and DEA agents want my Horn?"

It was even more fantastical when you suspected the DEA agent and the drug cartel might be on the same team, but I wasn't going to share that bit.

I leaned forward with my elbows on my knees and my hands spread. My instructor on body language use during collaborative negotiations would have been proud.

"It is hard to believe, sir. The whole thing is a little bit ridiculous, but it's also very serious. We believe the information on that device is critical to the safety and well-being of people across the country. You know I don't work for the government—"

He nodded. "Private security, like Rod's company."

"Exactly. And we're trying to protect our client by keeping them from being associated with this information in the public sphere. We fully believe this information should be put into the right hands, most likely the DEA, but we'd like to be the ones to do that in a way that also protects our client."

Tommy nodded. "I'll assume your client is the Horn of Glory Corporation itself."

I didn't say anything, so he continued. "Quinn explained that as long as I'm suspected of having this information, my family could be in danger."

"Yes. Absolutely. There is a very dangerous and powerful drug cartel that will do anything to recover this information and keep the government from getting their hands on it. We don't know how much they know right now in terms of the Horn's precise location, but we believe they're here in the Thicket looking for it."

"What makes you think that?" Tommy asked.

"We found surveillance tech in our office, and an

intruder was seen trying to break into Quinn's shop last night. Things are escalating, which is why we decided to come to you and tell you what's going on."

Tommy's piercing stare was meant to intimidate, but I'd been on the other side of much more intimidating glares than his. "Mr. Champion, I can't say I'm thrilled you used deception to weasel your way into my home. All this time, I thought you were here as Mr. Taffet's partner, and in reality, you were doing some kind of reconnaissance. Is that correct?"

I reached over and grasped Quinn's hand. "Not exactly. I *am* Quinn's partner. And I wanted to be here with him regardless of the Horn situation." It wasn't completely accurate, but it was true nonetheless.

Tommy nodded and looked over at Quinn. "Marissa said you really came through for her. She said you were the one who told her to follow her heart." He cleared his throat. The man was definitely not used to talking about emotions. "I never did like the way Trey treated my baby girl. I know Carlotta had a lot of things to say about the family and such. She told me to let Rissy handle her own love life, so I stayed out of it. But I'm glad you didn't, Quinn." He exchanged a look with Levi's dad before looking back at Quinn. "That's the only reason you're sitting here right now."

Quinn and I both nodded. "Yes, sir," Quinn said. "We appreciate it."

"The only way I'll do this is if I get that Horn back. I don't care what information you need to take off it, but you will give it back to me in working condition."

This time I was the one who said, "Yes, sir."

He pulled it out of a desk drawer and set it on the surface between us. The peach-color gaming device looked ridiculous in the sober situation.

Quinn stood and reached for it. "I promise Champ's team will get it back to you as soon as possible. In the meantime, Champ will give you the decoy for you to put in its place tomorrow."

I pulled Kev's collectible out of my coat pocket to show it to him. "If someone comes in during the wedding like we anticipate, it would be best if they could find this fairly easily. Maybe put it in a display box on a shelf as if you were going to bring a few VIPs back here during the reception to show it off? Then stay the hell away and let them come take it."

He nodded, but there was a stormy look on his face. "I'd rather shoot the fuckers. You know that, right?"

Levi's dad cracked his neck from side to side. Even though he didn't speak, I got the feeling he was planning on shooting the fuckers whether Tommy approved or not. I met his eye. "That would be a very bad idea. Your families will be on-site, and we don't know the size of the infiltration team. Better to let them get in and get out. The decoy Horn will have a tracker in it. We can always confront them later, once they're away from here."

Not that I'd ever share the location with Tommy, but he didn't need to know that.

Tommy stood and reached out his hand to shake again. "Quinn said you were going to spend the night at his place tonight, so I won't see you at breakfast."

That was news to me. I glanced over at him. "We'll still be here first thing. It's important to make it look like everything is still on track for the wedding."

He nodded. "Quinn explained all that. I'm sending Carlotta back to Nashville to get her out of the way—her crystal guy agrees it's for the best—but once

Marissa and Levi are back from Vegas, they'll be here to keep up appearances."

Levi's father finally spoke. "Levi knows his number one priority is keeping Rissy safe. She'll be covered. I'll cover Tommy. Your team will need to cover everyone else."

We agreed and said our goodbyes before making our way upstairs and out of the house. I took the Horn from Quinn and gave it to Riggs before following Quinn to his car and helping him into the driver's seat.

"I'll meet you at your place later," I said softly. "Lock the doors and call 9-1-1 if you—"

He let out a surprised laugh. "That's funny."

"What's funny? I'm not leaving you there alone."

"I'm not going to my place because we're not staying there. We're staying at Carter and Riggs's house along with everyone else. The only reason I told Tommy we were staying at my place was to have an excuse to be out all night."

I grabbed his chin and kissed him hard on the mouth. "Thank fuck. I didn't feel good letting you go home alone."

He pushed me away with a hand to my chest. "Then you should have said that. I know it's hard for you to get this through your thick skull, but we're a team now. I'm not saying I'm going to stay up all night noodling encrypted data, but I'm sure as shit going to be under the same roof and waiting for you when you finally fall into bed exhausted."

I inhaled the clean and cold night air and let it out slowly. My eyes wanted to water, but I blinked it back. "Thank you," I whispered. "I will meet you at Carter and Riggs's place. I don't want him to travel alone with the Horn."

Quinn nodded and grinned. "If you don't want to ride in Rebecca, just say so." He shot me a wink before shoving me away and closing the door. I walked over and climbed into the passenger seat of Riggs's truck.

"Let's go. Lots of work left tonight."

Riggs started the truck and followed Quinn's tail-lights down the farm's long driveway. "I'm really happy for you," he said in an unusually serious tone of voice. "I like Quinn a lot—we all do—and you deserve to have someone who adores you but also doesn't put up with your bullshit."

I huffed out a laugh. "He definitely doesn't make it easy on me."

We rode together in silence for a few minutes before I spoke again. "I'm trying not to assume the worst. That he'll leave. Just like Vince."

"Vince is an ass," Riggs said, full of venom. "He was *always* an ass, you just didn't see it because he was a high-achiever like you. He was smart like you. You were drawn to that so much, you failed to see he was the kind of guy who yanks others off the ladder to get to the top. Quinn's not like that. He'd climb the ladder with others on his back just to help them succeed too."

I rested my elbow on the door and leaned on my hand. The cold surface of the window seeped through my coat to my arm. "Yeah."

"You need to let him in, Champ. Stop keeping your damned walls up because of your past with someone else. Don't let Vince take this from you."

I looked over at Riggs's familiar face lit by the dashboard lights. He and I had been through so much together. There were few people who knew me as well as he did. "You're right, and I'm trying. Thank you."

He nodded and didn't say anything more because

he didn't need to. When we arrived safely at the mansion, the rest of the crew was eager to hear how it went.

I handed the Horn over to a reverent Hux, with Kev looking on with a mix of envy and awe. "Woah."

Hux and Kev sat down together and began to work seamlessly, as if someone had flipped a switch that removed all of their previous antagonism. I wasn't going to complain. Two Horn eggheads were better than one.

It didn't take long for both of them to start making disgruntled noises.

"Use words," I said. The anticipation of what we were going to find on that device was making me pace irritably between the large kitchen island and the countertops on the opposite side of the room.

Hux glanced up from his laptop screen. "There's definitely data here, but it's encrypted. Give us a little while to get through it."

"Define 'a while.'"

Hux and Kev exchanged a glance. "Anywhere from an hour to a month?" Hux said, giving me a look I recognized. It was the one the team gave me when I was being a pushy bastard.

I bit out a curse. "Okay, so for now we stick with our original plan. Let Vince take the decoy from the farm after we've loaded some super-encrypted data on it."

Kev frowned. "Data? What kind of data?"

"Jesus, I don't know. Any kind. Doesn't matter because I want it to be so encrypted that it takes them a decade to hack it. That's the best we can do until we get the real stuff unencrypted."

Kev looked at Hux. Hux looked at Kev. Then they broke out in identical smiles of unholy glee.

It was creepy as fuck, and I decided I was better off not knowing what could make Hux and his nemesis smile at one another like that.

Despite my advice for everyone to get some sleep, Hux and Kev stayed up working on the data encryption. I overheard them arguing about rainbow tables, Triple DES, bit keys, and weak encryption cyphers. I could only hope they'd get to the data before killing each other.

Quinn and I made our way upstairs to the guest room Carter had directed us to.

"Take a shower with me?" Quinn asked.

Nothing in the world sounded better.

I took my time running soapy hands all over his naked body. We didn't speak for a long time until I finally remembered something that had been nagging at the back of my mind. "I'm sorry about the wedding."

Quinn's mouth was busy kissing and licking my wet shoulder. He lifted his head up and smiled a lazy smile. "Oh, all of this is for sure gonna come up in your annual performance review, silent partner."

Despite the intense, draining day, I found myself smiling. "Just make sure you remember my flashes of brilliance too. Wedding piñatas full of glitter, for example. That was my idea."

"Noted," Quinn laughed, and then he sobered. "Seriously, though, it's okay. When one door closes, another one opens. I already found a replacement couple to get married tomorrow, and they'll take over much of the expense from the Drakes."

I blinked at him. "Wait, what? Some random couple

is going to use Marissa and Trey's wedding day? How's that going to work? Is it even safe—?"

Quinn sank to his knees and peered up at me through wet, spiky eyelashes. "Why don't you let me handle that part of things? It was Riggs's idea. I guess he wanted to make sure Vince didn't catch wind of the wedding cancelation."

Before I could argue with him, he ran his tongue along my shaft and engulfed my dick in his hot mouth.

And I ceased thinking about anyone or anything other than Quinn Taffet.

23

QUINN

If I could have stayed all day in Champ's arms, I would have. But the sun had risen, and I had a wedding to put on.

I closed my eyes and inhaled the sleepy scent of him one last time before trying to extricate myself from his possessive hold.

His arms tightened around me. "No," he grumbled.

"I have to go. I told the florist I'd come by first thing to make sure everything is packed right before they're loaded up in her van. Then I have to supervise the delivery of the cake and arrange for—"

He cut me off with a kiss. The scrape of his beard abraded my chin and cheeks while he tried making a very compelling argument to stay in bed.

If you'd told me a few weeks ago that getting Percy Champion *out* of my bed in the morning was going to be a problem, I would have laughed at you heartily, and so would my constant companion—

"Hercules!" I said, sitting up in bed. "Holy shit! Where is he? Champ—"

Champ snorted. "I asked Riggs to have Mrs. Clayborn take care of him last night, and I texted to check on him after you fell asleep." He grabbed his phone and tapped keys until he found a picture of Hercules sprawled on an enormous velvet blanket, munching a bone, like the pampered prince he deserved to be.

"Oh." I put a hand to my chest to calm my breathing. "Shit. I'm sorry, I—"

Champ dragged me down and pressed a firm kiss to my mouth before guiding me back to the pillows. "I know I have some shit to make up for where you're concerned, Quinn. You and Herc both. You were right the other night when you said that I didn't deserve him. Either one of you. But he's not a symbol of a dream that didn't come true. Not anymore. He's a part of the future I want to create with you. And you know how I feel about succeeding at a mission, right? From now on, you're my priority."

My vision suddenly went blurry with unshed tears. I knew it wouldn't be that simple, that *both* of us would have to learn how to truly believe in this relationship, but the fact that he was so committed to trying made my heart ache. It was everything I hadn't been able to admit to myself that I wanted.

I threaded my hand into Champ's hair and pulled him more fully on top of me, kissing him with all the joy and hope he made me feel.

It took me several minutes before I remembered what I was supposed to be doing. "Get off me," I said with a breathless laugh, shoving his shoulders away. "I have to work, and so do you. Maybe Hux has something for you."

That was enough to sober him up.

We shared a quick shower with one hundred

percent less groping and one hundred percent more focus on getting out the door than the night before. I drove straight to the florist.

The weather was glorious. The air was still very cold, but the sun was shining bright in a deep blue sky. It was wholly unexpected for a February wedding.

I helped facilitate a successful transfer of all the florals for the event out to the farm before returning to Taffet Events to pick up several boxes of decorations. When I approached the shop, I noticed a young woman on the front step setting down a plastic bag.

"May I help you?" I asked. I wasn't expecting a delivery today, but it wasn't out of the realm of possibility that it would be something for the wedding.

"I have a delivery for Quinn Taffet from a Mr. Champion. Are you Mr. Taffet?"

"I am," I said, unable to stop the grin.

She returned the smile. "I'm from Annie's. Mr. Champion came in this morning and asked us to bring you hot glazed donuts and a coffee to help get you through your busy morning. He says he hopes you'll be his Valentine."

I thanked her profusely and tried to tip her, but she claimed it was already taken care of. Once she was gone, I let myself into the shop and sat down to enjoy the hot donuts while I texted Champ to thank him for his thoughtfulness.

Me: *You're the best, Valentine.*

Delusional McBossypants Champion: *I love you.*

My heart flopped around in my chest like a frantic fish. Maybe I needed to change his moniker in my phone's contacts list.

I tapped on my screen while chewing on another bite of donut.

Me: *Stop trying to distract me. I have a lot of work to do. Heading over to farm in about an hour.*

Mine: *If I can't tell you I love you, can I tell you how much I want to fuck you?*

Me: *Great. Now I'm hard. Get back to work.*

Mine: *It's going to be a beautiful wedding. Riggs told me everything. You're amazing. I would tell you that I love you, but my boyfriend would get angry with me.*

I couldn't help but preen a little at the new title. *Boyfriend.* It was hard to imagine Percival Champion admitting to having one after all the times he insisted he wasn't interested in anything serious.

You did the same.

I closed my eyes and mentally thanked Aunt Cherry for helping me get over my commitment issues. I wasn't naive. I didn't expect things between us to run smoothly after such a rocky start, but I also knew that for both of us to admit to being in a relationship, there had to be something strong there.

Me: *I love you.*

I finished the donuts and coffee before loading up the final boxes into my car and heading to the farm. For as much as I complained about fickle brides and challenging wedding day events, I loved my job. Wedding days were definitely a roller coaster, in general, but this one was primed to be a roller coaster on steroids.

And I needed all of my wits about me if we were going to juggle a secret cartel op with an elegant outdoor winter farm wedding for the Nashville elite.

Once I arrived at the farm, the next several hours passed in a blink. Marissa and Levi had taken a private plane back from their whirlwind trip to Vegas. Instead of looking exhausted from the quick turnaround, they looked like a happy, glowing pair of newlyweds showing off their plain gold rings.

Part of me wanted to slap them for throwing everyone into a tizzy and flying off for a Vegas quickie after we'd spent weeks planning the wedding of Marissa's dreams. But the other part of me was thrilled to see the genuine joy emanating from both of them.

I remembered Diesel and Parrish Partridge telling me once that they were the marrying kind, not the wedding kind. I hadn't understood it at the time, but now I thought I did. Hosting an epic celebration was all well and good, but when you found the person you were supposed to be with, every day was kind of epic.

Levi was tender and sweet with Marissa, and I loved her enough to want her to be cherished like that for her entire life. Meanwhile, she doted on him, teasing him to make him laugh and ensuring her father knew that, for today at least, Levi was his son-in-law, not his right-hand man, ready to take orders.

At one point, Marissa pulled me aside to explain what had happened with Trey.

"He was upset, yeah, but he didn't seem disappointed so much as... secretly relieved? I actually wonder if he might be bisexual," she whispered.

My eyes widened in surprise.

"No, really. Hear me out," she said, misunderstanding my reaction. "I caught him kissing his best man one time during our friend Kaylee's wedding reception. He claimed he was too drunk to realize it wasn't me, but the whole thing seemed really weird to me."

She shrugged and changed the subject while I tried not to laugh. I would have to tell that story to Champ later. Drunken mistake, my ass. But maybe Trey would be a different kind of partner once he was with the right person. For his sake, I hoped he and his best man were having fun in Mexico.

Finally, Champ and his team showed up while Marissa, Levi, and I were finalizing the decorations in the large event tent.

The three of us all wore heavy coats over the top of our wedding clothes to ward off the chill while walking back and forth between the main house, bunkhouse, and event tent. My topcoat was black cashmere, a piece Cherry had bought me as a gift when I'd started Taffet Events. It looked great over my tux, and I'd already worn it as often as possible simply because it was so warm and soft.

The portable gas heaters were doing a great job keeping the space comfortably warm, and the rows of white rental chairs had already been adorned with silk bunting and floral arrangements at the end of each row. Overhead, a canopy of woven birch branches was festooned with thousands of twinkling fairy lights and long, trailing garlands of eucalyptus and roses.

The other half of the large space was filled with round tables covered in white linens. The glass center-pieces were filled with tall manzanita branches, from which hung hundreds of clear votive holders that looked like glowing orbs, sparkling and reflecting the candlelight within. After the ceremony, the rows of chairs would be removed to clear the dance floor, and the band would set up on the low stage where the wedding canopy now stood.

It was stunning, and I was reminded once again that you really could turn a pig farm into an elegant wedding venue if you had a big enough budget.

The catering trucks were already parked discreetly

behind the back side of the tent, and a gravel path flanked by tall, decorated fir trees in galvanized buckets wound between the tent and the bunkhouse where the bathrooms were.

Marissa sighed. "Okay, now I'm having second thoughts. I kinda want my big, gorgeous wedding back."

I laughed as I tweaked one of the flower arrangements. "Too late. You got your cheap-ass Vegas deal, and you'll have to live with it."

Levi shot her a look. "Tell me again about your regrets?" I could tell from the spark in his eyes he knew she hadn't meant it.

"Just promise me one day we'll get to hire Quinn to plan a big anniversary do for us."

He strode over and took her in his arms. "Anything for you." Then they kissed. Like newlyweds.

Eventually, I was forced to make gagging noises until my phone buzzed with a message from Champ.

Mine: *He's here early. Stay clear of the house.*

My smile dropped. *Fuck.* We hadn't expected Vince to arrive until the ceremony was in process, an hour from now. The guests were due to arrive in just a few minutes.

"He's here," I said softly.

Levi pulled away from Marissa. I saw his hand jerk toward the opening of his coat before he stopped. He was wearing a shoulder holster like Tommy, his men, and Champ's crew. For once, I was glad to be with someone strapped.

"We're supposed to stay out here, but…"

Levi turned to Marissa. "Let's go wait in the bunkhouse like we talked about."

I couldn't do it. Now that the moment had arrived, I

couldn't simply stand by and not know what was going on. "I'll meet you there in a few," I said before bolting toward the house. Levi called after me, but I knew he wouldn't chase me. He was way more concerned for Marissa's safety than mine.

I stopped at the catering trucks to remind them to stay put until it was time for the reception. They knew the house was completely off-limits.

Instead of going to the front door, I snuck in the side door to the mudroom and considered how close I could get without interfering with the op. I didn't want to mess up Champ's plan, but the man I loved was downstairs with his asshole ex. I wanted to be close by so I could help out if things went sideways. More than that, I wanted to be ready to hear all about it as soon as Vince was safely away from here.

When someone grabbed my arm roughly from the doorway behind me, I realized how stupid my idea had been.

I belatedly realized Champ's text hadn't specified whether Vince was actually in the house yet.

It turned out, he wasn't. Maybe he'd gone to search that outbuilding first the way I'd suggested. I wanted to kick myself for being an idiot in more ways than one.

"You're going to keep your mouth shut and do exactly as I say," Vince said in a low voice. There was a distinct thread of nerves in his tone, which only scared me more.

I nodded fervently, my heart slamming against my chest.

Champ was right. A wedding planner was not a security operative.

24

CHAMP

My team, together with Tommy and Rod, waited in the nearby guest room, watching the surveillance video on the monitors Hux had set up. We'd watched Vince park his car alongside the wedding guests, duck behind a barn, and emerge a moment later wearing a white jacket so he could blend in with the waitstaff. Hux had quietly announced over comms that he'd lost visual, as expected, once Vince passed beneath the trees toward the back of the house, but his tracker placed Vince near the mudroom, just where we'd thought he'd enter, and for one happy second, I marveled that this whole operation was going to run perfectly smoothly from start to finish…

And then Vince walked into Tommy's office with a gun to Quinn's head, and every muscle in my body seized like I'd been juiced by a live wire.

"Tell me I'm not seeing that!" I demanded to my team as I scrambled around the giant bed in the middle of the room to get to the door. My brain scrambled to make sense of the image.

How the hell had Vince gotten a hold of Quinn?

And Jesus fuck, *why*?

Over the past week, every revelation about the man I'd once been involved with made me realize how little I'd ever really known him, but the idea that he would take an innocent man hostage and literally hold a gun to his head? That was a factor I hadn't considered when planning out this op. Vince was a thousand times more dangerous than I'd let myself believe.

He wasn't just playing fast and loose with the law in order to get a promotion or financial gain from the cartel; he was actually putting a civilian's life at risk. There was no shred left in him of the guy I'd once tried to love.

And I would have no remorse about ending him if necessary.

I slammed my headset on the desk and strode out of the spare room. My team called after me to be cautious and make a plan, but I was too angry to be sensible. There was no way in hell I was allowing Vince Parler to threaten Quinn. Not for one second longer than necessary.

I pulled my weapon and stormed into the office. "Let him go right fucking now."

Vince's smile was unlike anything I'd ever seen before, and it made my blood run cold. "That's not happening. Put down your weapon, Percy."

"That's also not happening. *Vincent.*"

Quinn's eyes were wide and his breathing shallow. I tried to send him a reassuring look, but he seemed too scared to even process what was happening. My whole body was on fire with the need to rip him away from Vince and hold him safe and secure in my arms—and then to shake him for daring to put his life in danger when I fucking *needed* him like I needed oxygen. Letting my training take over to keep my emotions contained and my brain alert was the hardest thing I'd ever done.

"I'm here for the Horn," Vince said. "You're going to get it for me, Percy, or your sweetheart's going to die."

Jesus Christ. The man was talking like the mustache-twirling James Bond baddie.

"You don't want to do this. Let him go now and we'll let you leave with the Horn."

Vince snorted. "You play the part of the devoted boyfriend so well, Percy, I almost believe you. But Quinn and I both know you'd never compromise your mission that easily. Which is why I'm going to take the Horn *and* Mr. Taffet as an insurance policy."

"No fucking way—"

"You don't get to say no to me! I'm the DEA!" Vince screeched. His jaw tightened, and he angled his weapon toward Quinn. "Now get me into the vault with the goddamn Horn."

"The Horn's not even in the vault anymore, you idiot," I said disgustedly. "Weeks of work figuring out how to get into it, and Tommy moved it to a display case so he could show it off to his guests after the ceremony." I hooked a thumb over my shoulder to the shelf where Tommy had put the decoy Horn. "If you'd just come here with a warrant—"

Vince's eyes flashed to the shelf and showed a split second of relief before focusing back on me. "Do I look like I need a warrant? I'm far more powerful without one. Now hand the Horn to me. *Slowly.*"

Without taking my eyes or gun off him, I reached back and fumbled open the display box so I could grab the Horn. "Take it," I said softly, holding it out to him. "My client's reputation isn't worth anyone's life."

Vince's eyes narrowed suspiciously at my easy compliance, because the Percy Champion he'd known —the Champ who hadn't known what it felt like to have given his entire heart to one small, sassy, lovable wedding planner with a fondness for stolen T-shirts— would've been far more conflicted about giving up a piece of leverage like that, even under these circumstances.

Quinn found his voice, and scared as he was, my gorgeous man did what he did best—he adapted and improvised on the fly to seal the deal. "No! Champ, don't do that! I don't believe a word he says. That information is important—"

Vince grabbed the Horn and jammed it in his jacket pocket. Then he moved his free hand up to clamp around Quinn's throat, cutting off his words. "Shut up, you little fool. You don't know what the fuck you're talking about. You should have agreed to work with me from the beginning. What the hell do you think some Podunk private security firm in rural Tennessee can do with this information that a DEA agent can't? Give me a fucking break."

"Let him go," I said again through clenched teeth. "You have what you came here for. If you leave on your own right now, I won't even try to stop you, and I'll tell my men to stand down too." I lowered my voice an octave. "But I promise, I will hunt you to the ends of the Earth if you harm one hair on his head."

Vince tightened his hand, and Quinn whimpered softly. "Aww. You know, I'm actually starting to believe you give half a shit about this guy, Percy. How sweet.

You always did have a soft spot for little nothings, didn't you?"

"You mean, like you?"

Vince's nostrils flared, but he managed a smirk. "It was more than a soft spot with me. You loved me."

I huffed out a humorless laugh. I didn't want to antagonize Vince, but in case things went sideways, I needed Quinn to know the truth. "I didn't know what love was when I was with you. I know what it is now. And I know I'll do anything to keep it."

My voice didn't sound normal to my ears. There was a dull rushing noise from the blood thundering through my veins, and my vision was literally tinged red with the need to do violence. Shit was about to get real because I couldn't stand to see Vince's hands on Quinn for much longer.

"Anything, hmm? Then you'll let us walk away," Vince countered. "Mr. Taffet and I are going to go for a little ride, that's all. I'll let him go once I know I'm not being followed."

"Take me instead," I offered. "Let Quinn go. I'll put down my gun, and you can —"

Vince laughed. He sounded truly deranged. The man I'd once known was nowhere to be found. "You want to spend some alone time with me? Then you should've taken me up on my dinner offer a few weeks ago. Now take a giant step back, Percy. Good, good. And lay that gun gently on the floor."

There was no way I was going to let him move Quinn to another location, but I also couldn't shoot Vince or even get close enough to tackle him without risking Quinn until we were upstairs.

I knew my team had to be thinking the same thing because when Vince pulled Quinn out the door and shuffled him down the narrow hall, none of them jumped out to disarm him. Vince dragged Quinn up the stairs, and I followed, trying to reassure Quinn wordlessly that we weren't gonna let him be taken.

"Oh, God," Quinn moaned, stumbling. "Oh goodness, oh gracious. I can't… I… *Oh!*"

Quinn passed out cold and slumped in Vince's hold, his dead weight knocking Vince off-balance.

"Quinn!" I screamed.

"Fucking *move!*" Vince demanded, jabbing Quinn with the gun, but Quinn didn't so much as flinch.

I saw the moment when Vince realized that his choices were to drag Quinn bodily out to his car in the parking lot where the wedding guests were arriving or to leave him behind. At the last moment, Vince shoved Quinn down the stairs at me, then turned tail and ran. Quinn slammed into me like a wrecking ball, and the two of us went flying back down the stairs to land in a heap on the basement floor with Quinn on top of me.

My men came streaming out of the nearby bedroom.

"Fucking Christ," Elvo cried, reaching down to help us up.

Riggs and Jordan darted past us up the stairs, no doubt to watch Vince leave and to prevent anyone else from coming down here.

"Hands off," I barked at Elvo. "Hang on a minute. Quinn fainted, and he might be hurt." My own body felt like it had been tossed down a boulder field. I'd done my best to protect him as we fell, but there was no way he didn't have his own set of nasty bruises.

"Baby? Quinn? Sweetheart, it's over. Please wake up. Where does it hurt?" I cradled his face in my hands, smoothing my thumbs frantically over his cheeks.

Quinn's big eyes popped open immediately. "Is he gone?" he whispered. "Did I do okay?"

My heart, which had iced over at the idea that he might be unconscious, began beating at double speed. "What?"

"With the fainting. That was a last-minute improvisation." He rolled off me with a pained groan and settled on the floor. "I definitely hadn't considered the landing. But I couldn't think of another way we could make Vince leave with the Horn—and without *me* —without being too suspicious, you know?"

"*What?*" I repeated more loudly, rolling so I was braced over him.

"The… Horn?" he repeated uncertainly, looking up at me in concern. "You know, Tommy's Horn? Well, Tommy's decoy Horn. We wanted Vince to leave with it, right?" When I continued to stare down at him in disbelief, he frowned. "Baby, do you not remember? Oh, shit, did you hit your head?" He trailed his fingers gently over the back of my scalp, looking for a lump.

I grabbed his hand and pulled it down. "Are you fucking kidding me? You… you… were pretending?"

"Well… yeah? I mean, I did *not* intend to get taken hostage. That was a serious miscalculation and terrifying as fuck. But then *you* were there, and you looked like an avenging angel, telling Vince that you loved me, and I thought, 'Get it together, Taffet. Champ's fucking counting on you.' And… yeah. So. Did I do okay?"

I pressed my lips to his right there in the middle of the hall, and Quinn Taffet kissed me back. He tasted like life and hope and everything I'd never let myself believe I could have.

And I was seriously going to kill him.

"What were you thinking, coming all the way over

here? You were supposed to be out at the bunkhouse with Levi and Marissa! You were supposed to stay safely away from all this."

"I know, but I… I couldn't stand not knowing how it was going, not knowing if you were okay." His eyes shone with love and sincerity. It was impossible for me to stay angry when he looked at me that way, and I hoped he never realized that, otherwise, he'd have me wrapped around his finger even more firmly for the rest of my days. "I was just going to hide in the mudroom until it was over, but then…"

"Vince found you."

Quinn nodded. "I thought he was already down-stairs. I thought I could help if you needed me to."

I kissed him again, gently this time. "If the roles were reversed, I'd have felt the same," I admitted. "But baby, I have training you don't have."

"And yet, some untrained people get involved in their partners' business all the time." He raised an eyebrow at me pertly. "Isn't that right, Mr. Wedding Piñata?"

"That's totally different. You are not going to be my partner in the security business, Quinn Taffet," I informed him. I heaved myself to my feet and hauled him after me, running my hands over his cashmere coat to check him for bruises, but like me, he seemed to be mostly fine.

"Hush. I'll be your *silent* partner," Quinn said, patting my chest soothingly. "Don't worry, we'll work up to it."

I shook my head and fought hard against a smile. "This is the rest of my life now, huh?"

"Pretty much, yeah. You having regrets?"

I hauled him up against me and bit his lower lip. "Not a single one."

"Good," Quinn whispered against my mouth. "Because otherwise, you'd *never* get your T-shirts back, Percival." He sauntered toward the stairs while Elvo covered his laugh with a cough.

"Am I likely to get them back anyway?" I called after him.

"Probably not. They're faded to the perfect softness." He tossed me a look over his shoulder. "Come on. We've got a wedding to execute."

We made our way upstairs, and I kissed Quinn goodbye before convening a quick meeting with my team.

Elvo and Riggs confirmed Vince's departure.

Hux said he'd confirmed it from digital surveillance also. "The red devil seems to be headed for the private airstrip. Think the DEA is bankrolling him a private plane?"

I shook my head. I *still* didn't want to jump to conclusions, but the evidence that Vince was working for the cartel was mounting, and I was confident we hadn't heard the last of him. But I wasn't going to let that knowledge ruin the rest of this day.

I lifted an eyebrow at Riggs. "So have you told Carter yet?"

Before he could answer, his fiancé came walking in from the front hall to the kitchen. "Got your all clear. Are you guys okay? Have you told me what? And do the Drakes know my grandfather? Because I could swear I saw his Bentley parked out there, but he didn't mention he was coming to town."

Carter was dressed in an expensive tux and looked like a million bucks. Riggs stared at him for a beat with tiny hearts in his eyes before I nudged him. "Tell him," I whispered.

Riggs took Carter's hands in his and knelt down on both knees, right there in the hall. "Marry me," he said simply. "Today. Here. Now. Marry me."

Carter's eyebrows crinkled in confusion before he looked up at the rest of us. We probably resembled a flock of clucking hens anticipating Carter's response.

"Is this…" He lowered his voice to a whisper, and his gaze darted around. "Is this an op? Is it still happening? Are we not clear?"

"No op," Riggs said. "This is about you and me and the fact that I'm madly, passionately in love with you."

Carter's breathing kicked up, and he stared at Riggs in shock. "Here? *Now*?"

Riggs nodded. "You told me that the next time I proposed, I'd better have a minister in tow. So I spent all night last night swapping Marissa and Trey's guests out for ours. I got Judge Kelly to come so she can sign off on the license and make it all official. I even brought your grandfather's favorite pastor in to do the ceremony. Marry me, Carter Rogers. Please." He bit his lip. I could see he was terrified of Carter's disapproval. "You can tattoo a capybara on me whenever you're ready."

Carter's eyes filled with tears. "Really? Oh, God, and now we don't even have to plan our own big wedding? I just get to be… married to you from today on?"

Riggs kissed Carter's hands before nodding. "Rogers and Rogers, for the rest of our lives." His eyes were suspiciously shiny too.

"Then I say… yes." He cupped Riggs's face in both his hands and bent down to press a kiss to his lips.

I wished Quinn was there to squeeze my hand, but I knew he was scrambling to make sure the guests were ready and Carter and Riggs's dream wedding was set to begin on time.

"Hey," I said gruffly. "Save it for after the wedding, boys."

Carter and Riggs broke apart with a laugh. Then we all made our way out to the tent, where two of the best men I knew pledged to spend their lives together while everyone who loved them looked on with joy.

After the ceremony ended and I'd collected my own man at the end of the aisle, where he stood directing guests to the bars set up around the edges of the tent, Quinn leaned over and whispered to me, "Think that'll ever be you?"

I put my arm around him and pulled him close before whispering in his ear. "Only if you'll agree to stand up there with me."

Quinn's grin was huge and full of his usual teasing. "Are you asking me to be your best man?"

I met his eye and grinned right back. "No. You're already the best of men. I'm simply asking you to be mine."

25

QUINN

I'd never been to a wedding as elegant and laid-back at the same time as Riggs and Carter's wedding turned out to be. Their friends and family were an odd mix of blue-collar and blue blood, which for some reason made it eclectic in a good way. Everyone got along great, and by the end of the night, we were out on the dance floor with rolled-up shirtsleeves and alcohol-flushed faces.

The relief of the completed op contributed to the celebratory feeling, which might have explained why we danced as much as we did, but the next morning was full of regrets.

"Can't move," I mumbled into Champ's armpit. "Pretty sure I broke all my bones in the stairwell fall yesterday and didn't know it at the time because of adrenaline. I read that's a thing."

"Mpfh."

"You need to wake up and make me coffee. It's the least you can do after your ex-boyfriend tossed me down a cement staircase to land on a hard stone floor."

"He tossed you because you pretended to faint," he

grumbled, assaulting me with facts despite the early hour. "I know that because I'm going to be replaying that moment in my head for the next seventy years of our lives. Also, the stairs and floor are carpeted."

"You sure?"

"Very. I remember it from the *first* time you tackled me to that carpeted floor a few weeks ago when we were looking for the vault." His voice went deeper and roughened with arousal. "Remember?"

I blinked at him. I had no idea I'd made a habit of tackling him to basement floors.

I supposed there were worse things, really.

"Baby," I said. "If you were thinking about the *flooring* that night, I had to be doing something wrong."

Champ made a noise of sleepy amusement. "I also have a rug burn on the back of my hand from yesterday."

I lifted my head up to squint at him. As usual, he looked divine in my bed. "You sure that's not from the sex we had last night?"

"We had sex in the woods behind the catering truck," he said. "No carpet in sight."

"You sure it's not poison ivy rather than rug burn?"

Champ sighed. "Shit."

I laughed. "Just kidding. It dies off in winter. But we might need to remember that come summertime."

He shifted until he'd pulled me halfway onto his chest. "Who says I'll still be fucking you come summer-time?" he teased.

I pushed against him until I was sitting up. Then I made a big production of letting the sheet drop before stretching my arms over my head. "I'd say the stack of seventeen T-shirts I have hidden in my apartment say so."

He sighed sadly and tugged the sheet down further. "My boyfriend is a thief."

I batted my eyelashes. "And yet, I'm *still* a better bet than the last guy you dated."

"Not. Funny." He tackled me onto the bed again and began tickling me mercilessly until the sheet was gone completely and I was breathless for reasons that had nothing to do with tickling.

With the exception of a brief walk for Hercules's sake, we didn't make it out of bed again for hours, but for once, my joy in spending the morning in bed had nothing to do with *sleeping*.

It turned out, dreams of some fairy-tale Prince Charming couldn't hold a candle to reality when your reality included Percival Champion.

When it was finally time to either get up or starve to death, Champ casually mentioned wanting to swing by his house to pick up some fresh clothes on the way to eat.

I stared at him, my chest squeezing with genuine surprise and excitement. "You want to take me to your house? Man, this *is* serious."

We moved into the shower, where Champ's expression turned sober. "I'm sorry it took me so long to see what was right in front of me this whole time. I really do appreciate you, love you, and want to spend my life with you. So..." He took a breath. "So I want you to see the house and tell me what you think. If you want to live there, we can do that. If you want to stay in the apartment over the shop, we can do that. Or, if you want, I can sell the house, and we can pick something else out together. I just... I just want you to be happy. And I want us to be together."

"I don't want to live there if it's going to remind you

of Vince," I admitted. "Didn't you say you bought it for the two of you?"

Champ shook his head. "Vince never liked that house. I bought it more to serve my dream of settling down. I thought, if I got the house and the white picket fence all prepared for him, surely Vince would get on board. I see now that I railroaded him into it. Hell, he never even looked at houses with me here. I don't know why I bought a house without his input, but when I saw this house, I..." He let out a breath. "There was something about it. It felt like home to me. It doesn't have to be, though," he added quickly. "Wherever you are is gonna be home."

I was secretly glad something had pulled him to the Thicket strongly enough to stay. Even if that reason was a dream with someone else, the reality of the situation included me, not Vince.

"I can't wait to see it," I said.

Fifteen minutes later, we loaded up in Champ's truck and drove a mile and a half through familiar roads. When he pulled into a *very* familiar driveway, I wondered if he was trying to make a joke.

"Ha ha, very funny. I had no idea you knew where my aunt Cherry used to live."

Champ threw the truck into Park and turned to stare at me. We both realized it at the same time.

"You bought my aunt Cherry's house?" I asked with wide eyes and a growing smile.

"This was your aunt's house?"

"The place where I spent my Licking Thicket summers," I confirmed. "Broke my heart when she sold it, but it was too much to maintain and needed too much work."

"No shit," he said with a laugh. "It's been a challenge."

I remembered him describing it as a money pit rather than "a challenge," so I couldn't hold back a laugh. "Show me. I can't wait to see what you've done."

The house was stunning. It was everything Cherry would have wanted it to be with the modern conveniences I would have insisted upon had we been the ones doing the updating.

"Champ," I said with awe in my voice.

"Don't credit me," he said. "Jericho did all the work."

The fresh paint, new light fixtures, and clean windows made a difference in every room. Original woodwork had been restored to its original lustre, and the hardwoods shone with new stain and a clear coat.

Hot tears began rolling down my face as childhood memories mixed together with hopeful excitement about the future.

"Can we keep it?" I breathed, looking around the entry hall. From there, I could see the front salon, the dining room, the curving staircase, and the new, modern kitchen.

Champ pulled me into his arms. "Hell yes we can, I was really, *really* hoping you'd say that. It's yours."

I hugged him tightly, but after a few seconds, I heard a familiar voice coming from the direction of the kitchen.

"Quinn Taffet, mind your manners! Snogging a strange man in your own entry hall is considered *gauche*."

I turned to see a smiling Bunny Champion leading a group of people in through the back door. I saw Ava and

Malachi, Cindy Ann and her husband, and a bunch of people I didn't know. But bringing up the rear, holding the arm of a short, handsome older man, was my aunt.

"Cherry!" I took off at a run and hugged her almost as tightly as I'd hugged Champ. "He bought your house," I whispered. "Look what he did. He brought it back to life."

The warm, familiar strength of her was all I needed to finally feel like everything was right in my world. "He brought more than the house back to life, sweetheart," she whispered back.

After hugging me, Cherry introduced me to Terry, whose kind eyes had laugh lines that immediately put me at ease.

Herc hopped around, licking Bunny's wool slacks and then nipping at Kev's jeans until Kev dropped on the floor alongside Ava's toddler to pet him. The rest of Champ's team began bringing in trays of wedding leftovers from their vehicles and coolers of leftover drinks before mingling with my new Licking Thicket friends and their families.

Pretty soon, we had an impromptu housewarming party full of our closest friends and family. Riggs and Carter blushed every time someone commented on their wedding bands, and Carter looked at Riggs like he was God's gift to wedding planners.

"I still can't believe you went through with it," he said to his new husband.

Riggs kissed him on the side of his mouth. "I had to lock you down before you found greener grass."

"You know I was already yours forever."

Riggs kissed him again. "I've been wanting to marry you since that crazy-ass flight out of Venezuela. I had one condition in a man, and it was that he knew how to subdue insurgents with grace while I hijacked a plane." He shrugged. "Right place, right time, I guess."

Carter flicked him on his shoulder with his finger before leaning in and kissing him hard on the mouth. I saw him whisper *I love you* against his lips.

A banging noise came from upstairs, and we all jumped. "My bad!" a man called.

Champ sighed. "That's my contractor. Jericho. He's finishing hanging window treatments in one of the guest rooms."

Hux's phone buzzed with a notification. He sucked in a breath when he read it. "Boss, we may have a problem. I need to head back to Carter and Riggs's place to see if this can be right."

Champ's crew moved out of the kitchen and into the empty salon. I trailed after them next to Kev, who was clearly as curious as I was.

"What is it?" Champ asked once we left everyone else to set out the food in the kitchen.

Kev whispered to me, "Hux looks nervous. He's never nervous."

Hux took a breath. "The data on the Horn is about what we suspected. A list of names of cartel members that map to their in-game usernames. The DEA could use it to map illegal transactions to individual cartel members if they're using the game the way we believe they are."

Champ crossed his arms in front of his chest. "If it's what we expected, what's the problem?"

Hux looked at his screen and back up again before handing the phone to Champ.

"What am I looking at here?"

"One of the names is Vince's."

The room went silent as a tomb at the confirmation that Vince did, in fact, have ties to the cartel.

Champ's eyes raced across the screen as he took it all in. I could sense his emotional upheaval even though his reaction was pure confident Champ.

He looked up and met everyone's eyes in turn. "Okay. Tonight, the priority is celebrating Riggs and Carter, celebrating a job well done, celebrating my house being finished, and celebrating the fact that I managed to convince Quinn to move in with me. Tomorrow, we get back to work. Understood?"

Riggs's mouth tipped up in a knowing smile. "Yes, boss."

A chorus of other "yes, boss's" echoed in the room until the rest of the team filtered out.

Champ turned to me.

"I'm sorry," I said.

He shook his head. "Me too. It's like the man is a total stranger. How long has this been going on? Was he contemplating something like this even when we were together? What's his endgame?" The corners of his lips turned up. "But you know what? Those are problems for another day. Today, I'm going to get to know your aunt and her man, ignore my mother while she acts like you're her favorite son, and then when they're all gone, I'm going to use your body to christen every room in this damned house."

I stepped closer and put my arms around his neck before leaning in to bite his earlobe, and then I pulled him down the hall to the bathroom. "Why wait? Let's start in here."

EPILOGUE
QUINN

When my phone went off, I grabbed it from the nightstand and rolled to the center of my empty bed without opening my eyes.

"H'lo?" I whispered.

Champ's low, warm chuckle sent a shiver down my spine. "I see we're up and at 'em, ready to greet the day, hmm, baby? I thought you were meeting my mother at eleven."

I sighed, torn as I so often was between clapping back snarkily... and begging him to keep talking because his voice did alllll kinds of things to make my stomach wobble and my dick hard.

"S'dark," I grumbled. "Not time t'get up yet. M'notta M'rine, y'know."

Champ chuckled again. "No," he agreed in a tone that held endless affection along with his amusement. "You're not a Marine. But baby, it's after nine o'clock your time. Are you sure the darkness isn't just your eye mask?"

Oh. Crap. I lifted a hand and touched silk.

"That… could be," I allowed with a sniff, and Champ's chuckles turned to full-on laughter.

Okay, safe to say I was *still* not a morning person.

Many, many things had changed about my life in the months since I'd met and fallen in love with Percival Champion, but this one had not. My brain still woke up slowly, and I still preferred to lounge in bed rather than jump up to greet the day.

The only difference was that these days I preferred to do my lounging *with* someone.

A very *specific* someone.

Sadly for me, that someone was currently finishing up the fifth and final day of an op that had taken him out of the Thicket to a super-secret location he could only disclose to his most trusted associates—it was Las Vegas. He'd told me immediately—and he wouldn't be back until tonight.

"For your information," I said with as much dignity as a naked man alone in bed wearing a sleep mask could muster, "I was rudely awakened, and I've been extra tired this week."

Five days was the longest we'd been apart since… well, since the night we'd met. Even back when we'd been counting our nights together, we hadn't managed to stay away from each other for that long. It was genuinely hard to get to sleep without him now.

If I were going to get all sappy and sentimental— which happened more and more often these days—I might reflect on how cool it was that now we spent our time counting down the minutes we had to be apart instead of worrying about how many evenings we'd spent together. But also, as a realist, the unavoidable travel that came along with our otherwise-fulfilling jobs kinda sucked.

"Poor baby. You must miss your boyfriend a lot," Champ said softly.

I rolled my eyes beneath my mask. Of course I fucking did. Like, a *lot*. But I hadn't yet descended to the stage of sappiness where I was willing to accept *pity*, damn it.

"A little bit, I guess. There might be a tiny… minuscule… trace amount of boyfriend-missing happening," I lied. "But mostly it's that I've had a constant whirlwind of work and socializing this week. Truly exhausting."

That second part was not a lie.

On Monday, when Ava had heard that Champ was out of town, she'd invited herself to the shop for lunch. She'd also invited me to her house for dinner last night so I could spend time with her husband and babies. Since she was an unstoppable force who'd given birth to three immovable objects, watching her love and pride and frustration with her kids was enough to make me a bit broody (which was another thing I wouldn't be admitting), and I'd really enjoyed it.

Tuesday, Carter Rogers had also invited me over, since Riggs was out of town on the same job as Champ. We'd been planning to watch an artsy French movie, but then Horn of Glory had released a whole new collection of decorative rainbow gourds for Pride month—and they were making generous donations to LGBTQ+ charities for each gourd that was claimed too—so we'd ended up spending the evening playing HOG. I'd told myself I was doing it for charity, but the truth was that I'd gotten kinda-sorta addicted to the game. Honestly, any game with vigilante fire fairies *and* decorative gourds was a guaranteed good time.

Wednesday and Thursday, Bunny had called me no less than twice a day, absolutely *needing* to discuss my thoughts on such diverse topics as her and Cherry's outfits for their upcoming high school reunion (artfully sexy and classy, but no couture), my feelings about the feather-trimmed shorts trend (highly suspicious), the preparations for her autumn fundraising gala (it would be a guaranteed showstopper, and plans were coming along swimmingly), and most recently, whether I'd be willing to help her host a fun last-minute celebration for some old Thicket friends in our backyard this afternoon (a definite yes, as long as she supplied the food). I got the impression that she was pretty lonely, despite being a social maven, and if I were a betting man, I'd wager she'd be moving to the Thicket part-time, like Cherry and Terry had.

And if all that wasn't enough, I'd been positively slammed with actual work, now that wedding season was in full swing. I'd overseen Posy Martinez's nuptials over in Nashville last Saturday (including a last-minute switch from emu feathers to bouquets made out of marshmallows and gumdrops), and I had another wedding coming up in the Thicket next weekend too.

"Ah, true. You *have* had a lot on your plate," Champ agreed. "No wonder you're tired."

I squirmed guiltily against the sheets. It was undeniable that I had a ton going on. My lack of sleep, however, had nothing to do with being busy.

"Fine, yes, it's possible that I may have also gotten used to sleeping with someone," I admitted, then quickly added, "You know our new air-conditioning system is really *aggressive*. It gets quite chilly in the night. I miss having a human space heater next to me."

"I missed holding you too, baby." Champ's voice was a deep rumble in my ear that made my heart stutter and my breath hitch. "Missed your soft skin under my fingertips. Missed that lean body pressed up against me. Missed smelling your skin when you're warm and sleepy. Missed the way you download about your day before we fall asleep. Missed the way your voice gets all rough and hoarse after I make you —"

"Okay, okay, you win," I moaned, pushing a hand against the blankets over my rapidly hardening cock. "I missed the fuck out of you, Percival Champion! Now could you please, *please* finish off whatever you're doing extra fast so you can get home and finish *me* off?"

Champ sucked in a loud breath. He said nothing for a long moment while I heard a door close, followed by the sound of rustling fabric over the line.

"You're hard right now, aren't you?" he whispered. "Touch yourself for me."

If I hadn't been hard already, his words would have done it. "Wait, what's going on? Where are you?" I demanded. "Is someone overhearing you?"

The thought was not the deal breaker it probably should have been.

"I'm in a closet, and I... Yeah, I'm kind of on a schedule, and I don't have long. So *focus*, baby."

I bit my lip. When Champ got bossy, it was always really hard not to immediately give in. I gave it my best shot, though.

"I really shouldn't. I have to feed Herc. And... and..." *Fuck.* I blew out a breath and admitted, "Sex is just not as good without you, okay?"

Now *that* was some serious truth. The man had

hooked me so deeply that orgasms by myself weren't as satisfying as orgasms with him.

"Ah, baby," Champ said hoarsely, tenderly, and I let out a shuddery breath.

Being able to be honest and vulnerable with him wasn't something I was totally used to yet, but knowing that he understood that and that I could trust him... well, that was why Percy Champion was my everything.

"Herc's fine. He can wait a few minutes," Champ went on. "I want to hear you come." There was more rustling, and his voice went extra soft. "Touch yourself for me, Quinn. Just like you did the other night."

My groan was a sound of resignation because just hearing his voice and knowing he was thinking about me that way had gotten me too hard not to want to do something about it.

I fumbled for the lube on my nightstand, pumping some out onto my hand. I kicked the covers down and gave my cock a firm stroke. It felt nice—*obviously*—but something about it wasn't quite right.

The other night, we'd jerked off together over Face-Time, and it had been seriously hot. Seeing Champ's eyes go hazy and unfocused, knowing he could see his own passion right there on the screen, had amped things up, and I'd come in record time.

But in the present moment, without Champ to focus on, imagining him in a storage closet somewhere in Nevada needing me to hurry so he could get back to his mission, I felt strangely shy.

"This isn't working," I said in frustration. "Maybe later, you—"

"You remember the first time you jerked off for

me?" Champ whispered. "It was the sixteenth night we spent together, back in December —"

The sixteenth night?

"You remember each of the nights?" I whispered back, even though there was no one in my house to hear me except Hercules.

"Every single one," Champ said. "But that particular night... Fuck, I have thought about that night so, so many times this week."

"Y-you have?" My heart rate sped up, and I rubbed my thumb over the head of my cock, smearing the precum there.

"Mmm. You were a little tipsy from that holiday punch I brought over, remember? Your lips tasted like cranberries. And when I stripped you and laid you down on the carpet back in your apartment, you gave me the most desperate look —"

Wait, what?

"No, I didn't!" I paused with my hand still on my dick. There were parts of that night that were a little foggy, but some were incredibly clear. "You're misremembering. *You* gave *me* the most desperate look. And FYI, calling me desperate is killing my vibe. You suck at phone sex."

Champ huffed out a soft, deep laugh that had me biting my lip and stroking myself again. "I remember that while you were naked," he purred, "I was fully clothed —"

"Oh, God. Oh, fuck. I remember that." The details were coming back to me through a haze of champagne cocktails. "The Christmas lights were on."

"Mmhmm. You were dazzling. And I wanted you so badly, Quinn. So much it scared me to death. I wanted to do all sorts of uncivilized things to you — tattoo my name all over you, paint you in my cum. Ruin you for any other man who might ever come along and want what was mine. Because some part of me knew even then, baby, before I was brave enough to admit it to myself, that you and I were meant to be."

"Yessss," I said on an exhale, and it sounded like a whimper. My eyes squeezed shut behind my blindfold. "Fuck, I wish it was tonight already." In that moment, I'd have given anything to have him with me.

"The next time I see you, I'm going to fuck you so hard," he promised. "Hope you don't have much happening this weekend because I've been making plans. Gonna take you in the living room, spread out on the rug. And then out on the screened porch after the sun's gone down, when it's absolutely still and silent and every little noise you make will carry—"

By that point, I was full-on panting, like I'd been sprinting up and down the whole of Weaver Street. "Oh, God. Oh, fuck. I'm *close*. I'm actually... Tell me more," I pleaded.

"More about what I'm gonna do to you? How I'm gonna work you up, get you loose with that toy you used the other night until you're ready to take me—"

"You don't have to," I blurted incoherently. "I... I've been playing with that toy every night this week."

"Quinn," he groaned loudly.

"That way, when you get home tonight, you can just—"

"Oh, fuck this," Champ said from someplace far, far closer than a closet in Las Vegas.

Footsteps thundered up the stairs, and I heard his phone clatter to the hardwood floor of our bedroom in stereo before I dropped my own phone.

"Holy shit." I tore my blindfold off as something—

one of Champ's big, steel-toed boots—thudded against the footboard of the antique bed, and I blinked up at the enormous, rumpled blond with the world's sexiest blue eyes. He was standing in our bedroom doorway, attempting to shed his shirt and pants at the same time... and somehow succeeding. "You... baby, *how*...?"

"I had a plan," he grumbled from inside his shirt. "A plan to surprise you. A plan that didn't involve phone sex. But, *fuck*. Five days was too fucking long. I'm not staying away that long again."

That sounded like an excellent idea. But also...

"Wait, were you downstairs this whole time?" I demanded. "Leaving me up here all alone while you—"

Champ climbed on the bed and crouched over me on his hands and knees, beautifully, perfectly naked and fully, gorgeously erect. He kissed me once, firmly, to shut me up. "I had a *plan*," he said again, running one big hand down my body from nipple to hip, like he was reclaiming his territory. "A whole-ass romantic plan. But then you sounded so fucking sexy, I had to change the plan on the fly, and I..."

I wrapped my arms around Champ's neck and dragged his mouth down to mine, cutting off his explanation because it didn't fucking matter.

When your prayers get answered, it's churlish to question the hows and whys.

"*Mmmpfh*," Champ argued. But when I bit his bottom lip, he got on board really quickly, kissing me so hard and so thoroughly, there wasn't room for a single thought in my head besides *Champ*. He even managed to snag the lube on the nightstand without breaking the kiss.

"Get inside me," I begged, my dick already leaking thanks to his words in my ear and his sudden presence in our bed. My hands scrabbled against his shoulders, trying to pull his weight against me more fully, needing to ground myself in him. "I'm ready, I promise."

But of course, Champ being Champ, the bossy bastard needed to assess this for himself.

"*I'll* tell you when you're ready." His pupils were dilated, *hungry*, and his cheeks were flushed with arousal beneath his tan.

I sucked in a breath and fought against a swamping tide of arousal. Seriously, Bossy Champ was irresistible. "Excuse you. I know what I need, Percy Champion, and right now, I need you to—*oh, fuck*," I groaned as he impaled me with two thick fingers. "Fuck."

"You were saying, baby?"

"I was saying I love you," I babbled as he moved those talented fingers in and out of me. The man knew exactly how fast, and deep, and intense I liked it. "And that you should never ever stop doing that."

"Mmm. That's what I thought you said," Champ agreed, and I was way too busy pushing myself up to meet his thrusts to care just how smug he sounded.

When he finally moved between my legs and pushed his cock into me, filling me up body and soul, I nearly sobbed at how good it felt.

"Fuck," Champ groaned. "Fuck. *Now* I'm home."

And then he stopped talking entirely and showed me exactly how much he missed me while I begged incoherently for him to fuck me harder, to come inside me, to stay there for good.

One at a time, he grabbed my hands and threaded our fingers together as he thrust against me. His face was contorted into an almost pained look, his face was sweaty, and his eyes were wild. He'd never looked more perfect.

"Touch yourself," he gritted out. "Now, Quinn."

I obeyed instantly, freeing one hand from his and stroking my slick cock in time to his thrusts. Someone let out a high-pitched keening sound, and I realized distantly that it was me.

"Just like that. Just. Like. That." Champ punctuated each word with a thrust, sliding against my hole with exquisite friction, tagging my prostate and making me shudder. As always, every nerve ending in my body came alive when he touched me, and every one of them was on fire with arousal, needing release.

Champ stared down at me and said the words that were like a key in a lock. "Fuck, I love you."

That was all it took. I screamed out his name and came *hard* all over my hand and both our stomachs.

Champ fucked me through my orgasm, his eyes never losing their intensity. He gave one final thrust, and his eyes rolled back as he came inside me.

I loved that feeling so damn much, my whole body shivered.

Champ withdrew from me carefully, slid slightly to the side, then collapsed completely, splaying himself over the entire right side of my body and burying his face in my neck so he could breathe me in. Without a word, his fingers slid through the mess on my stomach and further down to toy with my sensitive hole. When he slid them inside me, I gasped, then sighed.

He had a total obsession with marking my ass.

Fortunately, I was equally obsessed with letting him.

"Five days *was* too long," I said, my voice hoarse as I traced patterns along his back with my fingertips. "From now on, take me with you."

Champ grunted in amusement but didn't move.

"Who'd take care of your brides? Someone needs to babysit Posy Whatshername and her emus."

"Oh my God! I didn't tell you!" I gave him all the details of Posy's last-minute change to carrying a bouquet of candy while Champ absolutely shook with laughter.

"Somewhere in the world, a flock of coral emus is extremely pissed off that they went to all that effort for *nothing*," he gasped, his breath warm against my neck.

I hugged him tighter and laughed along with him because when I held him in my arms, a tension I hadn't known I'd been carrying all week slid away.

Everything was simply better when he was there.

"So, Posy's happily married for now," I said once our laughter subsided. "Part of me thinks I should start thinking up ideas for her *next* wedding, but…"

"But?"

"I dunno." I shrugged. "I'm thinking… maybe this one will last."

Champ pulled back far enough to grin down at me. "You're becoming a romantic finally?"

"Maybe," I allowed. "A little. Oh, and speaking of romantic. What if you and I take a romantic getaway in November? If I can plan a week with no brides, can you plan a week with no jobs? I mean, we've already been fake-engaged, right? And we've *attended* ten weddings this year, even if we haven't done the vows," I teased. "I feel like we deserve a honeymoon."

Champ froze against me, and his eyes went wide.

"Problem? If not November, we could—"

"No! What? No. November sounds great." He pushed himself off me and rolled to the side of the bed. "I just forgot Hercules."

It had been a long while since I'd heard Champ say

those words, and I almost made a smart-ass comment… But I realized I'd forgotten the poor mutt too, so I quickly sat up.

"Shoot. Poor boy. Let me clean up, and we can take him for a walk." I began cleaning myself with some wipes from the nightstand.

"No! *Noooo.* Nope. Not necessary. I walked him already, and he was eating when I came up here," Champ said. He was already pulling his pants on, dressing nearly as quickly as he'd undressed. "You, uh… You just stay here."

I paused with a pair of shorts in my hand and peered across the bed at him. "But if you already fed and walked him, what's the hurry?"

"No hurry. I just have a…"

He paused at the sound of four happy feet running up the stairs, and his eyes widened in panic as Herc bounded in the room and up onto the bed.

"Aw, see?" I grabbed his sweet, fluffy head with both hands and ruffled his fur. "Here's my good, patient boy. He—"

I broke off instantly when my hands slipped over the place where Herc's collar should have been and instead found a wide, red satin ribbon that had been threaded through a shiny platinum band studded with diamonds.

I cut my eyes to Champ. "I don't… I, uh…" I cleared my throat. "What?"

Champ shut his eyes briefly, shook his head once, and sighed. "I had a *plan.*" Then his eyes popped open, and he grinned at me, wide and warm. "But I guess I shouldn't be surprised that my plan didn't quite work out, should I? That's par for the course now."

I gaped at him. I had zero words. None. For maybe the first time in my whole existence.

He made his way around the big bed without breaking eye contact, like he worried I might bolt. He reached out his two hands for mine.

"Quinn Taffet, when I met you, I had a decent life. A house. A dog." He nodded at Hercules. "My own business. A solid team of men and women behind me."

I swallowed hard, and my breathing accelerated.

Champ cradled my jaw in both his large hands. "But even though I had all of those things, I wasn't happy. Somewhere along the way, my priorities had gotten out of whack. I didn't *appreciate* any of the things I had. But you…" He ran his thumb over my cheek. "You came along, and you were…"

Champ broke off and shook his head.

I waited a second, but when it seemed he wasn't going to speak, I prompted, "I was…?"

He snorted. "You were feisty. And funny. And totally unwilling to settle for less than you deserved. You threw my careful life into chaos. You drove me insane. You made me re-evaluate every priority. You made me happier than I'd ever thought I could be."

"Oh." I sniffled just a little, because… wow.

Was there anything better than hearing the person who was the center of your world tell you that you were the center of his? There couldn't possibly be.

"So. My *plan* was to ask you to marry me. To be a family with me and Herc. To be my fiancé for real this time." Champ pulled the bow off Herc's neck and slid the ring free, then held it out to me. "Maybe we can have a ceremony *and* a honeymoon by November, since we've already established that taking a whole year to plan is for slackers." He grinned. "We can do it however you want. Elegant at my mother's country club in Nashville, some kind of Shakespearean-costumed extravaganza here in the Thicket. Whatever kind of wedding you've always dreamed of. Tell me what you want, and I'll provide the glitter piñatas. If you're happy, I'm happy. Just say you'll—"

"No," I managed to choke out. "No, absolutely not."

Champ blinked and straightened, his eyes going cool in an instant. "Uh. Okay." He nodded once and closed his fist around the ring. "Right. So is it a timing thing, or—"

Wait, what?

Ohhhh.

"Jeez, Champion, I didn't mean no as in *no*! I meant no as in *yes*, but without the wedding." I grabbed his hand and tried to uncurl his fingers. "Now show me the precious again."

He held tighter. "Nuh-uh. You're gonna have to explain in actual English, baby."

I blew out a breath. "I meant…" I licked my lips, stared up into those blue eyes I loved, and spoke exactly what was on my heart. "I don't want a fancy wedding. I don't *have* a wedding dream of my own because I never dreamed of that for myself. I never thought I'd want to get married, you know? And now… I don't care how the marrying happens, as long as it's with you. Turns out I'm the marrying kind, not the wedding kind." Just like Diesel and Parrish.

Champ's whole face brightened, and he slid the ring on my finger. "Thank fuck."

"Were you worried I'd say actually no?" I demanded.

"No." He cleared his throat. "Yeah, maybe a little at the end there. And that would've been really bad."

"Aw. Because you love me." I held out my hand so I could watch the sparkles catch the light.

"Well, yeah," Champ agreed. "That. But also... I kinda had my mom throw together a little party for us this afternoon."

I blinked up at him. "Oh my God. The gathering she had me organize? That's my own engagement party?"

The woman was beyond devious. I had so much to learn from her.

But then the meaning of his words clicked. People were coming in just over an *hour*, and I was a rumpled, sticky mess.

"Oh my gosh." My eyes widened in panic. "We need to get moving!"

Champ grabbed me by the waist when I attempted to leave the room and pulled me back against his chest, holding me from behind. "Hold your horses. It's been five days, remember?" His mouth worked at my neck. "I'm not done being reunited yet."

I tried to protest, but it came out as a breathless, curious "Oh?"

"Also..." Champ moved his hands up my torso to tweak my nipples. "I've never fucked an engaged man before."

I laughed out loud. "Is that right?"

I let him pull me down on the bed, and still cradled in his arms, I turned to look at him.

"Well, I suggest you enjoy the experience while you can, Percival Champion," I said softly. "Because this engagement thing? It's a one-shot deal for both of us." I kissed his smiling mouth. "And if I have my way, you and I are gonna be hitched before you know it."

Want to see what happens when Kev and Hux finally drive each other off the deep end? Turn the page for a sneak peek of Hacked or grab your copy of the final book in the Champion Security series, here → https://readerlinks.com/l/2453277

Want more Licking Thicket romance? Check out more hilarious reads set in the punniest small-town in America…
Fakers (Brooks and Mal
Liars (Diesel and Parrish)
Fools (Dunn and Tucker)
Turkeys (Charlton and Hunter)

SNEAK PEEK OF HACKED

KEV

SmittyKitty clearly needed my fuzzy dice… and I was in the mood to give them to him.

Watching new guys play Horn of Glory wasn't generally a hobby of mine. If I wanted to watch a bunch of cocky know-it-alls fuck around—and I did *not*—I could find a plentiful supply in my real life since my cousin-slash-best-friend Carter had fallen in love with a life-sized GI Joe doll named Riggs, who came complete with a huge entourage of overgrown "security expert" badasses including his boss, Champ, and in a shockingly unpleasant turn of events—my Horn of Glory archnemesis, Jasper "HogMasterHux" Huxley.

As of two weeks ago, Champ, Hux, and the whole crew of Champion Security had practically moved into our house while they pinpointed a vulnerability in their security, where they'd proceeded to steal my cheesecake brownies and gobble up the bandwidth in my dedicated internet connection.

Not that I was bitter about that or whatever.

But Smitty was the exception to my newbie rule

and had been since the first moment I'd noticed him trespassing on my HOG homestead looking for abandoned tools and seeds a few weeks back.

Not to blow my own, erm, *Horn*, but I was kind of a big deal in the game. Even the rankest newbie knew the only players allowed on my land were me and Carter, and encroachers would meet the business end of my rhubarb wand. I'd messaged Smitty to give him a chance to retreat before I turned him into compost, because I was a nice person like that.

HogDocKev: *You seem to have gotten off course, Swamp Minion.*

I'd waited for him to apologize or pretend he'd wandered past my wards accidentally, but he hadn't done either.

SmittyKitty: *Oooh, scary. *yawn**

I'd leaned toward my computer screen, my finger hovering over the obliterate button, but I'd had to admit, this was… new. It had been a hot minute since someone in the game—besides HogMasterJerkface, obvs—had dared to disrespect me. So I'd typed back.

HogDocKev: *You want to battle? *eyeroll* I don't battle newborn babies. Accrue some actual game play time and we'll talk.*

SmittyKitty: *Puh-lease. Like it would be a fair fight even then. You can't be killed. Not when you have BOTH the Apple Butter Booster AND the Hedgerow of Health booster. The odds are stacked against me.*

HogDocKev: *Yeah, cause I stacked them myself through hard work and commitment. I completed every quest needed in order to obtain both boosters. I have earned every pip I've ever spent in this game.*

SmittyKitty: *Sure you have. You're like a knight in shining armor, Sir Pipsalot. And did it ever occur to you that* *those quests were only open to ranked players? Just like almost all the quests required to compete in Ascendant's Class in the Conqueror's Tournament require a certain ranking. New guys have to work twice as hard, and it's still not a level playing field.*

HogDocKev: *I'm not apologizing for playing HOG longer than practically anyone. Move along.*

SmittyKitty: *Just saying, Pip, I could beat you in any fight... if the fight was fair.*

After that, he'd turned around and stalked off my land... and I'd let him go, for a bunch of different reasons.

For one thing, destroying a newbie would be a hollow victory. And for another thing... Smitty intrigued me. I liked his frankness and confidence. I liked the way he challenged me. And I liked that he made me rethink stuff I took for granted, like which players were eligible for quests and tournaments... and what I could do to make the game more fair.

Since then, I'd kept an eye on the guy, and what I'd seen had intrigued me even more. I learned he used he/him pronouns, lived in the upper peninsula of Michigan, and worked as a cashier at a pet supply store. The only thing I was unsure about was his age, so I ran his chat strings through an AI assessment tool, which estimated his age to be around late twenties, early thirties.

I also knew that he was a really talented player.

And that he continued to call me Pip, even though —or maybe *because*—it bugged me.

Tonight, I'd watched him swindle a marauding red panda out of his rubies—which required serious strategic thinking skills—but Smitty hadn't gotten ten paces in his air speeder before he was beset by a pack of lightning orcs who'd watched the whole showdown and wanted the rubies for themselves. Without fuzzy dice in his air speeder to up his transportation points, Smitty was a goner.

HogDocKev: *Hey, Smitty. Your air speeder needs these. Enjoy!*

After sending the dice as an in-game gift, I sat back and stretched, moving my eyes off my monitors for the first time in hours. I rubbed my eyes and adjusted my glasses.

It was late… or early, maybe. Somewhere in the 5:00 or 6:00 a.m. range, according to my internal clock. I'd been watching Smitty for maybe half an hour, but I'd been playing Horn of Glory since midnight. With the new Valentine's theme release, it had been easy to lose track of time. There were a million reasons I loved a theme update in the game, but this one had been extra special because Carter and Riggs had gotten married yesterday on Valentine's Day.

Riggs was a good guy—even if he had terrible taste in friends—and I was genuinely thrilled he was joining our family. He made Carter happy, which meant I was happy too. Mostly.

But I couldn't deny that Carter's wedding made me a little melancholy too, which was why I'd left while the party was still in full swing and jumped online. I wasn't a fan of too much socializing, even when I was in the best of moods, and my HOG life was way easier to deal with than my real life.

Now, I'd completed a scavenging quest through the Infernal Wood, my orc horde was surrounded by heart-shaped fairy lights, my villagers had enjoyed a cham-pagne toast, and the pink and red fireworks had continued on for hours over the icepack townships.

I was satisfied that my HOG world was running

smoothly, and it was officially time for me to get back to my real-world work — namely, investigating the security breach that had caused Riggs's team to invade the calm quiet of my house. The sooner I figured it out, the sooner they'd all leave me to my peace and quiet... and my cheesecake brownies.

But the moment I clicked the key to switch programs, the edges of my monitor flashed, and a cultured British voice that I may or may not have created to mimic Henry Cavill's said, "Good morning, sire. I regret to inform you that your internet speed is critically low."

My internet?

Motherfucker.

I growled, then typed the keys that would turn on the security feed I'd installed on the first floor the day that the Champion Security invaders had arrived.

Sure enough, the bandwidth thief was sitting at my kitchen table, bold as you please, where he'd crafted himself a mini-lair complete with three monitors.

HogMasterHux.

The man who'd not only attacked me in a cranberry swamp upon first "meeting" me in Horn of Glory last summer, stealing every pip in my pack and all my health nuggets because "That's how the game is played, HogDoc. Watch and learn."... but who'd then had the absolute *gall* to not be an utter ignoramus with a face like a potato and hair like a troll doll when we'd met in real life.

Why should Jasper Huxley get to be a muscular, brilliant, sexy, crinkly-eyed Zac Efron look-alike with a smile so bright it could power a small city? It was utterly unforgivable.

Also, the man was way too well-groomed and well-rested for this hour on a Sunday, damn it.

"For fuck's sake, Huxley," I said into my comms and had the pleasure of watching Hux jump three feet as my voice broke the silence. "Why are you at my house at this hour?"

"Because according to Riggs, we work here now." Hux scowled and addressed his words to the clock on the wall, then scowled harder and addressed the area by the refrigerator, unsure where my camera was. "And it's not a house—it's a fucking *estate* with ten billionty rooms. And unlike *some* people, I'm dedicated to my job, so I'm doing it. Go away."

I growled again, off mic. Go away? When he was in *my* home?

I really hated it when people assumed I was a free-loader who lived in my family's basement because I was too lazy to get a job and make money. I mean, I *did* live in the basement, but that was because I'd built my lair here. And I had plenty of my own money, both earned and inherited.

"Bold talk for a man who'd been working his Horn until I startled him," I spoke into the mic in a bored voice. "And don't try to pretend that you were on that Horn for work purposes, HogMasterHux, because I can see from here that the device sitting on that table is a blue star-sapphire third-gen Horn, and I know for a fact that the Horn device you're supposed to be analyzing for Champ is a sparkly peach first-generation one." Just to grind his gears, I added, "And I know this because I supplied the decoy Horn that saved the day on your mission, *remember*? I'm…" I paused for dramatic effect. "…kind of a hero."

Smug? *Moi*? Maybe just slightly.

I could practically hear Hux's molars squeaking. "I remember it a little differently," he told the light fixture on the ceiling. "Now, go watch cartoons and let the grown-ups do their work."

God, he was infuriating. I pushed my glasses up on my nose. "Stop stealing my fucking internet and maybe I will."

"You can't possibly need all of it," he bit out—*erroneously*—addressing himself to the vase of Valentine's Day roses in the center of the table. "What the hell was Champ thinking, making us work alongside a bunch of fucking civilians? If I have to spend one more day here, I'm quitting."

"Quitting? Oh noes! Oh, *gasp*! Wherever will Champ find someone with your amazing skill set, Huxley? Oh, wait, no, I know. Amos Nutter has that overly aggressive alpaca who spits constantly. Betcha five bucks nobody would realize he wasn't you for a full forty-eight hours."

Hux made a high-pitched teakettle noise of rage. "This is why no one wants you around, Kevin Rogers. Because you will do anything to get attention. But I'm *not* gonna give it to you anymore." He clapped a pair of headphones over his ears and began banging his head in time to some music I couldn't hear.

Oh. My. God.

Attention? Me? The guy who'd avoided attention his whole life like vampires avoid the sun? How could one human contain as much *wrong* as Jasper Huxley? I burned with fury at the injustice.

I briefly brainstormed ways to create a targeted signal disruptor that would work only on Hux's headphones so I could force him to listen to Neil Diamond's

"Girl, You'll Be a Woman Soon" until the resulting earworm dissolved his brain into applesauce.

When that vision didn't satisfy my lust for vengeance, I contemplated outfitting the kitchen with some kind of laser I could use to vaporize people—one particular person, really—at will.

Then I sighed. I was pretty sure this was how regular geniuses turned evil.

And the truth was, I didn't want Hux *harmed*, I just wanted his charming, poison-ivy-eyed, mean-spirited self out of my home as quickly and safely as possible… which meant getting to the bottom of Champion Security's infiltration problem.

I'd already begun checking over the scans I'd set up the night before, and even set a couple of new ones to run, when a new message notification from Horn of Glory popped up on my screen.

I expected to see some kind of acknowledgment from Smitty—was a thank-you too much to hope for? —but I quickly forgot about him because the message was from someone way more exciting.

Anomaly451: *Hey, honey! How's my Valentine? I missed you today!*

My heartbeat kicked up a notch at the endearment.

I'd waited a long time to be somebody's *honey.* Twenty-five long years, in fact.

Take that, Huxley. Plenty of people want me around, fuck you very much.

Anomaly451, whose real name was *Adam,* was a HOG player I'd "met" in an online tournament a little over a month ago. Unlike Smitty, who had a chip on his shoulder the size of my homestead, or HogMasterHux, who was the sort of person who'd commandeer a man's orc forces without so much as a by-your-leave, Adam was sweet.

When I'd harvested a record number of snowflakes and knocked him out of contention for the tournament prize, Anomaly hadn't been upset. Instead, he'd plucked a bouquet of snowflowers to congratulate me. Then he'd chat-requested me, and... well, the rest was history.

We'd been online boyfriends for weeks. We'd started having regular Tuesday night chats. I'd told him all about the computer lair I'd constructed. He'd asked my advice on system security for the projects he worked on. And, in a development that had filled me with 90 percent excitement and only 10 percent crippling anxiety, he kept begging to meet in real life so he could "see my setup"—which was code for helping me cash in my virginity card at long last—and I was pretty sure I was going to agree. Soon.

Like, *really* soon.

Could be any day now.

But I couldn't exactly invite the guy over to my house while it was invaded by a nest of hot-as-fuck security operatives, could I? "Pay no attention to the waves of high-octane testosterone luring you toward the ripply-muscled badasses, Adam! Come down to my dark lair and spoon me!"

Yeah, no. There were limits to how much humiliation a man could endure.

HogDocKev: *Hi! It was good. Haven't gone to bed yet. How was work?*

When Adam had told me he had to work on Valentine's Day, my brain had immediately tried sabotaging me by suggesting he had someone at home to celebrate with, but I'd resisted. I was not the doubting, jealous type. Besides, Adam told me all the time that I was the first thing he thought of each morning. That he'd never met anyone like me. That he didn't want us to rush into anything too fast or to become exclusive too quickly, but that he considered me his boyfriend. His *Valentine*.

Having him message me first thing this morning just confirmed it.

Anomaly451: *Meh. Work was a shit show because my boss is incompetent. And you remember that huge research project I mentioned to you? Looks like it's gonna be more time consuming than I thought, and the deadline is getting tighter. You know how it goes.*

Anomaly451: *Actually, I guess you don't exactly, do you? Lol. Trust me, it's annoying. Not nearly as fun as staying home and playing games all afternoon!*

I shut my mouth with a clack.

So, okay, maybe there were a couple of things about our new relationship that I wished I'd handled differently. One was the time I'd explained to Adam that I came from a long line of prestigious doctors, when he asked why my username was HogDoc. Another was telling him that I was a self-employed consultant, when he'd asked what I did for a living.

I hadn't explained things well enough, clearly, because he'd jumped to some conclusions about my work ethic that reminded me a lot of Hu—erm, *certain people's*—bullshit conclusions, and no matter how many times I tried to correct him, he didn't seem to get it.

Consequently, I never brought up his work anymore so he wouldn't make comments about mine.

HogDocKev: *You know I do other things besides play all day. I'm an inventor. I mentor college kids interested in STEM careers. I make a chicken tikka so good you'd cry.*

Anomaly451: *Sure, sweetness. I know. I didn't mean it*

like that! Just that I wish I had more free time. Time I could spend playing HOG with you.

Awww. I melted. Was that the cutest thing ever? Pretty sure it was.

I was being an idiot. A prideful, overly sensitive idiot. And it was Hux's fault. Just because *he* didn't take me seriously, that didn't mean Adam didn't.

HogDocKev: *Sorry. I'm a little touchy this morning, I guess.*

Anomaly451: *No need to apologize, darling. What's got you feeling prickly?*

See, this was what I liked so much about Adam. He asked me questions about my life and seemed interested in the answers. I debated where to begin.

HogDocKev: *Well… my cousin got married yesterday. You remember me telling you about him?*

Anomaly451: *Of course. KevsCuz. The guy you share your homestead with.*

I felt a bittersweet pang.

HogDocKev: *Yeah, him. But we don't share a homestead anymore. He and his hubby will be sharing their own homestead now.*

I'd even gotten them a rare pair of mated swans for their roof as an in-game wedding gift.

Anomaly451: *Ahhh. And now you're carrying on all alone?*

I blew out a deep breath, and stupid tears prickled behind my eyes. Adam understood me on such a fundamental level, it felt like magic.

HogDocKev: *Exactly! That's it exactly. Thank God you understand. I'm happy for him, truly. But…*

But Carter was my best friend. More like a brother than a cousin. He'd been looking out for me since I was a socially awkward middle schooler and my parents dropped me off at our grandfather's house for a visit… then decided it'd be better for all of us if I just lived there permanently.

It was hard not to feel a little lonely, knowing someone else was Carter's priority now.

Anomaly451: *Say no more, angel. Defending a homestead the size of yours all by yourself this close to the tulip harvest? What a pain in the ass!*

Anomaly451: *I don't blame you for being angry at your cousin!*

I blinked. Okay, so maybe Adam didn't magically understand me. But he made an effort, which was more than Hu — erm, *certain people* — did. Right?

Another new message notification popped up onscreen.

SmittyKitty: *What'd you send me this for???*

I rolled my eyes. Speaking of annoying people determined to misunderstand me…

I heaved a sigh as I switched chat windows.

HogDocKev: *It's fuzzy dice. So your air speeder will go faster. Buzz buzz vroom vroom? Maybe you can avoid the lightning orcs next time.*

SmittyKitty: *Don't remember asking for your charity, Pip. Also, FYI, air speeders aren't motorcycles. They don't make noise. And if my motorcycle started buzzing, I'd check out the bearings before I had a catastrophic engine failure, just sayin'.*

Oh, for God's sake.

HogDocKev: **eyeroll* First off, I was racing air speeders before your Horn was even manufactured, whippersnapper. Second, it's kindness, not charity. Don't people do nice things for one another in the UP?*

HogDocKev: *Third, stop calling me Pip.*

Three dots swirled next to Smitty's name for a long moment. Then finally, he responded.

SmittyKitty: *The UP?*

HogDocKev: *Dude. The Upper Peninsula of Michigan? Where you live?*

The second I sent the message, I smacked my forehead.

Wow, Kev, tell me you're a creeper who's been stalking the newb's bio without saying you're a creeper who's been stalking his fucking bio.

SmittyKitty: *They do. For friends. But you and I are not friends… Pip.*

HogDocKev: *We could be, if you wanted. I could help you out. No strings.*

SmittyKitty: *Not interested. I'm not playing the game to amass an empire.*

HogDocKev: *Lolz. That's what most players say when they haven't yet amassed an empire. You ever meet a player named HogMasterHux?*

SmittyKitty: *??? Should I have??*

HogDocKev: *Guess not. You two have a lot in common, that's all.*

SmittyKitty: *Incredible natural talent?*

HogDocKev: *A love of looted goods and a chip on your shoulder. Hux is a great Horn player, but he's not a *team* player. You can't trust him.*

I sighed. Why was I wasting time trying to explain fucking *Huxley* to *Smitty*, the only person in the world who disliked me as much as Hux did?

HogDocKev: *Just watch out for Hux, that's all. And try not to be like him.*

HogDocKev: *Anyway, the dice are yours. Go in peace.*

I closed the chat window and went back to my chat

with Adam, but the green light by his name had gone dark. He'd left me some unread messages, though.

Anomaly451: *One day, when you're ready, I can move into your homestead, and then you won't be alone anymore. I'm a kickass scout, and between my gift for strategy and your spellcasting abilities, we'll be unbeatable!*

Anomaly451: *#HOGPowerCouple!*

Anomaly451: *Which reminds me, what are you up to next weekend? I'm working remotely at the end of the week. I could be in Tennessee by Friday. We could celebrate V-Day in a whole new way. Lolol. *eggplant emoji**

Anomaly451: *I want to know what you look like. And I respect our promise not to google each other or send pictures, but a man has needs. *eggplant emoji* *eggplant emoji**

Anomaly451: *Plus we can quest together while I'm there! If you and I team up, I can qualify for the Ascendant's Class in the Conqueror's Tournament at HOGCon in Vegas in a couple weeks. You're going, right? Because the new HOG Power Couple needs to form an alliance!! We're gonna dominate.*

Anomaly451: *Hello? Earth to Kev?*

Anomaly451: *Guess you fell asleep without saying goodbye.*

Anomaly451: *When we meet in person, I'll have to make sure to keep you awake. *eggplant emoji* *eggplant emoji* *eggplant emoji* Let me know about this weekend!*

My stomach flipped. Next weekend was very soon.

Possibly too soon for all that eggplant.

But the tournament at HOGCon… Hmm.

I'd considered playing in the tournament more than once. Despite having some of the highest posted scores in the game, and maybe the highest number of game-play hours (Hux and I were usually neck and neck at the top of the leaderboard), I'd never competed in an in-person prizewinning tournament before. Social anxiety was a bitch sometimes.

But if Adam and I were boyfriends, a HOG power couple, and we could meet in Vegas, away from prying eyes and rogue badasses…

I toyed with the corner of my glasses nervously.

Anomaly451: *I have quite a bit of work to do today, so I've got to go, but starting the day talking with you is the best thing I could have hoped for, sugar. XOXO*

Damn it. I'd wasted my time chatting with Smitty and being annoyed at Hux when I should've been focused on the guy who actually cared about me. Story of my damn life.

I read the message again and again. *Sugar.* I didn't know anyone who used that endearment unironically in real life, but I decided I liked it.

I typed out a message he could read next time he logged on.

HogDocKev: *Sorry I missed saying goodbye. Good luck with your work! Let's talk about Vegas!*

I stared at the screen some more, thankful I was alone so no one could see the giant grin on my face. And then another message popped up on my screen.

SmittyKitty: *Thank you for the dice, I guess.*

SmittyKitty: *FYI, someone (not me) crossed your border and is looting your magical jelly and jam cellars. I think it might be the Hux guy you mentioned. Now you and I are even. Have fun storming the castle, Pip.*

What the…

I clicked over to the correct monitor and found the orc horde that was supposed to be guarding that section of my property wasn't just ringed by heart-shaped fairy lights anymore, they'd been *tied up with them.*

Meanwhile, HogMasterHux was systematically—

nay, *gleefully*—destroying my carefully organized jelly cellar, upending a ten-gallon drum of boysenberry preserves to the delight of my champagne-drunk villagers.

What. The. Fuck.

He thought *I* was the attention-seeking child around here? *Me*?

Ohhhh, the lasers in the kitchen were *so* happening. But first, I was going to march up there and—

"Pardon me, sire," Henry Cavill interrupted politely as my monitors flashed. "But your scan is now complete, and an ongoing vulnerability has been detected."

I clicked over to the tool I'd been running, and my heart sank when I saw the system vulnerability the computer had found.

Fuck.

This was going to make Huxley *miserable*, which should have made me happy. Instead, it was the absolute last thing I wanted to see.

Hux and I were going to be stuck with each other for even longer.

~

Grab *Hacked* here → https://readerlinks.com/l/2453277

A LETTER FROM LUCY & MAY

Dear Reader,

Thank you for reading *Hitched*! We loved returning to the zany world of Licking Thicket and hope you enjoyed it as much as we did. For more stories set in this quirky small-town, be sure to check out the complete Licking Thicket series.

In *Hacked*, the final book in the Champion Security series, the story of Buck Nutter's stolen Horn data comes to a close amidst Hux and Kev's steamy enemies-to-lovers romance story. We fell in love with these two geeks the minute they appeared on page in *Hijacked* and are so excited to bring you their story. Grab *Hacked* here: https://readerlinks.com/l/2453277

If this is your first book by one of us and you'd like to read more, we suggest you start with *Fakers*, book one in the Licking Thicket series, or Lucy's *Borrowing Blue* and May's *The Date*.

We would love it if you would take a few minutes to review *Hitched* on Amazon, GoodReads, or BookBub. Reader reviews really do make a difference and we appreciate every single one of them.

We've been friends and fans of each other's work for a couple of years, so we weren't surprised when writing our first collaboration went so smoothly. We were surprised, however, that it didn't end up being a stand-alone novel like we planned. There are plenty more stories to tell, starting with *Firecracker*, the first book in the Honeybridge series!

Be sure to follow Lucy and May on Amazon to be notified of new releases, and look for us on Facebook for sneak peeks of upcoming stories.

Feel free to sign up for our newsletters, stop by www.LucyLennox.com, www.MayArcher.com, or visit Lucy's Lair and Club May on Facebook to stay in touch.

To see fun inspiration photos for this book, check out the Pinterest board for Hitched.

Happy reading!
Lucy & May

MORE FROM LUCY AND MAY

Licking Thicket

Flakes

Fakers

Liars

Fools

Turkeys

Peacocks

Champion Security

Hijacked

Hitched

Hacked

Honeybridge

Firecracker

Mr. Important

ABOUT LUCY LENNOX

Lucy Lennox is the USA Today bestselling author of over fifty gay romance titles including the GoodReads Hall of Fame winner Wilde Love. Born and raised in the southeast USA, she is finally putting good use to that English Lit degree she earned before the turn of the century.

Lucy enjoys naps, pizza, and procrastinating. She stays up way too late each night reading romance because it's simply the best.

For more information and to stay updated about future releases, sales and audio news and to grab some free and bonus reads, please sign up for Lucy's author newsletter on her website at LucyLennox.com or to stay in the know, join her exciting reader group, Lucy's Lair on Facebook.

facebook.com/lucylennoxmm

instagram.com/lucylennoxmm

amazon.com/Lucy-Lennox/e/B01N0IOYPT

bookbub.com/authors/lucy-lennox

patreon.com/lucylennox

pinterest.com/lucy_lennox

ALSO BY LUCY LENNOX

Find me online → https://linktr.ee/LucyLennox

Read my books:

<u>Made Marian Series</u>

<u>Forever Wilde Series</u>

<u>Aster Valley Series</u>

<u>The Billionaire Brotherhood Series</u>

<u>After Oscar Series</u> (with Molly Maddox)

<u>Twist of Fate Series</u> (with Sloane Kennedy)

<u>Licking Thicket Series</u> (with May Archer)

<u>Champion Security Series</u> (with May Archer)

<u>Honeybridge Series</u> (with May Archer)

Find a complete list of my stand alone romances and novellas at www.LucyLennox.com along with audio samples, freebies, suggested reading order, and more!

ABOUT MAY ARCHER

May is an M/M author who lives in Boston. She spends her days planning vacations, mainlining diet soda, avoiding the gym, reading M/M romance, and when all other forms of procrastination fail, writing it.

Visit her website at mayarcher.com to sign up for her newsletter to hear about sales and upcoming releases, freebies and behind the scenes info and more! Or join her Facebook group, Club May!

facebook.com/may.archer.author

instagram.com/mayarcherauthor

amazon.com/May-Archer/e/B075JQVGLX

patreon.com/MayArcherRomance

bookbub.com/authors/may-archer

ALSO BY MAY ARCHER

Find me online → https://linktr.ee/mayarcherauthor

Love in O'Leary Series

Whispering Key Series

The Sunday Brothers Series

Copper County Series

The Way Home Series

Licking Thicket Series

(cowritten with Lucy Lennox)

Champion Security Series

(cowritten with Lucy Lennox)

Honeybridge Series

(cowritten with Lucy Lennox)

For a comprehensive list of titles, audio samples, freebies, suggested reading order, and more, visit my website at www. MayArcher.com!

www.ingramcontent.com/pod-product-compliance
Lightning Source LLC
Chambersburg PA
CBHW031642200726

48289CB00004BA/1142